T0375699

King Solomon's Baby

MELISSA BANKS

Editor: Fiona Zerbst

BALBOA.
PRESS

A DIVISION OF HAY HOUSE

Balboa Press books may be ordered through booksellers or by contacting:

Balboa Press
A Division of Hay House
1663 Liberty Drive
Bloomington, IN 47403
www.balboapress.com
1-(877) 407-4847

Because of the dynamic nature of the Internet, any web addresses or
links contained in this book may have changed since publication and
may no longer be valid. The views expressed in this work are solely those
of the author and do not necessarily reflect the views of the publisher,
and the publisher hereby disclaims any responsibility for them.

The author of this book does not dispense medical advice or prescribe the use
of any technique as a form of treatment for physical, emotional, or medical
problems without the advice of a physician, either directly or indirectly. The
intent of the author is only to offer information of a general nature to help
you in your quest for emotional and spiritual well-being. In the event you use
any of the information in this book for yourself, which is your constitutional
right, the author and the publisher assume no responsibility for your actions.

Any people depicted in stock imagery provided by Thinkstock are
models, and such images are being used for illustrative purposes only.
Certain stock imagery © Thinkstock.

ISBN: 978-1-4525-3197-7 (sc)
ISBN: 978-1-4525-3198-4 (e)

Printed in the United States of America
Balboa Press rev. date: 12/12/2012

Dedicated to the most beautiful child I've ever seen.
This is my love letter to you.

Contents

Preface

April 2002

Summer was drawing to a close. The African sun turned the sky from blue to pink as it set a little earlier each day. The earth was dry. There hadn't been much rain that month.

The township of Daveyton, 20km east of Johannesburg, South Africa, was alive, filled with the sounds of music, laughter, shouting, fighting and the barking of a dog. The smell of burning wood from fires made outside the corrugated iron sheet housing permeated the air.

The shanties or shacks were assembled closely to one another. There were no ablution areas, apart from a few communal taps.

A four month-old baby lay on a makeshift bed. It was made of crumpled-up newspapers and bits of foam rubber covered with a blanket to cushion him from the floor. Usually his mother, brother and sister would also sleep on the same bed. It was a bit cramped, but at least they could keep each other warm on a cold night. When it rained, water leaked between the corrugated iron sheet panels, which formed the walls and roof. The bitter cold of winter was on its way, and would mercilessly seep the entire shelter with icy wind and frost in a few weeks' time.

Tonight the baby was alone. He slept contentedly, completely oblivious to the extreme poverty he lived and slept in, with the candle beside him lighting up his delicate features.

He smelled of Elizabeth Anne baby cream. Thankfully, some baby products were provided for free from the clinics that underprivileged mothers took their babies to. His teenage mother had managed to scrape together enough taxi fare to go to the clinic just once. She had been given three months' supply of birth control tablets, condoms and free baby cream.

She was attending a party tonight. She'd had children from other men in her early teens. She hoped that the one she slept with recently would be the key to her future. It was his baby that lay sleeping at home.

She was afraid to get too attached to her children in case they were taken from her. Life as she knew it was cheap, anyway. She could barely keep herself alive. The new guy seemed really decent. Maybe this was the opportunity she needed: he hadn't run away when she had his child. She was 19, and already a mother to two when she fell pregnant again. The father was 21. Welfare had very recently taken her two older children as she was unable to provide for them.

A gust of wind blew through the hole that served as a window, knocking over the cup perched on the empty box that doubled as a table or chair. The noise woke the baby. He started to cry. Another gust of wind knocked the candle onto the bed where he lay.

Nobody outside heard the screams.

Sometime later, a fireman found a very badly burnt unconscious little form. He was still breathing, but only just. Screaming and howling pierced the air, as the small community sobbed. The young mother never saw her son again. She started drinking and took to the streets. Later she learnt from gossip mongers that her son had survived, but was likely to look like a monster, when he got older. She chose to leave him at the hospital forever.

The father committed suicide soon afterwards.

PART ONE –
A PRAYER AND A PROMISE

A meeting of two worlds

5 December 2007

The day of the company year-end party had arrived. It was hot and sticky weather, perfect for the chosen venue, a theme park in Boksburg called Wild Water. We all had to be at Wild Water, a water theme park in Boksburg, at noon.

I'd put sunscreen on at home, before putting my swimming costume on under my clothes. I was a little self-conscious in my shorts, but I'd be damned if I was going to sit around baking, in a pair of jeans, in 35°C heat. People at the office weren't used to me in flat shoes – boy, would they be surprised when they discovered I'm actually knee-high!

On arrival, we were given a little backpack with a green towel, matching hat, sun-block, a shot of tequila, and a tablet for the anticipated hangover the next day. This was not an unusual party pack for the advertising industry. The South African Broadcasting Corporation (SABC) was known to host legendary parties. Clearly, it was going to be a long day. I promised myself that there would be no hangover or sunstroke for me the following day, in spite of the tequila still burning the back of my throat.

The venue was an oasis in a desert of mind dumps and palm trees decking the waterslides. The day progressed as office parties do, with loud music, people swimming in their clothes, shy wallflowers and one or two uptight nerds turning into Justin Timberlake on the dance floor.

I'd spent most of the afternoon in the pool, on the waterslides or on the dance floor, dancing with my friend Christopher, the two of us entertaining everyone, as we often ended up doing. He was an awesome dancer, and made whichever woman he was dancing with look amazing. He was very good-looking and could easily have been a model. Although he swore he was straight, he had a habit of squealing when he was excited, and used words like 'fabulous' often. I'd yet to see him with a girlfriend.

I had never really questioned him, but appreciated that he was perhaps as confused with life and relationships as I was.

After sausage rolls and several glasses of wine, a few of us decided to move our party to another location, as you do, especially when you should rather be heading home. We agreed to meet at a restaurant in Parkhurst, an upmarket arty suburb in Johannesburg, where everyone had either renovated their houses, or turned their homes into little Art Deco street cafes – complete with tables, umbrellas and travelling artists peddling their wares.

"Want me to drive, Ruby?" Christopher asked as we headed to my car. We had decided to travel together. Grateful, I handed over my keys and climbed into the passenger seat of my Jeep Wrangler. In spite of my resolve earlier that day, I could feel the wine had hit me, and my shoulders and face were tender from the sun. Oh well, I'd just have water or a cold drink at the restaurant and go home.

The sun was about an hour away from setting. I put my feet up on the dashboard, and turned the music up. It was lovely being a passenger. I reflected on the year, and told myself, as I do every year, that it had been the best year yet. I'd had my ups and downs – and heartbreaks – but it had been a superb year for learning lessons, some of which I hoped never to repeat.

I wondered what 2008 would have in store for me. I knew the start of it was going to be exciting, because I'd planned to spend New Year in Amsterdam. I'd never been there before, but I imaged that a 36-year-old single woman with no responsibilities could have a blast there.

We approached Parktown. Although a run-down suburb, it still boasted beautiful Victorian buildings. We turned right into the main street. I observed the houses, and realised how much I didn't notice when I was driving.

We were swiftly approaching Parkhurst. In the distance, I could see a house with jungle gyms and swings. I smiled and got ready to wave at the kindergarten kids I expected to see. I saw little figures running in the garden, next to the green picket fence. I started waving, but the shock of what I saw made my arm weak. The little faces smiling back were not normal. In fact, they looked like tiny goblin masks. They saw me noticing them. They screeched, running and jumping, with one or two twirling in the air shouting "Sweets! Please buy us sweets!"

With horror, I registered the severe disfigurement I was seeing, but as quickly as I noticed their cruelly scarred little faces, I also noticed their glee and excitement. They were thrilled with life, it appeared.

"Chris, look at those kids!" I gasped.

"Haven't you seen them before, Ruby? We pass by here often; they're kids who have been burnt."

"Please stop the car!" I shouted. "I want to go over to them. Stop at the shop on the corner, so I can get them some sweets."

Chris pulled over and parked across the road adjacent to the shop. The car had barely stopped but I jumped out and ran across the road. The kids could still see me and, realising what I was doing, they started shouting even louder, in case I hadn't heard them the first time.

I ran up and down the aisles of the shop, unable to make up my mind as to what to get them. Thinking back, I remembered what I used to like as a child. The dilemma I always faced was whether to buy Cadbury's Chomp or five toffees. I preferred the chocolate, but the toffees would last me a lot longer. Generally, the toffees won.

I spotted the strawberry fizzer toffees. Perfect. I picked up 12 of them. At the counter, I picked up 12 strawberry fizz-pop lollipops, too. There were no packets available, so I walked out clutching all the sweets in my hands, with some nearly falling through my fingers. It was a lovely feeling.

I crossed the street, and the children's excitement was infectious. Little scarred arms and hands reached urgently through the picket fence. Some of the little damaged hands didn't have fingers. In fact, most of the children had either lost a hand or digits. I noticed one of them had even lost an arm.

Later, I learnt the reason for that. When a part of the body is exposed, or threatened, we instinctively reach out with our hand to cover or protect that body part. Sadly, it's almost always the 'doing' hand, so the child is forced to learn to use the weaker hand when the strong hand gets damaged.

There were two boys who were clearly the ring-leaders. The loudest, biggest one had a beautiful face on the one side. The other half of his face was badly scarred. He couldn't have been older than seven, but he had the deepest voice I'd ever heard in a child.

The second little boy was slighter, with a high-pitched little voice that I'd get to know only too well. His eyes were bright with intelligence. He appeared to have his head thrown back when looking at me. That was because the hairline on the one side of his face was just above his eyebrow, and he had no nose:

just two little cavities where the nostrils were. He didn't walk or run. He skipped. He was riveting.

I started handing out sweets through the fence. It felt like the most natural thing to do. But taking sweets from a stranger is a textbook no-no. Not surprisingly, a tall young man came out from the building to see what all the commotion was about. He couldn't have been older than 22 but he must have been a few inches over six feet tall.

"Please stop that! This is not a petting zoo! Make proper arrangements with management of the school if you want go get involved!" he scolded in his British accent.

"What? I don't think this is a zoo! I take offence at that statement. All I want to do is give the kids some sweets!" I protested.

I knew he was mostly right, but my indignation (or perhaps the wine) would not allow me to apologise or back off. I wanted to give the rest of the sweets to the kids, so I walked around the property to the entrance. The kids were there waiting for me. So was he. But I was ready for him.

"Okay, maybe we got off to a bad start," I pleaded. "Please will you open gate so I can give them the sweets I bought for them?"

By this time, Christopher had joined me.

"No, I can't let you in. Please go away and make arrangements, as I suggested earlier," he scolded.

What a pompous self-righteous ass! No man tells me to go away! Especially not one this much younger than me! Where was his respect for older women, I wondered, not fully aware of the irony of a drunk, dishevelled woman's looking for respect.

"What is wrong with you? Why are you like this? I feel like I'm being punished for doing something nice! Can I please just give them the sweets!" I shouted. Then a whine started to creep into my voice. I knew if I didn't leave, I'd end up crying soon.

"Some of these kids are HIV positive! Do you know what happens to their CD count when you give them sugar? It drops! Now go away and make proper arrangements," he said angrily. I was shattered. In my effort to be nice and share my favourite sweets, I could have hurt a child by mistake. Christopher took me by the hand.

"Come, Rubes. Let's go – the others are waiting."

"I feel like such a terrible person," I wailed, and started to walk away.

The kids were still shouting for their sweets. I had put the sweets in my bag, but the children knew where they were. I had raised their hopes for a treat; and now, in my ignorance, I had caused immense disappointment.

For the rest of the evening, I was upset and Christopher tried to cheer me up. I woke up miserable the next morning. My head hurt. I cringed, thinking about my experience with the children. I could never show my face there again.

It would be some time before I did.

Amsterdam

29 December 2007

I boarded the plane for Amsterdam. It was late at night and I looked forward to sleeping on the plane. I had decided a month before to travel overseas. It was a short space of time in which to get organised, but I managed to get leave from work, obtain a Schengen visa and some Euros.

An old friend of mine was staying in Amsterdam. We had always got along very well when he lived in South Africa 10 years beforehand. I had dated a friend of his for a few months and had moved in similar circles to him. I was quite excited to see him again. A little part of me wouldn't have minded if something came of the visit, especially if he was anything like he was a few years ago. But either way, I was excited to get out of the country and explore.

Tom and I had reconnected via Facebook, and he had invited me to visit. He had just come out of a two-year relationship which he seemed to be quite cut up about. It seems his girlfriend had already moved on. I understood how that felt, as I had been in a pretty serious relationship a year before, which had come to an end. Before that, I'd been in a seven-year relationship that had ended in divorce. I knew all about letting go and facing disappointment.

A lot of the disappointments had been my own fault. I had come to terms with that, but had decided that I still deserved to have my dreams come true. In fact, I'd started praying in earnest for a husband and child. I had a condition known as endometriosis, which had affected me for most of my life.

Every two years, I'd have to undergo a laparoscopy and have the little nodules lasered off my tubes and ovaries, which made fertility a problem.

Maybe – just maybe – there was a miracle waiting for me.

Tom and I had decided we'd spend New Year together, and that he'd show me around. He mentioned that we could perhaps drive to Germany as well for a weekend while I was there.

Unfortunately, I had lost my phone two weeks before and had not got to read a text message from Tom in Amsterdam, which was to confirm all our arrangements. A few days before I was meant to leave, I messaged him with my flight details. He called me back immediately, sounding annoyed.

"I wondered what had happened to you! I didn't think you were coming. Why did it take you two weeks to respond to me? Where have you been?"

"What? Sorry, I didn't get your text. I promise I didn't. You know I would have responded."

"How could you not have got it? Your text to me was a reply to my text. I'll show you on my BlackBerry. It has my text as well as yours in the same message. Something very strange is going on here. I'll send it to you."

"I really don't know how that happened, as I didn't see that text. I'm really sorry!"

He sounded unconvinced.

Oh dear, this trip was getting off to a bad start, and it was too late to cancel. I was embarrassed and explained that it was a bit late to do anything about the arrangements. He agreed and said he'd meet me at the airport.

I arrived at Schiphol airport in Amsterdam. It was icy. Tom kissed me hello and took my bag. He hadn't changed much, his hair was as curly as ever, but he'd gone quite grey. Tom's apartment was up three very narrow flight of stairs and had a lovely view of the city. He showed me where I was to sleep and put my bags down.

"Come, let me show you around," he said, picking up his large, scratched, straight-handled, black 'postman' bicycle, which was standing in his lounge. I followed him down the stairs.

"Pardon the bike, but it's really not worth getting an expensive one here. Quite often, they get damaged or stolen. Get on the back; you can sit on the carrier."

He balanced the bike as I climbed on the back, vaguely noticing how flat the back tyre looked under me. The bike even had an old-fashioned bell. Oh, this was going to be so romantic. The bike wobbled a bit, but we managed to get going.

Within five minutes, I had changed my mind about this bicycle stuff. The back tyre wasn't just a bit flat, it was very flat, and I felt every bump on that metal carrier. My hands and nose were freezing. This was not romantic or fun at all.

I forced myself not to focus on my discomfort and to rather see the city. It was indeed lovely in winter and surprisingly green. Unfortunately Tom had been called into the office for the next few days, so he couldn't show me around the city as planned. This didn't bother me too much, as I quite like exploring new places on my own.

"So where are we going for New Year? There's so much to do here. I honestly expected every second person be stoned on weed around here!" I exclaimed when we had stopped. Tom was putting a chain around the bike's wheel. I followed him into the grocery store.

"I don't really hang out in areas with people who take drugs. So I never go to those pubs or tea shops where people smoke weed," said Tom. "Although it's legal in this city, I don't intend to smoke it. I never have, and never will. I'm certainly not going to take you to any of those places."

I was slightly offended at his tone. I didn't want to smoke weed, I don't particularly like the smell, and just wanted to see where these types of places were, so I could say I've been. What was it with all of these bossy and judgemental men? This was definitely not what I had in mind.

The rest of the trip progressed along similar lines. Tom caught the bus to work, so I got to use the bicycle. I hadn't ridden a bike in years. I didn't own flat shoes, so it was going to be tricky in my high-heeled boots. On my first day back on the saddle, I was wrapped in my faux leopard print coat. I balanced the bike; heels hooked underneath the pedals, which I could barely reach. The ground was a long way down. Wobbling all over the street, I lost co-ordination and couldn't stop. I crashed into the traffic light. Three men sat at a bus stop sniggering.

"At least I have a bike and don't have to rely on public transport!" I shouted to them, getting off the ground and climbing back on the bike.

I had been there for a mere three days, but I'd had enough of Amsterdam and my host. I had eight days left of my trip, and I was already pedalling to Schiphol airport. Tom was a lovely person, and had tried his best to make my stay as pleasant as possible. But I could feel that I was irritating him, and I think I was a little irritated too, actually.

I had done my best not to get in the way. I tidied up after myself and cooked a few meals for him when he got home. I didn't go to any pubs or questionable places. I ate thousands of *olliebollen* (doughnuts) and visited museums. I bought two Vincent Van Gogh biscuit tins as gifts to prove it, too.

At Schiphol, I booked a train ticket to Paris, scheduled to leave the next day. When I got back to the apartment, I packed my things and waited for Tom to come home. He looked genuinely surprised when I said I was leaving, and was even more shocked to see that I had already packed. I explained that it would be a shame not to explore the rest of the continent, when I'd spent so much money on the ticket. I insisted on taking him to dinner to thank him for his hospitality.

Paris

I was on my way to France. Hooray! The train ride was four hours long, and I got to see Rotterdam, Brussels and many windmills along the way.

I didn't have a lot of money and I had no idea where I was going to stay. The train trip alone had cost me 100 Euros. I arrived in Paris and made my way out of Gare du Nord train station. I had no idea where I was, and hoped that the 'sortie' signs I saw everywhere at the Metro had something to do with everything being 'sorted'. I soon discovered it meant 'exit', and took delight in shouting "sortie" as often as I could. It just felt so good on my tongue and was a great addition to my French vocabulary, which consisted of "Je t'aime" and "merci".

I enquired at all the hotels in the vicinity and ended up finding one across the road from the station. I didn't want to wander too far from the station, as I doubted I'd ever find my way back. My bags were heavy and I needed to orientate myself. It was 50 Euros a night at the Picadilly Hotel. I could live with that, but there wasn't going to be much money left for shopping!

The hotel had rusty brass chandelier light fittings, and a few rusty brass-framed prints on the walls. The grey wallpaper in the foyer had a faded, lined pattern, which one could only see close up. A rickety old lift, which looked a bit like a cage, descended. Apparently it worked only sometimes. I chose to take the stairs, which were always dark because the light bulb on the staircase hadn't been replaced. Thankfully, the stairs were carpeted, so taking a tumble, if you couldn't see in the dark, wouldn't have been a disaster.

Eating and drinking in Paris is an expensive past time. No wonder the French make such a big deal of it! Mealtimes are special – you may even need to sell your house to afford them. Well, that's how it felt at the time. Drinking tap water wasn't advised and bottled water was more expensive than cold drinks so I essentially lived on bread, and red wine, which was the cheapest beverage on the shelf.

One night I got tired of my 'holy communion' and broke into the Vincent biscuit tins in desperation. My friends would just have to make do with empty tins, or I'd fill them with local biscuits back home. Now and then I gave into temptation and bought a bonbon from the chocolatier at the station. But I'd buy only one at a time. I knew I was going to have to fight a few additional kilograms when I got back to South Africa.

I bought a pass that gave me access to the underground train system for the rest of my stay. I couldn't wait to get to Notre Dame – it was the first place I wanted to see. As a child, I had watched the old version of *The Hunchback of Notre Dame*. It wasn't the Disney version, but an old favourite I watched on the black and white television in my parents' lounge. I remember crying as I watched this lonely, afflicted man swinging from those huge church bells, while becoming deafened in the process by the loud clanging sound.

I made my way to the island in the middle of the Seine, which houses the magnificent Gothic structure, and imagining that if I looked up into the bell tower long enough I might just see Quasimodo swinging from the ropes. He was obviously just too quick for me to see that day!

On my second day in Paris, I was crossing the road when the Frenchman walking beside me started chatting to me. I could barely make out what he was saying, but I was sure he'd invited me to see the Louvre. The famous glass pyramid was literally across the road from us. He hauled out a security card with his photograph – he was from the department of Culture and Tourism. It was my lucky day, because it usually costs 25 Euros to get in. We bypassed the queue and walked straight in. I handed in my belongings at the desk, which everybody has to do, and followed him. I felt very important.

The place was magnificent. The Mona Lisa was surprisingly small. Once again, we bypassed the queues to get a closer look at her. This was really working for me. I hovered around the statue of Cupid and Psyche, trying to see if the artist had captured Psyche's expression when she realised that the 'monster' visiting her every night, whom she was forbidden to look upon, was none other than the god of love himself. She was reaching out to him, but his wings were spread as he prepared to take flight, while he caressed her one last time.

"Next time, stick around when you decide to visit me, okay? I'm actually quite fun," I told him, before I moved on to the next headless exhibit. I could have sworn I heard him whisper back, "Oh, yeah, well why don't *you* ever stick around?" I wasn't about to have a full-scale argument with the god of love in the Louvre. So I walked away.

I sat in the foyer below the famous glass pyramid, and was thrilled with the grandeur of the huge, marble cavern housing the gigantic statue alongside me. Who would have guessed that this is what lay beneath that little pyramid above, on the street?

We made our way to Napoleon's apartment; I really wanted the details of his decorator! Today's equivalent of his decor budget would have been lovely, too. It was quieter there. I was busy contemplating how short Napoleon's bed was when my tour guide decided that it was a good time to try to kiss me.

"No! I'm not Josephine!" I pulled away.

I don't he think he understood exactly what I was saying, but he certainly understood that I was not about to lock lips with him. Somehow, we reached a compromise that I'd hold his hand. We walked hand-in-hand through the rest of the museum. It seemed like a fair trade-off at the time.

Later, he enquired where I was staying, I replied that I couldn't remember the name of the hotel. It was getting dark now, and he was with me on the Metro. I had to get rid of him. The train stopped – it was not my stop. Just as the doors were about to close, I jumped up and pretended that I'd just realised it was my stop while running for the door. He barely had time to stand up. The doors closed as I got off and disappeared into the crowd.

I lay in bed that night thinking about how much I missed my mother. I sent her a text message about my day. She'd be nervous about what happened with my Frenchman, but in her heart, I knew she'd love my story.

I wanted to call Brent, my friend in London, but felt it wasn't the best thing to do because I knew he was interested in being more than friends. He practically fitted my entire checklist regarding what I wanted in a man. But for some reason I had wanted to see Tom before I committed to anything. If I'm honest with myself, I think I was afraid of commitment in the first place, although I would never have admitted this to myself at the time. I would have considered that weak.

I decided to call a mutual friend of Brent's and mine, to help with my decision. I knew she was all for us getting together, but she also knew about Tom, and my commitment issues. She encouraged me.

"Just phone him! Do it!" she urged.

I called Brent, and he made a plan to come across the channel almost immediately. I couldn't bring myself to tell him the whole story, but he'd hinted that maybe it was best he didn't know exactly what brought me there.

Brent took me to the Basilica at Sacre Coeur during a service. This white cathedral is perched on a hill that overlooks the entire city. I could hear the nuns singing from the outside; their voices were ethereal. With the city of Paris sprawled out below, I breathed in the beautiful sights and sounds. I couldn't believe the naughty Moulin Rouge was almost a stone's throw from this deeply pious place. I loved the contradiction of it all.

Brent could only stay for the weekend. He had arrived late on the Friday night and left on the Sunday. I cried as we said goodbye; I didn't want him to leave. It's easy to fall in love in Paris, especially if you're a hopeless romantic. He promised he'd see me in a few days' time, when he was in South Africa – and he did. The walk back to the hotel was one of the loneliest ever.

I settled back for the last four days of my trip. I wanted to go home. I wanted to be back in South Africa, see Brent and get on with life. I thought I'd found what I was looking for and time couldn't move quickly enough. I was tired of being a 'pauper'; the shabby hotel had certainly lost its appeal, so naturally I wanted to be back in my lovely bedroom at home.

It was the last day of my trip, and I was in the process of congratulating myself on my financial discipline throughout the trip when I saw them …

The airport

They were soft brown leather, with the most adorable little heels. The sign outside the shop read '50% off'. So far, my credit card hadn't played up. It was still happily going through every night at the hotel. I had 50 Euros left in cash, and it was the last day of my trip. The boots were 50 Euros on sale. There was a good chance I'd be able to swipe my card here, buy those Tommy Hilfiger boots, and use the cash at the hotel for my accommodation.

The shop assistant swiped my card, and the little receipt printer buzzed away. I put the boots on immediately. They were soft and comfortable; blisters were unlikely.

I was triumphant. My card appeared to be 'unlimited' and I had cash. I went to the little bistro I walked past every day and decided I was going to treat myself to a lovely Parisian meal on my last night. I would use my card for the meal and stick to the plan of using the cash for the accommodation. I ordered a slice of quiche, and crepes for dessert. The bill was 23 Euros. I produced my card and waited for the waiter to return with the slip for me to sign.

He returned with an embarrassed little smile. "Madame, zees card, ees not werking."

I closed my eyes for a moment and took a deep breath.

I handed over my precious accommodation money, and waited for my change. Oh, how I loved my shabby little hotel room at that moment. I was sorry I'd every complained! I made my way back to the hotel.

I held my breath as my card swiped. The clerk at the hotel reception desk frowned. I asked him to try again. It was declined again. Oh, how could I have done this to myself! It was 8pm, and my flight home was at 6am the following day. What was I going to do for nine hours in the middle of the night? I was exhausted, and had really looked forward to my bed.

I climbed the two flights of stairs to fetch my things. I'd have done anything to smell that mouldy old smell in the stairway for the next few hours.

My pride wouldn't let me call anybody. I thanked the man at the desk. The porter seemed to sense my desperation and suggested I stay with his family for the night, which I politely declined. Since the Josephine incident, I was a little nervous of Frenchmen. I asked if he knew of any place where accommodation was under 25 Euros. Of course, such a place was unheard of. I lugged my suitcase out the hotel door for the last time. It was bitterly cold outside.

I sat at MacDonald's, sipping coffee. I'd finished the two books that I'd brought with me. It was getting late, and a man approached me to ask if he could sit by me. I asked that he rather leave me alone, but he sat down anyway. I called for the bill and left. It was 10pm.

I decided to make my way to the airport, but say goodbye to the Champs Elysees first. I'd heard of young people hiking through Europe and sleeping at airports and stations. Maybe I could spend the night at the airport. The Virgin store on the Champs Elysees was still open, and they were having a book sale. I bought Dan Brown's *Angels & Demons*. I had five Euros left for the night.

I arrived at a beautifully refurbished Charles de Gaulle Airport. I didn't see any loiterers or students sleeping there, so I hung around reading my book until the last person left the airport. I was homeless, but I had fabulous boots on! The airport was enormous, with not a soul in sight. I thought about doing cartwheels or something silly. But it doesn't take long for that liberated feeling to give way to loneliness and fear.

Finally, I saw movement in the distance. As happy as I was to see signs of human life, I had to remind myself that I was possibly loitering or trespassing. It was the cleaner with his floor polishing machine. I hid behind the Avis sign. What if they threw me out?

The cleaner passed by without seeing me. I left my luggage behind the sign, and ran with my book to the restroom. The wallpaper inside the toilet area was made of a bamboo print. I sat inside a toilet cubicle, reading – I managed this for 90 minutes. I had a three-and-a-half hour wait left. My life felt like a Tom Hanks movie.

I crept out of the toilet and decided to move from my spot behind the Avis sign. I wasn't sure where I was going. I spotted an instant coffee machine outside of the empty food area. It was one Euro per cup, so I bought another cup of coffee. The cleaner was coming into view again, although I wasn't sure if it was the same man. I soon found myself hiding away in yet another restroom. This one had wallpaper with images of pebbles on it. After reading Dan Brown for another two hours, I ventured out for coffee again. It was after 3am and the catering people had started arriving. I was thrilled to see them. I walked alongside them and hoped to just blend in. I was thankful my ordeal was over.

A few hours later, I boarded the plane, bleary-eyed, and slept all the way back to Johannesburg.

The charity

March 2008

The wild pink and mauve cosmos had started blooming alongside the road in Johannesburg – a sure sign autumn was on its way. Brent had come and gone. He had spent the first two weeks of January in the country and we'd seen each other every day. Eventually, we discussed how we were going to conduct our relationship in future. We both agreed that one of us would eventually have to move. He didn't really want to come back to South Africa, but I considered going to the UK.

This was happening so fast – although you'd think living so far apart would slow down a relationship. It didn't.

Brent had come back again in February for a week, so in a space of three months, I'd seen him for a total of three weeks. I had missed him while he was away. It was becoming apparent that I'd have to pack up soon, if I wanted to be with him. I felt the stirrings of fear in my gut but I stifled them. Brent was exceptionally career-orientated. His phone calls and texts started slowing down as he got busier. I carried on with my life and decided to do something constructive with my time, instead of waiting around.

The sight of those burnt children, at the home I'd seen in December, still haunted me. Since being back at work, I'd often chosen to drive past the home. I wanted to reach out to them, but I was still ashamed of my behaviour during that first visit. Hopefully the strict young man had gone back to Britain. Or perhaps he wouldn't recognise me. I took down the number that was on the board outside of the home, and called their offices.

A woman's voice answered the phone, and she, too, had a British accent. I introduced myself and explained that I was available to read to the kids or babysit from time to time. She asked me what I did for a living. When she heard I worked for a broadcaster she became quite excited. She gave me her address, as she wasn't based at the school, although it was within walking distance.

I rang the buzzer beside the wooden gate – it didn't appear to work. The gate was open and I peeped inside. I walked up to the door and knocked. Somebody from inside the building shouted to me to come in – there appeared to be a lot of activity. I opened the door. There were tins of food and bags of clothes everywhere. The walls were covered with photographs of all the children, and newspaper clippings. Phones were ringing and two young people were packing boxes, answering phones and appeared very busy. Thankfully, the bossy young man wasn't around. There was barely space to walk from all the bags and boxes I had to squeeze through.

As I made my way in, the woman who answered the phone appeared. She was one of the oddest-looking people I'd ever seen. She was probably in her fifties. She wore a blanket around her, beneath her armpits, which she had tucked in the front. She was wearing a blouse underneath, as well as what appeared to be tracksuit pants. Her long grey hair was parted in two plaits on either side of her head, like Heidi. Come to think of it, she resembled an Indian squaw; she just had the wrong accent and skin tone.

"Come in, I'm Barbara. We spoke on the phone," she said. "We're frantically busy here, packing for the Joe Slovo squatter camp." She picked up teddy bears, and a few stray tins of food, while busy talking, and moving towards the centre of the hurricane of goods.

"This is what we do when we have a surplus," she continued. "Sometimes people just dump stuff with us, which we can't even use. It's a nightmare trying to sort it all out."

"Let's move to the office where we can have some peace to chat," she suggested, walking through another doorway leading to what looked like an office.

"I'll bet Thando and Philemon lured you into buying them sweets? They're impossible. They do that to everybody who passes by. It's so difficult to manage, as we don't want their taking sweets or encouraging the wrong kind of attention."

I smiled silently. I followed her, thinking about how unfair it was that I got into so much trouble that day, when the little guys were actually the instigators. But the adult in me realised that I should have known better.

The office was strewn with papers, files, a broken computer and even more clippings and photos on the wall. A photo caught my eye.

"That's my Daisy ... doesn't she look great?" Barbara asked, as she admired the picture.

I politely nodded, shocked at what the little girl looked like. Her head was severely deformed, with no eyes, a cavernous hole for a nose and deformed lips. She'd lost both her hands, with one of the stubs at least having a bit of a forearm.

"Look at how much progress we've made," she pointed to another photograph of Daisy, which was the 'before' photograph. At that stage, the child didn't even have lips. It appeared she had no features; her face was just a blur of skin and bone. I swallowed hard (I've done a lot of that since first going there). Barbara had stopped talking for a moment. I took the opportunity to speak.

"I passed the school sometime in December last year and saw the children. I've been meaning to come back and ask what I can do to assist. I don't have money to offer, but I can offer my time. Maybe I can read to them, or babysit."

"Well it would be really great if you could come in and cook for them maybe one night a week. Do you cook?" asked Barbara.

"Yes, I'd love to cook for the children," I said excitedly.

We agreed on Wednesday nights. I had no idea what I was in for, but cooking was something I could do. It was a start. Barbara asked me more about my life and my job.

"I'm divorced, and currently single. I don't have kids. And I sell commercial airtime to advertisers, on behalf of the SABC. That's about it, really," I said, noticing her excitement at what I saying.

"We obviously can't afford airtime, but we desperately need some help. We've been badly defamed by a television programme, and we could do with some positive exposure. We've got some ads ready for airing, so it's just a matter of getting some airtime."

She proceeded to tell me about some disgruntled former employees who had made up stories about her. It seems they'd even approached a journalist that presented one of those extreme, shocking exposé-type programmes that supposedly uncover injustices. At the time, Barbara had no idea what the reporter would do, and had allowed her free rein on the premises to get her story.

All sorts of allegations were made by the reporter. One of the allegations showed the reporter standing in front of sealed cardboard boxes that had a well-known television manufacturer's brand and images printed on them. The reporter alleged that the some sort of other business was going on that involved buying and selling televisions. The reality was that the boxes were filled with blankets donated by another radio station, as well as other goods that had been donated. This is what Barbara told me.

The impact and implications of the exposé were devastating. Another company that was just about to sponsor the charity quite significantly pulled out due to the bad publicity. Unfortunately, the programme had aired that episode at Christmas time. The programme had undoubtedly done its job as far as ratings were concerned, but sadly the amount of support the charity usually enjoyed at Christmas time dwindled.

I was a bit suspicious. But the more I listened to Barbara and saw what she'd done to assist these children, the more I empathised. I didn't care that there was speculation around her. All I cared about was that the damage that was done had clearly affected the children. I decided to speak to all of my contacts in the industry when I got back to the office. Something had to be done.

"So, do you want to have children?" asked Barbara, getting back to the subject of my personal life.

I replied hesitantly, "Yes, but I doubt it would be possible at 36 with endometriosis and no man on the horizon. Ideally I'd like to know the man for at least two years before considering children. That would take me to 38. Then of course, we'd have to start *in vitro* fertilisation or whatever else I'd probably need to make pregnancy possible. That would take me to 39 or 40. My back aches just at the thought."

Barbara pondered.

"Would you consider adoption? I have a little boy who has asked me to find him a mum."

"No, I can't take on a child. I'd love to, but I'd be nervous. Maybe one day, as a last resort," I said. How could I possibly take on a child? I was one of the most irresponsible people I knew – I could barely look after myself!

I wondered if we'd be having this same conversation if she knew I was the inebriated lady insisting on sticking sweets through the fence and being snotty towards her young volunteer a few months ago. In spite of all of this, I asked her who the little boy was that wanted the mother. In my heart, I already knew which one it was.

"It's Philemon; we call him Phil – the little one with the hair just above his eye. He was in a shack fire when he was a few months old. He was never fetched from Baragwanath Hospital, where he was treated. So he is truly alone."

I fought an internal battle. My heart was jumping around in my chest and I wanted to say "I know exactly which one he is – give him to me now; I'll take him!" But I knew that would have been the craziest thing I've ever done. And what's more, this was a child's life and heart at stake. I could never risk hurting him – what if I disappointed him?

"Maybe one day, but in the meantime, I'll see what I can do about that radio and television airtime you're after. And I'll be there to cook for the children on Wednesday at 6pm," I promised.

We left it at that.

The school

I rushed around Pick 'n Pay after work. I'd planned to make chicken á la king. I couldn't buy the ingredients earlier, as we had no fridge for storage at the office.

I arrived at the green picket fence. This time, they were going to let me in, and I smiled to myself. The children were thrilled to have a new person cook for them. They knew there would be some treats in my grocery bags. The excitement was at fever pitch.

I stood at the gate, packets in hand, while the bossy young man appeared with keys. I blushed and looked down while he opened the gate. He didn't seem to recognise me, or he was just being polite. Either way I was relieved.

"Hi, I'm Kelvin," I heard him say amongst all of the shouting, as little hands tried to tug the bags from my hands. I tried to shout my name back, but by this time I was being grabbed by all sides. I followed him inside the school.

The yard was scattered with a few broken kiddies' toys. A toddler was crying while a very tall black man consoled him. Kelvin introduced him to me.

"Moses, this is Ruby." Turning to me, he said, "Moses is the teacher here, and is known as everyone's 'dad' actually."

Moses flashed a beautiful white smile and reached out to shake my hand. I liked him instantly. He had the gentlest manner, and such soft eyes. He was from Zimbabwe and he had three children of his own back home. But the deteriorating economy of his country had forced him to seek employment in South Africa. He was paid a small salary, lived on the premises and sent money and basic supplies back home regularly.

"Welcome, Ruby. The children have been looking forward to your cooking."

The kitchen was basic. There was a little bar fridge, a gas stove and one or two wooden cupboards where the doors were almost off the hinges. There were hardly any utensils. I was certainly going to remedy that next time.

Kelvin said goodbye to me and the children, while Moses showed me where everything was. He was looking forward to his night off, and said he'd be in his room outside. I was overwhelmed. I didn't know how I going to get everything done and look after all 15 of the kids that were hovering. It was out of control.

A girl of about 13, sensing my situation, came to help me. She shouted loudly, and the noise seemed to die down a little. I was so thankful to her. She had no scarring anywhere, but when she got close to me I could see that she was blind. Her name was Felicity. Apparently, the school also catered for blind children. I later discovered that they had the most exciting Braille room. It had fishing nets strung from the ceiling with objects hanging at different heights, so that they could orientate themselves.

Phil showed me how it worked.

"When you walk like this, and this thing knocks you on the head, you know where you are," he said, demonstrating on one of the other children's heads, and bounced one of the dangling lightweight plastic balls off of it.

There were tiles all the way around the room. They were waist-high, next to each other. They had big round bumps on them, in different combinations. The kids showed me how they used their hands around the room to learn the Braille alphabet.

There were another two classrooms. The lounge consisted of dilapidated furniture and a piano. A very pretty, rather plump teenage girl sat at the piano. She had opal-coloured cataracts over her enormous eyes. She was practicing on the piano, while Daisy sat on the couch behind her. In person, Daisy was even more difficult to look at. Not only was she severely deformed, but she was blind, deaf and mute.

"Who's got Daisy's nose?" shouted Phil. One of the other kids ran off to another room and came back with a little brown thing that looked like a piece of chocolate. He put it on her face, and between him and the pretty blind girl, led Daisy to the kitchen for dinner. Thando, the biggest boy, had gone in for surgery, so Phil had taken over the ringleader position. He never left my side, and continuously fiddled around with the groceries, sticking his fingers in wherever he could.

"Philemon!" Felicity shouted at him, making him jump and withdraw his hand.

I started taking out the groceries. Felicity came over to me with a chopping knife. I was about to take it from her, given that she was blind, but she insisted on helping me chop the vegetables.

"But what if you cut yourself, Felicity?" I asked, not wanting to dampen her spirits.

"I always chop vegetables," she said, smiling. I hoped she was telling the truth, and not just trying to show off. Besides, I really needed her on my side as the rest of the kids seemed a little bit fearful of her. I turned around to see Phil holding the lighter I'd left on the counter, while one of the toddlers tried to grab it from him.

"Stop that! You're going to burn yourself!" I yelled, with a silent 'again' at the end of the sentence.

"No I won't, no I won't!" Phil chimed back.

29

I couldn't believe it. The blind kids wanted to help chop vegetables and the burnt ones wanted to help me light the gas stove! This was crazy!

The food was taking too long to cook. The children started getting restless and whining. They were usually fed and in bed by 7pm. I had gotten to the school at 6pm and, by 7.30pm, the food was almost ready to dish up. One of the children ran out and rang the dinner bell.

I started dishing up into 15 old plastic plates, which were so old and scratched that they always looked dirty. Each child came and took their plate of food and a plastic spoon. Moses came in with a plastic double-sided apron, which he put on Daisy. He strapped a little brace that had a spoon on the end onto one of her little arm stumps.

Daisy used the spoon on the end of the brace and the other stump to scoop her food up and feed herself. It was unbelievable to see. Eating was one of the few things she could really enjoy. Her taste buds were still perfect and she loved to tuck in, albeit messily. She ate a huge amount of food and had a preference for protein and starch. Vegetables were definitely not her thing.

I once saw only courgettes and carrots end up outside of her plate. How she managed to do that without hands, or the ability to see, will always astound me.

Barbara was evidently doing something right. I left for home exhausted and happy that night.

The weekend arrangement

It had been a month since I'd started going on Wednesdays to cook for the children. I got to know a few of them quite well, and loved the reception I always got when I arrived.

The main reason for the school's existence was to facilitate learning while the children recovered from surgery. The charity sourced the surgery and the best care for the children: therefore, children came and went. Most came from rural areas to which they'd return when recovered. The treatment required for these children was mind-boggling – from plastic surgery, to physiotherapy, and of course the treatment of the emotional wounds.

Sadly, a few of the children had been burnt intentionally. Sizwe, now four years old, had been burnt by two teenagers, when he was two years old. They'd wrapped him up in a blanket and poured boiling water on his head and genitals. Thando had allegedly been burnt by his mother, which I found devastating.

Whenever I looked at Thando's face, and saw the beautiful, unscarred side of it, I'd feel tearful that any human being, let alone a mother, could do something like that to her child. However, most of the children had been burnt by accident. Paraffin stoves in shanty huts were probably responsible for the most of the burn cases I saw there.

Initially, I thought I wouldn't be able to handle the emotions that go with working with children who have been so damaged. Once or twice, I had to go to the bathroom to wipe my eyes and pull myself together. However, I soon didn't even notice their injuries. They were just normal, boisterous children.

Phil was always at my side. He almost seemed to 'own' me and was very helpful. Later it emerged that on weekends and during school holidays Phil often had to sit at the school, alone with Moses. Barbara had adopted Thando and Daisy, so technically Phil was the only child there without a home. It didn't take long for me to want to take him for a weekend. I made an appointment with Barbara.

"I think that's a wonderful idea," said Barbara, with a smile. "There is a couple in the States who has expressed interest in adopting him. In fact, there are a few people that want him. But I think it will do him good to come to you, anyway. You do understand he has a boney deficit?"

At my look of confusion, she proceeded to tell me about Phil's boney deficit. He had no forehead. His skull had been burnt, and then septicaemia had set in. The skull bone had disintegrated and had been absorbed into the bloodstream by the body. He had lost a huge portion of his skull, which is why his hairline was brought down to his brow. The only thing protecting his brain was skin and hair.

"So if a ball hits him on the head or somebody bumps his head, what happens?" I asked, nervously.

"We don't like to think about that, although it would be disastrous if something like that had to happen. It could be fatal," Barbara explained.

The thought that something could happen under my supervision, on my property, terrified me. I wanted to run away, but when I looked at the photo on the wall of his little face, I knew I wanted to give him a part of me. I wanted to make his world a slightly better place, if I could.

I decided to take him for that very next weekend.

Barbara made arrangements that Phil be dropped off by Kelvin and another volunteer by the name of Marie. Obviously, they wanted to see where I lived, and if everything was child-friendly. I had tidied up my little apartment in Fourways as much as possible.

The suburb was known to be relatively affluent, with lots of shopping centres and 'resort-style living' apartment complexes. I lived in a particularly attractive complex, which felt almost like a safari lodge. It had tennis courts, three swimming pools and a clubhouse. I glanced up at the thatched ceiling, glad to see there weren't any cobwebs. My large wooden dining room table had been polished. There was a loft room upstairs, which served as a lounge. There were three large fertility body masks on the wall from Tanzania. I hoped they wouldn't take offence at the shape of the pregnant tummies and breasts. The effect was supposed to be dramatic.

Phil arrived in scruffy clothes, with a dirty little green backpack on his back and holding a teddy bear in his arms. He looked nervous. I gave him a big hug and took his things to my bedroom. I didn't have a second bedroom. He was going to have to sleep in my bed, and I'd sleep on the couch.

Kelvin and Marie stayed for dinner. We finished eating, and Kelvin suggested Phil go and watch some television upstairs in the lounge while we chatted.

Kelvin pulled out some papers that he asked me to sign. He seemed a bit sheepish.

"Sorry, but we need you to sign these, in case anything should happen. It basically says that Phil is in your care and that you're aware of his injuries. If anything should go wrong, which I doubt it will, you obviously have to take responsibility. I also think you should consider making this a regular arrangement. It will give him some hope."

I was terrified; what had I done? Once again, I thought of his little face. I reached over and signed the papers with a prayer on my breath. I could do this monthly. One weekend a month would probably do us both some good.

Kelvin explained, "Phil has wanted to leave the school since he was five. The child psychologist was amazed that, at such a young age, he was so determined to get out. A child this injured is usually nervous to venture out into the world. He keeps saying he wants a normal life, with a normal family.

"He has been through a lot. He spent pretty much the first two years of his life at Baragwanath Hospital. He then ended up in another orphanage, where he was actually shunned by the other children.

"He used to hang out with the cleaner, so when he got to our institution two years ago, he used to run around cleaning up after everyone. It didn't take him long to lose that habit, though!"

I immediately reassured him. "I'll do my best, Kelvin. I believe there's a couple in the States interested in adopting him? Is that right?"

"Yes, but he needs to go for surgery first," he answered. "We're trying to get his boney deficit sorted out. He'll probably be ready for adoption then. He's actually supposed to wear a helmet all the time, but he keeps taking it off. While he's a child, they can't use a foreign substance to create a forehead for him, because his bones are still growing. To do it, he'd need a donor, and they'd be able to cover the deficit. They've never done anything like it here in South Africa."

I didn't really want to hear too much more. I was intimidated enough as it was. The prospect of Phil's having such a huge operation troubled me. And on top of that, they would have to somehow attach the skull bone of a deceased child to cover the hole, which also upset me.

Kelvin and Marie left, and I ran a bath for Phil. He wore an old T-shirt and shorts to sleep in. I gave him a fresh towel, and hung around wondering if I had to bath him. He didn't want me to. In fact, I could sense he didn't want me in the bathroom, so I gave him his privacy. He emerged a few minutes later in his pyjamas, and seemed rather tired.

He climbed into my bed, and I stayed with him until he fell asleep. I was so conscious of what was appropriate or inappropriate. Heaven knows what a child could go back saying to the others. Besides, neither of us really knew each other well, so I thought it best to be as respectful as I could and not make him uncomfortable. I went upstairs with some bedding and fell asleep on my purple couch almost immediately.

At about 4am, I heard crying. I jumped up and tried to get down the stairs as quickly as possible to Phil. I had expected him to wake up with a bit of a shock at being in a strange place. He was crying loudly, which I've learned is actually very unusual for Phil. I held him in my arms and rocked him. He seemed to settle down. I climbed in beside him and he rolled over, till he lay against me. We both fell asleep, with him in my arms.

Phil woke up at 5.30am. I heard him marching up and down the wooden stairs and running around the apartment. I was shattered! With bleary eyes, I made my way to the kitchen to see what I could get him for breakfast. I took a yoghurt from the fridge, and set it out for him, with a spoon on the kitchen counter.

"Mmm. I love yoghurt!" he exclaimed, as he wolfed it down. I realised that I wasn't going to be able to get back to bed. That was it; my day had begun.

It was a shock to my system.

The most beautiful child I've ever seen

The day started at a frantic pace. Phil was curious about everything and immediately commandeered the remotes for my television, satellite and DVD player. He was everywhere!

He had the concentration span of a flea! Not that mine was much better. I called my childhood friend Liesel, who had a nine-year-old son, for some ideas. She chuckled on the phone and welcomed me to 'six-year-olds and single motherhood'. Oh, she was such a comfort!

We needed new clothes for him as the ones he'd brought were definitely play-clothes. Phil was always in a rush and didn't really care whose clothes he wore. He often wore clothes that undoubtedly belonged to Sizwe, who was four years old at the time. At first, I thought that perhaps he had no clothes that fitted him, but when I bought him a few items that he took back with him, he still seemed to favour Sizwe's trousers.

We went to the mall, and I could see he wasn't comfortable. In truth, neither was I. We were being blatantly stared at. It wasn't just because of how he looked. In spite of calling ourselves 'the rainbow nation', post-apartheid South Africans are still curious about people of different races getting married or adopting kids. You see the "So, how's that working out for you?" question in their eyes. I've learnt to answer with a gleeful "You should try it sometime" stare back.

I sometimes also saw something else in their eyes. It looked like anger or accusation, which I also understood. I could almost hear them asking "How did this injury happen, and were you around?"

With Phil and I being of different races, it was quite obvious I wasn't his biological mother and that the accident hadn't happened on my watch. I sometimes wonder how I would feel if Phil was of the same race, and looked like me. People would assume I'd been negligent or somehow responsible for my child's accident.

I sometimes got uncomfortable with all the attention as I felt Phil was the hero, and I was simply the person lucky enough to have him in my life.

He spotted a pair of kiddies' sunglasses. I bought them for him, even though he battled to keep them on, because he didn't have a bridge for a nose that the glasses could balance on. A little while later, he asked for a cap. He was obviously having a difficult time and feeling exposed. So I bought the cap for him as well. It seemed to make a difference, although we still got a few curious glances.

I met Liesel later that day, at the Spur, which is a restaurant geared specifically for families with children. She was waiting there for me, dressed beautifully. I always admired her sense of style; she was shorter than me by about a head, which was awesome as I was always the 'shorty' compared to my other friends. Her dark brown hair, which always looked immaculate, was envied by most, including me.

Phil had never been to a Spur before and he quickly realised that it was like a little paradise. There were climbing walls, trampolines, jungle gyms, a TV viewing room and – the pièce de *résistance* – a PlayStation! He was so eager to play that he just ran off without me.

I was concerned about how the other children would receive him. The children stopped what they were doing and began to stare at him. I could see Phil become self-conscious once again in an instant; I ached inside for him, but I also knew that both he and I had to get used to the stares.

A little boy ran out from his group of friends and pointed at Phil's face, shouting "Look at this funny boy!" His friend began to laugh and my blood boiled. I felt rage stirring within me threatening to consume me. A scene from a movie called *The Hand that Rocks the Cradle*, directed by Martin Scorsese, came to mind, where the psycho nanny, played by Rebecca De Mornay, swears and twists the arm of the child who is bullying the child she's looking after.

I wanted to swear, twist his arm and say the nastiest things to this little boy who was being so cruel to my Phil.

I walked over to them and started talking.

"Hey guys, this is Phil. He's normal like you and just wants to play."

I continued, "The reason he looks the way he does is because he was in a fire when he was a baby. He is the strongest boy I know, because he lived through the fire."

I saw they were clearly impressed. Phil relaxed instantly. He ran off, and the little boys ran behind him, curious as to what he was about to do. I heaved a sigh of relief, and made my way back to the table. There was a television screen right by our table, where I could watch what he was doing, as they had the whole play area covered with security cameras. Everything seemed fine.

Phil came skipping back to the table, his face aglow with excitement.

"What would you like to eat, Phil?" I asked, holding up the kiddie's menu for him to choose from. He certainly didn't hesitate. He ordered viennas, chips and Coca Cola Light, before running off to play again. No sooner had he left when his food arrived. I approached the kiddies' play area and heard a distinctive voice shouting louder than the others. Phil had taken over and was on top of his game, totally confident. Well, I say once a ring leader, always a ring leader!

This type of thing happened often after that incident. I learnt not to interfere and I let him socialise without trying to be over-protective of him. But, sadly I could see from his face when someone had been mean to him. One day, after a little blonde princess in a pink dress had been particularly nasty to him, he turned to me and asked, "Why did you choose me? Why didn't you rather pick a girl like that? Or another one at the school?"

I looked him in the eyes and answered simply, "Because you are the most beautiful child I have ever seen."

Phil was very careful when it came to showing emotion towards me. I could see he didn't know what to make of what I had just said. I've said it to him often since, and I think he's starting to believe it.

Kelvin called me on Saturday night to see how Phil was doing. I was glad to report that we had both survived our first day together. When I dropped him off on Sunday afternoon, Kelvin asked if I was fetching him the following weekend. I thought about it and said yes for two reasons.

Firstly, I seriously had nothing better to do with my time. There's only so much partying one can do. I wanted my life to have purpose. The second reason I didn't say no to Kelvin, was that he had inspired me. I still wasn't sure if he had remembered me but I felt that, if a youngster like that could be so responsible and well-behaved, then what on earth was my excuse, when I was practically 100 years older than him?

My boys

Brent and I had called it off about one to two weeks before I had met Phil. It was the Easter weekend and we hadn't seen each other in six weeks, so naturally we were both a bit disheartened. I guess we were just preoccupied with our own lives. I didn't really have to go back to lonely 'singledom' because, in reality, I hadn't truly been part of a couple, what with Brent being on another continent.

In between taking Phil on weekends, and having some rather interesting conversations with him (including discovering he wanted to become a doctor one day), I managed to be active on Facebook. People don't admit to flirting or dating online – there seems to be some kind of sad stigma attached to it. For that reason, I intentionally didn't advertise my 'online' status. I would peek to see who was doing what, but nobody would have a clue that I was online on a Saturday night, because my chat said 'offline'.

I had kindly asked the charity to assist me as a single woman. Due to the nature of Phil's injuries, I couldn't really ask anybody else for help if I wanted to go out. If I had a date or if I was invited to a party, Phil would have to stay at the school for that evening. This was fair to everyone.

As early as Phil awoke, he went to sleep. His bedtime at the school was 7pm so I'd have Phil in bed and be sitting twiddling my thumbs by 8pm. Often, I'd go to bed early, because I was always mindful of the rude awakening I would get early the next morning. One night, I actually decided I was going to show some online activity, so I downloaded a networking application called "Are you interested?".

I used to have a fabulous time with this type of thing. I'd had some gorgeous professional photographs taken of me which, in actual fact, looked nothing like me. The next time I logged in, a pair of blue eyes looked out at me. My goodness – it was Daniel Craig! Well, close enough. This gorgeous man's profile stated the following: '35, divorced, has two children and is a loving father' (that last bit gets girls like me going). This one was definitely going to get a 'yes' from me.

By Monday, I had a match! Blue Eyes gave me a 'yes' as well. He was a general manager in IT for quite a well-known financial institution. I responded to his message immediately as I couldn't wait. I've always admired those cool, calm and collected Grace Kelly-type blondes. I've tried to be like that, but generally I want to explode after a couple of hours. It's much like sulking – it actually hurts me more than the person I'm trying to snub.

Phil could manage a good sulk. I battled with it initially, but I soon realised that perhaps it wasn't so much his sulking as protecting himself. He had learnt to fit in amongst his peers and to stay out of trouble.

In my family, we weren't allowed to sulk. In fact, most of our traumas and upsets were dealt with eventually with a joke. To be a Florence, (that's my surname) meant you dealt with whatever was troubling you and moved on. Cracking a joke, even if it was in bad taste, got you over whatever stress you were enduring.

Blue Eyes was definitely interested in me. We chatted for two weeks on a daily basis before I met him. I've discovered that you can get to know a person quite well by email correspondence, rather than speaking face to face. It takes the pressure off. However, I was still a bit nervous to meet with him. That's the problem with posting photos that make you look like a teenage pop icon. Although there's always the possibility that whoever you're meeting has also posted a few unrealistic photos.

He finally asked me out. We arranged to go on a 'treasure hunt' one Sunday afternoon. I have a penchant for antiques and art, so every now and then, on Sundays, I visit my favourite shops and I call it my 'treasure hunt'. I wouldn't always buy something, but I loved to just look at what was in stock. I'd taken Phil back a little earlier, so my date and I could meet without any distractions.

John came to fetch me at my apartment. I opened the door, trying to act nonchalant. He was just as good-looking in reality as he was in his photo. He wore a camel-coloured tailored jacket, with a white shirt underneath, paired with denim jeans. I hoped he wasn't disappointed in me.

I had never really lost the 5kg that I'd picked up overseas, even though it had been six months since my trip. I was very conscious of this, as I'm one of those people who immediately show weight gain, especially in my face. He didn't appear disappointed; in fact, I discovered that he had lost 35kg in the past year by being on a strict diet and gym regime.

We shopped around, and I showed him all my favourite places. Later, over coffee, he told me about his children and what had gone wrong in his marriage.

John had been divorced for several years. His son was 12 years old at the time, and his daughter was nine. It seems that the marriage had been rocky from the start. He told me that his ex-wife had been a compulsive liar, and had betrayed him on more than one occasion.

I started to feel sorry for him; he then proceeded to tell me about his rebound girlfriend, who was most definitely 'psycho' and an alcoholic. It seemed that he'd never had attracted any good relationships, and that everyone he'd get involved with was either crazy or evil. I was rather concerned that I might be one of the two – after all, he was attracted to me, too!

We finished off the afternoon. I'd had a lovely time and hoped he felt the same.

"Don't worry about walking me to my door," I said, breathlessly; and I leaned over and gave him a lingering kiss in the car. I hoped he'd get the message that I was interested, but didn't want things to move too fast. He responded afterwards with a smile, saying that he most definitely wanted to see me again. I giggled all the way up the stairs into my little apartment; waiting to get behind closed doors to do my little victory dance. I knew he'd be around for a while.

Sure enough, he sent me a text message when he got home and invited me to his parents' place the following Saturday. He was having a few friends around and he had his children over for the weekend. John thought it would be a good idea for his children to meet Phil. I was quite taken aback about the whole event as, on my side, meeting parents is usually a big deal. I agreed to go. The children wouldn't know that there was potential romantic interest – they would assume we were just friends, which is actually all that we were at that stage.

I looked forward to the following weekend, while we communicated via text or email. Saturday finally arrived and I followed the map and direction to his parents' place. His folks were down to earth, welcoming Phil and I as if they'd know us for years. I brought a bottle of wine, some snacks and a box of Turkish Delight for his mother. John kissed me hello and, after introducing his children to Phil, took me aside.

"I didn't know how to tell you this before, but I actually live here. I was worried you'd think less of me if you knew I was living with my parents. The truth is, I'm in the process of building a house in Edenvale, which is not far from here. I lived with my ex-girlfriend and left everything behind when I walked out."

I shrugged and said it didn't matter, really, as it was just a temporary arrangement.

The children were well-mannered, with John's little girl, Ashley, being extremely affectionate. She was the spitting image of her father, whereas the son, James, was darker in complexion and obviously took after his mother. He was quiet, and sat in front of the computer in his grandfather's office most of the day. Ashley took Phil under her wing; he was running around all over the place. I had to calm him down quite often, but he was out of control with excitement. It didn't help that he'd been given sweets earlier. I could see the difference in him after he consumed anything with sugar.

The day progressed nicely. I sat and chatted with John's mother for a bit. Every now and then I caught John staring at me. At one point he silently mouthed "you're sexy" to me, with a wink. I blushed and looked away. I didn't want the children to see, as I think it could possibly be unsettling when a parent gets involved with a new person. I wanted to make sure of whether we were right for each other before I got demonstrative in front of them.

I said as much to John, but he said that he wanted his children to see him being affectionate with me; after all, I was going to be part of his life and it was perfectly natural. He thought that we may as well get them used to it. I was thrilled that he'd also accepted Phil. Life was looking peachy.

A whirlwind romance

John had taken to visiting me every second night. We went out to dinners and to see the theatrical production of African Footprint, which his parents attended, too. We had been seeing each other for a month when we planned a trip to Mozambique. He didn't scuba dive, which is one of my interests, but he loved the country as much as I did, with its palm trees and white, sandy beaches.

Phil didn't like the fact that he wasn't coming with us. I drew up a calendar for him, and cut out pictures of *Kung Fu Panda*, to mark each day I was away, so that he knew exactly when I would be back. We had all gone to see *Kung Fu Panda* together, and I knew that Phil would enjoy the pictures and find a sense of comfort in them.

We made our way to Inhambane in Mozambique, which is a picture-perfect destination. The country borders South Africa, and is by the coastline, with the Indian Ocean lapping the beautiful beaches. We stayed at a place called Bali Lodge. John had found it while on holiday with his friends from work and decided it was the perfect place to bring a girlfriend. The place had a Balinese theme – wooden walkways led the way to the lodge, which boasted Indonesian teak furniture. The individual chalets were similarly themed and were well-equipped, although we had to prepare our meals in a communal area.

John liked cooking and food as much as I did. We didn't have much to do there, except go to the markets, cook and drink wine. Every day, we bounced along the beach in my Jeep with the soft-top roof down. I had a video camera and started filming while standing on the passenger seat as John drove across the dunes. I felt truly free and excited to be alive.

John, who was usually quite introverted, was also thoroughly enjoying himself, and got into the swing of things easily.

Our little breakaway came to an end and we realised that, between us, we were almost broke. Somehow, this seems to be the story of my life when on holiday in foreign countries. In Mozambique, it is essential to carry cash – if you get a spot fine, you're expected to pay money on the spot. We were stopped by a traffic officer, and had to pay a R500 fine for an expired licence disk, which I'd forgotten to renew. We had no money left.

Having just recovered from handing over all of our cash, not even an hour later, yet another traffic officer stepped out. Unfortunately, we weren't given a receipt or any paperwork from the previous officer, so once again we were expected to pay a fine for the offensive licence disk. We had no money, so instead had to trade a cap and designer shirt for our freedom.

We stopped in Maputo, with the fuel tank just off reserve. Before filling up with petrol, we asked the petrol attendants to see if either of our petrol cards worked. Neither of them did, so we didn't put in petrol and just hoped for the best. It was 90km to the border. Maybe our petrol cards would work once we got across the border, although both were in deficit.

I was once again counting on my card going through for under R100. You'd think by now I would have learnt my lesson. Scarily, John didn't seem that much more responsible than I was. He was supposed to be an IT nerd – they're not supposed to be like me!

We crossed back into South Africa with a huge sense of relief. We could practically cruise to the filling station in neutral. Unfortunately, things weren't much better back home in terms of finances, although the following day was pay-day. Both our cards were rejected. John ended up leaving his laptop and watch with the management at the filling station until such time as we'd paid for the fuel.

We stopped at the next town and both of our cards miraculously worked, so we made it home.

"I'm very impressed with how you handled the stress of what we've just been through," John kept saying. Little did he know that having a financial crisis in other countries was the norm for me!

It seemed our relationship had survived the first few tests – that of being together solidly for a few days, and not fighting; and then, surviving in a financially pressured situation. Although I wasn't quite sure I was comfortable with him being as financially irresponsible as I was.

Happy families

John and his children started to spend more time with Phil and I. For the moment, I was comfortable holding his hand and being affectionate in front of the children. They seemed to enjoy coming to my house, and started to bond with Phil and I.

We fell into a regular routine. John would visit on alternate nights during the week, and would bring the children over every second weekend, when it was his turn to have them. By this time, I'd bought a bunk bed for Phil, so that he and Ashley could share. James and John would sleep on both couches.

I could see Ashley was very protective of her father, and didn't particularly want to share him with anybody. I was fully conscious of this, and didn't want her to feel threatened in any way. Therefore, when she was around, I'd keep a distance and let her have her time with her dad. Eventually, she sensed I wasn't a threat and seemed happy to share him.

On weekends, we would go to gym in the morning and have a braai in the afternoons; either by the pool in my complex, or at John's parents' place. Phil had been asking to go to church for a while. Before we met, he apparently used to go every Sunday with the rest of the children from the home.

The same couldn't be said for me, however! Christianity made me doubt myself in the silliest way. It has taken me many years to realise that receiving God's *undeserved* love and kindness, doesn't mean I'm an *undeserving* person! Maybe I'm the only child who ever took that personally and formed a self-sabotaging, subconscious belief system around it!

Barbara had suggested I take Phil to the same church he had attended. If I couldn't get him to that church, I could take him to a non-denominational church, as long as they didn't push 'fire and brimstone' dogma or anything controversial.

Before meeting John, I'd attempted to take Phil to a normal church service. It was a church recommended for families. After having to sit still for about 20 minutes, the minister asked all of the children come forward to the front row of the church, which had been kept vacant.

I became excited and told Phil all the kids were going to the front. He got excited, too, and proceeded to run to the front. The rest of the children all sat obediently, facing the stage. Phil wasn't sure that was what he wanted to do and therefore decided to sit on the edge of the stage facing the audience, where he could keep an eye on me.

The minister carried on as if nothing out of the ordinary was happening. I tried to mouth to Phil that he must sit on the chair and turn around. He ignored me, swinging his legs backwards and forwards, kicking the stage. Nobody was listening to the sermon; everybody's attention was on Phil and I. He looked me in the eye, and then reclined on the stage as if he were at the beach.

By this time, I was furiously mouthing and showing him to sit up and turn around, with big gestures, trying to be quiet and not make a spectacle of myself. It was too late. The audience was fascinated with our commotion, while the minister continued with his sermon. Thankfully we got to the end of the service and all the children returned to their parents. Phil came skipping back to me innocently. That's just how he was.

John's children had also been regular church-goers, along with their mother. Therefore, on Sundays we took the children to Sunday School. I hadn't been too keen on a structured religious environment, but it seemed to be best for everybody.

James and Phil got along famously, in spite of their age difference. We'd often laughed until our stomachs ached at their antics. Poor Ashley was always the brunt of their jokes; she was a gentle little girl who genuinely wanted to please everyone. John said that his ex-girlfriend, who also happened to be an industrial psychologist, had said Ashley would end up being a stripper or falling pregnant as a teenager. I was determined that, while I was around, she's have a strong sense of self.

Strangely enough, I got the feeling that her mother was also determined to do the same for her little girl, in spite of John's telling me what a bad mom she was.

James, on the other hand, was having a rough time with his stepfather. John had custody of his children for the first four years of Ashley's life. There were initially issues in the mother's life, but she had since remarried, gone for counselling and settled. In fairness, she tried really hard to atone for her absence. She'd also had another two children with her new husband.

James was hell-bent on coming back to his father. John didn't want to take one child without the other, so the idea was to get both children back. John's parents had told me that he'd given up his children because his then-girlfriend (the 'mad alcoholic/industrial psychologist') didn't want them. Who could blame her, though? She was in her mid-twenties and wanted a fresh start. John had had a vasectomy but was prepared to reverse it for her.

In the end, it seems her drinking ended their relationship. John had lost his children, as well as a large sum of money. From time to time, she'd send a drunken text, which John would show me.

Mostly, I felt sorry for her.

School holidays had arrived, and we had John's children for the duration of their holiday. John would take them to work, where they behaved like angels. At his office, the kids were so well-behaved they were practically invisible.

James was prepared to do anything to go back to his father permanently, and had gotten up to all sorts of nonsense, such as self-mutilation and shop lifting. In the meantime, his stepfather had told him to pack his bags and to go and stay with his father. James was quite happy with this arrangement, and told me he was not going back to his mother and stepfather or he would start being naughty again. He wanted to stay with his dad, at my house, if possible.

I told John to let James stay as long as he needed to. James stayed for an additional week after school holidays had ended, before he agreed to go back home to his mother to give their relationship one more try. We hoped he would keep his word and not do anything else that could harm himself or anybody around him.

Germany

John had decided that the weekends he didn't have his children, he'd give Phil and I some alone time. Phil was always thrilled when I arrived on Fridays after work to fetch him. The feeling was mutual.

These weekends were precious, even though at times I'd be exhausted. Phil had never eaten a toasted cheese sandwich before. 'Toast of cheese',' as he called it, became a regular request – in fact, anything containing cheese was a winner. I was concerned that he wasn't getting enough nutrients in his diet, so I would buy Woolworths pasta dinners for children, where the vegetables were artfully disguised; and I always made sure the bread we used for the 'toast of cheese' was whole-wheat.

Phil had never been to a wedding or social braai. Obviously, I could organise the latter event quite easily, but a wedding would hopefully be an option sometime in the future.

Barbara had mentioned that she was trying to find a doctor who would be prepared to operate on Phil and fix his boney deficit, therefore constructing a new forehead for him. She had enquired both in the States and Europe. Thankfully, a doctor in Berlin agreed to examine Phil, and perhaps operate on him. A local airline was prepared to sponsor Phil's ticket to Berlin.

It was heart-warming and scary at the same time to watch the plans come together. To top it off, a number of radio stations ran commercials in order to raise awareness for the charity. All in all, the charity was doing very well. Barbara was hoping that the doctors would examine and operate on Phil immediately. Hopefully there was a suitable donor's skull available.

Phil's departure to Berlin came all too soon. I knew he would perhaps be far away for some time, and the operation would be risky. I worried that the bone might not 'take' and might disintegrate again. What if something went wrong as they operated so close to his brain? He could also return looking completely different, with a newly constructed forehead and his hairline moved back to its rightful place.

In my imagination, I saw the doctors getting really carried away, practically giving him a new face. My heart leapt with excitement and anxiety. I loved him so much the way he was. I loved the little cavities that were his nostrils, his lopsided eyelids and his top lip that had curved up on the one side in a little point, to just under his right nostril. I loved kissing his beautiful little face. He was perfect just as he was!

I had no leave days from work, and I was also out of money, so it just wasn't feasible for me to go with him. I felt helpless. However, I knew Barbara was accompanying him. I had every confidence that she'd get Phil exactly what he needed. Everything would be alright.

Barbara had a knack for getting what she wanted. She also had a nasty streak, though; she would humiliate, criticise or expose people in public, on her website or in her newsletters, when people let the charity down, or she couldn't get her way. I understood how former staff or volunteers could have the nerve to go to the press – there was no doubt her methods were controversial. I had heard that the old lady living next door to the house, where Barbara ran the charity, had physically slapped Barbara recently. God only knows what she did to the old lady to warrant getting a slap! She must have been particularly insolent.

As a child, I'd enjoyed reading a children's book called *The Water-babies*, which is a classic by Charles Kingsley. The story is about children who are able to breathe under water and live in a stream. They have gills (the concept is actually quite Darwinian, come to think of it) and are looked after by two archetypal women.

The illustrations depicting them were particularly memorable. One woman, known as Mrs Doasyouwouldbedoneby was soft, kind and epitomised love. Her cheeks are plump and rosy and the naked little water babies are sitting on her lap, hanging on her, with their arms around her, completely enthralled.

The other woman, known as Mrs Bedoneasyoudid, was haggard, bristly and dressed in black. She held a stick in her hand, representing discipline, and seemed terrifying. Whatever nasty or naughty thing a child had done to another, she would do in turn to the child. So if you were a water-baby and put a stone in another child's mouth, Mrs Bedoneasyoudid would put a stone in your mouth.

Both archetypes reminded me of Barbara. Sometimes, I wasn't sure which one she took after more. She seemed so soft and kind with the children, but she certainly turned into an angry, bristly lady of vengeance when dealing with adults and the public in general. In fact, she seemed to have general disdain for people.

I packed some new clothes for Phil. I also bought him pyjamas decorated with Grand Prix inspired images printed on the fabric. I included a pair of slippers that had 'whateva' printed on them; James had identical ones. I tucked a little figurine of Kung Fu Panda into the side pocket of Phil's little backpack. I gave him his Barney to cuddle on the plane.

We had to collect Barbara on our way to the airport. By the time we arrived at her place, she hadn't even packed. John was driving us to the airport, and I could see he was anxious about getting Barbara and Phil there on time for their flight. I mentioned to Barbara that I had already packed for Phil. She took the backpack from me and instantly started removing the clothing from his bag, replacing the new clothes with shabby, old clothing. I wasn't sure what that was all about. Maybe she wanted him to look poverty-stricken and have people feel sorry for him.

"He can wear his nice, new clothes when he's home with you," she said abruptly, handing the Barney toy back to me. I didn't argue; I was just thankful that she hadn't discovered the sweets and Panda, as they would no doubt have been confiscated, too. I was a little annoyed, but I respected the fact that she had her reasons for behaving like this.

We had 20 minutes to get to the airport. John drove as fast he could, with Barbara directing him all the way, although he lived right by the airport and travelled the route often enough. We arrived at O R Tambo airport with a few minutes to spare.

As Barbara checked in, Phil hugged me goodbye. He'd never been on a plane before and he knew it was going to be a life-changing trip. He was teary, possibly because he knew he was in for some surgery and it would doubtless be painful.

I didn't let him see how emotional I was. I watched him walk through the doors with his backpack on, which was nearly the same size as him. He was the bravest little boy I'd ever met. The doors closed behind him, and I collapsed into tears, while John tried to console me. I cried all the way home.

There is also another brave little boy worth mentioning. When we arrived to fetch Barbara, Temba approached me. He was 11 years old, and so badly burnt it was difficult to look at him. He had one eye, one arm and a very disfigured face – more so than Phil's. He looked as though he battled to breathe, and constantly had sinusitis.

He was quiet, but always the voice of reason, as he was a little more mature than the two ringleaders, Phil and Thando. When reading or speaking to all the children, they'd lose concentration and get boisterous, whereas Temba would volunteer an answer or add a comment to indicate he was listening. He'd often do this when the children were getting raucous. It was reassuring to have him around, as he brought some order to the hysteria Phil and Thando often caused. He was polite and tried his best to set a good example.

Temba approached me and said in his nasal little voice, "While Phil's away, can I please come to your house? Even if it's for one night only?"

I hesitated, as I'd already become so attached to Phil. I knew I could possibly get attached to this child, too. He saw my hesitation, and quickly added,

"Don't worry, I'll handle my own ARVs. You won't need to worry about that."

I was shocked! Temba was HIV positive on top of everything. I didn't know it, and only realised when he mentioned his anti-retroviral medication. He thought that was the reason I was hesitant, and the realisation of it overwhelmed me.

"I'm going to have to ask John if it's okay, Temba," I said, looking for an excuse to turn away and compose myself. I quickly ran to the bathroom, and the tears started flowing. I couldn't comprehend that one little person on this earth should be so afflicted. I made a mental note to have it out with God when I next prayed.

John readily agreed to have Temba over, even though I could see he was concerned that I may get caught up and take on another child. I could see he battled with the stares and attention we got when we were with Phil. I also battled at times, but John was not as open a person as me, so I really appreciated his generosity of spirit.

I organised to take Temba the following weekend. James and Ashley would be there, and hopefully they'd be as kind to him as they were to Phil.

As it turned out, the kids got on fine. James was happy he could have a fellow PlayStation fan to hang out with. When I went to fetch Temba, he came out with three plastic shopping packets. One had his old clothes in it and the other two were like grocery bags filled to the brim with medication, not groceries. We had morning and afternoon ARVs.

I couldn't believe how much medication Temba had to take. He was an independent little boy, I thought, as I watched him take his meds. Temba counted out his tablets from various bottles and I double-checked what he took against the list of amounts and times of medication Moses had given me. He didn't make any mistakes. He even managed, with his one arm, to open a bottle and suck up a few millilitres of liquid in a big plastic syringe and squirt it into his mouth. I was impressed and touched by his strength and the courage he displayed in taking care of himself.

I wasn't sure how to cope with HIV; I didn't personally know anybody in my life that had the virus. Temba always washed his cup when he was finished drinking. I had since noticed, when at the school, that the children sometimes ate off each other's plates, but never off his.

That weekend, he left his toothbrush next to mine, in a little puddle of water. I was initially alarmed, but I reassured myself that it was all right. At that moment, I realised how staggering my ignorance was. I was ashamed.

Temba's father had abandoned him and his mother, who was also HIV positive. He had contracted the virus from his mother. His grandmother took care of him most of the time, when he was home, and not at the school, undergoing surgery. From what I could gather, they lived in what I would consider extreme poverty. However, unlike Phil, who had nowhere to go and was at the school full-time, Temba was able to go home to his grandmother. He had already been to Canada for an operation.

Barbara certainly knew how to organise things. A few years back, she'd arranged for some surgeons in Toronto to construct a forehead for Temba, as he also had a boney deficit. The hole in his skull was substantially smaller than Phil's. The doctors there had used a metal plate in his skull, which according to Barbara was a mistake. I wasn't sure exactly why she felt Temba's surgery wasn't a success, but he was alive and well nevertheless.

The weekend with Temba came and went. Life went back to normal. Phil was away for an entire month. Barbara emailed the volunteers at the office, updating them on Phil's progress. It seemed they'd found the right surgeon, but they were going to use his own ribs rather than the skull of a donor. Barbara learnt that Phil wanted to be a doctor, and was quite taken with his choice of vocation. She also discovered his love of cheese. She said she'd noticed that, since he'd been coming to me, his food choices were definitely becoming unhealthier. She accused me of feeding him white bread and 'other such rubbish'".

I was offended as this most definitely wasn't the case. Most kids would have chosen a chocolate croissant over a whole-wheat sandwich. This was when I discovered how quickly she criticised people and continuously made assumptions. She'd sometimes be adamant, even though she was in the wrong.

Barbara is the only person I know who is capable of firing volunteers and being quite hostile in the process. There were often times when Phil would mention that someone had been fired by Barbara. Nobody ever resigned gracefully, it seemed. The word 'fired' was always used. I was quite shocked that this was commonplace, and that the information about the volunteers or teachers who had been dismissed would be shared so openly with the children. It seemed disrespectful to these adult helpers.

After what seemed like an eternity, Phil and Barbara finally returned from Germany. I waited for them excitedly, at the arrivals section at the airport. I was filled with anticipation, as I hadn't heard whether Phil had been operated on or not. I finally saw them! Phil didn't look any different. They made their way out of arrivals, towards me. Phil ran towards me, and I picked him up and hugged him tightly.

"I'm so happy to see you, my baby! I've missed you so much!" I kissed him repeatedly, all over his face. He hugged me back, and then struggled out of my arms to climb onto the luggage trolley.

When we were inside of the car, Barbara began explaining. They didn't operate on Phil, but they wanted him back in a few months' time so they could do so then. She then proceeded to tell me what it would take to harvest Phil's own ribs to create a skull cap, and which muscles and skin they'd also have to use. She explained how they would move his hair back to where it should be. The doctors had stated there was a 50% chance of fatality. She started to spell out the words, so that Phil couldn't understand, so as not to alarm him.

The tears streamed down my face, under my sunglasses. It was frightening, and a selfish part of me wanted to say that I would have him the way he was, and alive, than take such a risk or have him suffer in any way. Barbara seemed adamant that Phil should have the operation. She was right, of course, but I really battled with the reality of it all. She was confident, though, despite the risks.

Barbara mentioned that she had to give Phil a few smacks on two occasions while in Germany. She looked at me reproachfully at the time, and said, "You have to discipline him. Little boys need a smack from time to time and he is no exception. In fact, he's quite naughty."

I was a bit shocked. I knew Phil had the capacity to be mischievous, like other six-year-olds. I had always used a stern tone of voice, which seemed to do the trick. I sometimes felt the need to shout when I was frustrated. Barbara seemed to believe his boisterous behaviour was as a result of my lack of discipline. I was still annoyed about the 'white bread and rubbish' comment, but now I was being blamed for his undisciplined ways as well.

Incidentally, on his return, his bag was stuffed to capacity with imported chocolates and sweets, which Barbara had obviously purchased. I thought it quite ironic.

From that point onwards, I could sense that Phil was testing me to see whether or not I'd actually smack him. But I didn't want to. Growing up, I had gotten my fair share of hidings, and my avoidance antics were legendary in my family. It always started with that one nasty sentence: "Go to your room."

I wasn't sure what I was going to do with Phil. My family seemed to be entertained by my current dilemma with Phil's discipline. I could sense my mother's amusement watching me attempt to discipline this younger version of myself. Without a doubt, Phil was just like me and has the capacity for the exact same behaviour.

With each passing day since his return, I realised that my stern tone was no longer working on Phil. Reprimanding, cutting back on TV viewing and confiscating toys weren't having the desired effect, either. I was being challenged. It upset me to know that at some stage I was going to have to smack him.

I could see John watching me, to see if I'd actually go ahead with it. When I asked John if he would do the smacking for me, he shrugged and said: "I smack my own kids ... I'm not smacking yours for you – that's your job". Admittedly, there were a few occasions where Phil obviously deserved a hiding, but I just couldn't bring myself to do it.

One night, I had an idea which I hoped would work. As he stuffed his uneaten bread crust into the pillows of my couch again, I threatened:

"Phil, if you carry on doing that, I'm going to tell Barbara. I've heard she hits really hard. And I'll make sure she gives you a big hiding when you go back on Sunday."

His eyes widened. I knew it was a cheap trick, turning Barbara into the bad cop, but in reality, she was the one who started this whole 'hiding' business. I was happy to make it her problem.

But this was a temporary solution, as any parent will tell you. And it didn't take long for me to understand the challenge didn't involve Barbara at all. A duel was imminent. Either I had to win, or Phil would disrespect me for ever.

The showdown came in the form of yet another cheesy bread crust stuffed between the cushion and the armrest of my couch. It was just before Christmas. Phil kept one eye on the television and one eye on me, just finding his discarded crust in the couch. I was quick and efficient.

"Phil, is this yours?"

"Yep." He was now ignoring me, facing the TV.

"Well, that deserves a smack," I said; and before he could laugh at me or roll his eyes, I was at his side. I took him by the hand, pulled him to a standing position and used my other hand to deliver one sharp, hard whack on his bottom. Even though he was wearing denim jeans, my hand still stung a bit.

Phil looked at me in shock. I knew it was a painful smack. He didn't cry, but I could feel the tears in my eyes.

"There'll be more of those if you don't start behaving yourself. Life is hard, Phil, but it's much easier when you've got manners and respect. I really hate smacking, but it seems to be the only thing you will listen to."

It was the last smack I ever had to administer. From then on, Phil was quite obedient, and seemed to respond to the stern tone again. When he misbehaved I'd make him forfeit TV time or not let him play with his favourite toy, which was a fluffy, stuffed dog. I'd gotten him a Spiderman money box as well, which was great for teaching him to save, and was also for fining him for bad behaviour from time to time.

Breaking up, making up

It was October, and John and I had our first fight while Phil was away. John literally disappeared from my life for two weeks. I got to understand that this was his way of dealing with issues; he'd go into hiding, and it turned out to be a monumental battle to get him to open up again.

The argument started when he had brought the children to my house. We were by the swimming pool, and John was preparing a fire for a barbeque.

John suddenly went quiet. I could feel he was withdrawing, and naturally, as we women do, I tried to get answers. Eventually, I got tearful, and asked what was wrong. He shrugged and said there was nothing wrong. Come to think of it, we'd been so busy with the children, maybe we had been a bit disconnected and I hadn't noticed. So I suggested we started 'dating' again, and having some fun.

He shouted defensively: "Doesn't washing the dishes mean anything to you? What about all the little things I do for you?"

Okay, so he spoke a different 'language of love'. I felt ashamed and apologised. But we honestly hadn't had a romantic evening together for at least two months. I didn't think I was totally unjustified in my request, but I had obviously found fault before taking the 'little things' into account.

When John left that night, I felt there had been in a shift in our relationship. He didn't make eye contact with me and he left without kissing me goodbye. I checked the drawer I'd allocated to him for when he stayed the night and I saw he had cleaned it out. I knew he wasn't coming back. In a panic, I tried to call him. He ignored my call.

Eventually, I got a text message from him saying that he needed time out and that perhaps I did, too. He mentioned that he could see I wasn't comfortable with the situation with his children and I had taken to 'comfort eating'.

That did it! I was mortified. I didn't think I was comfort eating, but he had started to watch everything I put into my mouth. Maybe I was comfort eating. I would be lying if I didn't admit to turning to food a lot when I am stressed. The truth is, I hadn't lost the weight from overseas, or the additional 3kg I picked up in Mozambique.

For a petite woman like me, seven or eight kilograms are a substantial amount of weight. John, on the other hand, had come back from Mozambique and immediately applied himself at the gym to shed the excess kilograms he'd picked up.

It was devastating to hear that my horrible habit had been noted. I never wanted to touch food again. However, like my attempts at sulking, starvation doesn't last long, either. In spite of fasting for only a few days, I lost three kilograms. I played my usual angry, break-up music (a favourite of mine is by My Chemical Romance's song called *Famous Last Words* – it's a really good break up song and the lyrics say it all: "I am not afraid to keep on living. I am not afraid to walk this world alone.").

I deleted John's contact details so that I wouldn't break down and call him. It was almost a ritual for me. My resolve lasted only two weeks, though. I made contact with John's mother. She was clearly upset about what had happened and said how stupid her son was. I liked that. John had apparently told his father that he wasn't ready for a relationship.

I was annoyed that he didn't have the decency to tell me what going on. I messaged him, telling him he wasn't going to get away with disappearing like a coward, without an explanation.

I got his number (again) from his mother. He responded immediately, saying he would like to come over and that he was hoping he'd hear from me – he just wasn't sure if I'd be open to him making contact again, after his rude behaviour.

John arrived in the evening and somehow I ended up in his arms. He told me that I was looking hot and couldn't stop kissing me. We seemed okay for now.

The crying lady

In between John's weekends with us, Phil and I had formed certain habits and routines. Phil loved routine and didn't like change. A typical Friday would start like this: I'd arrive at the school to fetch him; he'd come running out and climb into my car, lean over and press the horn. Then he'd wave like mad to all his friends. He'd then press as many of the buttons, knobs and dials, on the dashboard, as quickly as possible.

We would go straight to the shopping centre next door to the apartment block I lived in. We'd usually walk side by side, holding a shopping basket between the two of us, chatting. We'd make our way to the dairy section, where he'd pick up a block of Gouda cheese, and I'd reach out to pick up a loaf of wholewheat bread for his 'toast of cheese'. We'd choose yoghurts – his favourite flavours were strawberry and vanilla.

Phil also enjoyed his cereal, so once a month we'd make it to the cereal aisle. I didn't allow Coco Pops, which would have been Phil's first choice, but we generally compromised with muesli or granola with chocolate bits in it. I thought that was fair.

Then we'd end up in the candy aisle, and that was where the real negotiations began. We often settled on a pack of Jelly Tots for Phil. I'd always take a Lindt chilli chocolate for me, which Phil resented as he felt it was a waste of good chocolate. He'd roll his eyes and go "Ooh, spicey chocolate again! Can't you just get nice, normal chocolate?"

"No, then I'd have to share it with you!" I teased.

"That's not nice," he said, hand on his hip, wagging a finger at me.

"Yes, you're right. Sorry. You can share it with me"

"Yuck!"

"Exactly."

Our last stop would be by the soap and hygiene section. I always had bubble bath in the house, as I believe little boys aren't always that interested in bathing themselves properly, even if you stood outside the bathroom, armed with a wooden spoon, threatening them.

At least I knew that while he played with the rubber ducks and soap suds he'd get clean in the process. That's what the bubble bath product's television commercial was all about.

We'd finish our shopping and then stop at Mimmo's, our favourite pizzeria, for a kiddies' pizza with a toy. If one of us needed the bathroom, the other would go in and order the pizza. Phil would always order a glass of Rosé for me – I'd be slightly embarrassed that my kid was ordering me alcohol, but decided not to make a big deal of it.

Every now and then I would order a mineral water, but if Phil got in before me, I'd get the usual glass of pink wine. I think he liked the way the word Rosé felt on his tongue (or maybe he realised that it was easier to get coins out of me for the tattoo-and-sticker slot machine when I'd had a glass of wine).

He'd sometimes order with me sitting right there; "She'll have a glass of Rosé and please don't forget my toy." Then he'd stand up and walk away with his nose in the air, one arm out like he was a waiter carrying an invisible tray, and then break into his Charlie Chaplin walk, which he knew was going to have me in stitches of laughter. He loved entertaining me.

Phil became something of a little celebrity at my shopping mall. All the store keepers knew the two of us by name. The waiters at Mimmo's, in particular, loved Phil. On one occasion, he had been begging me for one of those stick-on tattoos from the tattoo machine. I felt it was a bit of a waste of money, so I said no when he asked. I usually gave in, but that night, for some reason, I felt I had to say no.

The waiters saw his face. Bearing in mind that they all most likely had impoverished families, to whom they sent money and maize-meal, they all chipped in and each donated R1 to buy Phil a tattoo. I knew they earned, on average, between R2 000 and R3 000 per month.

I got a lump in my throat. David Gregory Roberts, in his book *Shantaram*, put it so well when he said, "There's nothing as humbling as the generosity of the very poor." I realised how much they loved Phil and wanted to see him smile. The love that was displayed literally made me feel like I was afloat. I believe we all were for that moment.

One night, Phil was sitting with me and a little boy of about three came wandering over to our table. He didn't see Phil's injuries and really wanted Phil to play with him. I looked for his mother. She was sitting there watching her son playing. She was a beautiful brunette with fine features. I'd have put her at about 28 years old. She seemed distraught. She was drinking wine at a rapid rate, and I saw that she had started crying. Her little boy was oblivious.

I continued to read my book, aware of Phil's movements. He was excellent with smaller children. He often carried the toddlers around at the school, although some were almost as big as him.

Eventually, the mother called to me. I looked up from my book and smiled.

"Sorry, but please would you come and sit with me? I want to talk to you."

I could see she'd had a few glasses of wine, but her eyes were still full of pain.

"I just want to tell you that you have a bright light around you but, as bright as your light is, your son's is even brighter – it's almost blinding."

"Wow! Thank you! He is special, isn't he?" I said back, proudly looking for my little angel.

"I couldn't help but see you're upset. Is there anything I can do?" I asked, without meaning to sound nosey.

She told me all about her husband, the little boy's father, who had left her for her best friend. They'd been having an affair for a while, apparently. The woman, Maggie, sitting before me, was at that stage of the break-up where the shock and disbelief make one almost delirious. She was quite disorientated.

I sat with her for a while, and encouraged Phil to distract her little boy. He understood immediately, while I tried to pacify her and sober her up a bit. But she continued to order wine. I gave the waiter a dirty look, and he just looked back at me, shrugging with a helpless "What am I supposed to do? I don't know how to handle this" expression on his face.

Later that evening, I called for the bill. When I asked Maggie where her car was, she couldn't answer me. She wasn't sure if she even had her car there or not. In fact, she wasn't sure how she had gotten to the restaurant. I asked her where she lived and she couldn't tell me that, either.

"Can you at least try to direct me to your house if I drive you home?" I asked.

She didn't answer me, and I decided that if we couldn't get her to her house we would just have to keep her at my place for the night. The little boy could sleep on the bunk below Phil, and she could sleep in my bed. I'd sleep on the couch. I paid our bill and got her up, while Phil picked up her little boy. We got them both to my car.

Thankfully, she managed to produce a set of keys. It was a good sign.

"Shurn here," she slurred, gesticulating with her arm for me to turn right.

We drove along the road for a while and she seemed to think we'd driven past her house. It had potential to be a long night. I turned back, and took the keys from her, pressing the remote control as we retraced our steps. The gates of one of the houses opened. I stopped outside the house and pressed the button again. This was definitely her house and she seemed relieved to be home.

We got them into the house. She immediately passed out on her bed. The little boy was wide awake and determined to continue the game with Phil. He was not going to sleep. I felt so sorry for him. We tucked him into bed, but he kept getting out. Eventually Phil and I went and sat in the lounge. I could tell we could easily fall asleep there, but there were no couches or beds and Phil was exhausted.

The toddler finally fell asleep and we let ourselves out. I locked the doors and threw the keys inside. Unfortunately the gate was going to have to remain open for the night, but at least they were home safely and their front door and security gate was locked. I was sure the mother and her baby would be fine, and said a little prayer for them.

We got in the car.

"Shew! That was a naughty baby. What happened to that lady?" Phil asked thoughtfully.

I thought about how to answer him and decided to be as honest as I could be.

"Her husband doesn't love her any more. He loves another lady."

"Is that really why she's crying?" He didn't seem to believe the situation warranted such tears. In fact, I could hear in his voice that he was actually a bit annoyed that she was such a 'sissy'.

"Phil, that's how girls cry. Their hearts get very sore when they love somebody and that person doesn't love them any more."

"Oh." He thought about it for a while.

"I'm never going to make a girl cry like that, ever!" he declared.

The woman was right – his light was blinding.

School holidays

It was our first Christmas together. Between myself a few colleagues, we managed to organise a year-end function for the charity. I had collected donations from everyone at the office for Christmas gifts. My boss was friends with the owner of a local restaurant, and they agreed to host the children there at no charge. In total, we managed to raise about R2 600, of which we gave R2 300 to Barbara, and used the rest to buy little gifts and crackers.

John had arranged to have his children over for the school holidays. His parents were taking the children with them to their beach house in the Eastern Cape. Barbara and I decided that it would be better for Phil to go to the school for Christmas, instead of being stuck with adults for the day. Apparently the school put on an excellent Christmas for the children.

In the end, we decided to do a traditional Christmas day on the 16th December for all our children. It wasn't exactly Christmas day, but we decided to make it as exciting as any Christmas day could be.

I watched an episode of *Nigella's Feasts*, and got some ideas for Christmas day. I'd never cooked a Christmas meal before.

I bought gammon, which I cooked slowly in nutmeg-flavoured brine. I baked a fruity Christmas cake and decorated it with golden, edible glitter and stars. The children helped me bake biscuits, which we had great fun cutting into various shapes and decorating with silver balls and icing. By the time it got to the turkey, I'd had enough of being the domestic goddess and bought one already prepared!

The 16th arrived. It was a wonderful day, which I don't believe any of us will ever forget. John had given me money to buy the children's presents. Ashley got a pink hairdryer set, James got an MP3 player (which was all the rage at the time), and Phil got a remote controlled car.

The children were beside themselves with excitement. We had put up a Christmas tree and decorated it with fairy lights. We took out the biscuits we'd baked for the reindeers, which Ashley put on a plate under the tree. John left a beer beside the plate, instead of milk, as he felt that Santa didn't get a stomach like that on milk alone.

After getting the children to bed, which proved to be a difficult task, we wrapped the children's presents and put them under the tree at around midnight. There wasn't a sound coming from the loft; the children were fast asleep. John and I ate the biscuits and he drank the beer and left the bottle next to the empty plate. So much for Santa and the reindeer – but at least the remains looked like evidence of their supposed visit.

I could barely contain my own excitement and battled to fall asleep. I really wanted to be awake and hear the children coming down the stairs in the morning. No sooner had I nodded off to sleep than I heard Phil stomping down the stairs. I heard little giggles and checked the time. It wasn't quite 5am, but the entire household was awake.

I peeped out of the room to see Ashley and Phil on the stairs, marvelling at the missing biscuits and empty beer bottle. Ashley loved the fantasy of it all. As for Phil, his excitement was bordering on euphoria. We had also wrapped boxes of sweets and chocolates and other little sock fillers, which had name tags attached to them. All in all, there were about three presents for each of the kids. Ashley and Phil quickly figured out whose was whose and waited anxiously to unwrap their presents.

John was still fast asleep. I eventually got him up all bleary-eyed so that he could enjoy watching the children open their presents. The children were thrilled with their gifts and proceeded to climb into the rest of the cookies. Phil ate all of his wrapped-up chocolates and sweets in one go – his blood sugar must have reached an all-time high.

John's father was coming over for lunch in the afternoon. His mother was already at the beach house, so she couldn't join us. Before we knew it, the morning was over and lunch was being served. It went down a treat, and I was glad I had put so much effort into the day. All the cooking and gift buying and, of course, the excitement had left me exhausted but wonderfully contented.

A few days later, Ashley and James left for the beach house and I dropped Phil back at the school, which would also give him the chance to enjoy his birthday with his friends, which was just before Christmas. On the way back to the school, we stopped at the supermarket so that I could buy him a big chocolate cake to take with him. I promised to fetch him a day or two after Christmas day, and also agreed to have Thando come over and visit with Phil.

John and I spent a quiet Christmas together. We went to watch the latest vampire movie on Christmas morning then popped in to join my relatives for lunch. They were happy to see us and the day progressed peacefully.

Two days after Christmas, true to their word, both Phil and Thando were ready for me when I collected them from school. Phil wanted to show Thando all the places we went to, and the activities we normally partook in whenever he came to visit. Thando's situation was better than Phil's in that Barbara had an official fostering arrangement with him, which actually made him her foster son, whereas Phil was merely placed at the home, as a 'place of safety'.

I believe Phil felt the difference, as Thando would go and sleep at Barbara's house or office and Phil was left to sleep at the school. It was obvious Thando would have been more 'favoured', and I suspect Phil wanted to show Thando that here, in his home environment, he was the favoured one. I guess it's the closest thing Phil had ever experienced to sibling rivalry.

We had a very busy weekend, with the two boys fascinating and entertaining everyone at the Spur, as well as everyone at our communal swimming pool the following day. A lady walked past in a white bikini, and Thando, in his deep 'gangsta' voice shouted "Yoh! Yoh! See that sexy chick in the white! I'm going to marry her!"

At barely eight years of age, they definitely knew the difference between 'average' and 'hot'. The girl in the white swimsuit smiled and said hello. Before I knew it, these two had walked with her to meet the rest of her girlfriends. I was thankful they were only seven and eight! I had seen enough of their antics, and how they charmed everyone, to make me shudder when contemplating them at puberty.

Not only were they completely adorable in spite of their appearance, they had the confidence of regular Don Juans.

In South Africa, we have a custom unique to tribes such as the Zulu and Sesotho speaking communities, where there is a bridal price that the groom or his family has to pay the bride-to-be's family – it's called lobola. Both Phil and Thando are descendants of these tribes, and I wondered morosely, if I ever had to adopt Phil, how much money I was going to have to start saving! And watching Phil and Thando, and which girls they approached, I knew that only the prettiest girl would do, and that was going to be damn expensive, or would at the very least cost me a whole herd of cows.

It was Saturday evening when Barbara called and she sounded extremely annoyed. She was under the impression that Thando was only visiting for one night and she wanted him back immediately.

"This is unacceptable. I never gave permission for you to keep Thando for the entire weekend. And I expect you to bring him back this instant!"

It was 8pm at night, and I was extremely shattered after looking after two active boys all day. The last thing I felt like doing was driving for 45 minutes to take Thando back home.

"Barbara, I'm sorry about the misunderstanding. I really thought it was okay for me to have both boys for the weekend."

Both boys stood anxiously by the phone, with Phil pleading with me not to take Thando back yet.

"I don't care what you thought. You can't just do as you please. I am in charge here, and I want him back tonight. He has plans for tomorrow."

"Barbara, I don't like driving into your area late at night. I don't believe it's safe. I promise I'll have Thando back by 8am in time for whatever it is you have planned."

"Well, you'd better," she said rudely and hung up before I could say anything more.

I put down the phone and the boys whooped with delight. I put them to bed and collapsed into my own bed shortly thereafter.

The next morning, I dropped both boys off at 8am, hoping I wasn't in too much trouble. Barbara wasn't around, and I left them with Moses at the school, who didn't seem to think there were any major events planned for the day.

Germany and bloody Valentines

John and I had a great Christmas and New Year's Eve together. We had toasted the New Year on my balcony, watching the fireworks display that our neighbours were hosting. Towards the end of December, he had to spend a week in Cape Town, setting up an office for his employer. He texted me every day, telling me how much he missed me. He promised that the minute he was back and we had some alone time we'd go down to his family's beach house. I had taken leave and made plans to go away for a week.

While on leave and in another province, I got an email from the school asking if I could drop Phil and Annie (one of the care givers) off at the airport. Phil was off to Germany again. It came as a shock to me. I'd had his imminent surgery at the back of my mind for some time but kept suppressing the thought, due to the accompanying fears which threatened to strangle me every time I contemplated the reality of it. I'd been informed of his pending operation two days before he was due to leave. This time, he was most definitely undergoing the life-threatening surgical procedure. His bed at the hospital was booked, and he was staying with the lady who had previously hosted both he and Barbara the last time he was there.

Unfortunately, due to my being so far away from the school, and with its taking at least another two days to pack up and drive back home, I had to decline. In a way, a part of me was relieved, as I couldn't face another tearful scene at the airport. I wanted Phil to be brave and I didn't think I'd be able to be the brave one this time. Given his 50%chance of survival, my nerves were on edge. I got a call from Kelvin, assuring me not to worry and saying he'd take Phil. This was probably better, as I knew he'd handle the scenario better than I could.

Phil was operated on within a day or two of landing. I called in at the charity to cook for the children that night, and Moses, the man with the big, white smile, told me that Phil was fine and that the operation had been a success. Apparently, although massively sedated, Phil had still managed to talk on the phone. Moses showed me a photo of Phil with his head bandaged, sticking his tongue out cheekily at the camera.

They had managed to harvest two of his ribs, weld them together and create a skull cap successfully. They had also used some tissue and muscle from his back. I wasn't sure how it all worked, and didn't want to ask too much, either. After all, it was my little boy's back, ribs and head being talked about!

It was the middle of January, and I could sense John withdrawing again. I'd given up trying to compensate for the long silences and sarcastic remarks, which would sometimes catch me by surprise. I learnt to leave him alone if he was in a bad mood. I knew he was also taking a lot of strain at work. So I also put it down to work stress.

As promised, we went down to the beach house and the situation didn't improve much. However, John had bought pencils and sketch pads for us to plan the layout of the house he intended to build in Edenvale. He had been steadily working towards building his dream home on the piece of land he'd bought.

Of course, the more he involved me, the more it became 'our' dream home. Thankfully, this seemed to bond us for some of the time. But other than that, I felt he wasn't with me. He was there in body but his mind was elsewhere. It wandered into secret places that I was refused access to.

The comfort eating wasn't a problem anymore. I was on my best behaviour. But something else had become an issue. Alcohol. This was partly because of the bad experience he'd had with his alcoholic ex-girlfriend. And on reflection, perhaps I had been swapping one crutch for another, but I didn't believe my drinking habits were any different from any 30-something party-girl's.

To keep the peace, I'd refrain from having a drink with him when he offered. He'd then get uncomfortable and tell me I shouldn't stop enjoying life because of him. It was strange that it was okay for him to have a drink, but then he'd resent me and watch me like a hawk the minute I put a glass to my lips. He'd quickly mention how badly his ex-girlfriend would behave when she drank. She certainly sounded scary, but I was nothing like her. If I did have something to drink, I'd be aware of what I said and did around him. That in itself was enough to drive a person to drink!

I started to think that maybe I did have a problem, and consequently became increasingly aware of how much I consumed as well as when and where I drank, which is never a bad thing. I believe alcoholism is a disease that can creep up quietly and, before you know it, you actually do have a problem. Moderation and balance is what I continually strive for; in my world, overindulging and abstinence are as extreme and undesirable as each other. I've experienced both. I'd rather be in the middle, enjoying life with the freedom that is mine, which is my responsibility to myself.

We drove for 10 hours, from the coastal town in the Eastern Cape back to Johannesburg. Upon arriving home, I felt a lot more tired than I was before we left for our little breakaway. Something just wasn't right.

Back home, we made plans for Valentine's Day. I called for a reservation at a lovely little restaurant around the corner from where I lived. Valentine's Day, that year, in 2009, fell on a Saturday. The day before had been a big day at the office. We had been under a lot of pressure. At 3pm, a few of my colleagues and friends left the office to go for a drink in anticipation of the weekend. I declined their invitation because I knew I would incur John's wrath. Fully aware of how much John hated my drinking, my colleague, Rina twisted my arm to join them. Rina reasoned that her fiancé wasn't fond of her having a drink, either, so she was likely to get into trouble. And if she was going to take the risk, so should I.

"Come on, Rubes! We never join the team for a drink. You're always off to fetch Phil on Fridays, and I'm always being the good wife-to-be. Phil is still in Germany. You can come this time – you have no excuse!"

I thought I would only have on cocktail, but ended up having two, as well as two tequilas, which were sent over to our table by a bunch of guys. I realised I definitely couldn't drive. At that point, John called and I froze. I knew he wasn't going to be happy with me. I answered the phone immediately, telling him where I was and what I was doing.

"Oh well, you know I don't like to be around you when you're drinking," he responded. "I may as well have stayed engaged to my ex girlfriend Francis," he snapped. "I'll see you tomorrow."

I felt a sense of relief that he wasn't coming over right then and I'd have to watch myself. And in my relief that I'd only see him the next day, I didn't really pay much attention to last remark about Francis. I was used to John being snide when it came to this type of thing. I was just grateful that I had to time to sober up without having to ask him to fetch me; or feeling like I had to rush home and pretend I hadn't had a single drink (which I did contemplate doing, by the way).

I had a cup of coffee and a glass of cold water at the bar, and made my way home much later. In spite of my attempts to sober up, the alcohol in my bloodstream was really too high for me to drive. I promised myself that, in spite of Phil's being away and me being a free agent, I would not do that again.

I called John and sent him a text, but didn't hear from him for the rest of the night, or the whole of the next day, for that matter. I called my friend Rina from work, who was also in the dog-box. We were both concerned, but I was even more so, as I was being blatantly ignored and I wasn't even sure if we were still on for Valentine's Day. I felt terribly guilty and remorseful.

I had so looked forward to going to the restaurant I had booked; I even paid a deposit. I didn't want it to go to waste, but then considered how sad it would be sitting at a romantic restaurant like that on my own. I also really didn't want a repeat of the previous year's Valentine's Day, either. I was aware that my neighbours could see into my house. So that year, in 2008, to cheer myself up on Valentine's Day, and also for the sake of the spying neighbours (I assume they spy on me, too, and it's not just me who is the nosey one), I bathed and got into a very sexy little nightdress and lit candles all over the house, in the pretence of getting ready for a romantic date, who was on his way.

I hoped my audience appreciated all the trouble I was going to.

I made a big show of closing all the curtains so that they could see I had 'plans'. Once, the curtains were closed, I changed into my baggy pyjamas, ate a chocolate, then took a mild tranquiliser to knock me out. The next day couldn't come quickly enough. I was grateful Valentine's Day happened only once a year.

This year, my options didn't look much better – in fact, they looked even more depressing. I imagined going to the restaurant anyway, and openly crying in front of everyone. If you made eye contact with everyone and stared at them you could really make all those stupid couples feel uncomfortable. That would serve them all right for being so deliriously happy.

That evening, I heard from John to say that he was on his way. I was ecstatic to hear his voice. I threw my arms around him when I opened the door. He was holding his kit bag, so obviously he intended to stay over. I was forgiven! Oh, happiness!

He was very subdued throughout the evening, and I felt significantly chastised.

"It's okay, babe, I'm just in a bad space," he eventually said, after I had hugged and kissed him, and launched into a thousand apologies. I considered I'd gotten off a lot more lightly than I'd anticipated.

I joked about what I had imagined doing to all the happy couples if I'd ended up at dinner alone. John knew all about the previous year, as I'd mentioned it when we made the booking, while rolling my eyes at my own antics. He smiled absently. I had thought it was all quite comical, actually. I had run out of conversation starters, and our silences were getting longer and longer. He ordered a bottle of red wine and was drinking very quickly. I barely sipped mine – I was very conscious that booze was what had gotten me into this awkward situation in the first place.

I looked around at the other couples and saw people communicating and touching. I hoped I would see another couple being distant or having problems. Nope, we seemed to be unique in our misery. I reached over and touched his hand, not saying anything, but pleading with my eyes. He smiled and looked away. I wondered how long he was going to be like this for. Last year's Valentine's Day suddenly didn't seem as miserable as I'd remembered it to be.

I cried myself to sleep that night, even though John lay next to me. I hoped he didn't realise I was crying; I didn't want him to see or feel how much the evening had disappointed me. He hadn't touched me or connected with me at all that night. I was confused as to what he was doing there when it was clear his mind wasn't with me.

New foreheads and revelations

There was some joy in my life, though. After years of living with nothing but hair and skin covering his brain, Phil came home with his promised new forehead. Initially he had two swollen sides, with the new scar down the middle, which had made the top of his head appear like the letter "m". I was hopeful that he had stabilised and that the ribs making up his forehead had 'taken' and were melding together nicely. It was a relief that there was now something a little more substantial protecting his brain than skin and hair.

After a month in Germany, Annie had gotten home sick and had returned before Phil. So Kelvin flew over, much to Phil's delight. It was a long time to be away from home. There were still another four weeks left of Phil's recovery at that stage.

Phil seemed to have settled rather well with Shelly, the lady he had stayed with previously in Germany. They had bonded, and I couldn't help but be a little jealous. It was evident that she was able to take care of him throughout the day as she worked from home. Phil also told me she never shouted at him ... ever! Shelly sounded like a saint. I hated her! I berated myself for my childishness, and in truth I had admired what I had heard about her.

My mother, as well as my younger siblings, Claire and Troy, accompanied me to the airport to wait for Phil's arrival. I often called Phil 'Troy' because they were so similar in spirit. It was almost uncanny. I'd waited more than six weeks to see my angel, so I was getting a bit restless at the arrivals gate. My mother had bought him a big, colourful balloon that read 'Welcome Home'.

Phil ran through the crowds; I held my arms open, waiting to be re-united, Hollywood-style. He ran straight past my outstretched arms ... into Troy's outstretched arms.

"Troyyyy!" he yelled.

"Well, thanks for that, sunshine!" I yelled, folding my arms in a mock sulk.

Troy picked him up and threw him in the air. Troy is about 15 years younger than me. Mom, Claire and I stood watching these two hug, as if there was nobody else in the room. It was a beautiful moment, and I was proud to have these two wonderful young men in my life.

Kelvin wasn't far behind Phil. He looked exhausted. "He didn't sleep on the plane," said Kelvin. "He actually hasn't slept a wink in two days! I'm completely knackered! What a handful!"

Phil was once again overwhelmed with excitement and, when he gets like that, he borders on being rude. I've given up explaining it to people – it's just the way he is.

I dropped Kelvin off at his quarters and dropped Phil off at the school afterwards. He was eager to get back to his friends and couldn't wait to tell them all about the sledding and the snow. It fascinated him, as we don't really get snow in South Africa. I quickly went to buy some biscuits and cake for the children; I knew they wanted to welcome him back. I arrived, cake in hand. The children were running around like mad things. Barbara was waiting for me. She wanted to 'chat'.

"Now that Phil had undergone the procedure, are you going to take him on full time? You know that's what he really needs," she said.

John had mentioned that he was prepared to have Phil live with us, and that he'd be allocated his own room when the house was built. Although we had our problems, the fact that John loved and accepted both Phil and I proved that he was worth every fight. I nervously responded to Barbara, "That is the intention – I'd love to take him, and John seems okay with it, but we obviously need to see how things go."

Ashley and James were thrilled to have Phil back. John was quite excited, too. But the next day when John read the newspaper and saw that a family had supposedly applied to foster Phil he became withdrawn. The headlines that rang out were something to the effect of "Boy Finds Forehead and Mom." I think it was all a little too real for John. He seemed taken aback and he knew that I was equally surprised by it; I'd told him about the casual remarks between Barbara and I the day before. I could see John had an internal struggle going on. In fairness, it put a lot of pressure on all of us.

Months passed by and May arrived. It was Mother's Day – the first time I felt entitled to think of myself as a mother. I can't remember what it was I'd done this time, but John had gone quiet again for a while. Once again, it made me question myself, and I was tempted to blame it on my weight again. I discovered I enjoyed doing that.

Phil had mentioned that he really wanted to go to Sunday school that day. I thought it was a good idea. Occasionally, I read him stories, as my parents had done for me.

Daniel in the lion's den was always a hit, but when I got to the story of the three Israelites, Shadrach, Meshach and Abednego, who were saved from burning in a fiery furnace by an angel, I was at a loss. "What's going on there?" he asked, as I tried to quickly flip past the story.

There was no getting out of it. I had to explain the whole story to him. He didn't even need to ask, I saw the question in his eyes, "Yes, your angel was there too, Phil. Why do you think you're here? He saved you!" Phil responded with a light "Okay," and I heaved a sigh of relief.

I dropped Phil off at the kids' area where school was held and walked past the entrance to the church. A woman stood at the door with a basketful of chocolates. As I walked past, she asked me if I was a mother. I hesitated, then said yes. I wasn't going to explain; all I know is that it just felt right.

She smiled and gave me a little chocolate and said, 'Well, this is for you, for being a mother." I wondered if she would still have given me a chocolate if she knew the whole story. I already felt like less of a woman because I wasn't a biological mother; imagine being deprived of a chocolate, too! After taking the chocolate (and lying), I thought it was best to go inside. Maybe I'd have some sort of epiphany.

I walked inside, with the hazelnut truffle melting in my mouth. It was absolutely delicious and worth lying for. The pastor's wife was apparently giving the sermon. I sat down thinking, "What am I doing here? I'm going to end up feeling bad, for not being part of the 'mommy' club." I started to switch off. I was already restless, and cursing my own weakness for chocolate that now put me into this awkward situation.

She began to speak. "As a mother, I want to welcome all the women of God who are bringing up their children in the Lord's way". Oh, enough already!

Then she said something so profound. I've never been back to that church, or any other since, for that matter. The job was done – I had heard God, and what I had to work with, was going to keep me very busy for quite some time. What she said that day influenced my beliefs and actions forever.

"I want to speak to the single childless women, if you'll permit. Young ladies, you may not be mothers as we know it on this earth, but you have been given the gift of femininity," she continued, "We are all mothers, whether we have children or not. I have a message specifically for these women. If a child in need has crossed your path, it has happened for a reason. We have a world filled with homeless, abandoned, hurting, abused children – aching to be wanted. I swear to you on this day, that child has come to you for a reason. Open your heart. You're needed."

I didn't hear much more after that. I never thought I would cry openly in a church, but the message was pure and true. I dabbed my eyes and got up to leave as soon as I had the opportunity. I didn't want to speak to anybody. I fixed my swollen eyes with a large amount of make-up; I forced a cheery smile in the bathroom mirror. I knew I had heard something of meaning.

I went back to the kids' area, where Sunday school was still taking place. I didn't feel like such a fraud, after all. Enjoying the warmth of the winter sunshine, I made my way towards my son. I wasn't sure how much I could provide for him, but I was certain of one fact – we belonged together.

The life coach

A friend of mine suggested that I go to see a kinesiologist. I'd never heard of kinesiology before: muscle movement is used to access the subconscious mind. It sounded a bit off-beat to me, but I was curious so I set up an appointment to see what all the fuss was about and what 'I' could tell 'me'.

The kinesiologist ran his practice out of a huge office park. The security process was tedious, with much signing, taking of photographs and interaction with security guards. They gave me directions to the practice. The place was like a maze! In no time, I was lost, and the fact that there were only one-ways everywhere annoyed me. I mistakenly drove out of the campus while in a one-way lane, and had to sign in all over again.

Once again, the security guards gave me directions towards the building. They spoke slowly, as if instructing a kindergarten child. I found the building, but then couldn't find the entrance. At last, I made my way to the second floor. I was running five minutes late and had become more anxious by the minute. After all, I was being charged R500 an hour, and those minutes were ticking by.

A man in what must have been his forties came out to greet me. He had a slight Afrikaans accent.

"Hi, you must be Ruby. I'm Kobus. Shame, you really battled finding this place. Don't worry – everybody does. Typical IT people designed it, with the entrances facing the wrong way." If it was an IT person responsible for the design, then I'm quite used to being lost, I thought grimly. I relaxed in the armchair opposite him.

"Right, do you know how all this works, Ruby?"

"No, but I heard that whatever it is you do is great, and people are getting results. I'm not sure exactly what it is I want from you, but I'm hoping you'll be able to tell me," I said.

He directed me to the massage bed. I must admit I was a little worried I may need to remove clothing, especially my boots! Yes, I was wearing those boots from Paris!

I unzipped them, and left white talcum powder footprints all the way to the massage bed. I hoped that was where my mortification would end. If I had to take off any clothes, if my memory served me correctly, I was wearing old, loose panties. Lovely! He must have seen the panic on my face.

"Don't worry, you can keep your clothes on," he reassured me.

Phew! Relief! I lay down on the bed and he took my right arm.

"I'm going to show you how this works", Kobus explained. "When I ask you a question that you're uncomfortable with, your muscle will unlock. As I press down, you need to hold your arm firmly. Don't resist; just hold fast. Say that your name is Ruby."

"My name is Ruby". My arm held fast.

Next I had to say,

"My name is Kobus."

Instantly my arm weakened. I realised it worked much like a lie detector would. Kobus explained that the body is the most reliable source of information, as it can access a lot more of your brain than your conscious mind does. I kind of bought into the theory and he started asking questions.

I was amazed at how accurate it all was, in terms of emotions and events in my life.

When he'd completed all the muscle checks and gotten a few answers out of me, he stood back, and said, "I don't want to be funny, but you're completely lost. I don't think I've come across anybody so confused and lacking in direction. Are you familiar with the biblical story of Jonah being swallowed by the big fish?" I nodded. "Do you know why he was swallowed by the fish?" he asked.

"He didn't listen to God?" I offered.

"That's part of it, but if you stand back and think about it, you'll see the story is mostly about direction."

He continued, "Jonah was heading in the wrong direction. When you head in the wrong direction, you would get swallowed by big fish, figuratively speaking. All sorts of things are likely to happen, and this may manifest as your having a really rough time. In short, when you're on the wrong road, the universe throws rocks at you!"

"Wow! That's profound!" I exclaimed. "I have obviously been heading in the wrong direction, as it's been really rough. But the good thing is the fact that you're going to fix it for me."

"The only one who can fix this is you," Kobus said firmly. "I'm trying to get an idea of what it is you want to do, but you're not responding. We can't set goals without knowing exactly what it is you want."

He made some notes, and looked up again. "I'm going to give you an assignment. Please go home, and make a collage. Just cut out pictures and glue them onto a piece of cardboard. They can be pictures of anything – anything that you want or anything you see that grabs you."

I was quite excited to do a project like that. I love drawing and cutting out pretty pictures.

When I returned the next week Kobus seemed quite impressed with what I had put together. I'd bought a bright pink piece of cardboard, and stuck so many pictures on it the colour of the cardboard underneath could not be seen.

I was very proud of my work, although I wasn't quite sure what he intended to do with it. I'd included pictures of Florence, Tuscany and passport stamps everywhere. Of course, he didn't say I only had to stick to pretty pictures I liked – so I had to include a few odd ones, too. Otherwise, it would be boring, just like any old vision board. And he hadn't said it had to be a vision board either, so I definitely wanted to make it as interesting as possible.

I had an image of a naked woman who looked cold, fat and uncomfortable in her own skin. Of course, there were also a few headless male torsos.

"I decapitated them," I explained to Kobus, when he pointed and raised an eyebrow.

Thankfully, there were a few men who did manage to escape the wrath of my scissor, and keep their heads. One man was playfully throwing a child up into the air. Isla Fisher (Borat's wife in real life) was doing a cartwheel on the beach, with Borat, holding their child looking on. There was a queen glued above everything. (Yes, I am the queen of everything.)

A little girl, with a guilty expression, had her hand in a cookie jar. Below her, Jack Black lay in a foam bath with curlers in his hair. Right in the middle I had a picture of a woman holding the hand of her husband – he was in a wheelchair. "Kobus, it's my expression of the ultimate demonstration of selfless love," I responded at his what-is-this expression on his face. He responded, surprising me: "I think you should get into some line of work where you do healing of some kind."

I thought about this, and asked him why.

"Because at least you'll be able to help your patients in a professionally recognised capacity. Hopefully then you'll stop dating them! All your ex-boyfriends were in a traumatic post-breakup stage, or they had lost their jobs or had some social issue. Isn't that so? And you put them nicely back on track – then they leave you – don't they?" he enquired. "No offence to anybody in a wheelchair, but do you need your partner to somehow be incapacitated so that he can't run away from you? Do you believe the only way anybody is going to stay with you is if they incapable of moving on their own?"

Oh dear, my arm was having a lovely time betraying me, while I blatantly tried to lie and deny these allegations. It seemed I had issues relating to food and guilt, which came as no surprise to anybody. The headless men showed that I wasn't sure who my future partner was, which didn't suit me at all. I really wanted it to be John – I was sick and tired of men and dating. It seemed I thought men were weak and women strong. Oh, and it appeared I was attracted to effeminate men – thanks to my fascination with Jack Black in the pink bathtub.

I couldn't wait to tell John the news – I could almost hear it. "Guess what, babe! My therapist says if you're gay and in a wheelchair, I'm likely to want to marry you!" I hoped to God that wasn't my truth, as it would mean something I wouldn't want to really admit deep inside myself: that I had deep-seated fears regarding men and my sexuality, and investigating that would open a can of worms I wasn't nearly ready to deal with.

"Of course I like effeminate men, Kobus! They're non-threatening!" I shouted in defence.

It was an exhausting session, but he wasn't finished with me.

"Do you know what the difference is between you and Jesus?" he asked.

My eyes went huge. Nobody had ever compared me with Jesus before. Goodness, that would have seemed blasphemous. Even somebody who didn't go to church would have been a little disturbed at where this analogy was going. (Although having said that, I have a very keen interest in theology and the Bible.)

"When Jesus healed the lame man, he told him to get up and pick up his cot. You would have healed him; you would have picked up his cot for him; and you would have carried it for him too, just in case he still had self-esteem issues. All of this while you still have all these people that still need to be healed and preached to, which is actually the real reason you are on this planet."

I got the point. I wasn't sure how I was going to do all this, though.

I had a second assignment. I had to go home and write a list of 30 goals, which was a task I struggled with. I realised that I didn't really want much, or maybe I was just scared to commit myself to anything. I had experienced quite a few disappointments in the past, so I had learnt not to expect too much. I realised my life was totally absorbed by John and the kids. I wasn't sure who I was anymore. John was working more weekends than usual. He had a new job and seemed to be at everybody's beck and call but mine. Often times, the children ended up staying with me on weekends, as they preferred visiting me to sitting at their dad's office.

I proceeded to write down my goals and couldn't get past eight. To be honest, I felt pathetic. At work, I had been asked to fill in a form pertaining to a career advancement programme. Tessa, my boss, had asked me to fill it in.

"Tess, you know I don't want your job. You know I don't want to be a manager – I'm good at sales and it would be a waste to place me elsewhere. I've been a boss before," I continued, "and I hated it, Tess. If I tell the truth, it's going to look like I'm not ambitious."

"I know, sweetheart, but you know this is a bureaucracy and we have all these tests and evaluations every couple of months," she explained, "And you know I'm the only one who is likely to read it anyway. Please just do it."

I walked away, form in hand. I sat at my desk, and started reading through it. It had all the usual questions, such as "Where do you see yourself in six months' time?" I couldn't help answering, "Exactly where I am, thank you very much. I like my desk."

The questionnaire continued, "Where do you see yourself a year from now?" Again, mischief got the better of me. I wrote, "Why, is something going to change? Am I moving desks again?"

I was starting to enjoy myself.

The next part asked if I'd like to be part of the management division. Obviously, that was a no-no.

"I think you'd be doing the company a disservice by putting me in management. I have been in said position before, and consequently hated it. The company will make more money by letting me do what I do best, which is selling advertising space. It's fun to break sales records. It's no fun to sit in an office managing people," I wrote.

There was another question about having sufficient tools to do my job. "No, I am useless at Excel. I need to go on a course or something," I wrote.

"Would you like to study further?"

My answer was yes.

"What degree would you be interested in obtaining?" "An Excel course," I repeated, knowing full well the difference between the words 'degree' and 'course'. But I was in a cheeky mood.

As Tessa read through everybody's forms, I heard her laughing. She shouted from her office:

"Florence, thank you for some honest bullshit. Everybody else, I'm sick of your dishonest bullshit!"

Now, in reality, I had to do the same with my life and I realised that I actually had to get serious and be honest with myself for a change. My situation was no joke.

Dreams and goals

I had completed my list of goals, and I ended up with a lot more than 30. Granted, some of them were more dreams than goals, but interestingly enough a lot of the dreams had actually started to manifest.

I wanted a house by the sea. Phil and I have an anthem – it's called *Ocean Drive*, by The Lighthouse Family. One day, he asked me to play that song about the sky being pink and blue. When I took Phil back to the school on Sunday evenings, the sun would be setting with the sky turning pink and blue. Everything would glitter with the last rays of sunshine. It was usually quite a sad time of the day. A part of me also wanted us to have a house, where we could live together with a sky that was pink and blue. This is when my daydreaming began.

I could imagine the house overlooking the ocean. If I closed my eyes I could almost see the dolphins. In my dreams, Phil and I are dancing around. We often danced around the house, anyway, but in my imagination we were on green grass in a beautiful garden with honeysuckle and the fragrance of roses in the air. The house had more than enough space for both of us and my husband and baby daughter. Yes, I'll admit there's a husband and a daughter in there. I've got a son already, but there's room for another one.

I'm usually skipping with Phil in the garden, while the baby is asleep. Sometimes she wakes up and wanders out sleepily with her pacifier and blanket; she's got wavy golden hair and wears just a diaper and little white vest, because of the heat.

The dream continues with me just having finished with a client who is feeling a lot better than she did when she arrived. My husband is due home in about two hours, as he is still at work. Clearly, I have no idea who he is yet, but what I do know is that when he looks at Phil, he must have a similar expression in his eyes to that of Kelvin and Moses. Of course, my future husband's daughter is his little pride and joy. As for when he looks at me ... nothing but ravishing looks should come to mind. It seems like a tall order, but there it is.

I've promised to help Phil with reading; but instead we run around the garden like lunatics, with our Labrador puppy. The dog is as excited as we are. I imagine Phil doing his mock-impersonation of me walking in my high heels and nagging him to pick his clothes up off the bathroom floor. He shakes his long hair, like someone in a shampoo ad, and puts his nose in the air. Or he does his little Charlie Chaplin walk.

So that more or less summarises my dream.

My short-term goals were vast and varied. I tried not to put too much pressure on myself – as if I don't pace myself, I start out with the best intentions and then burn out and give up. So I put time frames in place. I was very impressed with kinesiology and enquired about part-time courses. The course required one full weekend a month.

I knew that would affect Phil, but I believed that ultimately it would be in both our best interests for me to study it. I don't have a tertiary education, and have been extremely lucky most of my life, but the prospect of being a media rep in my more 'mature' years depressed me. I worked in a fickle, young industry. I knew I didn't look bad for my age, but I was painfully aware that I was close to being a 'has-been' if I didn't go into management or do something progressive.

At least a kinesiology practice would be something to fall back on. I could slowly start practicing and work my way towards building a little business that would allow me to work from home, and help people at the same time. The total course was four years long, but after 250 hours of practice, and a number of exams, one could already be considered a kinesiologist. According to my schedule, I would reach that level in about two years' time. I could live with that.

The other goals included belly dancing, doing a creative writing course and losing 8kg. Maybe I'd excite John again. There were a few chores on the list as well, such as cleaning out my CD collection. (I hate to admit it, but I did remind myself of Bridget Jones from time to time. We seemed to have the same self-image issues – she's just luckier in that she's fictional!)

Another goal was to travel to exotic places, especially Tuscany. Like everybody else, somehow meeting Nelson Mandela and Oprah Winfrey both featured in there as well. (We all want to meet them, regardless of whether they want to meet us or not!) And finally, doing the right thing for Phil – whether that would be to adopt him or set him up somehow for life. Perhaps both.

My list of goals was ever expanding, and I had great fun ticking them off my list as I achieved them. Plant herbs – tick; sort out music collection – tick. I was seeing less and less of John, but I hardly noticed. He had become so quiet lately that he was practically invisible. Every now and then, when somebody asked me how everything was going, I'd launch into everything I was doing. Then of course they'd ask how John was, and I'd say "very well". This wasn't really a lie, because he was so quiet, that everything indeed seemed well. Or maybe I just didn't care.

Coming together and falling apart

I hadn't seen John in a month. I had been working hard on my list for the last two months, so I was certainly feeling much better about myself.

My time was narrowly divided with work and Phil. I often felt like I was spinning out of control. At times, I'd wonder if I should be in a relationship at all. The problem was, I was very attached to John's children. One day he called me and asked me if I wanted to have a look at an apartment he was interested in renting, while the house was still being built. He assumed I'd being moving in with him, so he wanted me to see it. He desperately wanted to get out of his parents' house.

It had been 18 months, and only a slight amount of progress had been made on the building plans; he was still waiting for the council's approval of the architect's plans.

I met John outside the apartment block. The August wind blew my hair into my eyes when I opened the car door, and looked out onto the power station in the vicinity. We were in the suburb near the land where the building was going up. It was becoming more and more obvious that the children were going to live with John in the new year. James had been playing up again, saying that if he didn't live with his dad he'd cause untold mischief.

The apartment was tiny. My heart sank. I tried to imagine living there with John and his children, but I felt the walls closing in on me, while the power station loomed over us, imposing and austere. I choked back my tears. My father had worked at that very power station, and had died a very painful death of asbestosis just three years before. I thought of my little thatch loft apartment on the third floor where I stayed.

On a clear day, I could almost see the Magaliesberg mountain range.

I realised just how much natural beauty meant to me. I needed it like I needed air. I recalled growing up and walking home from school in a suburb not far from where we were standing at that moment. I hated concrete and tar. Often, the municipalities would tar the entire pavement. Now and then, thankfully, there was a tree planted in the tar, with concrete encircling it.

I used to feel a sense of victory when I saw the roots of the tree fighting and cracking through the ugly tar, which was hot and burnt through the soles of my school shoes. I couldn't wait to get to the next block with the grass pavements. I imagined the families living with grass pavements were much happier people than the ones stuck with the tarred pavements outside their homes.

As I stood in a daze, taking it all in and remembering my childhood, I knew I couldn't live there. I didn't say too much. I really wanted to try and get over myself and make this thing work. John told the agent that we'd let her know the next day. He seemed really keen on the place.

He called me later on and I broke down, telling him I just couldn't live there. I mostly blamed the view of the power station, which "killed dad", but John didn't seem to understand. He compared it to my wanting to avoid a street because somebody I loved died there in a car accident. The street wasn't going away, and I had to get on with it, according to him. I told him I needed time to think, and called my older brother. Greg told me exactly what John would have been going through at that moment. Here he was, doing the best he could to build *me* a house, in order for us all to be together and happy. According to my brother, I was being a bit of a bitch.

I called John again, and told him I'd had a change of heart. I pledged my allegiance to him. I would faithfully go wherever he went, without any complaints. I would try to be like my mother. Although it felt like it was martyrdom.

I'd always admired my mother's generation, although at times I have felt sorry specifically for my mother, who always did the best she could without complaining. Sometimes, I'm not sure whether she even questioned her life, as I question mine now. With her, it was always just a matter of getting on with life, being a lady and doing the best she could for her family. Unfortunately, for her, it led to all of our putting her on a pedestal. But how could we not, when she would even blush when we caught her shouting at "the blooming dog next door"?

I would love to take my mother to Italy, the land of passion and food. She's always had a crazy side to her that's irresistible, and I've no doubt we'd both end up behaving like teenagers again!

Just as I was about to contemplate my new life in my new home, I got the email that rescued me. It was from the children's mother. She felt it would be better if James came to live with John, and Ashley stay with her, as she was approaching puberty. I could understand the logic. I was often fearful of Ashley's being bitter at being taken away from her mother when it mattered the most. She practically worshipped her mother. I couldn't live up to that.

John emailed me. He said, "This changes everything. If it's just James and I, then you don't need to move."

I replied to both John and his ex-wife, Sue, saying that either way I respected their decision and would be there to support them. I also mentioned how hard it must have been for her as a mother to let her son go. I knew she'd occasionally questioned her own worth as a mother, because of giving John custody initially. I truly appreciated the sense of defeat and rejection she had to be feeling. I hadn't had much contact with Sue, prior to the mail, but I'd gotten to know her children well enough to appreciate that she was a caring, loving mother. She sent me back a highly appreciative response.

Everything seemed to have fallen into place. However, John was increasingly unavailable. I thought that perhaps he was sulking because I had acted like a nasty female weaver bird – when unhappy with the workmanship of a nest, these weavers destroy the nests their partners had worked so hard on.

It was obvious, though, that John and I both weren't happy. One of the recent that problems that had crept up on us was the argument about whether Phil would stay with us in the new house. John had become reluctant to allocate the spare room to Phil. Once he muttered something about it not being fair to expect me to "make the choice". He was right – if that 'choice' was choosing between him and Phil. He would lose.

I was busy, so I chose not to harp on about it. All I wanted was a clear-cut answer to my question, which I was still hesitant to ask. In our recent conversations, I'd mentioned that over the past few months we'd barely been in a relationship. The last weekend in August, I decided that somebody had to get the inevitable over and done with. I broke up with John over email, because his phone was always off. I didn't get a response; but later that night he came to my house.

"Are you really prepared to throw away everything we've worked on for the last 18 months?" He stood there, on my doorstep, pleading with those beautiful clear blue eyes. I could see he meant it.

I didn't know how to respond. I was confused, but what I saw in his eyes gave me hope. My resistance crumbled.

"No, I don't want to throw it away. We just can't carry on like this," I sobbed, as he held me.

"We can get through this, babe," he whispered into my hair. "Let's go away for the weekend. Just you and I. I don't have the kids, and maybe the school can look after Phil."

I brightened up instantly. That sounded fantastic!

The next afternoon, I collected Phil from the school, but sent an email to Barbara that Phil would need to stay at the school for the Saturday night as I had an event I had to attend. John and I found a lovely game reserve to go to for the night. I made the booking, and anticipated a lovely weekend of relaxation and reconnecting with John.

It was one of my best memories. We had an amazing time, being in each other's company and relaxing. There was a resident zebra that ate bread out of the back of a van every night at the restaurant. You could stand right next to him and he'd just carry on eating. There was a tiny little restaurant called Hedwig's overlooking a gorge that was lit up at night. The stars were so close I felt I could almost touch them. John was very relaxed and things seemed to be on track again.

Little did I know that the next three weekends were to pass by without John's being around. I was down with a bronchial infection. I unashamedly decided to look for sympathy. In this relationship I wasn't one of those needy, insecure women. I saw a distinctive difference to how I behaved now in a relationship, compared with how I had behaved in the past.

I put this down mostly to having Phil around. When the 'mommy gene' is taken care of, boyfriends don't get smothered. You love a little more 'appropriately' – that's the only way I can describe it. The right love goes to the right places. It just feels a lot healthier. Conversely, there is the danger of ignoring your man, which is also a common problem.

John and I had just finished talking on the phone. Half an hour later, I wanted to hear him say "I love you" again, which was very unlike me. I messaged him and he didn't respond. Twenty minutes later, I just had to call. What on earth was going on with me? The fever was turning me into a mad woman, like his ex-girlfriend, who would compulsively call or text John. He would just shake his head, and say: "She's been drinking again." I honestly felt sorry for her, and used to say things like, "Just be respectful, babe. Don't make her feel any worse than she already does."

John never answered his phone. I wondered if he used to do the same with his ex-girlfriend when he was with her. A part of me wished I could speak to her and ask if this behaviour was truly what he was all about. He had seemed sulky and distant for most of the year. I understood that changing jobs and fighting for custody could be stressful, but I started to wonder if he would ever go back to being charming again. His mother also mentioned that he had been distant, and she was extremely worried about him.

The next morning, when I was on the way to the pharmacy, my phone rang – I didn't recognise the number on the screen.

It was a woman, who introduced herself as Frances.

"Hi my name is Frances, are you Ruby Florence?"

Instinctively, I knew which Frances this was. The drunken, mad ex-girlfriend! I affirmed it was I on the phone, with a stammer in my voice.

"Do you know John Sinclair?"

"Uh ... yes, I do." I started to shake.

"Are you just friends? Or are you romantically involved with him?" she enquired.

"We are in a relationship," I answered, feeling slightly annoyed, but disturbed at her interrogation.

"What a bastard!" she shrieked. "He's been seeing both of us at the same time. I don't think you know he's been seeing me since the two of you got involved."

She didn't take a moment's breath. I was too stunned to stop her. She continued relentlessly.

"He was with me when you phoned last night. He had just bought me a R7 000 promise ring." There was no stopping her, now that she had my attention. "You know how good he is in bed, and he's got a great body," she giggled. "We even did it last month, when his kids were with us at the movies. We were at the mall, and at the movies, we snuck into one of the change rooms in the mall."

I was in disbelief; shock. John certainly wasn't like that around me, which I made the mistake of admitting.

"He actually said he's not that attracted to you." She paused. "Have you seen what I look like, Ruby?" Before I could answer, she continued "I don't think I'm that special; but somehow he keeps coming back."

This had gone too far. I couldn't breathe. I needed her to stop, but she was ruthless. I wanted to tell her to go to hell, but eventually broke down.

"Please stop, Frances. This is hurting me so much. Please just stop."

"Okay, I'm sorry. 'bye."

And with that, my tormentor put down the phone.

I tried calling John, and once again he didn't answer his phone. I decided that I needed an answer out of him – and if he wasn't going to answer his phone, I'd get an answer out of him somehow. I was feverish and started coughing. I could feel the onset of a panic attack. Why was this happening, when I was so weak and sick?

I reversed the car, and turned into the road his office was in. I didn't have the strength to make a scene. I stepped into the lift, and pushed the button indicating the third floor with a heavy heart. By the time I reached the reception area, my heart had gone from being heavy to thumping wildly in my chest. The receptionist looked at me and smiled.

"Can I help you?"

"Yes," I answered, "please call John and tell him Flo is waiting for him." I'd never used any abbreviation to my name or surname, especially with John. I doubted he would know it was me. A few minutes later he appeared in reception, and looked like he'd seen a ghost. He walked through reception, and walked past me. In fact, he sped up his pace, and said, "I can't talk now. I'll call you later. The whole system has just crashed and there are big problems. I'm just going to the toilet."

"Fine, I'll wait," I answered. "I'm not leaving here without an answer, John." I tried to keep my voice as low as possible.

After what seemed like an eternity, he emerged from the bathroom. I was amazed he hadn't climbed through the window and made some grand escape, as they do in the movies.

"So is it true? I think you know what I'm talking about."

He nodded his head in acknowledgement, "Yes, it's true."

"Thank you, that's all I needed to know," I said, turning around and walking away.

The offices were in a shopping mall, and I'd parked my car in the basement. I wandered around in a daze. I couldn't find my own car. I had been wandering around the parking for 45 minutes, when the phone rang again.

It was Frances again. "Did you phone him?"

"He didn't answer. So I went to his office," I replied numbly. I could hear her excitement at that news on the other end. I continued, "I didn't make a scene, though. I asked him for the truth. And he admitted it."

I wanted to get her off the phone, but she'd once again launched into another monologue.

"Did he buy you gifts? He was forever buying me gifts." Truthfully, he had hardly ever bought me anything, as he was always saving money for the house he was building. That hurt.

"No, he's never had to pay me for my services," I retorted. However, the snide comment didn't give me much satisfaction.

She hung up. I knew that this was all for the best, but I couldn't help feeling devastated.

I thought about the past few months, and realised how naive I had been. Nobody had ever cheated on me that I knew of. This was a whole new experience. It was horrific. My heart went out to every person who had experienced the feeling.

Sadly, in the past, I had caused somebody to feel that pain of infidelity, and for the first time I can say I acknowledge the personal hell they must have endured. It was torture. I couldn't get the image of John and Frances making love in a change-room out of my head. I felt totally worthless and undesirable.

The ugliness of it haunted me for a long time. I had many theories, as one does when these things happen. There were many factors that could have played a part in the destruction of our relationship. I spent hours and days agonising over each and every one of them.

PART TWO –
RUNNING AWAY

Truth and children

I wasn't sure how to break my news to Phil. I didn't want to tell him that he wasn't going to see John again. I was sure we'd somehow be able to make a plan to see the children.

It turned out that John felt it would be better that we cut ties completely. This was exceptionally difficult for me, as I'd grown to love those kids. I was literally pining for them, and swore to myself that I would never date a man with children again. When you break up, you don't just lose one person. I was trying to hide my heartbreak from Phil. I seemed to be doing a good job of it. However, I made it a point to be as honest as possible with him.

He had once asked me what a stripper is, when the presenter on the radio mentioned that Lady Gaga used to be a stripper.

I answered as best I could. "It's a lady who takes her clothes off in front of people, and they give her money for it." He seemed satisfied with that explanation and thankfully the subject never came up again.

Phil was also satisfied with my explanation about "John not loving me any more" as the reason why he wasn't going to be back. Phil had seen his fair share of people coming and going in his life. There were children who sometimes did not return to the school.

Sadly, there were also a lot of volunteers or people he got attached to that he had to let go of from time to time. He'd had some tough experiences in his little life, and didn't seem too disturbed about not seeing them all again. But from time to time, he'd say things like "I can't wait to show this to James and Ashley!"

I informed Barbara about the break-up. I had to keep her in the loop at all times. "Obviously, we will have to stick to the weekend arrangement," I concluded. I was afraid of being a single parent and felt that if there were other families or people who wanted Phil, as Barbara had always implied, maybe they should consider his options. It broke my heart to say this, but I really wanted to do what was right for all of us.

When John and I finally did speak again, he said that Frances had given up drinking entirely and that she was a different person. I respected that, but still felt humiliated. He had always loved her – it was just the alcoholism that kept them apart.

Phil told everyone that "John doesn't love Ruby any more", and that "He loves another girl, so he's not coming back." It hurt a little, but I thought it better that he get it out of his system.

That was until we were lying beside the swimming pool one day. There was quite an attractive guy in the pool, whom Phil had started chatting to. I was used to the attention Phil attracted, and people's fascination with him. Their reaction was varied, but inevitably it followed the same pattern. The shock in their faces would register first, at his appearance. You could clearly see the discomfort in their faces. Soon after, their expression would change to surprise at his attitude and confidence. You'd see the admiration, and finally relief in their eyes.

In fact, their expressions would often become quite joyous. They saw hope and somebody they needn't feel sorry for. He was cared for, loved and we were happy. We often laughed and teased each other, which is more than many normal families can say!

"Oh please, can I tell him what happened with John?" Phil asked, while rubbing himself dry with the towel. Even though he didn't have hair, he flicked his head the way James always used to. This was almost becoming a party trick. I wasn't that comfortable with how this was happening any more, and told him as much.

He usually started out the story with: "You know what happened to *her*? *She* got dumped. And John has a new girlfriend." He seemed to enjoy using the word "dumped". It had become his opening line to everyone we met.

The following Wednesday, I got greeted at the school by one of the five-year-olds with: "Hello. Did you get dumped?"

Eventually I decided to straighten this all out. Clearly, I'd done too good a job of hiding my emotions. I had to say something.

"Phil, do you remember that lady who was crying so much? Remember how sad she was? It was because the same thing happened to her. I don't cry like that anymore, but I did for a little while."

He asked me why, and looked at me like I'd lost the plot.

"Because it hurt. I didn't cry for long, but that's how I cried for at least two days and nights when John stopped loving me and chose another lady," I explained.

Phil pondered for a while. I didn't want him to be uncomfortable, but I realised that he needed to understand that these kinds of situations hurt. Needless to say, his way of introducing me to strangers has changed from announcing my recent rejection to something along the lines of:

"I used to have a hamster, called Ben, which *she* let escape."

I have a really bad habit of walking past pet shops and playing with all the animals. I had made the mistake of falling in love with a baby eclectus parrot. They are bright red, with blue wings and bellies and grow to about the size of an African Grey.

I love birds. A little voice inside me kept saying: "If you buy this bird, you're supporting an industry which you haven't supported for a while." These beautiful creatures aren't meant to be kept in cages, and most certainly they shouldn't have their wings clipped. I knew it was a bad idea to get a pet. As I stood staring at this bald tiny chick, with little tufts and spikes of red, a little girl reached into the cage, and fiddled with its fragile little wings.

"Mommy, I want the red one!" she squealed.

"You can come back and get it when you get your birthday money tomorrow," her mother answered.

There was no way I was going to let that little brat have my bird, especially with her pulling at it like a spatchcock chicken. I waited quietly in the background. Admittedly, it was nasty of me to buy the bird she'd set her heart on. I felt completely justified, though. If I was a bird, I'd have hated to be prodded like that.

I bought the bird, and called her Scarlett O'Hara, which I thought was quite fitting. Phil arrived that weekend; he wasn't as impressed as I thought he'd be. Besides, Scarlett wasn't much fun yet. She couldn't talk and made funny little squawks instead. She was too small for her cage, so I kept her in a box with blankets. The first night I checked on her, I thought she was dead. I realised that it was because her legs weren't strong enough to hold her yet, that she slept that way. Naturally, Phil thought it was hysterical. He decided he wanted a hamster like the one from the Disney movie *Bolt*.

I thought about it and contemplated as to whether I should take another trip to the pet shop. I loved having a hamster when I was a kid. Of course, with Phil only visiting on weekends, I would ultimately be the one cleaning the cage. But I thought it might be a nice little diversion and would possibly prevent Phil's missing James and Ashley too much. And maybe I'd also be too distracted to be heartbroken.

Phil managed to twist my arm, and we headed to the pet store. We left with a tiny, hyperactive hamster which was nothing like the fat one in *Bolt*. It was still a baby and moved with lightning speed. Phil would have to be really quick to catch it if he wanted to hold it. The man at the pet shop told us that the hamster would settle as it got older. Phil named it Ben 10, while we were still at the store. He walked out the proud parent of a hamster.

"At least my one is quieter than *her* pet," he told everyone, rolling his eyes at my squawking little bundle of spiky feathers.

While I was putting food in Ben's cage the one day, he darted out. I tried to chase him, but I couldn't catch him and lost sight of him. No matter, where I looked, I couldn't find him. Phil was coming to visit the next day, and I'd have some explaining to do. I contemplated buying another one that looked just like its predecessor. The problem was that I didn't want another little escape artist. If I did get a new one, I would choose one of those fat ones that sleep all day. And Phil would most certainly see the difference.

Phil arrived with the dreaded question, "Where's Ben?" I didn't want to tell him, but there was no other choice. "Phil, he escaped. He was so quick, I couldn't catch him."

"How did he escape?" he asked, in utter disbelief.

"I was feeding him, babes. I opened the cage, and he ran out."

Phil looked annoyed. I continued, "He's probably running around somewhere downstairs. We'll get another one, and if he comes back, he'll have a friend. What do you think?"

Phil thought it was a great idea, but I suggested that we put off getting another Ben for a month or so, as I was flat broke. I sorted of hoped Phil would forget about it, but that didn't happen. Even when I got him a new one, he would still tell everybody about my irresponsible actions and what a terrible 'hamster grandparent' I made. But in spite of all this, he still loves brushing my hair. Sometimes I wonder who is taking care of whom.

Sleepless nights

Phil often complained of a cough, just before bedtime. I soon realised it was because he wanted me to rub Vicks Vaporub on his chest and back. So when his cough cleared up, he'd still force out a fake cough. I took to rubbing body lotion on his chest and back, as it was the physical contact he wanted. It was the only physical affection he would ever give himself permission to request, even though I would grab kisses from him whenever I could, to which he'd go "yuck" and wipe his cheek or wherever I managed to plant a kiss.

Phil's skin was mostly dry and itchy anyway, especially in the winter months. So we developed another little ritual – I'd put cream on him, then I'd kiss him goodnight. Every now and then he asked me to say a prayer, which I did. I noticed he never wanted to say the prayer, though.

Phil slept with his arms and legs flung all over the place. Once, I had found him sleeping with his torso balancing on the bed, and his knees almost touching the ground. We also battled with winter colds and flu because he would kick his blankets off. I would then wrap him up snugly at night and make him sleep in his pyjamas and night gown. Sometimes he spoke in his sleep, too, and he'd be chatting to Thando or Themba.

One October night, shortly after my relationship had ended, I came to say goodnight to Phil and tuck him in. I could sense he was restless. I rubbed his back and shoulders and asked for the 'two big angels' to please watch over him while he slept. It seemed to settle him a little.

I watched Phil fall asleep, which he did in seconds. I suddenly noticed that he'd curled into a foetal position, and had started sucking his thumb as though his life depended on it. I was alarmed. He had never slept like this before, and he certainly had never sucked his thumb before, not even when he had first arrived in my life at the age of six. I gently tried to remove his hand from his mouth, but he clutched even tighter. It was devastating to witness.

Bursting into tears, I walked out of the room. I didn't know what to do, and could only imagine what had made him become so terribly insecure. I hoped it wasn't my influence somehow – then again if it was me, this behaviour would have been consistent from the time I got him.

I didn't sleep that night, and waited anxiously for morning to come. I needed to know what was going on in Phil's head. He woke up during sunrise, as per usual. While pouring milk over his cereal, I casually asked him if there was something worrying him at school. He said no.

"Are you sure, babes? You know you can tell me anything. Is somebody making your life difficult or sad at school?" I asked. He eventually nodded his head. "Yes, but I don't want to tell you," he said as he turned away. "But I can't make it go away if you don't tell me, my angel. What's happening? Please tell me so we can fix it?"

He hesitated, then said, "I sleep at Barbara's house and I can't really sleep. So most of the time I watch TV all night, in Annie's room."

"Does anybody know you do this, Phil? Does Annie hear?" I asked.

He sighed, "No, she doesn't," then shrugged, "I just can't sleep."

"Why can't you sleep, Phil?" I enquired again. I needed to know the reason why he was having such difficulty sleeping. "I don't know," he answered, eating his cereal, eyes averted. Somehow, I didn't believe him.

119

"Do you rather want to sleep in your old room at the school, there by Moses? Would that help?" He nodded, and answered yes. I promised to talk to Barbara and Moses. I was sure Moses would understand and let Phil sleep in his old room. It puzzled me why Phil had been removed from his usual quarters in the first place. There was no doubt I'd have to speak to Barbara as soon as possible.

I wondered what on earth had frightened Phil so. I needn't have worried for long. Looking through the TV guides, I realised that October was 'Halloween season', so there were plenty of horror movies on most channels.

No wonder he couldn't sleep. I don't know of anybody who could happily go to sleep, with Freddy Kruger hanging around waiting to attack.

I emailed Barbara about the situation and asked if Phil could go back to his old quarters. Her response was curt and not very comforting. She insisted that, as the school was filled to capacity and they accommodated the children based on age and gender, he had been assigned to sleep at her house and he'd just have to "deal with it".

I was quite surprised by her lack of empathy. I'm unsure whether she was being defensive, or irritated. Possibly both. She did, however reassure me that his new television habits would be censored. I wasn't quite happy with her response. I drove past the school to chat with Moses. He wasn't there, so I left him a note asking him to allow Phil to sleep in his old bed again, in peace.

Thankfully, when I called later to speak to Moses, he reassured me in his kind manner that he was in agreement with me, and that he'd move Phil back to his old dormitory again. Phil was visibly relieved when I saw him the following weekend.

Although he needed the light to remain on, and he requested that the door remain open, he slept peacefully again.

This made me realise that Phil didn't like change at all. Who could blame him? I, on the other hand, embrace change and hate when there is too much predictability. It could become a problem if there wasn't compromise from both sides. Perhaps more from my side than his.

A different type of Christmas

With John out of the picture, I was a bit concerned about Phil's future with me and with the lack of masculinity in my house. I'm what I like to call a 'pink blonde'. Think Reese Witherspoon in *Legally Blonde*, and you've pretty much summarised me, minus the pooch in the handbag.

I noticed that Phil was slowly starting to pick up many of my habits and mannerisms. From the hand on the hip to the way he held my handbag for me, one could see a Mini-Me developing, which wouldn't help him at all in his adolescent years!

So I had to think of a few 'boy' things I could do with him before he turned into a total princess. There can only be one princess in my household at the moment, and we all know who that is. I'm not quite ready to hand over the sceptre just yet.

And so began what I called 'The Butch Campaign'. It was obvious Phil wasn't partaking in enough physical activities with me. We had become two Hannah Montana couch-potatoes! We decided to construct a kite, which was supposed to be a simple task, according to the instructions on the packet it came in. After much fumbling and fiddling around, we were ready to fly it in the park. It was a battle to get it to fly and Phil got bored. I was determined to get the kite airborne, however.

Phil sat relaxing in the shade under a lovely big tree, while I panted and huffed my way around the park trying to get the damn kite to fly. Eventually, Phil suggested we go home to watch the Disney channel. I quickly saw his logic. Miley Cyrus was waiting for us....

Phil was undoubtedly turning into a bit of a little 'Fourways boy'. That would mean 'spoilt' in layman's terms. Fourways is a very affluent suburb, when one compares lifestyles in suburban South Africa, which can be quite extreme either way.

Christmas was almost upon us, and I was perturbed about what to do with Phil. I could see us spending it alone together. I tried not to allow myself too much time to mourn the loss of my relationship with John, James and Ashley. But Christmas was going to be painful without them. There was no getting away from it – there was an ache in my heart, from an empty space they used to fill. I had to toughen up.

Phil got breathless with excitement when he saw the decorations in the shops. He'd touch the tinsel like it was a magical substance. So our first goal was to get our own Christmas tree, as the previous year we had borrowed one from John's parents.

One Friday in early December, we were at the supermarket when Phil convinced me to buy a tree. It was our first Christmas tree, and certainly the first I'd ever bought. We marched out of the shop, each clutching a grocery bag in one hand and one side of the tree in the other. We decided to finish off our shopping expedition with a pizza, and settled at in at Mimmo's, after depositing the groceries and tree in the car.

"I can't believe it! We forgot the bubble bath!" Phil hadn't even sat down yet. He stood with one hand on the hip and was gesticulating with the other hand (the one that had the little stumps for fingers.) He mock-wacked his forehead the way I do when I've forgotten something.

"I'm not going back into that mad place; it's a mission, Phil," I complained, shaking my head.

"I guess I'll have to go and get it, then," he sighed.

"Are you serious?" This was a first. I raised my eyebrows and asked "If I gave you some money, would you go to buy it yourself?"

He was only seven, and although all the shopkeepers knew him by name, it was still a very independent thing for a child of that age to do. I didn't want to put him off, and handed over some money, which was a lot more than he needed. He grabbed it and skipped off. I was a little worried, and motioned to the waiter, Patrick, to watch my plate and that I'd soon be back.

"Ma'am, you must stay. Don't go after him. I will follow him, but I will hide so he doesn't see me. He wants to show you how clever he is."

I nodded, thanking Patrick while he quietly ran behind Phil. I'd make sure I tipped him well. Minutes later, Phil emerged with his bubble bath and my change. He put the change and the bubble bath on the table, with a flourish and exclaimed "See?!"

I was elated! I was so proud of him that I wanted to stand up in the middle of the restaurant and yell, "This is my son, everyone! Isn't he magnificent!? Find me another seven-year-old who could pull that off!"

I grabbed him. Knowing he was about to get a big kiss, Phil grimaced and turned his cheek, while rolling his eyes heavenward. I could barely speak.

"You are amazing, kiddo. I am so proud of you, my baby," was all I could get out in between the hug and kiss.

It had been an exhausting year. I felt completely drained, but a moment like that made everything worth it.

At home, we assembled and decorated the tree. Phil asked if he could keep it next to his bed, which I agreed to. It was beautiful – fairy lights illuminated the room, and tinsel reflected on the walls. We were definitely feeling more upbeat about Christmas.

Barbara emailed constantly, usually to check up on my plans for Christmas. She often asked if I was going to take Phil on holiday. I responded that I didn't have the means to leave Johannesburg for a holiday. I was hoping to be able to get away with him, but I wasn't in a position to confirm or get his hopes up just yet.

Birthday time was also rapidly approaching, so Phil already had started asking if Thando could come over. I emailed Barbara to ask for permission, and she responded rather tartly that Thando had other plans.

I mentioned to her that Christmas this year was going to be a bit lonely for Phil if we couldn't get away, especially without James and Ashley. I knew the previous year the school and some charitable corporate put on a spectacular event for the children. I suggested that if this was the case this year again, maybe he should join them instead of coming to me on Christmas Day. It was merely a suggestion, to which I received no reply.

A few days passed without a response, and another email came requesting to know if I was taking Phil away on holiday. I was puzzled. I'd said no before, but it seemed that something was up.

Sure enough, that Wednesday night, I went to make supper for the children at the school, and Phil told me he was going away on holiday with Maggie. She was one of the little girls from the school. They were going to Maggie's family over the festive season, and were leaving the very next day. I was shocked and a bit disappointed, from a selfish perspective. I'd looked forward to his birthday, and spending some time with him.

The following day I received an email from Barbara saying that Phil had requested that he go with Maggie, as he wanted to experience a proper family Christmas, as he'd never had one before. The email also mentioned that he realised that his circumstances were different to even Thando and Daisy who had a family (with Barbara being their 'adoptive' mother), whereas he clearly didn't have a family or anybody. I suspect this was intended to somehow hurt me, which it did. I had put on amazing family Christmas the previous year, and I was planning on trying this year as well, even if it was just the two of us.

When I think about it, there was some truth in what was being said, but the email appeared to be filled with admonishment and criticism.

I also sensed envy, and it wasn't the first time. At times, it was blatantly obvious. Sometimes, I got the feeling Barbara was threatened, that Phil loved me more than her, and that Thando wanted to come and live with me too, which he often asked to do. But I think what she really envied was my freedom, whereas she had become resentful of her lot in life.

Every now and then I caught glimpses of the social butterfly in Barbara. In fact, she seemed to thrive on attention and drama. So do I, to an extent, to be honest. However, I began to withdraw and avoid her as she had become an emotionally draining person. Being in her space was almost like trying to rescue a drowning victim who drowns you in the process through all the struggling.

There was one particular occasion on which the positive side of Barbara's love of drama really stood out for me. This was Barbara at her best socially. The Welsh choir was putting on a benefit performance for the charity. Barbara had completely forgotten about this, therefore she had overlooked the marketing of the event. Unfortunately, I had only heard about it the day before, so there wasn't much I could do from a publicity point of view. I was asked to fetch some of the children for the show.

I ended up with six children in the car and wondered how I was going to explain this if I was pulled over by a traffic officer. There were two cars full of kids, but no Barbara. I was told she'd made her own way there.

When we arrived at the venue, Barbara was already there ... resplendent in the Welsh flag! Her flag had been transformed into a 'dress' of sorts. She wore it toga-style. Draping a flag over oneself with nothing on underneath is brave, especially in the middle of winter! I was fascinated. She actually looked really attractive, and I told her so.

But back to the Christmas plans! I was somewhat dismayed that Phil wouldn't be around, although a part of me was relieved that he would have fun and be taken care of. I was excited for him and wondered how he would cope with a more rural kind of existence. What would he do without Mimmo's pizza and the Disney channel?

I could only imagine what life would be like in the mountains of Lesotho. I had visions of him fetching water from the river to wash and cook in. I wanted to remind him to take my number in case he wanted to come home early or was uncomfortable. But I thought better of it – maybe I'd interfered enough.

As much as I looked forward to Phil's coming home, I was having a great December relaxing and unwinding. At first I'd felt lost. I had taken leave from work for a few days to spend time with Phil. Now that he was gone, I had nothing to do. I had become so used to having children around that I truly did experience the 'empty nest' syndrome. I decided to paint my room back to cream. I don't quite know what had possessed me to paint it pale green a few months back.

My purple lounge suite had seen better days, so I decided to give it away as a thank-you gift to the gardener in the complex, who had very kindly helped me to paint and move the furniture around. I had moved my room upstairs to the loft and put Phil's double bunk bed in the main room downstairs, which used to be my (and John's) room. Maybe Phil would sleep better in my room.

Slowly, I settled into my own space again. I realised how tired I really was. Maybe it was time to make some changes. I was worried that I'd taken on too much, and maybe I was still holding or carrying the 'lame man's cot' for him somehow. I wondered if I was supposed to be so involved in Phil's life. What if I was a disappointment in his eyes? Had I done too much and then too little? Was he expecting me to do more? Barbara was clearly expecting a whole lot more from me.

Aside from my misgivings, I had received a dinner invitation from an estranged friend I hadn't seen in a while. Now and then, you meet people whom you don't get close to immediately. But somehow something happens that draws you together, and a close friendship is born. Out of the blue, Desiree called and invited me to dinner. It sounded like it was going to be fun. It was my first proper grown-up outing on my own for almost two years. I was very excited!

Grown-up time

It had been a while since I'd been to a formal dinner party, and I was very excited about Desiree's dinner. I had been on a 'detox' for a while, since the break-up with John. Maybe it was hearing about Frances sobering up that inspired me. Possibly, it was also a case of my blaming alcohol for the breakup, and therefore deciding to give it a wide berth. I also felt the need to cleanse my body and soul. Knowing John had cheated on me, while being intimate with me also, had left me feeling a little dirty inside and out.

Either way, I felt rejuvenated. I'd been going to gym as well as yoga, and the belly dancing was paying off. I had slowly started getting back my self-esteem, and was thrilled that the stubborn 8kg had finally shed themselves.

I felt in control of my life. There was no shortage of male interest, either. I thoroughly enjoyed returning to the world.

Desiree's dinner party turned into a fun and raucous evening. Her husband, David, wasn't there, and she'd invited only her single friends and acquaintances. It wasn't surprising as she and David always appeared to live quite independently, together. I had always quite admired that, but I sensed there was more to it this time. She seemed different, somehow. She had an excitement about her, almost as if she was having her 21st all over again. It turned out it wasn't far off from being just that.

"I knew I just had to see you," she told me afterwards, with a twinkle in her dark eyes. How right she was. We both needed so much from one another. Desiree was in the process of splitting up with David, and she really needed her friends. I was a recently recovered 'singleton' who couldn't make decisions when it came to the child in her life.

I was honestly enjoying my freedom, and started wondering what the right course of action was for Phil. I realised that I had missed my adult time, and found myself pondering over how to have both. But that was a decision for later. Right then, I was single, childless and it was the festive season – it was time for some silliness.

Desiree had an 18-month-old daughter, whom I hadn't officially met, as Desiree and I hadn't had the opportunity to get together. Jody had been put to bed before the guests had arrived. I decided to stay over the night of the dinner party, knowing I would meet Jody the next day. It was delightful to wake up to her little voice. She stood in the guest bedroom, staring at me with her baby bottle hanging out of her mouth, her teeth clenching the teat, and her blanket in tow. She looked like an angel, full of fun and innocence. She had similar features to her father, but possessed Desiree's lovely brunette complexion and eyes. I knew Phil would love her, too, when they met.

Desiree also had the biggest Rhodesian ridgeback dog I'd ever seen. Her name was Chocolate, and she added to the enchantment of the home. It's amazing how certain people and spaces can still remain sanctuaries, in spite of their own inner turmoil.

I started spending more time with Desiree, Jody and Chocolate. In spite of all the fun I had been having, thanks to my newly recovered freedom, I realised I was missing Phil and the family situation of yesteryear terribly. Desiree and her family filled that gap.

There were many opportunities and decisions which I now had a bit of time to think about. For instance, I read up about costs and timing for 'Spiritual Therapy' courses in Hawaii, which appealed to me no end – although there seemed no way I could afford it. As I've mentioned before, I believe that God uses angels as messengers. I believe that, due to our physiological make up, where we live and what we eat, we have lost our ability to 'see' energy and 'Godly vibrations'.

I believe that if our bodies and minds are clear, we have a better chance of making contact with God. And if one goes to an unspoilt destination where the air is pure, one may even somehow catch a glimpse of God. I was convinced that I'd somehow see a sign of Him or an angel at the volcano in Kona on the big island in Hawaii.

Mysteriously, I found a flyer under my door within that same week on behalf of a company looking for properties to rent during the FIFA World Cup. The rentals and dates matched the costs and dates for the course exactly. It was a sign. And I was not to be disappointed – the trip proved to exceed my 'fantastical' expectations, which we'll get to later.

I also happened to meet a new and exciting male friend. I was definitely not ready for a relationship, but I appreciated the attention nonetheless. I met Eugene at a restaurant in Melville. I was sitting there with my sales manager and her immediate boss. I thought Eugene was gay, initially, because the young man next to him was most definitely gay. The Melville coffee shops and restaurants were renowned for their gay patronage, as well.

He was a good-looking guy, the type that girls are just in awe over. Pity he wasn't straight, I thought to myself.

The restaurant was crowded, and I became aware of the awkward angle I was sitting at. I apologised and adjusted the seating arrangements. Suddenly, I became aware of being gazed at, and started to feel slightly uncomfortable. Mr Good-looking Gay Guy was openly staring at me, and smiling. What was this guy's problem? Was he mocking me? Was I wearing the wrong shoes? He was looking me up and down, brazenly.

Eventually, I couldn't take it anymore and was curious as to what this was all about.

"Excuse me, why are you staring at me. Is there something wrong?"

He carried on smiling, shaking his head.

"No, I just think you've got a beautiful profile."

I blushed. Every now and then, it's nice to be appreciated by gay guys and arty types. Maybe he wanted to paint me, or do my hair. Self-consciously, I finished my lunch and we decided to move inside the restaurant. As I got up to move, Mr Good-looking's definitely gay friend leaned over.

"My friend here wants your number; he'd like to take you for coffee."

I was a bit confused. Maybe he wasn't gay. I generally prefer to take down numbers, instead of giving mine out. I was caught off guard this time and I was more than a little curious. He certainly was very handsome.

"Sure, I'll meet you for coffee," I responded to Mr Good-looking, looking him in the eye.

"Would you seriously give me your number? That's great. I'm Eugene, by the way. You must think this is so strange."

"No, not really," I said casually – as if this happened all the time. I gave my details and walked away tossing my head. I was aware of him watching me for the rest of the afternoon. I was intrigued. What I couldn't help noticing, though, was that when looking at his profile, Eugene had a bit of a long nose like mine. No wonder he thought my profile was beautiful! He looked like me!

Later that day, Eugene messaged me. The text read as follows: "They say honesty is the best policy, so I'm going to be honest with you and tell you that I think you've very attractive."

We made arrangements to meet. He told me he couldn't see me that weekend, but wanted to see me the next week. He wasn't desperate or pushy; he was prepared to wait a few days to see me. It was sounding better by the minute.

It turned out Eugene was an actor. In fact, he was (and still is) a known Afrikaans soap opera star. I had never watched an Afrikaans soap opera back then, so I naturally had no idea who he was. It was a bit embarrassing to be working for the SABC, and not know who he was – when he had been in at least two drama series, where I had sold airtime in the ad breaks.

The following week we went on a date. He put me at ease instantly with his chattiness and crazy sense of humour. But he kept reaching over to me to touch me. I wasn't sure how to respond or how I felt. I wanted him to touch me, but I was a little shy and nervous. It was thrilling and scary all at the same time.

I have since watched Eugene on television once or twice, and its odd seeing him behave in character. In reality, he is totally different to the character he is portraying.

Being six-and-a-half years younger than me, I knew Eugene wasn't the man I'd end up with. At the time, there were a couple of other guys who far better suited to me, if I happened to be looking for a boyfriend, which I wasn't. His age and the fact that he was a good-looking actor definitely didn't make him relationship material for me. Unfortunately, people stereotype actors, and I was no exception. Maybe I was being unfair, but because he was so obviously 'unsafe', he was safe for me, in that I knew never to take him seriously.

Melissa Banks

Our conversation during our first date established exactly what our options were in terms of what we were going to mean to each other. He broached the subject.

"So if you're just out of a relationship, what do you think about the whole 'friends with benefits' thing?"

He was so forthright! He had caught me off guard again, and I had to think about it. In fact, maybe it wasn't a bad idea to review the concept, anyway, as I hadn't really given it much thought in the past. I always had steady relationships most of the time. Here I was, single, and I had options.

Now in truth, whether we want to admit it or not, no woman ever wants to be just somebody's sex partner. There's something insulting about it, even though that is indeed, what we sometimes end up being, willingly. If we're not that interested in the man, and have accepted a date just to pass time, we still mostly want them to want to marry us. Even if we don't want them. So let's just admit it; no honest woman (unless she was a smitten groupie, which I certainly wasn't) would jump up and down at that offer.

I shrugged. "It's not first prize, Eugene." I didn't have much more to say on the topic.

"Would you come away with me this weekend to a friend of mine's farm?" he enquired, after a pause.

"No, I don't know you well enough at all." I was so afraid. He left it alone, and we carried on with idle chatter.

The rest of the evening was lovely, which led me to review the situation. There was no way I was ready for another relationship. My entire being was fragile, but maybe I needed to take a risk. Maybe a hot, passionate, simple relationship was just what I needed. I smile as I say this, as I still wonder whether such a thing exists. A few dates later, I decided to explore my options.

134

Eugene had auditioned for the role of toy-boy/friends with benefits in my life. And this is what I discovered.

'Friends with benefits' truly is just that. And it's not always about sex. By its very name, it suggests conditional love, which is quite selfish and not how I love. Secondly, the sophisticated older woman role isn't something I've ever really aspired to. I found this out the hard way.

One night, after a particularly intense conversation over spirituality and philosophy, before reaching over to touch my breast, he murmured "You're like my guru ... is it wrong to touch my guru like this?"

I came to with a jolt. Yes, I like to play the stronger, more dominant role – but this was too much! I don't want to be anybody's guru. I've nothing against learning from each other, but people must form their own ideas and opinions and not make their salvation my problem. I certainly don't make mine anybody else's problem. I'd have to tell Kobus I was going to make a shocking preacher at this rate!

"I'm not your guru!" I hissed, grabbing his hand and holding it to my breast, desperate for him not to put me on this pedestal and kill my mojo!

It was all way too grown up for me. I wanted to play. My friends and lovers must be playful and not put me in some kind of parental role. Or maybe, if I'm truly honest ... and this is hard to say ... I wanted to be the controlling person (because I'm insecure), but didn't want to feel old!

The relationship remains a firm friendship to this day, which I am thankful for. He signed up for a role in my life – no more, no less – which I accept and am thankful for.

Admittedly, I ended up wanting him to sign up for a more important role in my life, but it seemed like I was signed up for the guru/older lady friend role in his life, whether I liked it or not. Or at least that's how it appeared.

New Year resolutions

The previous year's activity had left me exhausted. There was no way I could over expend myself like that again in the New Year. I had to start negotiating some sort of compromise for the sake of my health and sanity. Thankfully my friend Tracy offered to alternate Wednesday night cooking at the school with me.

Tracy was a friend I'd met 17 years ago, when we both started out in the advertising industry at a well-known publishing house. She was blonde, a little taller than me, and must have weighed about 120kg at the time I met her. She had the most exquisite face, and the kindest, gentlest heart. Recently, she had lost 50kg for her wedding, and looked fantastic.

After two years of cooking every Wednesday night, I felt I had done my share, and was quite happy to share the responsibility. Phil's visitation programme didn't change, however. We stuck with the original plan, with him coming over every weekend, except when I was on my kinesiology course.

I received a text from the charity. Apparently Phil had returned from his vacation, and was dying to see me. I was thrilled he was home. I couldn't wait to see him and hear how he had coped without DStv and the kind of amenities we have in urban areas.

I had bought Phil a bicycle while he was away. I couldn't wait to present it to him and see the look on his face. I didn't want him to see it at once, so I arranged for Tracy to fetch him. The idea was for me to arrive at the Spur at the Brightwater Commons (a park-like facility in the suburb of Randburg), pushing his bicycle, where he would already be seated with Tracy. Or if I arrived before them, I'd have the bike leaning against his chair at the table.

Phil had told me he wanted a motorbike for his birthday or Christmas. This particular bike had the finishing of a motor bike, so it appeared like a small off-road bike, but obviously had pedals and no engine.

Tracy seemed to be running late. Eventually she called. Apparently Barbara wouldn't allow Phil to leave with her, although she was known at the school and had volunteered before. Phil also knew her well, from all the time we had spent together. Barbara specifically wanted to see me, right there and then. It didn't matter to her whether I had a surprise for him or not. Both Tracy and I explained this to her, but she insisted on my coming to see her, saying I was being disrespectful sending Tracy.

I got into my car fuming. I knew that Barbara wanted some kind of interaction and acknowledgement. I didn't necessarily want to be her friend. I found her exhausting and quite insulting, actually. She had sent out the strangest email late on Christmas Day about how badly children who had been burnt had been let down by society. It was a sad email, and I'm very glad I didn't open it on Christmas Day or my day would have been spoilt indeed.

As I had ignored her email on Christmas Day, I decided to ignore her quest for emotional attention that day I drove to fetch Phil. It was evident she was in a bad space, but I didn't have the energy to give her the fight or the sympathy or whatever it is she wanted that day – at her office, away from the school.

I would be kind, but brief and to the point. She had tried to bully me in the past, incessantly nagging for airtime, money, more involvement from me in Phil's life. It was like trying to fill a bottomless pit of need. I could understand why volunteers left and didn't come back.

Generally companies and individuals would work with the charity once and then not want to get involved with it ever again. They would end up avoiding Barbara at all costs. I'd had first-hand experience of this – many of the people and corporates I'd corresponded with, who had done work with the charity in the past, were reluctant for any further involvement. As I didn't represent the charity officially, my hands were tied at this stage.

For Phil's sake, I decided to indulge Barbara a little. I arrived with a smile and spring in my step. I didn't want to give Phil the bike in front of the all the other kids. I had to hide it and it was impossible to do so in my Jeep. Also, Phil and the all the children had arrived at Barbara's office from the school, so there was no time to even throw a jacket or jersey over it on the back seat.

The minute I arrived and Phil saw me he started screaming about the bike in front on the other kids. I had to announce that it was my bike, actually ... which was true right then and there as I hadn't given it to him. I felt completely deflated, but would make it up to both Phil and my inner child at the Spur when we got out of there.

Barbara sat me down. Tracy had disappeared. She had somehow managed to avoid meeting Barbara in person again. It was amazing how she got away with it. For quite some time, she had managed to assist me on Wednesdays, drop off blankets and all sorts of goods which she felt the children needed (which Barbara inevitably complained about) without ever coming face to face with Barbara. Barbara had asked for her number once or twice, which Tracy had reluctantly agreed that I give.

They had one disastrous conversation, in which Barbara asked Tracy "what the hell she was supposed to do with all the blankets and warm clothes" Tracy had dropped off, after witnessing all the children shivering in flimsy clothing one particular evening. When Tracy arrived the following week, the children hadn't received the clothing or blankets. They were still freezing, and a sorry sight.

Thinking back, I wouldn't be surprised if the 'slanderous' programme that had aired, that Barbara was suing for defamation over, was actually closer to home than anybody suspected.

"So, Ruby, it's the New Year and we'd like you to state your intentions with regard to what you want to do with Phil. If you're going to adopt him, then at least we need something in writing that we can show the social workers," Barbara said, sitting forward on her faded couch, feet on the floor, clasping her hands together. She meant business.

"Okay, Barbara. First of all, I don't want to change anything with regard to Phil's and my weekend arrangement." Sitting there under her scrutiny, I wanted less to do with her than ever. I wanted Phil around, but I wasn't prepared to deal with her anymore. I was terrified of her reaction if I pushed back, but a part of me was angry with her bullying me, so I decided to bite the bullet.

"I must admit I'm exhausted from last year, and I need a break from the cooking on Wednesdays."

She was silent for a while.

"All right, Ruby. Please just put in writing what your intentions are with regard to Phil. Send me an essay and we can take it from there." She stood up and showed me the door.

I was relieved that I'd relinquished the arrangement and that she'd taken it so well. Or so I thought.

"Great! I'll write an essay and send it to you this week," I said as I stood up and moved towards the door, my escape in sight. It felt like resigning from working for a particularly tough boss, but one whom you still need to freelance for from time to time. It's a relief, but you can't say what you really want to say as you can't afford to burn your bridges entirely.

Phil was waiting for me outside, playing with Temba in the garden. We made our way to the Spur.

"So, Phil, how was your trip? Did you have everything you needed? A toilet? Did you have to fetch water from a river in the mornings?" I had a lot of questions, which he patiently answered with a touch of exasperation in his voice.

"No. We had taps. We slept on the floor, and the toilet was outside. Otherwise, we had TV, sweets and everything we needed."

It didn't sound nearly as bad as I thought. I was relieved. A part of me was embarrassed at my lack of knowledge about rural life and the differences between white suburbia and the rest of the country. But as the proverb says, he who is ashamed to ask is afraid to learn.

Then it was Phil's turn to question me about everything, from what I had for breakfast that morning, to where I'd gotten his bike from. Finally he asked,

"So are you going to fetch me every weekend from now on?"

"No, Phil, I need one weekend off a month so that I can carry on going to school." He leaned over and smacked me hard on the hand.

"Barbara says I must smack you if you go back to school, because you're not allowed to!"

I was furious! I had to remind myself to not let her spoil my first day back with Phil.

Firmly, but kindly I responded: "Phil, I need to do this – I didn't get a chance to study at university when I finished school. I want to get another qualification. Barbara might be the boss at the school, but she is not my boss and I will not allow you or her to smack me. I'm glad you like your new bike."

I was anxious to change the subject and get our spirits back up to where they were supposed to be on our first day back together with his gorgeous new bike.

He was absolutely thrilled with his bike, and he proceeded to ride off into the park when we got to the centre. I didn't need to teach him to ride, as the bike had training wheels on it. I watched him happily whizzing around, with his little black helmet on. At this point, I realised that I had missed him terribly, and couldn't imagine my life without him. I smiled that I had even contemplated cutting back an additional weekend, let alone the one for studies. One weekend away from him – as necessary as it was – was difficult enough. I felt like I was missing a limb without him!

I sent Barbara my essay around mid-January. It was titled "My plans for 2010". I was working on my goals with a belief that the great authors and life coaches would be proud of (although in hindsight, and while writing this now, I realise I wasn't being too realistic, but we all have to start somewhere).

It went as follows:

"I would like to continue my weekend arrangement with Phil for the year. However, as you are aware, I am attending a course which takes place on weekend per month. On those weekends, Phil will unfortunately have to remain at the school. I have sent

you the dates for the first year already. My second year commences July 2010, and I could open my kinesiology practice after year one, already.

I will be renting out my apartment during the FIFA World Cup as an additional way in which to make money. Therefore, there will be a period of six weeks when I won't be staying at my house. Depending on where I stay, there may be a weekend or two where I won't be able to fetch Phil, but we would have to sort this out closer to the time. I will also be overseas for two weeks in June, so I won't be able to collect him at all for those two corresponding weekends. (I'm on yet another course!)

Hopefully, things will then return to normal and we can continue with our normal weekend arrangement.

I do not want to stay in the advertising industry in my current capacity. Therefore, I am unlikely to remain at the SABC after October. I may even leave earlier, as I want to open up a kinesiology and holistic healing practice. The great thing is that once I have had 250 hours of practice – I can start charging people, which will hopefully happen by October 2010.

This is a year of change and learning for me. I want to change my life for the better and, as much as I would love to foster Phil full-time, I cannot foresee that happening at all this year. I realise just how much Phil wants to be part of a family, and I would love to provide that for him. My goal is to foster Phil full-time as of 2011. He is going to have to be patient with me this year, though, because I'm building something that will be beneficial for both of us, and provide us with the stability we need in the long run.

I would also like to make arrangements for Phil's schooling in 2011. Because of Phil's natural talent for dancing and singing, I would like to explore the option of enrolling him at the National School of Arts. Additionally, I would love to buy us a house with a garden – this is part of my plan – towards year-end, but all depends on finances.

I envision a really beautiful future with Phil in my life, as my son. I know I have frustrated him, as I've needed time to make these decisions, and he has wanted to be adopted right away. But I am coming around. It is obviously a huge decision, and it has taken me a while to figure out what I want and how to go about it. But I have absolute faith that, despite all of my fears, we will be a family soon."

It was a big day for me. I sent the email feeling like I had turned a corner with myself. I had admitted that I wanted Phil in my life, properly, as my *son*. I was terrified as all hell. But I'd said it, and that was that. It was now just a matter of when.

Friends, family and dancing

Phil had been introduced to Desiree before, but had had never met Jody or Chocolate. He was introduced to both the 18-month-old toddler and the hound – a great friendship was formed. He was also forming an attachment to Desiree. It was wonderful to watch him open up to her, as he had with Tracy and my family.

It had become second nature for us to pop in at Desiree's house. Sometimes we even bathed and slept there. Initially, Phil had been nervous of Chocolate, as she is indeed an enormous dog! She had sensed his fear – this had made her nervous and there had been a bit of a standoff between the two of them, where Chocolate had barked and Phil had backed off. But then Phil relaxed, and allowed Chocolate to sniff around him.

In no time, the two were running together and were inseparable. Jody was too small to play with Chocolate the way Chocolate wanted to play, but Phil could play nicely with her. Jody would stand there thrilled, watching the two rolling together, while she clapped her hands and squealed with joy. She was still talking baby gibberish. Now and then, Phil would carry her around. She had him wrapped around her little finger. One night, he had slept in the little bed next to the cot. The following day he reported back.

"You know what? That baby Jody kept me up all night. She just talks and talks and I don't know what she's saying. But she stood in her cot all night and spoke to me. She made me very tired." Ah, there's justice in the world! Phil had certainly exhausted me at times, especially right before he was meant to go to bed.

One evening Desiree decided that we needed to take off our maternal capes and go for a night out on the town. She organised it so that Jody's caregiver, Mpho, could work for the night. She briefed her about Phil (who of course didn't think he needed a babysitter).

I was nervous about leaving Phil with a babysitter, in case he bumped his head by accident, which would be disastrous, both from a health and legal perspective. After a great deal of persuasion, I agreed for Mpho to take care of Phil for the night. Mpho was also staying over, and it would be quite fun to wake up in a house full of people. But I was a tad nervous to leave him.

One of Desiree's childhood friends was picking us up and taking us for dinner and to a nightclub afterwards. His name was Alan. He was 46 years old and new in town. He was pretty much 'The Bachelor' – blond, blue-eyed, gorgeous (in fact he could have passed as John's older brother) and he was six foot, six inches tall. He had worked hard and put his life on hold for success, which had worked out very well for him, as he had become quite wealthy. He was now ready to settle down, and the single women were lining up.

I had met him before, and we got on really well. I was at Desiree's house on the first night we met, which was during the Christmas break. We'd stayed up until the early hours of the morning talking. We were lying on the lounge floor, while the music was playing. I was lying on the one side of the coffee table, and he on the other. Ever since that night, and because he was like Goliath next to me, I insisted that if he ever wanted to talk to me (seriously) again, we'd have to get on the floor again, and discuss whatever it was, under the coffee table. My neck hurt after long conversations looking up at him!

Desiree had actually called me the next day to tell me that Alan wanted my number. I wasn't sure about all of this ... my life was chaotic. Too much was going on, and I was still recovering from John. Besides, he was enormous! I laughed and told Desiree to tell him I don't date belly buttons, because at my height, that's what I'd be spending most of my time looking at!

Phil wasn't accustomed to my new lifestyle of dressing to the nines for a night out. Pacing outside Desiree's room, he seemed to be sharing my excitement at going out. I heard him ask Desiree, "What's she wearing? Is she dressed yet? Does she look nice?"

Desiree came in with a big smile. "Phil can't wait to see how you look. It's so sweet."

I was used to his comments on my clothes. They ranged from "You can't wear that to the shops, it's for gym," to "When did you get those trousers?"

I stepped out in a little black number with hair blown dry, straight and smooth and my make-up carefully applied. Phil stood with his hand on his hip, looking me up and down – he seemed satisfied that I looked as good as I possibly could. He reached up and stroked my hair. I picked him up. He was getting so tall. I knew he was proud of me, but I was continually proud of him.

I tucked him into bed before we left. He seemed content. Just before I switched off the light he asked if we could stay with Desiree, Jody and Chocolate forever. He loved the huge house, park-like garden and, of course, the long driveway, where he could whizz up and down on his bike. I wanted so much to give him all he wanted. I kissed him again.

"Yes, this house and our friends are special, but we can't stay here. I promise you one day we'll have our own house with a magical garden, and a long driveway, for you to ride your bike. And you'll have lots of friends to play with." I would love to have been able to promise him a sibling, but I obviously couldn't.

We had a fun evening with Alan, who thoroughly enjoyed having a lady on each arm. He didn't seem particularly fazed about my not giving my number previously. We drank French champagne, and danced till the early hours of the morning, before Alan, 'The Bachelor' left.

We knew we were going to experience an early, rude awakening by the children, the next day, but we continued partying as if we were 18.

True to form, the children didn't disappoint. In fact, we heard a loud commotion – Jody was howling loudly. She had climbed into her stroller, expecting Phil to push her up and down the driveway. He had wanted to watch Barney instead, and had chosen to ignore her. She was having none of it. Her chauffeur wasn't interested and her life was falling apart. I understood completely!

Our life was serene, yet fast-paced and exciting. I could sense Phil and I had settled nicely since the sudden departure of John, James and Ashley three months earlier. It was a relief and we were happy.

Phil was sleeping well and we had decided to take him to a hip-hop dance class. Initially, I found a dancing school that was open on Wednesday afternoons. I wanted to take Phil, in my lunch hour, but the very first day presented problems. I had a business meeting which had run into my lunch hour, and furthermore, Phil had been receiving laser treatment for his hairline, and was in another part of town, where I'd have to collect him. I had to cancel, which disappointed him. However, I managed to find a Saturday class at the gym we went to.

At home, Phil and I often danced to Michael Jackson's music. We had one of Michael's live concerts on DVD, and danced around imitating his legendary moves. The hip-hop dance class would be great for Phil. Even his school report came with a suggestion for me to try and take him to a dance class to boost his confidence. His teacher felt it would be something that he would be good at naturally, and had mentioned this when last I fetched him from the school.

As soon as we arrived at the dance class, Phil began to withdraw. It was evident he felt self-conscious. The class was full of teenagers in baggy pants with caps worn back to front. The instructor was a really 'cool-looking' guy with dreadlocks, and the whole pimping outfit going on. I hoped Phil would relax, and I introduced him to everyone, as I usually did when at the Spur, hoping he would snap into his usual cocky, confident self, as he normally does.

For some reason, this didn't happen, which I couldn't understand. If there was one thing he was good at, it was dancing. All of a sudden he didn't think it was a good idea for us to be there at all. Maybe it was the big mirrors all around that made him feel self-conscious. He also battled with concentration at the best of times. So between battling with concentration and being exposed, it may just have all been too much for him. He looked at the floor, as if he wanted to disappear. I didn't want to embarrass him and walked quietly over to him.

"Do you want to go home, Phil?" I asked quietly.

He shrugged, and I understood his apprehension and predicament. He had been nagging to come to dance class and had bragged to the kids at the school that we were attending, and now he was uncomfortable. I could see where this was going. The last thing I felt like doing was a hip-hop class with a whole bunch of kids – especially in my grown-up, sophisticated clothes. But for him to do something he really wanted to do, I offered, "Phil do you want me to do it with you? That way, you can watch me and laugh?"

He brightened immediately. I felt a bit foolish for being nearly 40 years old, in a kid's dancing class. I could only imagine the rest of the gym members watching my awkward movements through the glass, unable to hear the music. But I bobbed my head, spanked my bottom and hopped around just as the instructor was doing.

The following weekend, Phil didn't want to go to the dance class. I contemplated approaching the dance instructor for some private lessons for Phil. I could barely afford it, but somehow we'd make it. I'd budget for it the next month. I didn't want to force Phil and decided to play it by ear. If the private lesson was a disaster, then we'd tried everything.

Changing jobs

I'd been for an interview for a job, several months previously, in November. The position was for selling advertising space, which I was used to doing. The company specialised in selling advertising on two major airlines in South Africa. The one carrier had just installed TV screens in all their planes, for content and 'advertising space'. With South Africa hosting the FIFA World Cup, there were a plethora of opportunities for advertisers – and airports were a no-brainer.

I had been approached by a recruitment agency on the company's behalf. I wasn't sure about moving to a smaller organisation and said as much in my interview. I was transparent about my daily life and my requirement to have the time to practice kinesiology and do creative writing. I was prepared to work hard for as long as necessary in this industry, but my plan was to eventually exit advertising sales in the capacity as I knew it. Little did I know, the company wanted me on board! Even with my needing two weeks' leave in June to do my Spiritual Therapy course in Hawaii!

The company had also instituted a customer relationships management system for all their employees, so they didn't have to manage people from an office. That way, they didn't have to pay for office space (apart from renting a boardroom in an office park from time to time). It made sense in our virtual world, where mobility is imperative and flexibility is a given.

The CRM system ensured that everyone who worked for the company accounted for their own time, while 'Big Brother' was watching – without cameras, of course. It suited my needs exquisitely, if I could get the deals in and do my creative writing, and practice kinesiology in between. After 17 years of selling advertising, I was desperate to branch out and try something else. But I needed to make money in the meantime.

But in spite of the appeal, it was still a new company and a small one, at that. And I needed my security, especially if I was going to take Phil full-time, as was my plan. One of the pros of taking the job would be the flexibility it would give me to assist him with getting ready for school, and fetching him in the afternoons.

Phil was adamant that he wanted to try a 'normal' school, and not go to a school for children with special needs for handicaps. He would often ask me to drive past one of the primary schools in our suburb. At mealtimes, he always asked me to put sandwiches and juice in a lunchbox from him instead of on a plate. I believed going to a normal school and having a lunchbox packed by a mom was a dream for him. I hoped to make it come true.

With this in mind, the employment opportunity seemed particularly appealing. It would be another tick in the check-box on my goal-and-dream list to be able to do all of that for Phil, and be available to him as a mother during the day. All I had to do was put energy and effort into the job, which is exactly what was going to be necessary to get a small advertising company off the ground. My final interview or job-offer situation had been quite extraordinary.

One of the partners at the company, Sean, really wanted me on board. He was my age, and absolutely dynamic in setting up businesses and putting together sound business plans. He wanted to make me an offer, but was away for the week. He was back in town on the weekend, and was determined to get a signed agreement that weekend, so that I could resign the following Monday. I explained to him that if I met him on the weekend, I'd have my little boy with me, and that it wasn't really appropriate. He assured me that it was fine, although I hadn't told him the details about that part of my life yet.

The Saturday morning I took my iPod (with Michael Jackson and The Lighthouse Family programmed in), Phil's activity books and crayons and we headed to the designated shopping centre. I introduced Phil, and Sean shook his hand. Suddenly Phil turned to me,

"Rubes, please can I tell Sean about John and that he dumped ..." I stopped him before he could complete his sentence.

"Absolutely not," I said firmly, settling him at the table alongside me. I took out his crayons and books and handed over the iPod.

I turned back to Sean, "Sorry about that. But I've just spared you the gory details of the collapse of my last relationship."

"No worries," he chuckled, while Phil sat colouring in, singing *Billy Jean* at the top of his lungs in the restaurant, thinking because he couldn't hear himself nobody else in the restaurant could hear him. We had ended up at a quaint seafood restaurant with a vibey atmosphere. Phil was hungry, but he didn't want anything on the menu, which was quite sophisticated.

"What? No toast of cheese here?" he sighed. He didn't want chips. He just wanted something with cheese, and asked for cheesecake, which of course they didn't have. The closest they had was tiramisu, which I ended up ordering. To my embarrassment, Sean reminded me that there was brandy in it a few moments later. It was too late – the tiramisu was already on its way.

It felt like the longest interview of my life, with endless negotiations. The sugar in the tiramisu had made Phil more energetic than ever, and I could barely concentrate in the busy restaurant. It seemed like a great offer. I promised to revert on the Monday and went home to think about everything.

I had been promised a basic salary, which was the equivalent of what I was earning at the South African Broadcasting Commission. It took a lot of tenacity and good salesmanship to earn commission at the SABC at that time, as there was a lot of disarray and management issues. That's if you didn't have to reapply for your job, which seemed to have become the order of the day. There was as much insecurity there at that time, as there was in any new or restructured organisation. As it was, I had to re-apply for my job, which I'd already been told was unlikely to be successful as there was a senior manager who was determined to fill positions such as mine with friends and family.

Thankfully, the unions intervened or many of us would have lost our jobs unfairly. But from my side, the damage had been done and I felt my relationship with my employer had been harmed. I had lost my heart for the place.

That Monday, I resigned from SABC and let the new company know that I would be on my way 1st March 2010.

The Austerity Plan and the boy who almost bought me a Ferrari

My final day at the SABC was on a Friday. The entire team congregated and planned a farewell party for me at our favourite restaurant – the one where I'd met Eugene. I tried to not drink, but it was impossible with everyone wanting to continually toast my new life. I kept reminding everyone that I need to still fetch Phil.

My boss, Tessa goaded me, "Come on, Florence! This is your farewell. I can't believe you didn't make provision for this, and let the school know you can't take Phil." I whined in response, as fetching Phil was also a good excuse to escape early and not have a big party. Now I was indeed starting to feel like a party pooper. I eventually caved in. "Okay, Tessa I'll quickly go to the school and explain, but I'm going to owe him. I hate disappointing him."

She came with me, and before long we were standing outside the green picket fence. I walked around to the gate, and Phil came running out, expecting that his lift had arrived. I gave him a big box of candy, as I sheepishly told him that I wasn't taking him right then, but would be there first thing tomorrow morning, so we could still have the whole of Saturday and Sunday together. He accepted the candy, but looked truly annoyed. He wasn't very forgiving at all. It wasn't fair.

The next time we were together, I made sure to explain that sometimes I needed time out with my friends, as an adult – but that it wouldn't happen often and it would never be a full weekend, apart from my kinesiology weekends.

I had put a new budget together in the new year, and it was a bit tighter than previously. The new job would possibly increase my earnings, but I wasn't going to pre-empt that. I would budget and cover all my expenses and any commissions would be the cherry on the cake. We had to be conservative, as I wanted to eliminate the debt I'd accumulated through the years. Simplifying my life would assist me with my goal to be in a position to take calculated risks with my life, and not endanger any of my assets. However, quality of life and a job that allowed me some kind of creative freedom was all I wanted for Phil and myself.

It is easier to equate being 'broke' to being on a detox diet. It is such a lovely way to get out of things or situations that you can't afford. "No thank you, I'm on a detox and am only drinking water," goes down a lot better with your friends than "No thank you, I can only have water – it's all I can afford."

Detoxing earns you respect, although climbing into your friend's wine during your 'detox' period certainly doesn't. It's a dead giveaway!

My days of strawberries, French champagne, Danish blue cheese and cocktails were going to be over. Living debt-free at that stage meant we were down to the emergency soya and frozen vegetables at the bottom of the freezer chest. However, it was a decision that I'd taken to ultimately improve the quality of our lives, and Phil didn't seem too concerned. His tastes were simple.

I considered selling my Jeep Wrangler, as it was becoming increasingly expensive to run, with the fuel price climbing constantly. I'd initially bought it because it would enable me to go scuba diving in Mozambique. This certainly hadn't been happening often enough to justify the expense of the day-to-day running of the car!

Something else I started considering a luxury was going to the hairdresser every six weeks. It was much more cost-effective to colour or dye at home. Although one fatal morning, this decision was definitely up for reconsideration. For the first time, I put a colour rinse in my hair.

After leaving the dye on for 35 minutes, I foolishly decided that it needed an extra few minutes. During those additional minutes, I disrobed to get into the shower, used the toilet and washed my hands. Two very disturbing things happened. Firstly, the tap water pressure suddenly reduced to a trickle. Secondly, there was no sound of the toilet cistern filling up with water after flushing. The water had been obviously switched off, and I had peroxide in my hair. The situation was dire.

With seconds to hair loss, I rushed around my apartment naked looking for water to rinse my hair. The water bottle in the fridge had a mouthful in it and the kettle was almost empty. There was a small soup bowl filled with rinsing water, including the remnants of the previous night's tomato soup in it. I threw the meagre dirty little bit of soupy water over my head. It barely made a difference.

Time was running out. Throwing on a gown I sprinted outside into my complex, facing the morning traffic. My options were limited. There was the fish pond closest to my apartment at the main entrance and exit of the apartment complex. The problem was it was in full view of everyone, and the fish would probably die with all the chemicals on my head at that moment.

I hesitated at the fish pond, my conscience stopping me from killing the fish. I carried on running to the bottom end of the complex towards the pool, where the highly chlorinated water would most certainly add to the quality of my lovely new hairdo. Suddenly I noticed three men in overalls digging. It looked like they were working on the plumbing.

"Did you switch off the water?" I screamed.

Melissa Banks

"Yes, ma'am."

"Well would you please turn it the hell back on for five minutes?" I yelled, sprinting back in the direction of my apartment.

A few days later, I was in a swimming pool with Eugene (on one of our few dates) who suddenly pulled me close. Not to cuddle. He had noticed my 'patchwork' job on my hair! He was polite.

"Who does your hair for you? It looks ... different."

How did I know it would one day all come down to the hair! I didn't want to tell him the whole mortifying story. Although I did confess that it was my masterpiece. Later that day, he mentioned a well-known supplier that sponsors him with hair products, and suggested maybe I try some. I made an appointment at the hairdresser shortly thereafter.

"I would have blamed the hairdresser!" screeched my sister, Claire (between fits of laughter) when I told her and my mother the story. When they had recovered from their hysteria, we got down to the car business and what I was there to do.

Claire's old car, a bright green Hyundai accent, with a spoiler or fin on the boot, had become the family 'emergency' car. I was set on a private sale of my Jeep, as the trade-in price a dealer would give was far below its true value. So while my car sat on a showroom floor, it was my turn to use the green car.

It was very seldom that I asked my family for help, but now and then it's good to permit assistance. It definitely makes everyone feel more loved. Leaving my Jeep on the showroom floor was sad, but getting into the car belonging to my family, who loves and cares for me, made it easier.

Phil didn't mind the car. But he definitely had a taste for sexy, fast cars – possibly as a result from one of my 'butch' campaigns. I had taken him to a showroom full of sports cars and taught him the difference between The Bull and The Stallion ... as in the emblems of Lamborghini and Ferrari. I believed that to be an essential part of a boy's education. I'd also taken him to Kyalami, a race-track in Johannesburg, to watch superbikes and Formula 1 racing. Phil's brand of choice was Ferrari.

One day he enquired, "Why don't we buy a Ferrari, instead of this green car?" I explained that I couldn't afford a Ferrari, which he felt wasn't a good enough excuse.

"Why don't you just work harder?" It really wasn't making sense to him at all that I possibly couldn't afford such an item. And come to think of it, how do you explain it without destroying a fantasy or dream that could well become a child's reality one day if he or she is given the permission to dream it?

"Phil, Ferraris are special, expensive cars. But it's not just about hard work or being special. There are many people who are special and work very hard, like Moses who looks after you and teaches you at the school." I didn't really know what else to say. Phil mulled everything over for a while and then announced, "I'm going to buy you a Ferrari on day." Then he changed his mind, "No, I think I'll rather get you a Mini Cooper, because that's for girls. Ferraris are actually for boys."

And with that settled, he relaxed into his dreams in the passenger seat, while I drove us home in the trusty, green family car.

The ugly truth

The upsetting news that it was Kelvin's turn to be 'fired' from the charity didn't come as a surprise – but I still didn't understand it. Phil was going to be devastated as he loved Kelvin very much. It had been just over two years since that fatal December day that I'd first met Phil and Kelvin had shouted at me for giving the children sweets through the fence. I wondered whether he had indeed been 'fired' or if the charity was in some kind of trouble financially which, given the noises Barbara was making, was a possibility.

I bumped into Kelvin shortly after hearing the news, at the local supermarket, and he explained to me that he and Barbara had parted on very bad terms. He seemed reluctant to talk, but I really needed to understand what was going, as I knew it was going to affect Phil. I could see Kelvin's devastation, too, and pressed him for answers.

"Look, I don't really want to say too much. Barbara is already trying to get my work visa cancelled and get me sent back home to the UK. I'm trying to find work, and I've moved in a few houses away from the kids so I can still see them. I really don't want this messed up any more than it is."

It was shocking that somebody like Barbara, who always complained about being understaffed and busy, had the time for such nastiness. Until then, Kelvin had been one of the longest serving volunteers.

I had started to form a very unsettling picture of Barbara, which was getting less flattering by the day. So far, I'd given her my support and understanding, but of late that was only for Phil's sake. This feeling was further punctuated by two little 'neighbours' who had become good friends.

Two very pretty little girls, who were also housed at the charity, ended up living across the road from me. They had been adopted by a gentle and kind but glamorous Zulu lady called Nandi. Like me, Nandi hadn't any biological children, was single and in her mid-thirties. Her adopted daughters, Susan and Treasure, were truly beautiful.

I remember the first time I saw Susan – it was at the school. I hadn't seen Treasure yet. Susan looked like a young version of Beyoncé, but the back and one side of her head was burnt, with a scar reaching across to her ear. Her face was exquisite though; I just couldn't stop staring at her. She was 10 years old at the time, yet seemed oblivious to her incredible beauty. I didn't want to make the other children feel inferior, but I eventually took Susan aside.

"Susan, you're so beautiful. I haven't seen a little girl as pretty as you in a long time. You're going to be just fine in life," I told her, smiling.

She was thrilled and opened up like a little flower in front of me. I then met Treasure, who was equally as beautiful, but her scars weren't on her face or head. Her body was badly burnt, so she always wore winter clothes, in order to hide her scarred torso and limbs.

Tragically, as Susan matured I noticed that she eventually started covering her neck, and eventually the side of her beautiful face that had been affected. At times, one would see a lonesome little figure walking alone, with her jersey stretched partially over the back of her head. It was a particularly disturbing sight in summer, when the heat must have been suffocating beneath the fabric.

Susan took to paying me visits. In my new job, working from home, this happened quite often after school, which was thoroughly enjoyable. Often Treasure would join her, as her lessons ended later.

On weekends they'd pop by to visit Phil, who was always delighted to see them. They gave us both hope that adoption or life outside the charity was possible.

During the previous December school holiday, when Phil had gone off to 'Rural Africa' (as I teasingly called it), Susan and Treasure came to visit me. It was evident they wanted to tell me something important that day.

Treasure began: "Ruby, while Phil's away there's something we want to tell you. We didn't want to say anything in front of him in case it embarrassed him." Her tone was serious. She continued, "One day when we were still at the school Barbara pulled Phil's trousers down and smacked him hard on the bottom in front of all of us."

It was appalling to hear. I heard myself ask, "Did she pull his underpants down, too? Were his private parts exposed to everyone?"

"Yes," they answered in unison.

My throat constricted and my stomach turned. Anger, anxiety and deep sorrow for my child threatened to come out as bile, but came out as salty tears. Phil could barely cope with my walking into the bathroom when he was naked. How would he have coped with the kind of humiliation this would have produced?

I bitterly recalled Barbara telling me, in the car on the way back from the airport when she and Phil had returned from Germany, about smacking Phil on his bottom like that. At the time I didn't believe my limited parenting skills or knowledge of child rearing gave me the authority to question her methods. However, I knew I would not have coped with that as a child.

I was furious with Barbara, myself and the situation. Hatred has never been a close ally of mine, but that day I knew a hatred and anger that could destroy anything in its path.

As quickly as the anger came, so did the despair. If I was going to go to war, I'd have to be ready for it and no doubt Phil would be the casualty. I'd end up in exactly the same situation as Kelvin. The only way was to get Phil out of there permanently. It was tempting to throw caution to the wind, drop everything and go and get him. But I had some selfish plans for 2010, which would ultimately cost me more than I would have been willing to part with. Both Phil and I paid a hefty price for this decision.

Due to his poor choice in direction, Jonah was about to get swallowed by the big fish ...

Fun and games

It was a lazy Sunday. Phil and I were winding up another leisurely weekend at the clubhouse swimming pool. It was that sad time of the day again, when bicycles get packed away, old clothes get put back on and the fairytale ends.

I used to buy Phil new clothes, which he'd wear back to school, but as his clothes were always being lost or stolen I had stopped. Once or twice, I'd asked Phil where his clothes were and he'd said that Barbara had taken them and was keeping them at the office at her house. She'd previously said it was useless buying clothing for Phil as everybody shared (even though the school's clothes were often in tatters).

My phone rang, and I recognized the number as Barbara's. I answered with a mixture of annoyance and anxiety. Her tone was crisp.

"When you drop Phil off later, please would you come by to fetch his stuff? Everything has to go."

Anxiously, I asked why. With Barbara, one never knew what to expect. In a very calm, matter-of-fact tone, she explained, "Well, I've just lost the sponsor that has been paying money into my personal account. Their last payment is at the end of this month, February. So from March onwards everything will be falling apart and I will be closing the charity's doors."

Keeping my voice as calm as possible, I fought back the panic. There was no way I was ready to take Phil immediately. My email had outlined the reasons as to why I wasn't ready to take him just yet. Having promised to pop around after dropping Phil, I turned into Desiree's street. I had to see her, and get my thoughts in order before meeting Barbara. We said our goodbyes, and left to drop Phil and face Barbara.

Phil had no idea what was going on and I was careful not to share too much. He hopped out the car and I drove off towards Barbara's house. She was waiting for me with a garbage bag in hand, stuffed to capacity with Phil's 'stuff'. There weren't any other boxes or bags around so she'd presumably only just started the process of packing up.

"What's going on, Barbara? I can't take Phil now. He's back at the school and he doesn't know anything about this."

"You're going to have to take him. I'm closing down the charity and am likely to lose my house in my personal capacity," she said.

This was all happening far too quickly. Something had to be done – and fast. I felt the walls closing in on me. With conviction, I promised to see what I could do.

"There must be a way out. I really can't adopt Phil yet. I've told you this before," I said.

She shrugged, about to walk away. It was all too terrifying to comprehend. Admittedly, a part of me was suspicious. But whatever Barbara's motivation, which would soon be revealed, her strategy had the desired effect. My reaction was one of sheer panic and adrenalin that would have moved mountains to assist rather than have to commit to something I wasn't ready for.

I had one last question. "Barbara, what if you sent all the other children back home and I took Phil?" I said imploringly. "I know you've adopted Thando and Daisy. So if Phil is taken care of then we only need to worry about you and your children for now."

"No. Why should I lose everything I've worked so hard for? I've sacrificed everything I own financially. And what about the other children?" she wailed. Very gently, I replied "Barbara, maybe this shouldn't be your problem anymore. I'll take Phil and maybe somebody else can care about the others."

"Who? Nobody can do what I do!" she yelled.

"Yes, I understand that. But maybe this shouldn't be your problem anymore," I repeated. "Let's find some corporate that has funding for social responsibility. Perhaps they can take the school over from you, including the debt."

She sighed. "That's not the answer to my problems. I need to keep an income and my house. I want to be able to leave something to Thando, Daisy and my biological son, Charles. It's just so unfair for me to have to lose everything. Let me get back to my packing."

I believed her completely. It wasn't right for her to lose everything she'd worked for, especially when she had done so much good. No matter what I thought of her, or her modus operandi, she needed help and I would do my best to assist. As depressing as the situation was, I believed it to be something that could be rectified, if I put my back into it.

I hugged her goodbye in spite of my anger and frustration with her.

Minutes later I was again at Desiree's in a daze, a little teary-eyed. Desiree immediately set to work calling her network of contacts and friends. Being a corporate lawyer had its advantages, and she wasn't averse to pulling out all the stops. There was a chance that, between my network and Desiree's, we'd be able to find a corporate sponsor. It was certainly within my power to secure some immediate radio airtime for an urgent fund raiser.

I had left Phil at the school that night. It seemed they were still having lessons the following day. It made no sense for me to take him until the school was actually closed, which Barbara swore would happen within the next few weeks. I opened the bag with Phil's things in it, including all sorts of baby clothes, old duvets, a toy telescope and only one or two items for a boy of his age. Clearly, it wasn't Phil's stuff. I was too disturbed to give this much more thought.

The following day I set about calling all my contacts and had over R500 000 worth of airtime shortly thereafter. This would give the charity two 30-second live announcements a day on a very popular radio station, in drive-time, for a week. Hopefully we could make some money quickly.

It was thrilling and I felt privileged to be in the position to assist in such a powerful endeavour. I called Barbara's office to tell her the good news. Apparently Barbara wasn't in, according to the volunteer who answered the phone.

"Ah, pity! I've organised some airtime," I said breathlessly. "So how is the packing going?"

"What packing?" the voice on the other end enquired rather curiously.

"Barbara was packing up everything last night!" I said, puzzled.

There was a sigh on the other end of the phone. "Nobody's going anywhere. She does this from time to time." I recognised the voice and accent to be one of the female Swiss volunteers who had been there for some time. Perhaps almost as long as Kelvin.

"Teresa, is this some kind of ruse?" I almost whispered in disbelief.

"No, I think there is some legitimate financial trouble. But I really don't want to get into the politics. This is the charity I support and I love those kids. So please let's not talk any further. There's no packing, moving house or anything of the kind going on from what I can tell."

It was all rather suspicious. But given the fact that Phil was one of the children I was raising money for, and we were so far along in the process, it was easier to give Barbara the benefit of the doubt. Possibly the reason Teresa didn't know anything was due to Barbara's not wanting to worry the staff or make them feel uncomfortable, I rationalised.

Desiree and I continued with our campaign to assist Barbara, in spite of my fears. Desiree had set up a meeting for the Tuesday evening with two agents who specialised in fund-raising and social responsibility programmes. Both had potential corporate clients whom they were confident they would be able to present successfully to. Both believed we would be able to access funding in time to avert the impending financial crisis.

I fetched Barbara from the charity at the prearranged time that Tuesday evening. She seemed quite buoyant, which certainly made me feel the more positive. En route, we discussed the situation, and once again I suggested we find her a solution that would allow her to take a break. We could set up a new Trust Fund or a whole new organisation, if necessary. If there was too much debt, perhaps we could even start the whole charity from scratch, paying Barbara as an employee. This would take the financial responsibility off her shoulders, which at this stage she seemed to be single-handedly responsible for.

It didn't seem fair that one woman had to handle so much responsibility in the first place. No wonder her behaviour was tempestuous and difficult.

But while we were discussing possibilities, Barbara suddenly turned to me. "I don't want to have to end up reporting to you, Ruby."

It was incredulous. The last thing I wanted to do was get involved in the management of the charity! That would mean I'd have to work with Barbara, and the prospect of that terrified me more than even adopting Phil!

"Where on earth did that come from?" I gasped. "I certainly wouldn't want to be responsible for all of this, Barbara! I would suggest some sort of committee be formed also that it doesn't rest on any one person's shoulders again."

We arrived outside Desiree's house.

Barbara was slightly anxious, which was perfectly understandable. Asking a whole lot of people for help was no doubt extremely trying. Putting myself in her shoes, I imagined how I would feel asking people to assist the charity I'd given everything to. We all settled in at Desiree's house and held thumbs that we would come out with some kind of solution. Barbara had brought along photos and press releases outlining everything she and the charity had accomplished. It was really impressive and I was proud to be associated with her and the organisation. She had done some outstanding work.

She told us how she'd started the charity with Daisy, her adoptive daughter, who had the worst case of burns I'd ever seen. The story had captivated many people for many years. Barbara had done the best she could for Daisy, but it seemed interest was always drying up. People were fickle, and as Barbara said some time ago, the Haiti earthquake had been a competitor at the time

And then of course, another disaster had struck in Chile. It was as if there was never enough time to focus on what was happening at the charity. There are many charities that need assistance, but unfortunately where the media's attention goes, the money and energy flows. And that is usually governed by sensation, whether we like it or not.

Melissa Banks

We summarised the situation that the charity was facing. There were more than a few sympathetic ears that night. A few companies and clients that were likely to assist with a bail-out were identified. However, Barbara was going to have to hand over bank statements, balance sheets and some sort of business plan. We suggested she include a salary in the plan that covered all her requirements. This was common and acceptable practice in all charities, and she was assured that she would be looked after. She was also required to disclose who the trustees were.

Prior to the meeting, I'd actually been advised by the agents to have these requirements ready if possible, which I in turn advised Barbara to do. It was disappointing that she hadn't brought any of it along except for the 'before and after' photographs and news clippings.

Even more disappointing, and a trifle disturbing, was her reaction to this request. There was no way she was going to disclose bank statements, she argued. Her rationale was based on the pending lawsuit between the charity and the TV programme that had allegedly defamed her. She didn't want to be seen to be taking any money from the charity.

We all sympathised and again stressed that it wasn't untoward for her to take a salary. It wasn't at all irregular for employees of a charity to draw salaries, even if they were trustees, provided the whole process was above board and approved by the rest of the board of trustees.

Barbara was adamant about not drawing a salary, though, and said she wanted money paid directly into her personal bank account. She argued that any disclosures about the charity's financial status were unnecessary. It was a disconcerting and suspicious argument.

The meeting was adjourned without any resolution. It would be impossible to find a corporate partner to sponsor anybody

170

in their private capacity. The sponsor that had withdrawn support had questioned how Barbara had ended up on their payroll as an 'employee'. This had led to the termination of an arrangement that had provided her with a salary, as one of their employees, in her personal capacity. She was looking for a similar arrangement and none of us thought it possible or appropriate.

One of the agents responded the following day, hoping that Barbara would change her stance, as she had a client who had expressed interest in assisting.

The agent, named Tammy, suggested her client offer Barbara a bail-out package of sorts to take over the whole charity, offering Barbara a salary in the hopes she'd stay on to manage it. This was communicated to Barbara in writing. But again, the necessary financial statements had to be submitted.

Barbara responded with a lengthy email outlining her hopes and dreams for the charity, including building special facilities for the children, but wouldn't disclose financials.

We seemed to have reached a stalemate.

Two days after the meeting, Barbara sent me a surprising email, outlining the details of Phil's 'new bank account', which she had just opened for him. She would apparently have signing power. Her stated intention was not to touch any monies deposited into it until he was a lot older, but it would provide for the 'what ifs' of Phil's life on a day-to-day basis.

Barbara hadn't exactly asked me to deposit money into the account, in so many words, but I could read between the lines. The unspoken expectation was that I would pay her to look after Phil, or have to take him off her hands. Of course the charity and school needed money, but her methods of acquiring had become tantamount to blackmail. Her email ended with her complaining that her request to my friends with regards to her personal circumstances had 'obviously fallen on deaf ears'.

I pretended not to read between the lines and played ignorant. Although her insult was annoying, I indicated in my responding email that it was a great idea to have some kind of fund for Phil, but that it probably wouldn't be necessary to touch any monies invested for his future as I'd be happy to provide for 'what ifs,' as and when they occurred. I wrote that if I were to invest in some kind of financial plan for Phil's future, it would be preferable that I do it through the investment company that handled my portfolio.

Although my correspondence was very polite and controlled, an inner voice inside of me raged that his woman was trying to sell a child to me, and not just any child but my priceless boy, Phil. I hated her for it.

I didn't get a response to my email, and thankfully didn't hear from Barbara throughout the rest of the week or the next. My next encounter with her was imminent; I just didn't know when it would happen. I was thankful for a reprieve for the next few days.

King Solomon's baby – Part 1

My younger brother, Troy, was getting married. Phil had never been to a wedding before, and of course he loved Troy immensely. We were all unbelievably excited about the festivities. The wedding was due to take place on the South Coast, by the sea, which was even more thrilling. I fetched Phil the weekend prior to the wedding, which happened to be the weekend two weeks after the frustrating meeting with Barbara.

Phil kept asking me if I'd arranged with Barbara for him to leave school on the Thursday and have Friday off. This was necessary, as my older brother Greg, and I were planning to take the seven-hour drive together.

We were scheduled to leave on the Friday morning. I didn't think it would be a problem as, if it came to the worst, we could leave at noon on the Friday and fetch Phil en route, and then he would miss only an hour or two of school. But of course, first prize was to fetch him after work on Thursday. I dreaded the negotiation with Barbara, especially since there had been no contact, and I could only imagine what was going on in her mind.

Phil and I spent the Friday night at the Spur, and went to gym as usual the following day. It was Desiree's birthday and she had organised a party at her house that Saturday night. Jody was going to her father, and Desiree wanted to have a big singles bash.

I explained this to Phil, who was disappointed to have to go back to the school on Saturday night. "Can't you just get me a babysitter again? Why do I always have to go back?" he vented.

"Babe, it's better for the school to look after you while your head is still getting better from your operation," I tried to explain. But he just wouldn't accept that.

We stopped in at Desiree's so that Phil could give her some earrings he'd chosen for her. We left at 7pm to drop Phil off at the school, when the first of the guests started arriving. Phil was really sulky that he couldn't stay and was very quiet all the way back to the school. It annoyed me that he could make me feel so guilty.

"Hey, Tiger! Remember I'm coming early for you and we're going to a wedding next weekend!" I shouted cheerfully.

"Okay, but don't forget to call Barbara," he said sulkily, pepping up just a little.

"I promise I will call her and organise it," I promised, grabbing one last kiss before he got out of the car.

I put off the conversation with Barbara until the Wednesday, when I finally gathered the courage to give her a call and ask for permission to take Phil the following night. My brother and I were quite prepared for difficulties, so we had already discussed leaving on the Friday afternoon.

Before calling Barbara, I said a prayer, as I always do when confronted with my fears. When I pray I like to feel like I'm actually in the temple of God, in the 'most holy' area, so I burn frankincense and myrrh to make it smell like it, too. I believe the aroma of our prayers is pleasing to God and maybe a personal little ritual makes me believe in my own prayers more.

"Hi Barbara, it's Ruby, Phil's mom," I said politely when Barbara answered the phone. "How are you doing?" "Suicidal," she replied.

I felt her hopelessness, but a part of me wanted to throttle her. We had potentially secured adequate financial assistance. Furthermore, Desiree and her colleagues had offered legal assistance and marketing support with regard to protecting her assets and image during the lawsuit with the TV programme, if necessary. But still she refused to co-operate, behaving like a victim without options.

I suppressed my annoyance and persisted with my mission to get Phil out of school. I didn't feel like engaging in an emotional blackmail, tug-of-war conversation. So without meaning to sound insensitive I responded, "I'm sorry to hear that Barbara." I paused, then pressed on, "My brother, Troy, is getting married at the coast next weekend and we'd like to take Phil down with us. May we please fetch him after work on Thursday, so we can leave first thing Friday morning?"

"We don't usually allow children to take off school for that kind of thing. They only leave early if there's an emergency or pending surgery," she responded tartly. She was determined to get as much mileage out of this conversation as possible. I felt my anger bubbling inside of me, but for Phil's sake I kept my cool.

"All right, I accept that. We'll leave on Friday afternoon then. Surely Phil wouldn't be missed if we took him an hour before school ends?"

At this point I was sorry I'd even attempted this conversation. We should have kept quiet and left late Friday afternoon, and arrive at our destination at midnight. Barbara would have been none the wiser. But here I'd stupidly given her the perfect opportunity to somehow exploit or torture me.

If I couldn't give her the money or whatever it was she was after, she was likely to try to punish me, as she did all the other volunteers she had disagreements with. I waited for her response.

Suddenly she sounded very tired "Email me with the details with where you are going and where you are staying, so we have it for our records." I heaved a sigh of relief, and thanked her sincerely. Before I could say another word, she said, "I'm not saying yes. In fact, I really don't want to talk to you anymore," and hung up rudely.

I was surprised but elated that I'd managed to get a vague yes from her. I drafted a respectful email. Although Barbara was angry with me, I remained positive as I didn't believe she'd hurt Phil.

I was wrong. The blow arrived the following day by email, and it was worse than I anticipated. The devastating piece of correspondence read as follows:

"Hi Ruby

Unfortunately we will not allow Phil to go with you to the wedding this weekend. Moira, the director and I have explained this to him.

Phil is doing relatively well at school, but can't afford to skip any days. School lessons continue until 2pm each day with supervised homework and extra-mural activities until 4pm. There are often educational activities on the weekend, including additional reading lessons.

With Moira being his guardian, it puts the charity in a precarious position should anything go wrong while he is away and out of our care.

Phil needs to be in a stable and dependable family environment, and for this we need to have him adopted, so that he can have a family to call his own. Phil's weekend visits seem to be occurring less frequently and even the dance classes (which he was so excited about) have not happened at all. It's not fair on him to have to experience the disappointment that is accompanied by these occurrences. He gets so excited about his weekend visits and it's terrible to see the look on his face whenever you let him down, or pick him up late because you're at a work party, or brought back early on a Saturday because you want to attend yet another party.

Therefore, for Phil's sake we will not be able to allow him to go with you to the coast. For now, we will need to stop his ad hoc visits to you, until you get in contact with a social worker and begin with the formal process of fostering Phil.

Moira will provide you with telephone numbers for counsellors and social workers (as previously given to you).

We do not doubt that you love and care for Phil, but at the moment that is just not good enough. Phil needs a firm commitment and a stable family. He cannot wait forever for the chance of being adopted or fostered. And if you are not going to commit, we will have to make other arrangements.

As he won't be visiting you, we would appreciate you return his belongings, so that he has access to them while he's here.

I hope that you will begin the formal step of adoption. If not, you will need to allow us the opportunity to find a Phil a family he can call his own.

Regards

André Botha"

It was shattering news. The message was crystal clear, in spite of the content. If I didn't pay Barbara, I couldn't see Phil. But she'd so cleverly orchestrated the whole thing that I had no choice but to review the validity of the content of the email.

My entire being screamed with anger, frustration, guilt and finally deep sorrow for Phil. And who the hell was André Botha? Where did he come from? I'd never had any dealings with him at the charity.

It was also the first time I'd ever heard that Moira had been appointed as Phil's guardian. She was a 19-year-old burn victim herself and had been schooled and treated at the charity. Having just completed her schooling, she now worked in the capacity of a volunteer – possibly with a small salary, I wasn't sure. I had the feeling she stayed at the school during the week, helped at the office, and in return got the on-going surgery she required on her neck, chin and chest area. She stayed with her grandmother on weekends. And they certainly had never given me numbers of any social workers working on Phil's case.

I suspected Barbara to be the true author of the email, and quickly dialled the charity's number to speak to 'André Botha'. Moira answered the phone, and confirmed my suspicions. Neither Barbara nor André were there apparently.

Shakily, I called Desiree. She was a lawyer, and had good sense in such situations. Desiree answered my call. "She's bluffing. Call her bluff. Tell her you accept her email. Phil will just have to miss out on this weekend, but you can make it up to him later. She's desperate for money, and you are her lifeline at the moment," Desiree advised.

I felt sick. Phil was going to be devastated that he couldn't go to the wedding. If he'd experienced disappointments with me in the past, this one would top them all, but I'd make it up to him and repair whatever damage a blow like this could make.

With a heavy heart, I drafted my one-line email bluff. "That's fine – I accept your decision."

I didn't contemplate that Barbara may just remove him from my life permanently. All I could think about was him not accompanying my family and I to the coast to the wedding. As the day wore on, I became increasingly upset. Was money that important to Barbara? Or did she have some sort of psychological disorder that enjoyed pain and cruelty?

I started doubting my initial response about accepting her decision. It didn't matter if I got bloodied and wounded. Like any mother, I realised I'd sacrifice anything for my child's sake – his disappointment and devastation was too much to comprehend. He didn't deserve this.

So I gave in and wrote another email, where I begged and promised Barbara anything, from airtime to money, to let me take Phil for the weekend and continue with our arrangement. I'd deal with all the promises I made later. An even nastier response arrived in my inbox, and it included banning me from all contact with anybody from the charity until I'd found Phil's social worker and started the adoption or fostering process.

Clearly, money wasn't as big an issue as she had implied – or revenge was more important.

I had no idea what Barbara would tell Phil and I couldn't let it go. In spite of the warning to stay away from Phil and the school, I got in my car and drove as fast as I could. I parked outside, knowing Barbara was probably at the charity's office, around the corner. If I bumped into her, I might have struck her, as her neighbour did some time ago.

I approached the green picket fence, like an unwanted stranger. It felt like *déjà vu*. A few children were playing in the garden – Phil wasn't among them. The children told me he was inside. One of them went to call him, but he wouldn't come out. I called out his name until he eventually emerged. He walked out slowly, staring at the ground, and when he looked up I saw emptiness in his eyes that nearly drove me insane with guilt and grief. He was beyond emotion and had totally closed himself off.

I needed to stay calm. It took every ounce of strength not to break down. I reached out my hands through the green bars of the fence towards him, a lump in my throat.

"Phil, please come here! We need to talk." He came closer, but stood just out of arm's reach. "Phil, I really don't want to cancel the wedding with you. But you see, Barbara and I have got some grown-up stuff we need to sort out. I'm so sorry, Phil. I will make this one up to you. I promise. In the biggest way you've ever seen."

It was best to take it on the chin, and not blame Barbara, as I didn't want Phil to be bitter towards the woman who fed and schooled him. Possibly it was too late for that, and he had lost confidence in both of us. I hoped and trusted that he would be as resilient as they say children are. But Phil is different, I said to myself – his emotions run deep and at times he's unreachable.

I continued desperately, "Phil, what did Barbara say about coming to my house?" His response was barely audible, as he murmured something softly, looking at the ground continuously, not wanting to make eye contact with me. "I can't hear you, babe," I enquired gently. He finally looked up again, looked me in the eye and said, "She said I'm not coming to your house anymore."

It was crushing to hear. She hadn't been bluffing at all.

I couldn't accept that she would hurt Phil so deeply. My mind raced with possible solutions – getting to the nearest social worker or centre would be my first port of call. Of course, I'd adopt or foster Phil earlier rather than never see him again.

As much as I believed that the reasoning as set out in the email wasn't the real reason behind Barbara's decision, there was some truth to it. I had to ensure that when I got Phil back, we wouldn't have the same thing happen again. I had to find out what he wanted, and felt. And he had to learn, for both our sakes, to deal with the fact that I was allowed to go out and be an adult from time to time.

But how do you tell a child to put on a happy face when the natural reaction is to withdraw and sulk?

I felt it might help our cause if he started to nag to come to visit me. It might make him feel more empowered. This quiet acceptance wasn't like him and I wanted him to keep his spirits high.

"My baby, I want to try to fix this. Do you want me to?" I asked. He didn't respond. I continued, "If you don't want to come to me at all anymore and feel you'd rather just stay at the school, it would be okay. I want you to visit me, but you must be honest with me. If it hurts you too much to sometimes come to me and sometimes not, I'll understand. Phil, do you want to come to me still?"

The silence continued. I knew I'd find him in there somehow if I just waited. Eventually he whispered, almost afraid to be heard, perhaps out of fear of the crushing disappointment that can come from when you've had the courage to risk asking for something aloud that you don't end up getting. "I want to come to you."

He said it softly but it was a breakthrough! I grinned at him, and then started talking quickly, so that he would know what to say and how to behave when the social workers met with him.

He had to tell them that he wanted to come to me full time, and if he couldn't have that, then he would be content with any other time to come to me. He had to promise to try not to sulk, and deal with me sometimes needing adult time. It was critical that I made it clear that the reason all of this was happening was not because he had sulked or had somehow brought this on himself. It was because Barbara and I had to sort out our grown-up stuff with the social workers' help.

In fact, I wanted Phil to know he was quite lucky to have *two* mothers fighting over him! In parting, I reminded him to nag at every opportunity.

"I love you, Phil. We'll fix this," I promised. We said hasty goodbyes as I didn't want to draw much more attention to myself. He seemed in better spirits.

Driving back, I contemplated what an extremely disturbing conversation it was to have had with a child. It was unfair to put him in this situation. But he needed to know that he had the right to an opinion as to where he wanted to be, and I'd make sure he was heard.

My grief and confusion were consuming and I battled to see through the tears that kept welling up into my eyes and spilling onto my cheeks. What had happened was unfair on both of us. Barbara had used Phil's disappointed reaction as a perfect weapon to annihilate a beautiful thing.

As much as I comforted myself with what I would do going forward, in terms of finding a social worker, a terrible nagging guilt constricted my lungs and threatened to choke the life out of me.

I had the feeling that I had done something terribly wrong in getting involved in Phil's life and that I may spend a lifetime trying to rectify it.

I rang the bell at Desiree's house. Mpho's voice crackled over the intercom. Desiree wasn't home and I needed somewhere to run and hide from the ugly, cruel world. Mpho was Jody's caregiver, who had babysat Phil the night we went out. She was a tall, stately, full-figured Zimbabwean woman with a gentle but dignified manner. She automatically opened the gates for me. Jody came running excitedly towards my car. I put my sunglasses on, so that Jody wouldn't see my distress. I got out my car and picked up that little two-year-old bundle of joy.

Jody, who normally wriggles like a worm, put her head on my shoulder and rested quietly as I wept silently into her hair. Mpho gently removed Jody from my arms and managed to hold Jody and put her other arm around me, drawing me close and holding me tight.

Seconds later, Jody wriggled out of Mpho's arms and ran to hug Chocolate. It was as if we were all in mourning for our lost little family member. I had barely recovered from losing James and Ashley and my previous family situation. I couldn't lose another child I'd taken into my heart and home. Compounding that was the still smarting wound of rejection.

The mourning didn't last long, and soon Jody was sitting in Chocolate's food bowl sharing dog chunks with her. I walked over to them wiping my eyes, and watched Jody put a do- chunk in her mouth then take it back out and offer it to Chocolate in her grimy little fingers. Chocolate gently took it from her. Then it was my turn to have the grimy little fingers put a dog chunk in my mouth.

Jody smiled, satisfied that she'd fed us and that we were all happy and okay. And in that tiny moment of tenderness my heartbeat regulated, and I was able to catch my breath.

Mpho brought me a cup of tea. She turned to Jody, "Jody you must be a good girl for five minutes. I need to talk to Ruby."

Jody carried on feeding Chocolate ignoring us, thoroughly absorbed by her task.

"What happened, Ruby?" Mpho enquired gently.

"Phil is not allowed to see me anymore. They say I make him unhappy." I told her, knowing and hoping it was a lie.

She took the cup from my hand. "I think you must go lie down on Desiree's bed," she said, leading me away. I followed obediently and climbed onto Desiree's bed lying back. Mpho set the tea down and left me to sob some more, until I had no more tears left to cry and could talk. A few moments later she returned, sitting on the edge of the bed, asking me to tell her everything.

I repeated the entire ordeal to her. She listened patiently. After a while, she responded in her Zimbabwean accent, "Ruby, God has given you that child. Phil knows who his mommy is and God will bring him back to you. That woman who did this is going to have to ask God's forgiveness. You must stop worrying, he's coming back."

She stroked my arm as she continued, "Maybe God gave you Phil to get you ready for the birth of your own child. Your tears show that you are a good mother. God is going to give you everything you want. He will give you your own baby."

I appreciated her sentiment, but I needed her to understand that Phil was the baby I wanted right now.

"Mpho, I want Phil back! He is my baby, too. I don't care about another baby now. I want Phil back!" I cried again.

"Yes, God will bring him back to you. But remember that Phil is God's child – not yours. He knows you are the woman who loves him as his mommy. Nobody will ever take your place in his heart."

I appreciated her insights, and felt a little better. But for me, it wasn't about who took up what space in his heart, it was about justice and righteousness. Both seemed to be lacking in my world right then. Maybe in the bigger scheme of things all is just and as it should be, but right then, I would not accept that there was anything right about our situation.

I wiped my face and got off the bed, eyeing the chair in the corner of Desiree's room, I walked over, and curled up in the chair, with my feet tucked in under me, momentarily enjoying the warmth of the sun's rays as they fell on me. I smiled at Mpho as she put a blanket over my lap. God had chosen the right angel to comfort me in my time of distress.

It was going to be all right.

Desiree arrived home. I had cried out most of the tears, and wasn't in too much of a mess. Desiree was very matter-of-fact when she saw me. In her opinion, I was to march into Barbara's office and have it out with her, for once and for all. "You have to draw your sword, Ruby. You have to demand what's right for your child," she said passionately.

I wasn't sure I was up to declaring war yet. I'd just learnt the hard way that battling somebody with no conscience doesn't make for a fair fight. I had to use 'the system' to get this right.

The following day, I called the Teddy Bear clinic, which is a government institution that does psychological evaluations with the charity from time to time. It was the only contact Moira had for me. It seemed Phil didn't have a social worker.

An appointment was set up for the following Friday, and I emailed Barbara with the date and time, confirming that Phil's attendance would be necessary. To my surprise, she agreed. Then again, she had promised that I could have contact only after adoption proceedings had begun. On Friday, at twenty minutes past nine, I arrived at The School. Phil wasn't there. He was at the office, at the charity, with Barbara. My heart sank. I anticipated her sabotage, but made my way there, anyway, with a sinking feeling.

Thankfully, Phil was waiting outside the office and saw me coming. I hadn't seen him in two weeks, but he seemed fine. He rushed towards the car, and I noticed Moira, his 19-year-old 'legal guardian' coming out the gate behind him. It didn't bother me in the slightest – I was just so relieved to not have to deal with Barbara, and be able to get to our appointment on time. On reflection, I thought it would be a good thing to have a witness from the charity at the meeting.

Once in the car, Phil asked about the wedding, and I told him that it was fine, but just not the same without him. The wedding had been lovely, but I had been tearful the entire weekend. I didn't tell Phil, who reached over for my iPod.

This gave Moira and I the opportunity to get into a discussion about the situation without exposing Phil to too much information as he had earphones in his ears.

Evidently Barbara hadn't told Moira that she was withholding Phil from me because I hadn't put money into a personal bank account. I didn't tell her either, as she too was a vulnerable child at the mercy of an organisation that decided on her future and care.

Barbara had done a good job convincing Moira of the correctness of her decision to prevent me from being in Phil's life until I'd started the adoption process. She used the afternoon dancing class that had been cancelled as an example of how badly I had let Phil down.

"Did you ask Phil about the dancing class we did end up attending, Moira?" I questioned, trying to hide the annoyance in my voice. "No, I didn't know he went with you to a dancing class," she replied.

"Well the fact is I did get him to a dance class, and he didn't enjoy it, Moira," I explained. That didn't change her mind, though – she kept describing Phil's desperation when I didn't fetch him or I was late.

I responded as reasonably as I could to what she had just described.

"Moira, since the beginning of the year, I have only let Phil down twice, according to our arrangement. It's now March. You have had the schedule of which weekend per month I have kinesiology class, since August last year. I've actually sent it to Barbara more than once. That part of our arrangement is not new. In fact, not even a month ago, Barbara thought I would make a good foster parent. Now all of a sudden I'm a bad parent who keeps letting Phil down and am therefore a threat to his psychological wellbeing."

As we drove towards central Johannesburg, the streets got dirtier. The buildings were dull and grey. Moira was now silent. I wanted to shout "Something's not making sense, Moira! Haven't you wondered what changed within the last month that suddenly made me a bad parent?"

I wanted to explain that I felt that Barbara was looking for money and if the school went bankrupt it would be because of her pride or greed. But it wouldn't have been appropriate for me to share these fears and suspicions with Moira.

Instead, I continued, "I gave Barbara that schedule long ago, so you could prepare Phil emotionally for those weekends, which I am entitled to, and which I need. As for the two parties I attended – I don't think as an adult two functions in the space of three months is irregular or irresponsible at all."

Moira didn't comment, but if she was indeed Phil's legal guardian, and aware of that fact, then she needed to hear my side of the story. I could sense her confusion, though, and realised she was also a victim in all of this.

We pulled into an empty parking space. A few homeless men fought over whom would take care of my car and its hubcaps, and then stopped to stare at us. We were an unlikely trio. We approached the rather dilapidated-looking building which housed The Teddy Bear Clinic. We were sent to the fourth floor, to room five. A woman with a big smile greeted us from her desk. I liked her immediately.

"Hi I'm Nokuthula, you can call me Nox. You must be Ruby and this must be your boy, Phil," she said, looking from Phil to me, beaming.

"Yes, that's us. And this is Moira, from the charity. Thanks so much for seeing us, Nox," I responded warmly.

She told Moira and I to sit down and led Phil to a play area so that the adults could chat in earnest. He went with her, bobbing, iPod in hand, speaker in ear. I wondered how many times he'd listened to Michael Jackson's *The way you make me feel* on the way. I knew it was his favourite at the moment, because the introduction to the song had an electronic sound that could be mistaken for the growl of a lion. In fact, Phil was convinced it *was* a lion.

Nox returned, and we discussed the situation. We didn't talk about bad blood between the charity and I, only whether or not I was a fit parent for Phil. She asked me what we did together and seemed satisfied with my answers. The only problem was that Phil didn't have a social worker assigned to him to make official decisions on his behalf.

I turned to Moira who assured me that Phil definitely had nobody assigned to his case.

"What does it take to get a social worker assigned to a child?" I asked both of them.

Nox leaned back in her chair and sighed. "It's quite a long process; one has to be appointed by a court. But first you need to find out exactly who the social worker was that placed Phil at the charity."

I turned to Moira again. She vowed that the charity had no details of any such social worker. Apparently he had been dropped off by some anonymous good Samaritan with no paperwork whatsoever.

"How am I going to find out who this person is?" I asked uncomfortably. Nox responded, "My darling, it's going to be like looking for a needle in a haystack. I wish I could help you more, but I can't. We don't have access to that kind of information. All I can tell you is that I approve of your being Phil's parent from what I can already see."

I was pleased and discouraged at the same time.

From what I could gather, it didn't matter whether Barbara and I were friends or foes – if Phil didn't have a social worker to officially make decisions on his behalf, nobody could actually lift a finger. He was stuck at the charity, and therefore Barbara could act on his behalf, as his unofficial guardian, until such time as a social worker was allocated to him to assess his needs and situation. I contemplated all of this, while Nox went to fetch Phil.

It was now my turn to leave the room for Phil's meeting with Nox. I walked out, hoping for the best outcome for all of us. About 10 minutes later, all three of them emerged from her office, and Nox openly said, "Go to your mommy, Phil. There she is ... and she's waiting for you!"

Phil ran into my open arms for a big hug. Nox came over and hugged me. It felt very reassuring. I couldn't get over what a lovely, warm person she was. I thanked God for sending yet another human angel to me.

It was time to head back to the school and we were all in high spirits. We had hope.

"Are you coming to fetch me next Friday?" Phil asked, as I dropped him off and kissed him goodbye.

Moira was standing close by. I looked at her, and she shrugged her shoulders. I trusted that the visit had gone well enough to prove my commitment, but felt reluctant to make Phil more promises, especially if Barbara wouldn't allow me to see him.

Kneeling down, I looked into his eyes, "Phil, I'll pick you up as soon as I can. This will be fixed. I'm going to ask Barbara if you can come to me next weekend. If she says no, it might be because there are rules we have to follow. She wants us to be a family, but we may need to visit other people from the government first, before she lets you come. Try not to be cross with her. She is trying to look after you properly, but she's only making me want you more," I finished off with a smile, and a kiss on his forehead.

It wasn't really a lie. As angry as Barbara had made me, in my heart of hearts I knew one day I'd be glad everything went exactly as it did. Although it wasn't right to corner me the way Barbara had done, it had certainly forced me to evaluate my feelings for Phil and how much I wanted him in my life.

Like Phil, I was also afraid to say it aloud, for fear of disappointing both of us. For now, my only concern was that Phil might be bitter or angry in his environment. Although he felt protected there, I was still worried that Barbara had exposed his genitals when she'd given him a hiding. At least he had a roof over his head, education and good medical care, though.

As Mpho said, he was God's child and I had to trust that he was as safe and as well as possible.

King Solomon's baby – Part 2

I got to the office later that afternoon, and set about drafting an email reporting back on our meeting at The Teddy Bear Clinic. It read, *"After a successful meeting at The Teddy Bear Clinic, I am pleased to inform you that I am committed to finding Phil's social worker and starting the process towards fostering or adopting him. In the meantime, please confirm whether I can fetch Phil next weekend or not. Also, if you do have any details of any social worker affiliated to him in your archives, please forward their details."*

Whoever it was who was now responding on behalf of the school wrote back saying that Phil would not be allowed to see me until I had completed a 'parental training course' or gone to an 'adoption workshop'. This was a supposedly legitimate requirement and part of the adoption process.

I was bewildered. There was no mention of a social worker or details of exactly what course I had to do. It was upsetting that the meeting at The Teddy Bear Clinic hadn't been sufficient for Barbara to allow Phil back to my home for weekends. I was aware that the adoption and fostering process could be long and tedious, and I was concerned that Phil wouldn't be able to hold out emotionally if it took too long.

I called Nandi, Susan and Treasure's mother, to find out exactly which classes she had attended, when she had gone through the process of fostering them. At least she had gone through the procedure with children from the charity. I reasoned I could do what she did if the charity didn't give me information.

Nandi answered my call and told me that she hadn't gone to any workshops or classes. The girls had a social worker assigned to them, who had visited her and approved of their coming to stay with her. It had been a simple, painless procedure, from what I could tell.

It was annoying to realise that Barbara was once again trying to make me feel unworthy as a parent and giving me tasks that she knew would waste my time, or throw me off track.

I researched 'parenting courses'. After what I'd just experienced with Barbara and The Teddy Bear Clinic, no matter what I did, she was likely to put obstacles in my path. She would play games with me, and play for time. I had to bypass her, and the only way was to find Phil a social worker, or track down a social worker who had worked with him in the past.

To my frustration, this proved easier said than done. I tried getting hold of Treasure and Susan's social worker, who said that she couldn't do anything as we had to find out who had worked with Phil in the past, as they were more than likely still assigned to him. I tried calling a few other social workers, and got the same response when they eventually answered their phones.

I didn't have Phil's ID number, or details of the shelter he had been at before, so trying to find him in the system became impossible. I called more than one office on the East Rand, the district he had originally come from, and there wasn't a trace of him in the system according to them. The task before me was staggering, and the realisation dawned that the only way to get anything to happen was to find a senior contact at the department of Social Services.

In vain, I made enquiries. Eventually, after exhausting all my contacts with senior officials, politicians, media moguls, I tracked down Kelvin. It was all becoming so complicated – possibly he had some ideas and insights.

I was also concerned about Phil's emotional state, and knew that Kelvin was still popping in at the school from time to time. My friend Tracy had faithfully kept the Wednesday cooking arrangement going, too, and she'd allowed Phil to call me once or twice when she was at the school.

I realised we'd have to tread carefully, though, because the last thing I wanted was a restraining order against me.

Kelvin answered the phone. Apparently, he too had now been totally banned since being fired. However, he was living in the area and walked past the school all the time, so he could at least still see the children – it was his turn to be on the outside, and have to reach through the green picket fence. He sighed deeply before advising me.

"Ruby, I don't want to say too much or get too involved. I've found a job, but Barbara is still trying to get my work visa cancelled. So I have to be careful. I think you should call the lawyer who was appointed as the curator when Abdul was removed from the school."

This sounded promising. I got a pen out, ready to write down the details, "By the way, Kelvin, do you think there is something Barbara's doing that is suspect? Do you think that TV programme was on to something?" I asked.

"I don't think she's guilty – I think she's just completely insane," Kelvin sighed.

I readily agreed with that statement. I took down the details of the lawyer and thanked Kelvin. He ended the conversation with a warning. "You do know this will push Barbara over the edge. And you know who she will take it out on ...."

I understood exactly what he meant. Abdul's being forcibly removed from Barbara's care was a very sore point for her. He had been removed by lawyers as a human rights issue, and it was this very case that had generated the interest that had sparked the TV programme that had defamed her. At the time, according to Kelvin, apart from being suicidal again, she had taken her frustrations out on the children by smacking and humiliating them.

Needless to say, using that particular lawyer could potentially stir up a hornet's nest. She would be enraged. Kelvin provided the details of the lawyer.

In parting, I asked Kelvin that if for some reason Barbara was removed from the charity he might be able to pick up from her. He assured me that he would be more than willing and able.

Even with that consolation, I was still nervous. If Barbara was as unstable as I believed, she could possibly take it out on Phil personally. She was very open with the children regarding all the people who disappointed the charity, convincing them she was their only hope.

Volunteers came and went (mostly 'fired'), but she remained there for them – their hero, their god. If she didn't take it out on Phil physically, she could tell him that like others I didn't care, and that she alone was the only one who 'cared' enough to save him.

She had once asked Temba what he thought would happen if she had to leave the charity, and he had responded with a helpless "Then who will help me get my surgery?" She had enjoyed telling me that story.

Once I'd gotten authorities involved, there was no turning back. What was left of my already frazzled relationship with Barbara would be over for good. In fact, it would be war. I followed my instinct, though, and dialled the number.

A softly spoken yet masculine voice answered the phone. I heard an Afrikaans accent. "Pieter speaking."

Nervously, I began, "Hi Pieter, my name is Ruby Florence – I believe you are familiar with the charity, and have worked with them before?" He responded, "Yes, I am familiar with it – what can I do to assist you?"

I blurted out my story. When I was done, he thanked me and asked me to draft an email – in point form – summarising the situation. He continued, "I'll then forward this to the professor of child law in South Africa, as well as the Department of Social Services and get the relevant people together for a meeting. I understand the sensitivities (I'd told him Barbara got suicidal and abusive), but we have to do what's right for these children. I am almost certain we'll find some sort of solution that is both lawful and beneficial for everyone. Obviously, we are sympathetic to what Barbara is going through, and we certainly don't want to disrupt the children or schooling. We'll handle it as gently as we can.

I drafted the email. It read:

April 2010

"Thank you so much for assisting me. This a brief summary of what has happened. The list of dates outlining the incident I wish investigated is below.

Two years ago Phil began to stay with me on weekends. I've him for three weekends every month in this period.

The charity has been putting pressure on me to adopt him. I have agreed to do so in 2011.

In the meantime Barbara, who runs the charity, has stopped me from seeing Phil altogether. This happened on the 11th March 2010. I had planned for Phil to join us at my brother's wedding in Natal, which I called for permission to do. I was told however, that not only was he not allowed to join me but I was to cease contact with him until I start the adoption process.

I have since done this, and taken Phil to The Teddy Bear Clinic, where our relationship was evaluated positively. Unfortunately, I cannot take any more action until I make contact with Phil's social worker, whose details have 'disappeared' from the charity. Tracing this person in the system has become impossible, especially since I don't have Phil's ID number.

The reasoning for putting a sudden stop to the weekend visits was that I was skipping weekends and partying instead. This is certainly not the case, as we have a roster of the weekends I take him, which I have adhered to, except on two occasions this year. As a single woman, one weekend off a month and attendance at two events doesn't seem unreasonable or make me an unfit parent.

Furthermore, due to Phil's injuries (he recently had a boney deficit on his forehead, which was repaired with his own ribs) I am uncomfortable leaving him with babysitters, friends or relatives as if something went wrong it could lead to major complications.

I believe the current situation with Phil's being unable to see me at all is actually doing more harm than good.

Herewith some facts and incidents in chronological order that led to the school's decision to end our weekend visitation arrangements.

22ⁿᵈ January 2010 – Requested to send an essay outlining my intentions with Phil, which I did, outlining my intention to keep our weekend arrangement and foster him in 2011.

14ᵗʰ February 2010 – Barbara calls me to fetch Phil's belongings, as she's losing her house, closing the charity and is busy packing up everything.

15ᵗʰ February 2010 – The charity sent another email requesting me to formally adopt Phil. They further informed me that they already had passed on his details to Child Welfare for possible adoption. Having unpacked his bag of belongings, I discovered that the contents were random items from babies, and not his belongings at all. Furthermore, when I spoke to one of the volunteers and enquired how the packing was going, she responded that the charity wasn't closing.

I responded to the email saying I would apply, but for it to please be a last resort, as I'm not ready to adopt Phil this year. I would be renting out my apartment to tourists for the month of the FIFA World Cup, and would be away overseas for two weeks. Therefore, if he urgently needed adoption right now due to the school's closing down, and other families came forward to take him, I wouldn't stand in the way. However, I would appreciate some contact or a weekend with him from time to time if the new family would allow.

Please note, at this stage I was getting annoyed by the pressure (which I believed was misleading) and was 'pushing back'.

16th February 2010 – Had a meeting with potential corporate sponsors and Barbara with a lawyer present. She explained that she needed sponsorship in her personal capacity and didn't want to take money from the charity. She was not interested in drawing a salary from the charity, nor in submitting financial statements and business plans to the charity's trustees.

22nd February 2010 – I was notified via email that Barbara has just opened up a bank account for Phil, in his name.

10th March 2010 – I started avoiding Barbara as she had been making me feel increasingly uncomfortable. She was unwilling to allow Phil permission to attend my brother's wedding and stated she felt 'suicidal' and would get back to me with a final decision the next day.

11th March 2010 – I receive an email asking me to refrain from all contact due to my 'absence' on weekends and my 'partying. The email came from one André Botha, whom I had never heard *of before – I believe the correspondence was more than likely authored by Barbara.*

20th April – Phil and I visited The Teddy Bear Clinic for psychological evaluation, with a witness from the charity present. Our evaluation was favourable, but I have still been refused all access to Phil. I believe the charity is using Phil unashamedly, expecting me to deposit money into his account then calling me an 'unsuitable parent' because I refuse to do so. There have also been incidents of abuse reported, including the public exposure of children's genitals when they are smacked. These are issues that could affect the children psychologically.

I know of ex-volunteers from the charity who would be prepared to step in and assist if necessary if Barbara is removed from her position. Please also be aware that Barbara is looking to re-locate the charity to another African country at some stage, and has been opening up affiliate branches in other countries. This would mean even less control over what happens to the children and any charity funding. I hope we can resolve this situation as soon as possible. I'm missing my little boy terribly.

Regards

Ruby Florence"

I felt liberated the moment I clicked the 'send' button. At least I knew I had done the right thing. It was time the state intervened, properly, as Barbara and I weren't very rational at that moment.

In my mind, we needed a wise King Solomon. I recalled the biblical story of King Solomon and the two harlots that were brought before him with a baby they were fighting over. Both women lived in the same house and had newborn babies. However during the night one of them had rolled over onto her baby and smothered it to death. Having discovered this, she quietly crept towards the other sleeping women, and stole her baby, replacing it with her dead child. A serious crime.

To find out which woman was the rightful mother, King Solomon ordered that the baby be cut in two, and each woman given a half. The rightful mother, of course leapt forward crying out to rather give the living baby to the other woman than have it die. The other woman had no such qualm.

I had reached the stage where I wasn't sure which of the two mothers from the story I identified with. I'd be prepared to let Phil go if it was the right thing to do – but I was terrified that I was also the one okay with having his soul 'split in two' by my putting up a fight.

Obviously, the details and dynamics of our story were different. My hope was that we'd get to the bottom of everything and that the truth would come out and justice would prevail. I waited anxiously to hear from Pieter. I didn't hear from him for nearly three weeks. I was frantic and had left messages to see whether he had received my email.

I lay on Phil's bed, and found myself pleading for spiritual guidance. It was a Sunday, and I prayed I'd hear something that would give me an indication that I had God's blessing. I was starting to seriously doubt myself.

The next morning, I woke up feeling nauseous. It felt like a train had run me over. I mustered up my strength for the sales meeting I was to attend, but my energy and conviction had been depleted. It had been almost two months since the start of the whole ordeal. I'd been so consumed and disheartened by it that I had no desire to be around people, or go out. I had no Phil, no boyfriend and I'd successfully managed to isolate myself. It hurt to go to any places or be around people that reminded me of Phil, and how I'd let him down.

I had no choice but to re-evaluate my life and my headspace. Over the years, I'd worked hard on myself, and was relatively happy with who I was. But right now I had to acknowledge that there were issues I wasn't dealing with. Although I hadn't been bulimic for a few years, this bad habit had reared its head again. I'd eat almost as if to gag myself from speaking my truth. Then I'd throw up my food as punishment, and a release. I was in deep distress.

I sought to control the bulimia by barely eating and taking antidepressants, but my distressing relationship with food wasn't really resolved. Arriving home after the Monday sales meeting, I collapsed onto my bed. My contribution to work and the business was pitiful I retreated under the covers, painfully aware that my behaviour was typical of a person suffering from depression. And that was one of my greatest fears. I was terrified of not being able to get out of bed. I knew what that looked like. I'd seen my father live like that for two years and it was terrifying to behold. It's equally as debilitating for people who love the person suffering, as what it is for the person 'under the covers'.

I was no good to Phil like this. I somehow surfaced on the following day, which was a Tuesday. I'd missed an entire day of living, and felt ashamed. Eventually I downloaded my emails. There was one email from the day before not from Pieter, but from the charity! It was an advert for a parenting course. I scanned it with excitement only to see that there were no contact details or phone numbers – just a generic email address. There was no company name or organisation name either.

That didn't matter to me, though – I took it as a positive sign. Maybe the situation could still be resolved in time, before we went the legal route. I quickly emailed both the generic email address and the charity, asking them if they had any contact details or any more courses they'd recommend. The response came quickly: "Ma'am, we cannot spoon-feed you. If you want to be a parent, you need to take steps to educate yourself." It was signed 'André'.

So much for goodwill.

"André" was dangling a carrot, then slapping me down for trying to reach it. Perhaps Phil's nagging had prompted this grudging offer. I decided not to respond.

I switched my phone on, and there was a message from Pieter! He had set up a meeting with the head of professor of the head of Children's Law, his assistant, and requested my attendance.

I had received two signs that I was on the right track and had to keep the faith ... that Phil would return to me. I called Pieter to confirm the meeting, but also to let him know about Barbara's 'peace offering' of an email.

Pieter didn't seem to think much of the email, and didn't believe we should relax in our pursuit of justice. To be honest, I was terrified of a big legal dispute. I wanted everything to be handled in as just, righteous and loving fashion as possible.

The meeting was scheduled for a week's time at their offices in Pretoria, a city north of Johannesburg.

I was longing to see Phil, just to show him I was still around and working on resolving the situation. Of course, I couldn't tell him exactly what was happening, but every now and then I liked driving past the school in the hope that I would catch a glimpse of him. He never was around. Puzzlingly, when I asked the children in the yard where he was, they would say 'At the doctor' or 'On a school trip'.

Thankfully, Tracy was still cooking dinner for the children on Wednesdays and reporting on Phil's wellbeing, or I would have panicked that he had been sent away somewhere. My greatest fear was that I'd never find him again. Unbelievably, Tracy had still managed to avoid meeting Barbara, face to face, or have any dealings with her. Barbara didn't have her details, and Tracy would pitch up at the school, a block or two away from the office, feed the kids and leave quickly. No questions. No interference. How I envied her!

I arrived at the offices in Pretoria 10 minutes early. I had left early with plenty of time to spare, in case I got lost on the way there, or in the corridors of that big grey building I found myself in.

The reception area was full. There were construction workers, bedraggled looking women who appeared homeless, with children in their arms and foreign passports in their hands, and many others. All were waiting patiently in a waiting area. Walking to the receptionist's desk, I hoped I didn't have to sit and wait for too long.

The receptionist was friendly. "I have an appointment with Pieter. My name is Ruby Florence," I said, watching her pick up the phone to dial his office. She confirmed with him that he was expecting me, and told me he would be there to collect me shortly. I had barely sat down when a young dark-haired man with a Canadian accent walked up to the desk. He was possibly in his late twenties or early thirties. He seemed to work there.

"She can come with me. I'm going up to Pieter's office now," he offered. I smiled graciously and followed the young man out of the building.

Pieter must be have been in his forties, with light brown floppy hair and very striking blue eyes. He was very handsome indeed.

My inner vixen got very excited. "Hot lawyer! No wedding band! Game on!" But I quickly quietened her down and reminded the vixen we were not there to find a man but to get some justice for a child!

"Ah, Ruby, I'm glad you made it. I hope my directions were okay," Pieter said, reaching out to shake my hand.

I smiled. "Yes, they were perfect. Thank you so much for setting this up. Do you mind if I quickly use the bathroom?"

Washing my hands and brushing my hair in the ladies' room, I contemplated my reflection in the mirror. Was this what a good mother looked like, I wondered? The reflection that stared back at me was that of a woman prepared to sacrifice her very freedom so the voice of the child she loved could be heard. I didn't know whether that made me a martyr or a mother.

A little voice of doubt kept telling me I was guilt-driven and I shouldn't be so involved. It was a very difficult time and my faith in everything I believed in about myself and God was put to the test, and for a long time thereafter. I found my way back to the office.

Pieter officially introduced me to the Canadian man, who had collected my from the reception area. His name was David. A few minutes later, an attractive woman walked in, dressed in a long red coat. She had bobbed blonde hair and was immaculately turned out. She was possibly in her early forties.

"Hi everyone, sorry I'm late!" she said, removing her coat. I stood to shake hands, and she introduced herself as Dr Angela Fraser, head of Children's Law at the University of South Africa. Sitting down, she produced a printed version of the email I'd sent Pieter, who was in the process of welcoming us all to the meeting. I was asked to please re-tell my story, especially for

David's sake – he hadn't had the opportunity to read the email. Summarising the events as they had happened, I hoped I'd covered all the necessary details as coherently as possible.

Now and then, they'd ask me a few questions while they jotted down notes. When I'd completed my story, Angela sat back and sighed.

"I'm concerned that you're being bullied into adopting this child when you're not ready."

Although I agreed with her, I reiterated that I still wanted Phil on weekends, and would most definitely be ready to take him the following year.

Angela responded: "All right. Although we don't want to disrupt the charity and potentially destroy something that is 'working', we are going to have to investigate the organisation. You do understand that this won't just be about your little boy. What we will be doing could possibly affect all those children. But it would start with your officially requesting an investigation on Phil's behalf."

My response was careful. "Yes I'd be happy to do that. But what about all the other children? If Barbara leaves, and the whole structure collapses around her, who will be responsible for the kids left behind?"

The prospect of having to step into Barbara's shoes was terrifying – even if Kelvin was around. And I knew I would feel responsible as I had been the one to blow the whistle! I was afraid I'd be obliged to run the charity and would become bitter, just like Barbara.

"Social Services would have to step in, because we're just an organisation of lawyers," Angela explained. I quickly interjected, "If Social Services needs this, I have details of ex-volunteers who would prepare to step in, so that the charity and school don't collapse."

Everyone listened intently as I relayed Kelvin's story.

"Sounds like he could do with some help, too," Angela mused, jotting down Kelvin's number.

She warned me that Phil himself could be removed from the charity at any time as Barbara was not his legal guardian at all – the state was. Phil had been placed in the 'safe house' of the charity but his status in this regard was up, because he had been there for four years – the period of residency was three years. And yet without a social worker he was effectively stuck there.

All this was incomprehensible to me – I struggled to get my head around the fact that Barbara didn't have any rights and nobody could make decisions on Phil's behalf. Nor did he have a legal right to be at the charity any more. In effect, he was floating around in limbo.

"If Barbara has as much right to Phil as I do, what stops me from going to the school right now and taking him?" I burst out passionately, knowing I'd get instant negative responses all round – it was worth a shot, anyway.

Pieter hadn't said much throughout the meeting. He spoke slowly and with authority. "Right, we're going to have to appoint a curator. David, would you please take that over and be Ruby's point of contact from here on?"

David nodded his head.

Pieter continued, "Angela, would you please contact Social Services and get the enquiry going into whom Phil's social worker is, and get him investigated?"

Angela readily agreed.

The meeting adjourned, with Pieter promising that I'd hear from David in about two weeks' time. Thanking everyone, I picked up my bag and walked out, feeling relieved and excited. I smiled at the security guard who had scowled at me when I arrived. I crossed the street, with a little hop in my step.

I called Kelvin on the way home and told him all about the meeting, including mentioning his name. "What did they say?" he asked a little nervously. "They said it sounds like you could do with a little help, too."

He sounded as relieved and excited as I was. He was missing the children terribly. Suddenly, he was anxious. "You do know that it's war now, don't you, Ruby? She's going to come after you, and she's nasty!"

Bravely I responded, "Kelvin, if Barbara is going after anybody she'll have to go after Angela and Pieter, because they are the ones now questioning on Phil's behalf. The state is the 'parent' or legal guardian now that I've got authorities involved. Hopefully, they're going to start acting like a parent. This isn't just my battle any more, it's theirs."

I tried really hard to convince myself that I was out of the direct line of fire. In fact, my plan was to be completely and physically out of the firing line ... in another country!

Moving out

It had been two weeks since I'd met with the lawyers, and two long months since I'd seen Phil. Thankfully Tracy was still faithfully continuing with the Wednesday night cooking arrangement, and I lived for that phone call I'd get from her and Phil from time to time. Tracy had proved herself to be a friend in a million, and I will always be grateful to her for keeping both Phil and I going emotionally through an exceptionally difficult time.

The last time I spoke with Phil, I listened to hear if his voice had changed. It was obvious I was being neurotic, but I was sure his voice sounded somewhat older. I wondered where his jeans were taking him, and if we'd have to take out the hem. I wondered how much he would have grown when we measured him against his previous marker on the door frame, with the ruler resting on his head. I was desperate to have him back in my life. I couldn't bear missing out on even a centimetre of his life.

Pieter had reverted. Apparently the lawyers were preparing a document requesting an enquiry into the charity. The story of the enquiry would likely break at the charity while I was in Hawaii, on my pilgrimage to find God. At the time, that was my story and I was sticking to it. The fact that there was an opportunity for my costs to be covered by renting out my apartment during the FIFA World Cup gave me all the more reason to believe I had to go.

When I think about it, though, I was probably subconsciously terrified of the confrontation and I'd planned to be at literally the furthest point in the world from Barbara's desk the moment the papers arrived.

We had also outgrown my apartment. I needed an extra room to conduct the business I wanted to start, which would include kinesiology and working with people's energies, helping them to find their true purpose. This would involve accessing the subconscious, assisting them with removal of their 'blockages' and helping them to find their purpose.

I also wanted to grow my own herbs and vegetables on the ground, rather than in flower pots all over my balcony. At the same time, I wanted a view. Another tall order for God!

I had found a tenant to take over my apartment from the 1st August, so I had to set about finding a new place. Desiree was quite happy to have Phil and I as tenants until October. This suited me perfectly as it would allow me to get a little business going, and enrol Phil into a new school. I was getting ready to adopt him from July, when I returned, if necessary.

In the meantime, Desiree, Alan 'The Bachelor' and I had registered a children's trust. The idea was to set up a children's home, which would be equipped to absorb the children from the charity in the event of Barbara resigning. If she didn't resign and everything at the charity proved to be in order, then the trust would cater for other children. But right then, I believed we needed some sort of contingency plan in my place from our side, and of course it included Kelvin, and some of the other ex-volunteers.

Alan had some wonderful ideas for the one or two teenage boys at the charity. He had already spent some time at Desiree's house, when Phil and I were there, and he'd been impressed with Phil's technical abilities. His dream was to pass on his welding trade. He believed that because some of the children had such extreme facial disfigurement that they may battle to find work when they got older, and at least he could give them a trade.

"Once you have a welding helmet on, nobody knows what you look like," he had commented, while suggesting that he'd even be prepared to start a little business for the young adults to partner in, which would possibly set them up.

It made a lot of sense.

I started packing up my apartment after having lived there for seven years. Our lives were about to change again. As much as Phil hated change, I believed at the time it had to happen.

Then the news came.

The local company that had planned to rent out furnished apartments during the FIFA World Cup had gone under.

The agent from the rental agency who had assisted me until that moment took my call and was profusely apologetic. It was true. It seemed she didn't have a job anymore, either. It was a big blow to many of us. I had banked on the money coming through to pay for my trip to Hawaii. (Yes, I know it's typical of me to spend money I don't yet have, and this is a lesson that started to hit home!)

My ticket was booked, and paid for in full, as was my Spiritual Therapy course, which would allow my dream of actually seeing a physical sign of an angel come true, I hoped!

There was very little chance of a refund on either the flight or the course at that late stage. I was due to leave in two days' time. It was a disaster. However, in spite of my failed World Cup rental deal, it was a catalyst to get to Hawaii on the trip that would change me forever.

Had there not been an opportunity for some kind of 'sponsorship' of my trip, I would never have booked anything in the first place. I would have considered such a trip way too expensive and unnecessary to justify – especially when faced with the looming costs of the school fees, medical aid and other necessary expenses I'd have to cover when adopting Phil.

Now it was too late for guilt. I had to go through with the trip.

I called the new tenant, who was due to move in August and advised her about the situation. I suggested she move in sooner if she so desired. Thankfully it suited her needs perfectly, so at least there was an additional month of rental income that made me feel a little better about the whole sour situation.

My return from Hawaii was scheduled for 18 June. That would give me a good 10 days to prepare everything for storage and move in with Desiree, who was excited to have a housemate. This arrangement was not meant to be permanent, but would certainly assist both of us.

Desiree had been struggling with her divorce, and she desperately needed company. We arranged nights out, as women do when their hearts are hurting. Generally, the best friend takes 'the patient' and drinks and cries with her. Then the two dance like idiots on the dance floor, trying to look sexy. If the two have really had too much champagne, they dance like lesbians and show these men that they're not needed, anyway, knowing full well they've just become an unattainable fantasy to the men watching.

Of course, the men never quite believe this, because, like the friends, they've also had enough alcohol to believe that they're utterly irresistible Brand Pitt lookalikes. One night, Desiree and I went out and did all of the above. Like most people going through a divorce, her need for release and fun was insane. Jody was at her father's and Desiree was determined to do an 'all-nighter'.

At some late point in the evening, when it most definitely was past home time, Desiree went and invited two guys over coffee. A very dangerous situation indeed, considering the amount of alcohol we had consumed. What was even more irresponsible was Desiree was determined to drive all of us home in her car. Cringing, I recall all four of us getting into her car and heading back to her place. Once we had arrived at her house, she opened yet another bottle of wine. A little while later, she went to the bathroom and disappeared. One of the guys went to look for her, and came back reporting that she had gone to bed, and complained that she wouldn't allow him into her bed with her.

I wasn't particularly interested in either one of the guys romantically, so I relaxed and carried on chatting. But irritatingly, the man who had tried to get into her bed with her kept getting up and going to her room. It was getting uncomfortable, and I was nervous that at some stage he might turn his attention to me. So far, his friend had been relatively well behaved, but also kept asking if he could share my bed. They had no transport home, and I was in no state to drive. Eventually I excused myself and went to Desiree's room.

"Des, what must I do? Where's the key for your bedroom door?"

She mumbled some inaudible answer.

I was getting annoyed, as she was the one who got us into this situation. "Des, you better have a plan or I'm going to have to stay awake all night trying to keep that man that *you* brought home, in *your* car, out of *your* bedroom!"

Finally she sat up, and reached into her drawer. Suddenly I saw a wicked smile cross her drunken countenance. "Give them shleeping tablets," she shlurred.

212

What an evil plan! I loved it! I looked at the packaging and saw the pills were the strong kind – salvation at last!

Ten minutes later, both men were fast asleep on the couch and floor, having consumed what they were led to believe were 'recreational drugs' or some kind of stimulant that would improve the party!

The next morning both men were woken up with coffee and herded into Desiree's car. I drove them back to their cars, which were still parked outside the bar. Neither of the two seemed to remember much, which is probably better in the long run. Thankfully, neither of them had any allergic reactions to the drugs either. I'm sure we were not the first women to resort to those drastic measures.

Desiree wasn't the only one going through a divorce. Sadly, the cracks had started to appear in Tracy's marriage too. I feared that if left alone, she'd end up running off with some skipper or dive instructor in Mozambique, with nothing but a rubber duck and pair of boxer shorts to his name!

Since she had lost the 50kg, which she joked was the equivalent of a Backstreet Boy, she had gone from a European size 22 to a 12. She had worked really hard to look as great as she did, and was quite the blonde bombshell. She had been a large girl all her life, and her new look was actually more than she or her husband could handle. She too was moving into a fabulous but very fragile space.

Having two friends going through a divorce at the same time is almost like having twins. It's intense! You have to be there for both at the same time, and nurture as much as you can with as much time as you have, making sure they don't run around hurting themselves due to their vulnerability.

The bonus was that I actually now had three friends with empty houses, and they were only too happy to have somebody in their guest rooms, filling up the void somewhat. It was reassuring to know that, whatever happened, I'd have a roof over my head, while finding the right property, when I got back from Hawaii.

I chose Desiree's house as a base, especially as it reminded me of Phil, and would be the ideal 'in between' home, if he returned before I found our new place of residence.

Dating the "belly button"

Alan, 'The Bachelor', had gone to great lengths with setting up our little trust fund that would hopefully form the basis of the charity we hoped to get off the ground. He felt passionately about getting things going, which was impressive, given his very busy schedule. Part of what he did for a living was buying and hiring out of industrial welding equipment, which meant that he was constantly on call if anything went wrong.

His dream was to own a helicopter and be able to fly off shore, anywhere in the world, to fix whatever piping or steel problem there was. I envisioned him flying on his chopper, out to oil rigs out in the middle of the Atlantic, doing repairs off the coast of Africa.

Recently he had made it clear that he didn't mind dating girls who took him to his 'belly button'. The first time we'd met, I'd refused to give him my number – now I was starting to wonder if dating the man 'who I took to his belly button' wasn't such a bad idea after all. He virtually checked out in terms of everything on my Checklist of Requirements for a Suitable Mate. However, I was incredibly nervous. Although it had been nine months since John had hurt me, I still felt vulnerable. Also, I wanted to go to Hawaii and feel truly free, answerable to nobody but myself for a while. But my head kept warning me not to close myself off too much or I'd be sorry.

After going on a few dates with Alan, he invited Desiree and I to his farm for a weekend. The farm was actually a plot of land where he had built a warehouse which housed samples of the massive equipment he specialised in. He also intended to start growing crops, as part of the regulations of the area were, that the land needed to have a certain percentage of agriculture growing on it. Of course, the idea of open spaces, and growing herbs and vegetables appealed to me enormously.

There was a little river that ran at the bottom of the property. Most evenings Alan would take his four dogs for a run, and they would swim in the river. Alan's brother, Roland, also lived on the farm. He was even taller than Alan, as well as overtly gay. We clicked instantly.

"So, Ruby, when are you bringing Phil here? We really want to develop a little animal petting zoo for the kids, so please bring Phil and his friends. It's part of our dream."

Alan's blue eyes danced and he put his huge arm around me, as he said "Oh, she'll be coming around with Phil, all right. Hopefully a lot!"

That night, after the four of us had consumed a few bottles of wine, Alan and I went outside to look at the stars. It was a clear, bright night, and we were far from the smog of the city.

"I want to ask you if you will come on a journey with me, Ruby. I have always liked you. You know that. And I'm really serious when I say that I want something meaningful. I'm not trying to have a fling with you." I listened carefully, unsure of what to say or what I wanted. He continued, "I ultimately want a wife and kids. Shall we take this journey together and see where it takes us?"

I was shocked. Alan certainly knew what he wanted, and his honesty was admirable. But we hardly knew each other, and I wasn't nearly ready for such an intense conversation. A voice inside me screamed, "He's saying all the right things! This is what you've been asking for!"

He was easy on the eye, hardworking, with a good heart. And he appeared to be able to offer me the life I'd been dreaming of. But the timing was just so bad. And he was so tall! Uncomfortably so, for a petite woman like me. Maybe I was making excuses out of the sheer terror!

After listening to him, I responded, "I don't know what to say to you, Alan. Let's just take each day as it comes. I'm really tired; would you mind if I turned in?"

Not wanting to put him off, I gave him a lingering kiss good night and went to the guest room, which was allocated to Desiree and I. That night, I had the strangest dream. I dreamt I was with Alan, and Eugene (of all people!) was in the room, looking on, and I felt guilty. Then I remember feeling annoyed with him for the intrusion. I was perfectly entitled to move on.

The next morning I awoke feeling confused, my mind playing tricks on me. But I was surprisingly happy and refreshed. It felt good to be appreciated and wanted, even if I couldn't reciprocate it. I most definitely had a little bounce in my step. I said my goodbyes to everyone and drove through to my mother's for the day. Alan sent me a text that night, saying that he already missed me. He asked when we could see one another again.

As much as I enjoyed getting the message, it was getting a little demanding and I wanted my freedom for just a little longer. I wanted to fly out of the country, free as a bird, and not be hankering after some man that I couldn't wait to get back home to before I'd even left. I texted back that I was busy that following weekend and that it would have to be the week after that. So we'd have to make a date for two weeks' time.

I could sense he was a little disappointed.

When the date drew closer, Alan informed me that he'd been called out of the country on business, and that he wouldn't be able to make it. The calls and messages from him started drying up. I was mostly relieved.

Hawaii was looming, and I hadn't heard much from the lawyers working on Phil's case. I'd called, left messages and sent an email indicating that I was to be out of the country soon, but they were to email me of any progress or updates. Alan was continually on my mind. He seemed so perfect for me. But my need for freedom and space was winning out. I had even contemplated staying on for a few weeks in Hawaii. Possibly, I could get a little holiday job, and fly back the minute I heard anything from the lawyers.

It may have seemed like a childish fantasy at the time, but I wanted that freedom to choose in my own head, even if something that crazy never happened. Over the years, so much had been put on me, and so much taken away.

Those two years had left me questioning my ability to make my own decisions and questioning and second guessing the decisions I finally did have the courage to make. Until now, my crazy decisions had affected only me – now they were affecting a child, too, and forcing me to question my own emotional maturity.

The week before leaving for Hawaii, I attended a barbeque at Desiree's house. Alan, who was back from his business trip, was there. He hadn't been in contact since I blew him off that day I left his farm. It had been three weeks, and I was truly happy to see him. When it was time for me to leave, he walked me to my car.

"I really didn't mean to scare you off last time," he explained, "and I'm sorry I made you feel awkward. I was just being honest. I just can't understand how you appeared so open, especially just before you left, and then shut me out in that text message. One minute you were happy to be with me, kissing me, and then you didn't want to know me. It's weird."

I replied, confused myself, with my own mixed emotions and reactions, "You did nothing wrong. In fact, you've done everything right. You've no idea how I've wanted somebody just like you to ask me with on their life's journey. It's what I've been waiting for all my life, and it's terrifying. I don't know what else to say, other than can we please go on that date we were supposed to?" I smiled, hoping for a positive response.

Alan smiled his beautiful, dimpled, oh-so-similar-to-John's smile. There really was a resemblance. The sudden discomfort in my gut instantly reminded me that the last man who smiled me like that had hurt me very badly. I chose to ignore the sensation, pushing myself to bypass and ignore it. It was time to move forward.

"Okay, how about dinner on Friday before you leave?" he asked.

"Great, it's a date!" I kissed him on the cheek and got into my car, smiling all the way home.

The next day, I had a serious meeting scheduled with Sean, my boss. I had brought one decent sales deal in, which only covered my costs to the company. My contribution had been disappointing to both Sean and myself, as normally I would over achieve. It was obvious that my heart was not in his business, and if not dealt with, I would become a liability.

Ideally what I wanted was to be able to go to Hawaii, and if I wanted, come back and work as a freelancer on a commission only basis. But I wasn't passionate about Sean's business, either – there was no brand or message that I could represent that I resonated with. I was merely selling advertising space, and, it felt like it never mattered.

If necessary, I'd grin and endure it, which was unfair all round. Financially, though it would take time to build up a kinesiology, esoteric healing-type practice, so I had to acknowledge that I needed income from media sales, while I weaned myself off of it.

I wasn't in the mood for a long 'detox' period at all. There's only so long you can get away with that excuse to the world – it does lose its charm for both you and your friends eventually. Furthermore, I had to find a way to be creative and put my need to assist people together somehow.

Although I had done a little writing course, I didn't feel nearly ready to earn an income from my writing. If I put all my passions and talents together, it was evident that for me to be happy, I had to find a way to write, entertain and speak about things that really mattered and uplifted, if I was to be in media. Obviously, I had a lot of work to do on myself first, but I was upbeat that I would heal from the past and be strong enough to follow my dream. I just didn't count on how long it would take or how intricate the process would actually turn out to be.

During our meeting, Sean seemed quite relieved that I wasn't expecting to come back as a salaried employee. Throughout the meeting, I realised that I probably wouldn't even want to freelance for him when I came back, which I was honest about. So we parted on respectful terms.

I gave back the laptop which I had done so much writing on, and felt excited about the new chapter of my life that was about to begin. Being honest, though, didn't solve the dilemma of what I would do for an income when I returned. I would have to find something to do quickly, but I'd worry about that when I got back.

In summary, my apartment was rented out, I had resigned and was therefore jobless, the Jeep I was still paying for wasn't sold (it was sitting on a showroom floor), and for some reason the process of getting Phil back was dragging. From what I could gather, it could take a few months, even if handled really quickly and efficiently by the lawyers.

Alan fetched me for our date. I wore a little black dress, with a black jacket and long, matching boots. He looked very dashing in a black shirt and beige pants. We went to the most beautiful little Italian restaurant and sat downstairs in the wine cellar, where it was quieter. Alan poured over the menu, then selected a bottle of good red wine, which the owner of the restaurant assured us was the best wine in the house. We clinked glasses and drank to my trip.

"I promise I will come back, Alan," I said. "I'm sorry about what I put you through."

He responded thoughtfully, "You must do what's right for you, Sunshine. This is your life and it's not a dress rehearsal. Go and enjoy yourself. You're worth waiting for." Then he leant forward and said, on a lighter note, "Even if your hair does stick up all over the place," and ruffled my hair, then tried to smooth the cow's lick in my fringe.

My heart did a little skip and I reminded myself to stay grounded and not get carried away. I had to go to Hawaii and keep the promises I had made to myself.

Hawaii

The date of departure finally arrived and I had packed up for two weeks. I went on yet another last date with Alan – call it an insurance policy. My instinct was to run but logic told me I'd be sorry if I did. It was a conundrum of note.

I'd made a deal with a car dealership for a reasonable trade-in on my Jeep – and would buy a little Citroen C1, which I really liked. Everything was working out perfectly. The finance had taken two weeks to be approved. On the day I was about to leave, the finance had been approved, and I was delighted at the prospect of coming back from Hawaii to a new car. I was told the dealership lost the paperwork. But be that as it may, I was determined to take delivery of my new car before I left.

My older brother, Greg, and I arrived at the dealership. I handed over the keys of the Jeep yet again, but this time I took the cute new Citroen in return. We transferred my travel bags out of the Jeep and transferred them into the sexy little car. Greg got into the passenger seat as I drove myself to the airport with us both singing to Neil Diamond's song *America*.

Although, I wasn't going to the continent of North America, Hawaii is one of its states!

I've always enjoyed playing Neil Diamond's music and it's often been the soundtrack to significant events throughout my life. As a little girl, I used to stand on a chair and sing at the top of my voice, "I am I said … and no-one heard at all, not even the chair." Then I would get off the offensive chair and kick it, to prove my point, to my mother's alarm.

Thinking back, when God had shown himself to Moses, he had introduced himself as "I AM", and I wouldn't have been surprised if in those days I was really calling God, doubting He was listening to me.

I recently wrote Neil a letter (which I never got around to posting) thanking him for introducing me to 'Shiloh' the imaginary friend, whom I believed to be Jesus. Shiloh was a great comfort to me throughout my life. I also mentioned how much as a child, I'd enjoyed *Girl, you'll be a woman soon*, where I had dreamt somebody like him would literally come and take my hand. Since he'd always been married I had given up on him being my prince but, in my letter, I asked him to please consider adopting me anyway. Besides, I really liked his surname!

As we arrived at the airport, the dealership called. Apparently, the bank had just called Sean to confirm my employment, which I'd just terminated that week. He told the bank I no longer worked there, so the bank declined the finance at the 11th hour! If the dealership hadn't have lost the paperwork two weeks prior, the finance would have been approved, as I would technically still have had a job. The car had to be returned immediately, and the Jeep returned to me. I turned to Greg helplessly.

"Sorry, dude, you're going to have to return this baby and take the Jeep. They're not going to finance the new car. Goodness, that's the shortest time I've ever owned a car!" and with that we both started laughing.

When we had sobered up, I implored him on a serious note, "Please will you sell the Jeep for me while I'm gone? I can't afford these payments. They're killing me."

"Shame, Rubes! I'll take the car straight back and sell your Jeep. Just have a good time and forget about all of this, okay? Get out there and live!" he said passionately.

"Thanks. I love you so much!" I responded, as we stood outside the soon-to-be-returned car. "I'm going straight through to departures. Don't worry about hanging around, please just get the car back."

We hugged and kissed goodbye, and he drove off waving.

I took my bags, huffing and puffing my way to the check-in counter. I was not going to allow a disappointment of this nature to spoil the excitement of the trip.

I contemplated my arrangements, and the lack of planning for my accommodation. As intimidating as that was, I knew I'd be taken care of and that was the end of that. I didn't have much money, therefore I'd packed my own food. I used to hike, so I had similarly organised my backpack the way I would to go on a hiking trail, with energy foods and basics that would keep me going in the event of my ending up homeless. Of course, one also has to have an outfit fit for meeting the queen, just in case. On the whole, I was pretty organised. I was not going to end up starving like I did in Paris.

After check-in, I made my way to the waiting area, where one could watch the planes take off, and ordered a cocktail.

"Well, here goes, girl. To the craziest and bravest girl I know."

I toasted myself and set about texting my friends to say goodbye. Within hours I'd be flying over the ocean, far away from home, Phil and, sadly, the Soccer World Cup. I consoled myself with the upcoming adventure, though. It was exciting to anticipate or try to guess the outcome of my pilgrimage, which is what I believed this was.

The flight to Sydney was a pleasure. Nobody sat next to me and I was able to stretch out over three empty chairs. Needless to say, I slept very comfortably on the plane.

We arrived at Sydney Airport and I had to wait for five hours until the flight to Honolulu. I read my book and sent out a few text messages again, updating everyone. I've always been able to daydream for hours at a time, so the five-hour wait wasn't much of a problem for me. Thankfully this wasn't an airport I needed to spend an entire night in!

The flight to Honolulu wasn't quite as comfortable. The plane was full, and I certainly wasn't going to be able to stretch out over any empty chairs. At least I had an aisle seat, and only one passenger next to me to contend with, and he seemed all right. One is often tempted to just ignore a fellow passenger, much like one does in a lift. But doing it for 12 hours can be more bothersome than it's worth, so I decided not to ignore the man seated next to me, who looked like someone straight out of *Jesus Christ Superstar* or the Seventies play *Hair*, with his beard and long hair.

I decided to be polite when he greeted me. His name was Stacy, and he appeared very laid-back, in fact, he got quite comfortable. We ordered copious amounts of wine and solved the problems of the universe. Stacy was a surfer, and made beach or surfer jewellery for a living. He was actually on his way to give a course on making jewellery. Suddenly, there was some turbulence, and he reached out and stroked my arm, so that it tickled. It was very relaxing. Then it happened again, and eventually he just continued. I passed out contentedly, with the hippie tickling my arm. All in all, life was good.

I arrived in Honolulu, anxious to catch the connecting flight to the big island. My lack of accommodation arrangements had started unnerving me. Once again, I said a little prayer and got the answer shortly thereafter, when I picked up a brochure advertising hostels in Hawaii. They looked affordable, and I had my own food, so I felt relaxed again.

We flew directly into Kona, on the big island, which has the largest active volcano in the world. The river of lava and fire that flows into the ocean, especially when seen at night, can only be described as spectacular. After two days of flying, with a day lost in between, due to the changing of time zones twice, I was exhausted.

I walked past a statue of three dancing Hawaiian ladies, where the movement was still in their twirling skirts and thick-set calves. People were walking around with lays of flowers, their floral scent wafting in the air. It was incredibly hot, and I struggled to get the heavy hiking backpack onto my shoulder. Eventually I managed to straighten myself, said goodbye to the dancing ladies and walked towards the information kiosk.

The lady greeted me with a warm "Aloha!"

"Hi, I'm looking for a youth hostel, a map and transport. Could you please assist me?" I enquired.

She obligingly gave me details of a cab, an affordable youth hostel and a map, where she very kindly circled exactly where the hostel was.

I was set to go, and hailed a cab. Upon arrival at the quaint hostel, it was pleasing to see how clean and functional it was. Grateful for a bed, I snuggled in and slept for two whole days before I was able to converse or get know anybody. When I awoke from my coma I discovered, to my delight, that there were three other people on the same course I was on.

We quickly introduced ourselves. There was a single woman from Boston, by the name of Tamara, who was a Pilates instructor. She seemed a bit shy under her thick, red fringe, which almost hid her beautifully long-lashed, sea-green eyes. Eva, who was married and a mother with two children, was originally from Ukraine. She had a tan, and golden spirals of curls that fell delicately on her shoulders. She was gorgeous. Then there was George.

George's wild, curly, jet-black hair bobbed as he spoke with his American, part-Colombian accent. At times, though, he sounded just like a black mama from the South, complete with gestures and eye-rolling. He was dressed, in long flowing white robes, with many bracelets and amulets on his wrists and around his neck. He blessed the dorm, his bed and thanked Jesus, Mary and all the saints for getting him to his destination safely. He then complained about the weather, the turbulence on the plane, his on-going sinus problem and finally, after kissing a photo of the baby Jesus, said goodnight to all of us.

The next morning, we discussed travel arrangements and Eva offered to drive us to the conference centre, in the car she hired. I offered to pay towards the costs, which she politely declined, smiling. "You can buy me lunch sometime, okay?" she suggested. I hugged her, and promised to do so.

In the meantime, we had to reassure George (twice) that he looked great in his white outfit. He still seemed unsure as to whether it was working for him or not.

The course

The course proved to be interesting and life-changing for all of us. On my first day, I got the confirmation or the sign I was looking for! I didn't expect to receive it so soon, or just outside the conference centre. I thought it may happen near the volcano, or swimming with the dolphins, but I was in for a surprise.

I was taking photographs of the entrance to the centre, and all the people gathered for the course. Some were dressed up in angel outfits, others looked like fairies – it was magical. I took a photo of George and when looking at the photograph, I saw something breath-taking. Above George (of all people!) there wasn't just an orb – but a mauve, pinkish outline of a being. It was definitely feminine, one could almost make out the flow of the robe or gown. Running up to George, I excitedly showed him.

One or two other people glanced at the photo and confirmed that it was indeed more than an orb. Of course, George was thrilled that the image had appeared above him, and took it as a personal sign that he was indeed "The Chosen One".

However, my ego or left brain, governing logic and limitation, held me in check and reminded me that possibly my camera was merely reflecting light, and it was nothing supernatural.

With my enthusiasm slightly curbed, I went inside where the instruction was about to begin. Unfortunately, I am unable to elaborate too much about what we learnt, as it's a very personal experience. But during the first morning session, the first lecturer, who had just arrived, without having any contact with me or the people I'd shown my photo to, mentioned that there was an angel present with us.

She described how she had recently started working with Jophiel, who had a feminine energy and mauve light around her. I was shaken. I still didn't quite believe it, and sometimes still battle to do so.

Since then, I've often glanced at my phone, and can't help but notice a very definite outline, and think 'maybe' ... It certainly dovetailed with my theory of being able to 'see' in the right vibrational environment, if clear-minded.

During the course, there was plenty of time for meditation, and some people experienced intense emotional healing that would affect their lives and decisions as a whole forever.

Of course, there were fun elements, too, where we played 'dress up', and nobody seemed to mind that I thought I was Tinkerbell permanently. We formed quite a large group, with many of us having studied other healing modalities, which we all endeavoured to share with one another.

On day three, a Frenchman called Ocean introduced himself to me. He always wore a sarong, and if he didn't have a flower in his hair, he'd wear a wreath made of bougainvillaea around his head. He had very blue eyes, sun-bleached blond hair and a good-looking face. He wouldn't share his age, but I guessed him to be around 50, with a very youthful spirit. He was a huge hit with the young girls on course.

He was a singer, and not just any singer, but a tenor as it turned out. I discovered that he'd changed his name from Patrick and believed 'Ocean' to be a much better fit to his personality. He had just been for a swim. He sat down beside me, folding his wet Speedo swimsuit on the floor at his feet. I looked meaningfully at the sarong, then back at him (the way one does at a Scotsman in a kilt). He quickly comprehended my wordless question, and replied with a wicked smile, "No, zer ees nosing under," glancing down pointedly at his sarong.

It was shocking and amusing at the same time! Goodness, these Frenchman are the same wherever you go!

Throughout the discourse, he would continually lean into me and whisper things I couldn't make out in his French accent. He was constantly in my ear, and in my neck! It was flattering, but I reminded myself that I had a man waiting at home for me, and pulled away.

Finally, we were told to do energy work on the person next to us, which Ocean seemed very happy about. In spite of all his flirting, he was amazingly insightful. He 'saw' a little boy with me, with something on his face. He surprised me even more by holding up his hand, "and zees hand ees somesing wrong" he muttered, eyes closed in his thick French accent.

Excitedly, I asked him "Is he coming to me? Am I going to be his mother?" Ocean, held my hands, deep in concentration. I could almost feel him reaching into my mind, searching to help me find my truth. Slowly he shook his head, "No, ees not coming to you. But you are 'elping him wis money".

I quickly withdrew my hands. That was not what I wanted to hear. Firstly, I believed I had gotten a message from God, in church. If God were here too, which is what I'd been led to believe, in that Angels are His messengers, why would He be contradicting Himself? Maybe the church was right about all of this type of New Age thinking. Possibly it was evil, and this 'prophecy' was sent to trip me up.

It was very confusing, but a part of me whispered, "What if he's right? What if these are my troubled thoughts he's merely accessing?"

Ocean could see I was agitated. I didn't want to argue with him, when he'd acted out of the goodness of his heart. He truly had nothing to gain or lose personally by the message he delivered.

I explained the situation to him, from my endometriosis and inability to have children to my story with Phil.

He looked thoughtful. "You can change ze future – you have ze choice. What I see is 'ow you feel and your energy now. Also, I can fix zes endometriosis. Come wis me to see the sun go down later at ze bar." Looking into his eyes, I saw some playfulness but there was a fundamental genuine compassion there too. I was intrigued, but also knew enough about Frenchmen to be a little wary.

"Okay, I'd like to see the manta rays. I believe they come to the surface after sundown, and we can see them from the bar."

Ocean seemed to think this a good idea too. I told Eva about our plans and asked her to join us, and eventually there were a few of us who decided to watch the sun go down. At the end of the session, we traipsed through to the bar, with Ocean singing en route, his magnificent voice echoing through the corridors. On arrival at the bar, Ocean took me aside purposefully, gently guiding me by the elbow to the railing overlooking the bay. The sun was about to set.

He put his hands on my stomach, eyes closed once again, saying, "Now, whatever zis sing is or zis person is zat 'as caused zees problem ... you must see ze end of it when ze sun goes down, while I move ze energy in your parts." He motioned towards my abdomen. I flinched, and he sensed my alarm. "Ees safe Ruby ... I'm 'elping you," he said gently.

And with that, I relaxed, truly wishing and hoping for healing. I knew exactly where the pain came from. I wanted so badly for it to be 'fixed' and to rid myself of the memories, as well as the manifested corresponding physical pain, induced by the years of anguish and guilt, of an indignant child inside of me that I had refused to listen to. I had effectively shut her up, telling her 'it was her own fault' that so-and-so touched her inappropriately, and that it actually wasn't that big a deal, anyway.

What was worse for my inner child was that she had attempted to stand up for herself at the time, but it had become an embarrassment and very painful.

Indeed, the pain of that incident and what it had cost her to fight for her boundaries had been too painful to comprehend. What it taught her was that life would have been easier had she just kept quiet. That was where it all began, resulting in a lack of faith in my own judgement, bulimia and confusing relationships with men.

I felt the tears forming as the sun rapidly set. I had to let go of everything I'd held onto, a failed belief system that no longer served me. Given what I was letting go of, I couldn't help but be conscious and a bit fearful of this man, wearing nothing but a sarong and a wreath on his head, moving his hands over my abdomen.

I focused on what I perceived to be his pure intent, and allowed myself to bid farewell as the last sliver of red sun had disappeared from the horizon, taking my pain with it.

When I opened my eyes, there were a few curious glances. I could only imagine how it had all looked! As crazy as it was to have somebody looking like Puck from Shakespeare's *A Midsummer Night's Dream*, with his hands over my stomach, our eyes squeezed tightly shut in concentration, I trusted the process as much as I could.

That day, I honestly felt liberated from the past. The sun was gone, the stars were out, and the hotel turned the spotlight on the sea. A big manta ray surfaced and floated by, looking like some ocean-dwelling UFO. Slowly it glided by, totally oblivious to the attention and excitement its presence had stirred with us. Drawn from the depths of darkness, instinctively attracted to the light. It was a perfect moment, a fitting metaphor for my life's journey at that moment.

"Isn't he magnificent?" Eva sighed, in awe. I responded, beaming, "Yes, life itself is magnificent, Eva." She hugged me, and we held on tightly to each other for a few seconds. Ocean, obviously out of 'work mode' and back to being a typical Frenchman, seemed a bit deflated when I decided against going to his room for some more 'healing'. I told him, with a chuckle, that he'd worked hard enough on me for the day.

Eva and I headed back to the car, with George in tow, complaining that we had taken so long and he had wanted to go back long ago. All the way home, Eva and I were quiet, while George discussed how everyone complimented him on his healing and psychic abilities, repeating the same stories over again. He needed reassurance that he was on the right track, too.

It seemed to have been day of significance for everyone.

The job offer

While on the course, we became quite a close-knit group. We even got to know George's children, whom he spoke to on the phone every day. I had always thought George was gay, but it turned out he wasn't.

In case you're wondering, as much as I'm supposedly attracted to effeminate or shall I say 'metrosexual' men, George was definitely not my type. But I listened to his conversations with his children and realised things were definitely not what they seemed. In fact, his situation was quite complicated.

Both his children had severe learning disabilities. They went to special schools for the mentally handicapped. I never asked what happened, or if they were born that way. George's wife seemed quite flighty and took to disappearing from time to time. I suspected she wasn't on the scene at the moment. It seemed to be a rather weird setup. Although, by now you may have figured that 'weird' has never been a problem for me! I think we're all a bit weird.

I also discovered his 17-year-old daughter was severely bulimic. She had been in and out of hospital a few times, which deeply saddened me. It was all too familiar, and my heart went out to her. So when George asked me if I would like to be their nanny over the summer break, I seriously considered it.

George had to attend a court case in New York, which was why he needed a nanny for the children. There was a good chance I'd get to go to New York with the family, too, which excited me no end! So I'd be paid a small allowance, have accommodation and get to see the United States. It was sounding better and better.

Except for one thing. Alan. How on earth was I going to explain this to him?

A little voice in my head said "Unfortunately, this is something you have to do and, if he really loves you, he'll understand and wait for you."

I called the airline to re-route my ticket – instead of flying via Australia, I would go to Florida, where I would be staying. The airline was of no help. I was unsure of the next step and I truly believed that for some reason, I had to do a 'Mary Poppins' stint.

Bulimia was something I understood only too well – I truly wanted to help the troubled teen. I've also always been sorry that I never took a gap year after school, where I could au pair and travel. Unfortunately, my circumstances forced me to find work immediately after school, and I'd never been on leave for longer than three weeks since starting my career. I wanted a sabbatical. It was long overdue.

I called my friend Liesel who was in the removal and relocation business. If I were to stay overseas, I wouldn't be there to pack up properly before my tenant moved in. I needed her help.

She assured me that everything would be in order. She said, "I'll sort it all out for you. I'll pack up your apartment myself. If you can't afford storage, my brother is prepared to buy all your household contents. He's moving into a new place, and would be happy to take your stuff. I'll just keep your clothes for you, and tell Jackie to keep Scarlett the parrot, a bit longer."

It was a great idea. True, I couldn't afford storage and the cash would come in handy at that moment. I'd been toying with the idea of self-publishing a book, which would cost me half of what I'd get for my household contents. It would be a testimony of my experience with Phil, and what those two years we spent together meant to me, regardless of what happened in the future. It would be his and my book.

That said, I confirmed the sale of my goods, and confirmed my bank details with Liesel so the money could be transferred instantly.

"Relax and go and see the world, my friend!" Liesel said.

Then I called Tracy. "How's Phil doing, Trace? I have an opportunity to stay on overseas for another four to six weeks. Have there been any movements at the school?"

It made no difference whether I was in the country or not, as I wasn't allowed to see Phil, until everything was resolved. But I needed to know he was all right.

Tracy responded, "There don't seem to be developments from what I can see when I'm there on Wednesdays. He always asks after you, Rubes, but don't worry. I'll keep him going until you're back in the country."

"Thanks, Trace, just tell him I love him when you see him again."

We disconnected, and I set about drafting an email to the lawyers, to ask them if there had been any further developments with the charity and Phil. I mentioned, I'd be away for a short while, but would appreciate regular updates. If anything changed, they were to notify me immediately and I'd return sooner if necessary.

Checking my bank balance, I said a prayer. Money from the sale of my household goods hadn't come through yet. Bearing in mind we were approaching the July 4th weekend, I could only afford a ticket to Florida if I flew from Honolulu to LA. I would then have to travel by bus to Florida, which would then be safely within my budget. Flying back home didn't seem to be a problem, provided George paid me as promised. I made the decision to go, booked the airline and bus tickets and gave George details of where and when to collect me in Florida.

When arriving at Honolulu airport, I was asked to produce my credit card. While handing it over, the man at the counter explained that it hadn't gone through because they didn't recognise the bank I banked with. I froze.

"What do you mean by that? Has the money not been paid to the airline yet?"

I was getting anxious.

"No, ma'am, but it's gone through now," he smiled, handing my card back to me.

I was petrified. What if the same thing happened in LA with my bus ticket and this time there weren't enough funds? I truly doubted there would be enough after my little spending spree in Honolulu, thinking that the money had already been deducted from my account.

What made it worse was my LA bus ticket was for a midnight bus, and I wasn't sure where the bus pick-up point would be. If it was downtown, which I suspected, and my card didn't go through, I'd have nowhere to sleep. There might be enough money for one night's accommodation, and I could face my problems the next day. Or perhaps I could see what was in my bank account and see how far the bus could take me across the country with what I had.

If I got halfway, I'd call George and ask if he wouldn't mind paying for the rest of my passage from wherever it was, to his place. My heart was in my throat. I boarded the plane praying and saying affirmations to myself for the full six hours of the flight.

We landed in LA, and I made my way around asking for help. I found a city shuttle and paid $16 to get to downtown LA, where the bus terminal was. The shuttle driver changed his sign from 'Hollywood' to 'downtown'. A little part of me was disappointed.

"Have you just come from Hollywood?" I asked.

"Yeah, it's one of the routes I drive," he replied.

"Oh! That must be so cool," I sighed wistfully, wishing I could hang around and explore the city. But it wasn't on the agenda for this trip. I had to get to Miami with what I had, and that was that.

I was supposed to be at the bus terminal an hour before the bus left. By the time I got to the bus terminal, my bus was scheduled to leave in 10 minutes. And there was a long queue! Things were getting extremely stressful, and once again I said a little prayer. In fact, my prayers had become one long dialogue with God. I didn't believe He'd allow anything to happen to me that I couldn't handle.

In spite of my anxiety, I stood in the queue, and before I knew it, my bag was loaded, my card swiped and a booklet of tickets handed to me.

"Enjoy your trip, ma'am. I suggest you hightail on over there. Bus is leavin' in five minutes."

I nearly kissed him. I don't believe he'd ever been thanked for a ticket like that in his life! I was incredibly grateful and relieved.

"Thank you, dear Father in heaven. I know I must be keeping your angels really busy, but I believe it will somehow be worth it," I murmured, running towards the bus, where the engines were already rumbling. Stumbling in, I found my way to the back seat. It was empty, and I luxuriously spread myself across all four seats. Oh, the relief!

I was on my way to Miami, Florida. I had $10 to my name, eight sachets of hot chocolate, three sachets of instant soup and two tins of tuna. I would survive.

And so began the longest bus trip of my life.

From LA to Miami

Upon checking the map, I discovered we'd be travelling across seven states. It was satisfying to know that I would indeed be seeing most of the country. We'd be stopping from time to time. The longest lay-over would be three hours, but other than that we'd be travelling through night as well. I wanted to see and experience as much as I could.

We drove out of LA, and I tried to absorb as much as possible in the dark. At least I got to see the famous control tower at LAX, which resembled a space ship.

I fell asleep as we crossed over into Arizona. Waking at dawn, I drank in the beauty of the desert and dark sky, where flecks of light blue and pink started to appear. It was hot out there, even in the early hours of the morning. Whilst contemplating the heat and emptiness of the desert, I noticed a sign indicating we were approaching Phoenix. The red Phoenix sun burst into the sky, like its namesake – a bird of fire. I saw potential of the new beginnings it symbolised. Death and rebirth through fire: a fitting symbol indeed.

The city bustled with peak-hour traffic as people went about their business. It was like a concrete oasis in the middle of the desert, with a busy airport from what I could tell when I looked up at the sky.

We stopped at the bus terminal, where I hoped there would be an opportunity to shower. No such luck! Not many people travelled by bus for days on end from what I could tell. We were barely off the bus when the announcement came. "Everybody please take their seats." Grabbing a coffee, I headed back to the bus, barely managing to comb my hair, brush my teeth and go to the bathroom. It was all there was time for.

We were entering New Mexico. It looked dry, dusty and very flat. Every now and then, a trailer home could be spotted. I wondered how people could survive in the middle of nowhere like that.

I chuckled to myself, as I thought about a television series, I particularly enjoy, called, *"My Name is Earl*. I was sure if I looked carefully I would see his dark-haired figure and trademark moustache, with his large, somewhat dim brother Randy alongside him. I imagined what it must be like for illegal immigrants to try to make their way through that kind of terrain. I shuddered, contemplating the possibility that I too could have been in that situation had I not had the funds to afford the bus ticket.

Night became day and day became night. I had lost track of days, bath times and sleeping hours. My feet were so swollen they could barely fit into my shoes. The opportunity to stretch out on the back seat hadn't presented itself again since we had stopped in New Mexico.

Although I was now penniless, I consoled myself that I'd soon reach my destination. There I'd be fetched, able to finally take a bath and get some sleep.

On the third day, a large family made their way to the back of the bus. The father looked like a Mexican version of Hulk Hogan, and the mother looked like a Mexican version of Hulk Hogan. It goes without saying what their three daughters looked like! All three of them decided to sit with me at the back of the bus. They were friendly, but it was awfully cramped. Thankfully their bus trip lasted only one day. But by the time of their departure, I was sitting with my knees under my chin, and my feet resting on my rucksack.

Stumbling, bleary eyed and stinky, I hobbled off the bus toward the bathroom at the El Paso bus terminal in Texas.

I returned to my seat to see a young man dressed a bit like a rapper sitting in one of the back seats. He flashed a big white toothy grin at me. "Hi, I'm Jarvis." He extended his hand, which I shook while introducing myself.

Somehow he decided that he would be my protector for the rest of the trip. He'd wake me up every time we stopped, always waiting for me and making sure I had my bag when changing buses. In short, he was an angel. When we arrived in Atlanta, Jarvis bid me farewell. It was a sad moment for me. We hugged and he disembarked, on his way to another bus taking him up north.

We finally arrived in Miami, significantly behind schedule, by a day, so George had been expecting me the previous night. I had let him know that I'd only be arriving at 6am the following morning. He said he'd be there at 9am. We actually ended up arriving at 3am.

While setting my bags down, I ran to the bathroom to wash myself. I'd washed as best I could in Dallas the previous night. In fact, I'd washed my hair in the basin and dried it under the hand-drier, as a hair dryer.

With some soapy water, and wet wipes, I'd done the best I could without a shower, yet still felt disgusting. It had been five days since I'd showered or bathed.

After my 'bath' at the Miami bus terminal, I tried to settle into a comfortable position. It was impossible due to the steel chairs that had steel armrests welded between each chair. It was definitely not a place that encouraged loitering of any sort. Disorientated, hungry and incapable of reading anything, I stretched my legs out over my bags in front of me, hoping that they'd be safe if I happened to nod off to sleep.

A young man, apparently of the same mind, opened one eye to look at me, from under his cap. He was slouched in his chair. I was starving, and wondered if my credit card might work at the vending machine. I was desperate for something in my stomach as my supplies had run out. I got up and swiped my card, but it was declined. I sensed the young man watching me. After a few minutes, he got up and approached me. He could barely speak English.

"You watch my stuff?" he asked, removing his bright-green backpack and handing it to me.

"Sure," I answered groggily reaching to take it.

"Is all my stuff – my whole life," he explained.

Taking in his expression and appearance, I asked, "You live here?" gesturing towards the seats in the terminal. He nodded, and then walked off. Placing his bag next to mine, I was starting to fall asleep when he arrived back with two cups – one with steaming coffee, the other with instant noodles. He handed both to me. I was astounded – a homeless person had just bought me breakfast!

"But you have no work? No money?" I asked, tears forming in my eyes. He hauled out a little ID card, and smiled. "I got food card. No job but I got food card for month. So I get you coffee and food," he said, pleased, putting the card back in his wallet.

"Thank you. My name is Ruby and I'm from South Africa," I said, deeply touched. "I'm Ricardo from Puerto Rico." He reached out to shake my hand. "I here for six months. I build, I tile, I make bricks. But no work. Is hard," he shrugged, as he opened his wallet again to produce a photograph of a little girl. "This is my baby. I do everything for her. She back home in Puerto Rico."

In between mouthfuls of noodles, I took the photograph and looked at the little face peering back at me. She had the same green eyes as her father, who was looking at me expectantly. "She's beautiful, Ricardo! I see she has your eyes."

He grinned even more widely, "Yip, I'm her daddy. Would you look my stuff again?" I nodded, wondering where he was off to now.

He wondered off again, and I spotted him talking to a couple outside of the building. Then he walked off, and came back with another two cups of noodles, which he handed over to them, before making his way back to me. "They hungry. From Russia. They not eat in three days. Only water. So I can help them too. Maybe one day I need help and somebody help me," he said with a shy little smile.

"I'm sure you will have all the help you need Ricardo. With your personality, I'm sure God has a lovely job for you," I assured him warmly.

"And you, Ruby. I want you to have my lucky penny. So you never forget me."

"How could anyone forget you, Ricardo?" I chuckled, taking his lucky penny and reaching into my bag, wondering what to give to him. It was obvious that I didn't have cash. I had carried a little harmonica with the name 'Puck' engraved on it. It reminded me of my older brother, Greg, who called himself 'Puck' too from time to time on Facebook. And as you can now see, I enjoy the character of the woodland pixie from *A Midsummer Night's Dream* enormously.

I looked at Ricardo. He looked like just like a woodland pixie as well at that very moment. I handed it to him.

"This reminds me of my brother, whom I love very much. I keep it close to me every time I miss home. Please have it."

He opened the little box and, realising what it was, started blowing on it with delight. It was very noisy – but he didn't seem to care – he was just thrilled with his gift.

"I learn to play! I learn to play on beach!" he said, in between breaths.

It was an extraordinary exchange; one I will treasure for the rest of my life.

George arrived at 10am, huffing, puffing and complaining about the heat, his sinuses, traffic and the poor directions he got from the staff of the company that owned the bus service I'd used.

"Hi, George! I'm so happy to see you! I'm sorry if I smell terrible!" I said, hugging him.

He barely heard me as he continued with his earlier monologue.

"We nearly died on the runway, taking off from Honolulu. Oh my God, I prayed to Jesus, Mary and all the saints. The plane stalled on the runway just before we were about to take off. I keep telling my kids they are lucky to have me alive."

I had no doubt he was doing just that, and suspected his kids had to constantly let him know how lucky they were to have him. He certainly needed a lot of reassurance.

A family in crisis

I took in the sights of Miami and the surrounding suburbs. There was water everywhere. We pulled into the driveway of a townhouse complex, where there was a picturesque lake, with ducks floating around contentedly. From what I could see, there was also a swimming pool, clubhouse and barbeque area. It seemed like a lovely place to live.

"I haven't told the kids about you. I wanted to keep it a surprise. They are to call you 'Miss Ruby' at all times," he said, as we drove in. Goodness! He sounded like a regular 'Captain von Trapp' from The Sound of Music. One thing was for sure – there was no way this 'Maria' was going to fall in love with him.

I was aware of my dishevelled appearance, and doubted I looked like much of a 'Miss' there and then. I squared my shoulders and walked in confidently, in spite of my lack of grooming. George obviously didn't want his children to really see me in that state, and ushered me very quickly into the bathroom, past two very surprised little faces, without any introductions. It seemed rather rude, but I was too tired to argue.

George put my bags in his daughter's room, and brought me towels and some clothes, which surprised me somewhat. Thanking him, I waited for him to close the door behind him. I had never been so grateful to take a shower. It was the best shower I'd ever had. I dried myself with the soft, fluffy towel and plugged the hairdryer in the wall. With my hair done and fresh make-up applied, I put on the golf shirt and Bermuda shorts George had given me. They weren't quite my style, but I graciously wore them anyway.

I headed back to the sitting room and met the children properly. They seemed quite shy. "This is George Jnr, and this is my beautiful daughter, Isabella," he said.

In a split second, he seemed to have a severe mood swing. He was suddenly furious at his daughter's appearance.

"Isabella, get into that room and fix yourself! You look disgusting! You know you're not to walk around *my* house looking like that!"

I watched the tall, dark-haired teenager quickly run to her room to change from the tracksuit she was wearing. It was all quite alarming. Minutes later, Isabella emerged from her room looking glamorous in her jeans and a tank top. She was wearing lip gloss, and very fashionable earrings. I thought she looked lovely.

George snapped again, this time with even more alarming words. "Take that tank top off! You look like a slut!" he yelled. I was shocked. It was harsh to witness, and what was more, I mostly wore tank tops! What had I let myself in for?

I followed Isabella to her room, and smiled at her, closing the door behind me.

"Want me to help you choose something to wear?" I offered gently. "Yes please, I'd like that," she answered. I could see she was angry with her father, and embarrassed in front of me. Walking over to her cupboard, we went through the clothing she had, and we both chose a pretty little pink gypsy top, which she looked beautiful in. I started unpacking my clothes, and saw George had left me some more Bermuda shorts and golf shirts. Bizarrely, there was also one pair of what I would call 'granny knickers' left out for me.

"Hey, I got shorts and a shirt just like the ones you're wearing. But I got too fat for them," Isabella commented.

I realised that George had given me his daughter's clothes, which she had outgrown. I didn't believe it to be a good idea to wear the clothes that a young girl with a severe eating disorder had outgrown. Gaining that extra weight, must have been very alarming.

George obviously didn't want me running around in tank tops in front of his daughter, but putting me in her clothes could easily send her straight into her purging patterns.

"Miss Ruby, do you think I'm fat?" Isabella asked, looking at her reflection in the mirror. Sitting on her bed admiring her, I responded, "I think you've got a beautiful body, Isabella. And your face is gorgeous, too. Your dad told me you've been taking good care of your body. That's great, and I think you're awesome!" Adjusting her hair, she answered "Yeah ... I don't wanna end up in hospital again."

"Well, if it's any consolation, Isabella, I know what it feels like to go through what you did. That is why I respect and understand you."

She looked surprised. "You had bulimia?"

"I did and I still need to watch myself from time to time. So how about this I'll watch out for you and you can watch out for me?" She smiled back, "Okay."

Little did I know how powerful this agreement would be. I had run out of anti-depressants, which I believed successfully controlled my bulimia. I had also run out of my thyroid medication, which meant I was likely to gain weight. There was no choice but to eat what I was given, so there was a good chance I wouldn't be fitting into Isabella's clothes for long anyway. I felt a sense of panic.

As I mentioned, my bulimia had made a little unwelcome appearance before I left, but it had been under control on my trip. I was anxious as to how I was going to cope under these new circumstances. I had decided to pray and trust. And that included visualising myself standing on a bathroom scale every morning and night, imagining my perfect weight.

I even went as far as mentally putting a Post-It note with the amount of kilograms I wanted to be over the actual dial, as my ego often visualised the scale dial on some nasty unwanted amount. It was a clever trick and I've used it successfully ever since!

Isabella seemed pleased. She lay on her bed with crayons and paper. Handing over a page and a few crayons, she asked "I'm gonna make you a card. Will you make me one, please?" Taking the crayons, I said "Sure", as I began to draw a little cupid-type of angel for her. Ten minutes later, we swapped cards.

I was stunned by her card, which was really beautiful, but extremely juvenile. I realised what I was dealing with, and felt very touched. The writing itself could have been that of a seven-year-old child's. There were no full stops or commas. The letters were all in different sizing, some in random capital letters, with a few repetitive words, straight consecutively after each other. It was incomprehensible, but the message was clear ... she was grateful to have a friend.

Finishing off with her, I made my way to the kitchen for a bite to eat. George sat me down, with a sandwich. He described the children's routines, which included meetings with psychologists, social workers and even a parole officer. Apparently Isabella had assaulted one of her previous care-givers. It did make me a bit nervous.

"These pills in the blue box are for George Jnr, and are to be taken morning and night," He instructed. Isabella's were stored in the white box.

According to George Snr, George Jnr would sometimes to try to spit his pills out, or hide them under his tongue. "But open his mouth and make sure he swallows them," I was told.

George continued, "When you give George Jnr his pills, only give him a little water, as he urinates in his bed."

George Jnr was 13! I was shocked that he wet the bed still, although I had been exposed to bed wetting with Ashley when John and I were still together. I had researched it, and from what I could gather it often correlated with paternal fear. I realised that I had my hands full, but I wasn't afraid – just respectful of the responsibility I'd been given.

Suddenly, George had another outburst.

"Why aren't you kids in bed yet? I am the father in this house! I am the man and I ... will ... be ... res-pec-ted!" he boomed, enunciating the last words and syllables, with his eyes half-closed, bangled hand on hip. He tossed his curly, dark locks with his other hand and flicked the hair out of his eye as he stalked off down the passage. This was incredible. He needed to be on stage! I was to hear those very words, in that dramatic fashion, often.

George Jnr seemed shy initially. He soon overcame that, when it came to having to take his medication. Looking me squarely in the eye, he said "Why ... do ... I ... have ... to ... be out of it all the ... time? I hate it! When ... people ... come ... here ... we always have to be..."

He searched for the right word, but eventually gave up, with a helpless little smile.

He didn't quite stutter, but spoke like a robot – very slowly and precisely, with a pause after most of his words. It was difficult not to finish his sentences for him and allow him to speak.

I smiled at him, "I think I understand what you mean, George Jnr. But I don't make the rules here – they are your father's rules. So please take your medication?"

I pleaded with him. He reached for the glass and the handful of pills and swallowed, then opened his mouth to show me that he had indeed swallowed everything. It was understandable that he didn't want to be drugged. There was nothing I could do except try to make the process as easy as possible.

In spite of George Jnr's slow speech, I realised he was actually quite 'switched on'. He was obsessed with *Star Wars*, and I wondered if the 'robot speak' was actually more inspired by the movies than an actual real impediment. Possibly bit of both.

It appeared George Snr enjoyed playing power games with his children. For example, he would promise George Jnr an ice cream for good behaviour, but then 'forget' all about buying the ice cream, in spite of George Jnr's nagging about it. George Jnr would rebel and then of course the ice cream was definitely out of the question.

Whenever the children or I needed or asked George Snr for anything, he would always answer 'later', knowing we would have to come back and ask again. It was as if he needed to extend this authority and power over us for as long a time as possible.

It felt a bit like being around Barbara, with her bottomless pit of need for any kind of attention. Both were energy thieves and had no qualms taking their energy or power from their children if necessary.

The longer I stayed, the more out of control George Snr seemed to become. Maybe it wasn't so much a case of that, as of showing his true colours. I liked his children immensely, and I hoped it gave them some comfort that I had witnessed their lives. Granted there wasn't much I could do about them, but sometimes one just needs to know that what happened to you as a child was noted by somebody and that it did matter.

It was clear the 'absence' of George's wife and the children's mother was a permanent situation, which I didn't ask much about. The children spoke about visiting her and her boyfriend every second month. I could understand a woman running away from George Snr. He was impossible. If he hadn't have been then, he certainly was now.

George Snr and Isabella had a strange almost nightly ritual. Isabella was supposedly allergic to cats. She had allegedly once been hospitalised, unable to breathe due to the asthma caused by her allergy to a big grey fluffy cat the family owned. In spite of the severity of her reaction – which I'd only heard about – Isabella insisted on the cat sleeping with her in her bed. In the middle of the night, George Snr would storm into the bedroom, which I shared with Isabella. He would throw the covers off her, remove the cat and slap her hard!

The first night it happened had come as an absolute shock to me. We were asleep, and not only were we rudely awakened by the light being suddenly turned on, but then there was harsh smacking and swearing. I wished I could smack him and treat him exactly as he did his daughter, but I daren't interfere.

Then something really strange happened. After all the fights over Isabella's allergy and the cat, George went out and bought yet another cat! One would think with the 'life-threatening' allergy Isabella was supposed to have (which warranted her being smacked almost nightly), the last thing a loving parent would do would be to bring home yet another animal their child was allergic to. It was bizarre.

I expressed my sentiment and George explained that the new kitten was for him, and that he had warned Isabella that she should stay away from it. In my opinion, George was a lot more 'sick' than his daughter. His disturbing behaviour was further evidenced by an even more bizarre conversation he had with me one day.

He took me aside, to speak confidentially.

"Just to let you know that we don't dispose of toilet paper in the toilets in this house. You need to wipe yourself and then throw the toilet paper in the bin beside the toilet. I'm not paying for toilets to be unblocked, and the water pressure is weak anyway. So everyone here in Florida rather throws their toilet paper away."

I was astounded. This was the first time I'd seen or heard of such a practice. I believe in water conservation, and understand one may want to conserve water when it comes to urination. But leaving soiled toilet paper in a bin, especially after a bowel movement, was just too disgusting to contemplate.

I was firm. "George, there's no way I'm doing that. Not after a bowel movement. Understand?"

He tried to argue, but I glared at him. Stalking away from him, I announced over my shoulder, "I'm not discussing this further. I'm going to the swimming pool. Can I please take the kids?"

Of course, he wasn't going to let me take his kids when he was in a lovely, strong position of authority.

"Only after they have cleaned their rooms and done their chores," he said.

"Fine," I responded. "Just to let you know I'm going with or without them."

I ignored him further, and got the kids and their rooms ready for his inspection. I barely acknowledged him while he endeavoured to appear as important and difficult as possible. The children and I hadn't been out of the house in three days, due to George Snr's having endless chores for us to always have to do first.

The children were ecstatic at the prospect of getting out of the house and going to the pool. Isabella asked if she could borrow one of my two-piece swimsuits, which her father overheard, and of course he shrieked that under no circumstances could she do so.

We were finally ready for the pool, and George emerged with a towel for himself in his hand. He explained, "You can't get into the clubhouse area without my identification card."

He walked alongside me and chatted closely with me when we got to the pool area. I could barely stomach him in my space, but he truly wanted everyone to see and believe that we were an item. A happy family with kids. It was nauseating.

After a few minutes of my ignoring George and the children playing in the swimming pool, he got restless. He wanted to go back inside his house.

"Sure, but I'm staying and I'm sure the kids will want to stay with me, George. They worked hard to get here, and it wouldn't be right for them to have to go back indoors after five minutes."

He didn't argue, and thankfully left the clubhouse area. The children played together and didn't interact with the hordes of other children around them. It was apparent Isabella was extremely self-conscious about her body.

My heart ached for the children and I swore to do my best to help them both grow in confidence for as long as I could handle to be around their father and his home. While the children were drying themselves, I organised a visitor's security tag for the pool from the security officer. It was valid for the duration of my stay. George Snr looked crestfallen when I showed him my tag triumphantly. The children looked thrilled, too!

That night, George Jnr approached me. "I've ... asked ... my dad to look in his ... closet ... he has some ... Lego ... they're from my mom for me ... he said ... he'd find them ... could you ... ask him too ... please?"

When we arrived home, I knocked on George's bedroom door, which he always kept locked. At times, he'd lock himself in his room for hours on end, and would later emerge either in exceptionally good spirits or in a foul temper. One never quite knew what to expect. He hardly ever answered his door after the first knock. There would be a five- or 10-minute wait. Then one would have to knock again.

Eventually George answered the door, and I quickly asked him about George Jnr's Lego. While chewing on some white bread and cold meat, he agreed to look for the Lego. I saw the small refrigerator in his bedroom was open. I could see items such as butter, sugar, white bread and cheese, which could never be kept in the kitchen. This was because the children, especially Isabella, raided the fridge constantly.

I understood bulimia, and therefore knew why it was better that 'trigger' foods that set off bingeing should be locked away. But what was fascinating was how George would buy treats and never share them with either of the children. I also noticed that he himself consumed huge quantities in short spaces of time. Initially, I'd wondered whether he was imbibing recreational drugs alone in his bedroom. However, the evidence the children would constantly find – much to their chagrin – indicated somebody bingeing on vast quantities of junk food.

George never ate meals with us, and lived on cheese, cold meat, crackers, candy and soda, whilst the children and I lived on rice, beans, oats and corn, which were much healthier anyway.

Isabella's eating disorder was indeed quite extreme, and her efforts to control and suppress it broke my heart, but made me proud at the same time. One night was particularly profound, certainly in shedding light on where this godforsaken disease may come from. Whenever I dished up a plate of food and set it before Isabella, I would see a reflection of my own emotions all over her face. It was the first time I'd truly witnessed it openly in somebody else, as I'd kept my condition hidden all my life and had no 'throw-up buddies'.

I've heard of bulimic girls sharing their bulimic behaviour, much the way drug addicts associate with each other, and make each other feel better about their behaviour. There's nothing wrong with girls with eating disorders 'hanging out', but it becomes very dangerous when the addiction starts governing the friendship.

Isabella's first facial expression would convey excitement and relief that meal time had finally arrived. Most of her day would be spent obsessing over the next mealtime, anyway, and this was to be expected given that her living 'space' had been so confined by her father's rules.

Some of the rules were undoubtedly necessary, but they were compounding her obsession. Her expression would then turn to concern. And I understood that, too. It was fear of weight gain, fear of having to get rid of the food and – worst of all – fear of getting caught heaving over the toilet, with your finger stuck down your throat.

That particular night, though, Isabella had quickly taken one large mouthful from a decent-sized plate of food. I looked into her eyes and saw a haunting fear. She needed to say something, she chewed and swallowed fast. I waited for her to speak.

"Ruby, is there more?" It was an alarming question. She barely had her first mouthful and still had a whole plate of food before her to enjoy. But suddenly everything fell into place for me. I had never acknowledged the fear of there not being enough!

Perhaps it was never about being overweight, but more about being a 'starving child', so to speak! Oh I knew that haunted look all right – it was all about emptiness and there being not enough of anything. It was the same look a child gets when they're being dropped off at a party and they have one of those parents who 'warns' them that they'll be back to fetch them in an hour, but sometimes it's more like 40 minutes. That 'hour' actually becomes a crippling fear, as the child is too afraid to actually have a good time, because for them, it will be over before it even began.

Pleasure and enjoyment become too much of a delicious risk to even have a little nibble, and once tasted could possibly guarantee dissatisfaction with the rest of your life.

Alternatively, the child goes wild and tries to get as much out of the party as they can. And generally they're not invited back again anyway!

My behaviour was mostly of the former group, but I had a tendency to fall within the latter category, too. On close inspection of my life, I realised it was never about food. It was actually about time.

The reason it had manifested as food was because, as a baby, I had been complimented extensively on my good appetite and ready smile. It's only natural for a parent to express joy when their child eats, but I had obviously cottoned onto this, and interpreted it as behaviour that what would make me good and acceptable. The 'time enemy' had snuck in, with me being the eldest daughter born to a large and very actively religious family. There were plenty of chores, homework and religious meetings, and not nearly enough opportunities for creativity and silliness for my liking.

Perhaps Isabella's eating disorder hadn't been born out of the exact same circumstances as mine, but I would put money on the fact that it was also as a consequence of having to give up the nice fun stuff too soon compounded with making some hard-working, insecure parent (who doesn't have time for their own silliness, let alone yours) happy by putting a spoonful of food or a pacifier in your mouth.

I had lost weight living on carbohydrates and eating without thinking of consequences. As difficult as the living circumstances were, being truly set free from an eating disorder without the usual anti-depressants I believed I needed was incredibly liberating, and worth every moment.

Two days later, George Jnr approached me again. His father had still not bothered to look for his Lego. It took yet another two days of nagging, including George Jnr's constantly pleading with me to intervene on his behalf. "Ruby ... I ... keep ... being ... good ... but ... doesn't he know ... he's messing ... with my feelings?"

I'd had enough! Barging into George Snr's room, I demanded "George Senior! You are messing with your son's head! You find his Lego now!"

He was reclining on his bed, downloading emails. He looked quite shocked, then smiled. He honestly seemed to respect and almost enjoy my tantrum! He rolled his eyes and got all playful with me. "Oh, get off your horse, Cleopatra!" he said, head thrown back, hands on his hips.

I wasn't about to play some sort of 'diva' game with him. I ignored him, calling George Jnr to tell him he'd have his Lego shortly, which surprisingly did happen within the next 45 minutes. It was exhausting.

I had to be careful as a guest in an environment like that. One can end up walking a fine line between building up an insecure child's confidence due to an abusive parent, and causing a revolution in a household. I was becoming increasingly intolerant of George's parenting skills and it was concerning that if I showed my disgust too openly the kids would see me as sympathetic to their cause.

Up until now, their situation was abusive, but predictable, which is a weird form of stability in itself, if one could call it that.

Despite my misgivings about George Snr's behaviour, I could tell he and the kids loved each other endlessly. One could see it in their eyes when they weren't fighting. Beneath all the anger, all three souls had a deep love for one another and it was their journey together that others would bear testimony to.

It had been almost four weeks, and I suspected that George Snr wasn't going to be able to afford to pay me. Things had started looking a little suspicious when there wasn't enough money to fix the car to get George to New York – the whole reason I was actually there, from his point of view. The car was in desperate need of a service and would not have made it to the next state. I noticed basics such as bread and milk weren't being replenished. It was clear something had gone wrong financially, and George wasn't telling me.

I approached him. "George, something is not right here. You and I both know it. Are you really going to be able to afford to pay me what you promised?"

He looked embarrassed. "There was a deal I had expected to come through that hasn't," he admitted.

It was just as I thought. It was deeply annoying that he had treated me like a servant, expecting me to be on call constantly, never wanting to allow me time off to go to the pool.

"George, I've seen you literally don't have two cents to rub together. So please know that I will start making other arrangements. I love your children, but while I'm making alternative plans, you will refrain from introducing me to people as one of your staff members (something he loved doing!) And my time will be my own. Looking after Isabella and George Jnr will be a favour to them, when it suits me."

George didn't argue.

The money from Liesel's brother had been paid into my credit card that day. I had just enough money for a small second-hand laptop, a plane ticket back to Honolulu, as well as the contract to self-publish my book. It was exciting to be able to pay a sizeable deposit on my publishing contract and buy a laptop.

Writing my story would keep me sane, and having a computer would certainly assist in my keeping touch with the world, as George Snr hadn't wanted me near his laptop too often.

At times, I'd been desperate to find out what was happening with Phil, but whenever I managed to check my emails there would be no response from the lawyers. It was disappointing to say the least.

One night, George exploded at his children. It was a weekend night, during school vacation. I'd warned them that their dad would probably want them in bed by 9pm. They had ignored me saying that it was the weekend, and it would be okay for them to stay up later. I was doubtful. "You guys sure about this? I really don't want a scene."

They shrugged, continuing to watch TV. A few minutes later, as predicted, George Snr came blasting down the passage from his room. His language was appalling, "Get the fuck to bed! You bastards!" he screamed hysterically.

It was the worst tantrum I'd ever seen from him. The children jumped up and rushed off to bed. I got up and went to bed too without as much as a backward glance at him.

The next morning, I gave him a piece of my mind.

"I am disgusted by your language and the way you speak to your kids. I hope you apologise to them!" I could see by his face that an apology would somehow be an admission of defeat from him. It wasn't really an option in his opinion. But he did apologise to me.

"I'm sorry you had to hear that, but I really take strain with these kids," he said, suddenly becoming the victim, looking for my sympathy. I wasn't about to give it to him.

"George, you need to set some rules for your kids, and then stick with them. And if the rules are going to change if and when you please, respect your kids enough to tell them in a civilised manner that you've changed the rules! You were in the wrong last night. And if you don't apologise to your kids, they're going to start doubting their own self-worth and sense of right and wrong."

He didn't look like he got what I was saying. His ego was way too fragile to get it. In that moment, I realised I couldn't stay any longer. I couldn't stand around watching children's instincts of right and wrong being eroded. They instinctively know right and wrong, and when you force them to accept 'discipline' or your own lies for the sake of your own need for respect and control they begin to doubt their own integrity, or inner voice, and lose themselves.

I made a mental note to myself that I'd never do that to Phil. It happens so easily, and one has to be totally confident within oneself, as an adult and a parent, to allow one's children the freedom to trust their own instincts.

I went online on my new computer to book my flight back to Honolulu, to finalise my flight back home to South Africa. I opened up my bank account and got a nasty shock! There was an annual debit order for an automobile insurance membership I'd forgotten about. The exact amount that would have sufficed for a ticket back to Honolulu had been deducted from my account!

It was ironic that insurance for potential transportation issues back home had actually prevented me from going home!

Once again, I avoided the panic and onset of bile that arose in my throat from fear. There was an option. I could ask Alan for help. During my travels, I hadn't really kept close contact with anybody, but I had texted him from time to time to let him know where I was. I had stayed 'faithful', but had needed this time for self-exploration.

Asking Alan for help was the last thing I felt like doing as I wanted to get home and have a new start with him, on an equal footing – not from a place of indebtedness.

However, at this stage there wasn't much choice, and my pride certainly wasn't going to get me home. I called Alan and explained the situation and that I needed a flight back to Honolulu. He sounded busy but concerned. "When do you want to come home?" he asked. "Tomorrow!" I almost yelled.

"Cool, I'll get onto it. Just send me your ticket and passport details."

Tears of relief gathered in my eyes. It had been a difficult month with George and the children.

Two days later, I still hadn't heard from Alan. It was disconcerting. I texted him, only to find he was battling with the arrangements. I don't think he had listened properly. All that was necessary was a flight back to Honolulu from Miami, not all the way back to Johannesburg. He was talking about getting me a ticket straight back to Johannesburg. I didn't want him buying a whole new ticket home for me, when I already had an open ticket back home from Honolulu. It seemed like such a waste of money, which I expressed. He promised to get back to me with details soon.

That night, George screamed at his kids again, this time in Spanish. When the children were settled and in bed, George walked into the kitchen where I was making coffee.

"Good night, George. Incidentally, you do know that 'fuck' sounds the same in Spanish as it does in English?"

I didn't wait for an answer and went straight to bed. The next day, I walked to a coffee shop with free internet usage, and opened my Facebook page. One of my childhood friends, with whom I'd lost contact, was in Miami and wanted to meet up with me. She suggested I share her place for a few days, which was a Godsend. It was an answer to a prayer!

I was excited to pack my bags that night, but very sad to say goodbye to the children. I was to leave early in the morning, before they awoke. We said our emotional goodbyes that night. As disappointed as they were that I was leaving, they understood that I needed to get back to Phil.

George Jnr came to me with a boy's shirt and little orange teddy bear for Phil. Isabella handed over a Bratz doll, saying "These are for Phil. He shared you with us, and we want you to give these to him."

I hugged them both, tears filling my eyes. The big fish of guilt that had swallowed me was finally ready to spit me back onto the shores of South Africa.

"Are ... you ... leaving coz ... of ... us?" George Jnr whispered as I hugged him.

"Definitely not, George Jnr," I reassured him. "I really do need to get back to Phil."

He was still concerned.

"All ... our sitters leave ... coz they say ... he's too strict. But ... I know ... you must go ... to Phil ... I just wish ... you could stay."

I held them both tight and responded, "Yeah, your dad's tough. But he loves you so much. He does make mistakes, but there are other dads out there who make even bigger mistakes. Try and think only of the good times and when he makes you happy."

I believed it was the right thing to say to the kids. I wasn't impressed at all with George Snr, but believed that my explanation then, and writing about them in this book now, was necessary for them to ultimately function and heal. Somebody saw their pain, joy and humiliation ... somebody witnessed their lives. Hopefully, when they're much older, they'll read this book and recognise themselves in it.

I left early the next morning. George Snr let me out quietly. I gave him a brief hug, angry with him but trying to find compassion and love underneath it all. Without a doubt, he was a tortured soul. I had heard him singing and knew that once upon a time he had a promising musical career – in fact he had all the makings of a real 'diva'! I suspected he had known lots of frustration in his life. That didn't make abusing his children right, but it was obviously coming from his own very abused inner child.

I arrived in a very festive Miami. Soccer world cup fever was in the air, and the Spanish sector of Miami was alive with colours, flags and a few vuvuzelas – which was very interesting to hear, so far away from home. My friend Tamara, who met me at the station, was quite homesick. I was a little sad to be away, especially on the day of the finals, but I'd learnt so much about myself and life that it didn't matter where I was in the world. Each day was a gift and I'd always be fine.

The previous few weeks had been intense, and I welcomed the light-hearted festivities. This including eating a marijuana-laced brownie given to me by somebody I'd met on the beach, called Doctor Therapy. He was a hypnotist. I had never eaten such a thing in my life! I got the giggles instantly.

Tamara was shocked when I arrived home, sunburnt and a little high from my brownie. I relayed the hypnotist story to her, thinking it was very funny. She was alarmed. Maybe it was time to come home. Thankfully, the next day Alan got back to me with flight details. It was just as well, as I'd been contemplating going back to the beach to look for the good doctor and his brownies. I had to remind myself that I'm against drug abuse, and that eating delicious, moist chocolate brownies laced with marijuana definitely constitutes that!

My inner dialogue argued it was a natural plant, like rosemary or lavender, but on the other hand it killed off brain cells, unlike herbs you normally add to your food.

The phone rang. It was Alan, and it was a relief to hear his voice.

"I'm having fun here in Miami, babe. But I still want to come home," I said, "and if you don't get me out of here soon, I'm going to end up fat and in drug rehab!"

Maybe, it wasn't the best thing to say, but it was certainly my truth at that moment. Alan had a slight chuckle in his voice, but I could tell it was nervous chuckle.

"Things happen on holiday ... relax and tell me all about it when you get home. I'm buying you a whole new ticket straight home. My secretary will send you confirmation."

I thanked him from the depths of my soul. "One more thing," I quickly added, "thanks for being so patient with me."

He responded a little wearily. "It's okay. Just come home now. No stopping in Hawaii, no partying in Sydney. Just straight home."

Twenty minutes later, the email confirming details of my ticket arrived. The ticket was not for Honolulu, but straight back to Johannesburg. Although I still wanted to see Sydney properly and would have fancied an extra day or two back in Honolulu, I knew I'd had enough. It was quite impressive the way Alan had taken control like that.

My story often reminds me of the folk tale about the little girl with the red dancing shoes that never stopped dancing. At first, after putting them on, the dancing was fun. But being unable to get them off meant she would never stop dancing.

In the story, about to die from exhaustion, she dances, wild and ragged, to the woodcutter's door and begs him to chop off her feet. He takes pity on her and gives her back her life by taking her feet.

As grim and sad as the story is, I felt that Alan was ridding me of those crazy red dancing shoes – and his no-nonsense approach was sexy! I was looking forward to going home.

Back to life, back to reality

Desiree and Jody were waiting for me as I walked through the doors at international arrivals. We rushed into one another's arms.

"Alan and my dad are also here to greet you – they're at the pub," Desiree said, reaching into her bag, hauling out a hairbrush. "Come here, let me fix your hair!" she said while Jody laughingly screeched and squirmed in my arms.

"Don't worry about my hair, Des – this is how he knows me," I protested, having too much fun with Jody to worry about my hair. Desire still managed to get a few brush strokes in, though.

Walking towards the pub, I was anxious and excited to see Alan. He stood up, with a warm smile and twinkle in his eye. Putting Jody down, I ran towards him and flung my arms around his waist. "Oh Alan, I am so happy to see you!" It was the truth. "Same here!" he responded, holding me close.

I felt something needed to be said about my little sojourn in America. I knew he doubted whether I'd be back for good, or whether I was serious this time. I couldn't say I blamed him. I'd heard later that when Desiree walked back into the restaurant ahead of me (I had quickly popped into the bathroom with Jody) he had said, "She didn't get on the plane, did she?"

I wondered how one could ever make up for the continual disappointments I had caused this man. Then again, he was somebody who could have any woman he wanted, but for some reason he had picked me. It was concerning that he had put up with so much rubbish from me. I'd never put a man through anything remotely close to what I'd just put Alan through.

"Alan, this is the way I am – a free spirit. I want to be with you. I just needed to get this out of my system. The thing is sometimes I have this desire to explore. I get inspired to write and create. One day I may even want to write bodice-ripping romance novels. I see myself renting a room in some exotic destination from time to time to go and write, even if my work doesn't get published. I love stories, I love adventure!" I said passionately.

"I want to share your journey with you, but I have a journey, too. I want to share most of it with you, but there are times when I need to do what I've just done now. Maybe not for six weeks, though, as I can't see that being viable with children. And I do want children. I want you, a baby and Phil in my life."

I took a deep breath. It may have sounded like a contradiction, my wanting freedom to create and explore and be a mother and wife at the same time. But in my heart I believed it was more than possible – even inevitable.

"I get it," was all Alan said. He didn't say much more and I could only hope he did 'get it', as I didn't want to lose him. Obviously, it would take a special man to understand me, and I had hoped it would be him – it certainly seemed to be. Part of being understood by somebody else also meant I had to take responsibility for understanding myself.

My time alone had always been a great teacher to me. Alone, I truly got to acknowledge my loves and fears. Most of my life had been consumed with pleasing others and often playing some role to make others happy.

I trusted I could finally relax and share the real me with Alan.

Having settled this in my heart, I focused on Phil. I'd had no feedback while I was overseas, so it was obvious it was going to take a good deal of pushing and nagging if anything were to get done.

A little voice inside of me nagged, "When you have to struggle so much for something, sometimes it is also a sign in its own right. That it's just not meant to be."

That little voice was supposedly my voice of reason, and perhaps wanted to protect me from getting my heart broken any further. A stubborn, determined voice rose up, though.

"Of course it's tough!" the voice protested. "This is a child's life you're dealing with!"

These opposing thoughts fought a royal battle in my head. The only way to attain any peace of mind was to get Phil heard, no matter what it took. But what it took had become intimidating.

Would I ever find peace in my soul if I just walked away? I doubted it. That beautiful little face, belonging to the most beautiful child I'd ever seen, would haunt me for the rest of my life. We both deserved a happy ending. I believed mine to be in sight, certainly with Alan, and I couldn't continue my life happily without ensuring Phil had his happy ending, too.

My phone rang for the first time in months. It was Tracy.

"Welcome back, my friend. I'm so glad you're home, because you need to help me at the school tomorrow. I can't make it." She quickly added assertively, "I think it's time you did this."

I knew I would possibly get into some serious trouble for trespassing, after the last correspondence from Barbara, but the prospect of seeing Phil was enticing. I responded, "Trace,

I can't tell you how much I'd love to do that. But I'm worried Barbara will have me arrested."

Tracy became even more assertive. "Phil needs to see you. Enough of all this. Just go and see your boy. Deal with the consequences later. Besides, I have a date."

She was right, and I gave in easily. I couldn't resist asking, "By the way, who's the guy?"

"You haven't met him yet. But I'll fill you in on all the news when I see you," Tracy responded. "We'll hook up tomorrow and I'll get the groceries for the meal in the meantime."

"Trace, thanks for this opportunity. You're one in a million," I whispered, with a lump in my throat.

"See you tomorrow, my friend." I heard the smile in her voice.

That night I could barely sleep from the excitement of seeing Phil again. I had envisioned our reunion so many times. In some fantasies, I fetched him in a borrowed Ferrari. In others, I spoke to him through the fence. In most of them I got tearful, and he would look at me in his usual way – rolling his eyes, and sighing his "Oh, she's just being a silly girl, crying again," sigh.

Tracy and I met up later the next day to do our grocery shopping. She was becoming increasingly excited about Phil's and my reunion. In fact she then decided it would be way more fun watching Phil's and my reunion later than going on her date with her 'mystery man', so she arranged to meet up with him much later.

I was grateful for this, because if Barbara got word that I was there she would most likely come swooping in like some nightmarish creature of darkness, from a Harry Potter movie, eager to make a scene in front of the children.

A confrontation with her terrified me. I wasn't sure if there had been any correspondence between her and my lawyers yet, which made it even more terrifying and unpredictable. All my contact details had changed, so she wouldn't have been able to send any correspondence or venomous emails, which I had no doubt would be a source of huge frustration for her.

Tracy and I threw supplies into the shopping cart and headed to the school in my Jeep, which had remained unsold.

I parked some distance from the school. Although seeing the Jeep would have been wonderful and comforting for Phil, it would also have reminded him of a time when things were secure and predictable.

Tracy was as excited as me. Phil wasn't around but the rest of the children, who hadn't seen me in months, started squealing. She gestured to them to keep quiet, and told them to tell Phil she had a surprise for him.

"Phil!" she called, while I hid away behind a bush. He was inside the classroom still, watching television. He came out, and I jumped out from behind a bush.

"Ruby! Ruby!" he screamed. I ran towards him, and grabbed him without a word. I picked him up and held him tight, finally letting out my own screech of glee. Once I started squealing with excitement, I thought I'd never stop. His arms were tight around my neck, and I thought he'd throttle me. It would have been a wonderful way to go!

"What's the Jeep doing here? I thought you sold it? When did you get back? Are you coming for me on Friday?"

So many questions.

"Nobody wanted our Jeep, babes," I laughed, "so I had to fetch it. And I won't be able to fetch you this Friday and I still need to do some lessons for Barbara to let me fetch you. But I'm back from overseas and I've missed you so much."

I stepped back from him. "Goodness, you've gotten tall! I'm going to have to get you some new clothes, sunshine!"

He wriggled from my grasp, running towards the Jeep, yelling over his shoulder "I can't believe nobody wanted the Jeep!"

He got to the car and opened it, blowing the horn and putting on the indicators and wipers in less than a few seconds. "Come Phil! We've got to go inside and cook. We can talk about the Jeep and when you can come back to me another time. Please help me carry this? Everyone's hungry!"

He came skipping back, clearly excited to have me home. He took one of the shopping bags from me, whistling. It was such a privilege to have his love.

Together, we walked inside with our groceries and started preparing the food, as we'd done together for so long, many months ago. I kept having to remind myself that I hadn't seen him in almost four months. It was as though no time had passed at all.

Moses was delighted to see me, although he did look concerned. I took him aside, after the exuberance had died down somewhat.

"Please, Moses, don't say anything, but we are going to work this out. And it's going to be sorted out properly."

"I won't tell anybody," he assured me. "But we need help here, Ruby. I can read between the lines. I know what's going on. We can't keep losing help and volunteers. And some kids have been sent home because Barbara is angry their families aren't

273

paying her money. We need volunteers and we need money. Barbara makes it difficult to get both."

I didn't quite understand what he meant about families having to pay the charity to keep their family members at the school. From what I could understand, the school ran on a charitable/voluntary basis and was merely an informal arrangement for in-between official 'schooling' while the children were recovering from surgery. The children were generally from impoverished backgrounds, needing assistance, but they weren't necessarily from families who didn't want them.

Only Daisy, Temba and Phil were orphaned and abandoned. The rest had families – possibly poor, but still families nonetheless.

Obviously these families had to pay the charity to educate their children. Barbara was constantly looking for donations and pleading poverty. Now there seemed to be some kind of school fee system in place!

I recalled Barbara's once mentioning something about certain families sending welfare grants when they couldn't take care of their children. Maybe it had something to do with that. Even then, I wanted to give Barbara the benefit of the doubt, as it was easier than facing what the alternative was. She couldn't possibly pose as a charity-only organisation while threatening families for lack of payment. Somehow that didn't make sense.

"I'm busy getting help, Moses; I haven't left this thing alone. I have been working on something and I'm sure we'll have a good outcome soon," I reassured him.

I couldn't explain too much more. It was time to get the food ready and get going.

"Moses, I think we should get this food cooked and leave it for you to feed the kids."

Tracy agreed. She truly didn't want to be caught with me by Barbara!

"Yes, Moses, we really don't want her to come here and fight in front of all the children," Tracy said, as one of the toddlers clung on to her neck, kissing her cheek. Moses was in agreement and seemed as anxious as we were to feed the kids and get us off the property quickly.

After we'd set the plates and rang the bell for the children to come and eat, we prepared to leave. Phil walked out with me. "I'm coming back, Phil. I'm sorting this out," I promised.

"Okay, Rubes, I'll see you soon." I could see he believed me and was content that I'd be true to my word. His resilience was incredible. I would do everything possible to ensure he wasn't disappointed.

The next day, I called the lawyers. We set up a meeting immediately and agreed to meet at the Johannesburg offices the following day. I was to meet David, the Canadian man again, who had subsequently taken over the case.

Arriving in downtown Johannesburg, I was excited to see what had developed since our last meeting. Did Phil perhaps have a social worker? Maybe I would even be able to take Phil the following weekend.

Sadly, very little had been done. In fact nothing had been done except the drafting of a very short letter, which had never been sent and made no sense at all whatsoever to me. Staring at David in disbelief, I put the letter down. David was apologetic and explained that he'd been away from a month. Also, the Department of Social Services had apparently also not gotten back to him regarding a social worker for Phil. I read through the letter slowly again, and spoke through clenched teeth.

"David, why didn't you use the details from the email I sent? All the details were there. This correspondence looks like it was thrown together five minutes ago, by somebody who actually doesn't know a damn thing about this case."

"I'm sorry. Our system crashed and I didn't have your email. We've been really busy and I understand you're upset, but we're working on so many human rights cases it's staggering," he said helplessly.

I was furious. Once again, the system and the adults had let Phil down. I couldn't stomach it.

"I'm sorry, David, but at our very first meeting I provided all of you with copies of a very comprehensive email reporting exactly what had happened. Firstly, you don't have Barbara's correct details here. You haven't even got her surname right! Secondly, I only agreed to immediate adoption of Phil if there were no other options and the charity was in real financial difficulty, which I don't believe is the case, in spite of what I was led to believe. And I never agreed to go on a parenting course! Pieter, your boss, told me to ignore that! What the hell is going on? According to Pieter, Barbara had no right to put the demands she did in place. Since when did that change?"

My voice had gotten louder. I waited for David's response. He squirmed, "I'm really sorry, but I drafted that from what I could recall from our last meeting. As I said, our system crashed and I had no records from the previous meeting."

It was too much for me. I hauled out my laptop, opened the document and read through the basics all over again for him.

"David, this isn't about my parenting skills and taking a child out of school early to attend a wedding. This is about *money*.

Don't you get it? Since when did it become right to use a child for blackmail and financial gain?"

I was becoming hysterical.

"Maybe four months isn't a long time for you! But for a kid, it's a lifetime! You guys are messing with us! I'm going to fetch him this weekend! I will take him and I don't care what happens, because none of you care either!"

The tears were streaming down my face, and I was yelling. Somebody or something needed to be punched. But all I could do was shout, a bit incoherently. "Do you know what you're doing? You're breaking a child's heart! You who were supposed to help! You're a bunch of liars! Go and sue some corporate for human rights by all means! But why couldn't you just say we weren't big or important enough for you to help! Why lead me along and waste the precious time of a child who needs me?"

David was embarrassed and silent as I attacked him verbally in the open-plan office. He looked like he wanted to run away. Wiping my eyes, I threatened "I'm going to write a book, David. I'm going to write about everything that has happened, including your apathy."

He shrugged and responded "Do what you need to do, but you can't publish anything until this is resolved."

"What are you doing to resolve it?" I shouted.

"Next week Tuesday we'll send a letter to the charity," he promised. "Please could you re-send me your email so I can update the facts?"

I sobered up and readily agreed. I pleaded with David to just get my weekend arrangement with Phil reinstated as soon as possible. I would approach the matter of full-time fostering again in 2011.

I gathered my belongings, and walked out of the grey building towards my trusty old Jeep. My mind was racing. If this was how long they were going to take to draft a simple document, at this rate, I'd probably only see Phil again in his teen years.

I felt like it was time to make a decision. Exposing Barbara and demanding an enquiry or justice was going to take precious time. Getting access to Phil was another matter completely, and of far greater importance to me. Hopefully the two issues could be separated and Barbara would see the wisdom of that.

I was desperate to see Phil, and was almost prepared to make myself vulnerable to Barbara again, if she would allow it. She had been known to 'punish' volunteers in the past by literally banishing them, which was understandable at times. I certainly didn't believe I'd be the exception.

In fact, she most likely would have built up quite a vendetta.

Toying with ideas such as getting the charity more airtime, and putting money into whatever account she demanded was nauseating. But my love for Phil was starting to override logic. Truly, what wouldn't a mother do out of love for her child?

The biblical story of Moses comes to mind – his biological mother agreed to be a slave to the Egyptian princess in order to be near her son, and for him to remain alive. Not that Phil was Moses by any means. But in a sense his mother gave him up for adoption!

I certainly wasn't Phil's biological mother. But something inside me refused to be silenced. It couldn't possibly be motherhood. I didn't know what it was – how could one who has never given birth? I wondered whether it was the "voice" of motherhood or the "voice" of my soul crying out for redemption. My Bible knowledge was confusing me, anyway. There were so many stories I tried to find parallels in, hoping the trusted biblical answer was there. Finding my own original 'story' through God terrified me. I wasn't even sure who He was any more, anyway.

The kind and loving choice to make would be to withdraw the entire case. There was still time, the letter hadn't been sent yet. Perhaps I could negotiate to see Phil, and Barbara would see the logic in it, rather than face a head-on fight which could ultimately lead to some serious allegations being made against her. The justice system certainly wouldn't like the fact that, within a space of a month, I had emails showing that I had to adopt Phil, as the charity was facing bankruptcy and that Barbara was looking for financial assistance that would come to her personally.

The fact that there was no mention of the charity's bank details would definitely not be seen in a favourable light.

Of course, I didn't want to have to use the evidence against Barbara – I would rather just get Phil back on weekends, with a view to fostering or adopting him full time.

As the eternal optimist, I had two hopes. One was that a 'curator' or social worker had been appointed for Phil. The Centre of Children's Law had seemed quite on the ball and actually seemed to care at our meeting. My second hope was that Barbara wasn't all bad and that her behaviour merely revealed a personality flaw.

Alan seemed to be a lifeline in the middle of all this overwhelming madness. He would be able to take care of me – so far, he seemed to understand my 'inner wild woman'. I'd barely gotten back from the States and Alan had taken me away for a weekend to Knysna, a beautiful coastal town in the Eastern Cape.

We weren't alone (which would have been preferable) as he was there to play golf with his friends. However, it did provide a wonderful opportunity for reflection and writing. Alan, Phil and I all deserved happy endings. I deserved to find a way to make a living being creative and making people feel better.

As entertaining as my journey had been, my behaviour hadn't always been rational, in spite of the medication I had been on. This was of grave concern to me, and I feared that something was wrong with me.

I hadn't recognised or fully acknowledged that my crazy behaviour was triggered not so much from being a dysfunctional human being but rather being a frustrated artist with a gentle touch and a passion for people. I had been contemplating going back onto my anti-depressants, even though my bulimia hadn't returned.

Staying off anti-depressants and ultimately adopting a special needs child, when I myself may have been one, seemed irresponsible. But George Jnr's words haunted me. "Why do I always have to be out of it all the time in front of other people?" I didn't want to have to be "out of it"either. I wanted to be fully present for my life.

I was soon to figure out exactly how it all worked in my head!

Having decided that my first priority was to get Phil back on weekends, at the very least, I decided to draft an email to David. The email indicated that I'd drop the enquiry into Barbara's behaviour and rather just focus on Phil. I went as far as saying I'd be prepared to work through Barbara, in the event that a curator wasn't appointed. I resolved to also find a parenting class. As annoying as that seemed, if it would do both Phil and I good, then I would submit to it.

In spite of Barbara's harsh, peculiar handling of the situation, I still felt a deep sense of compassion towards her. I never doubted what she was doing, and ultimately accomplishing. I believed that she needed rescuing from her situation as much as Phil did. She just didn't know to accept help or give up the reins. Maybe her conscience wouldn't allow it, or she was afraid that she wouldn't have a sense of purpose if she let it go.

It also went without saying that I'd have to enter some type of financial rehabilitation programme, as my shopping habits and financial choices had been risky. Selling one's entire household of contents to self-publish a book could possibly have been considered irresponsible behaviour by some.

In my mind, though, there was a method in my madness as the book would leave Phil some sort of legacy. Especially if, for some reason, he didn't re-enter my life.

Sometimes those precious two years together seemed like a fantasy, and I was desperate to record it for both Phil and I. One day, he would be able to read it and recall: "Yes, it did happen like that," and yes, our love mattered. *He* mattered.

I also hoped the book would inspire other women and give comfort to all the women who have doubted their maternal capabilities. This would probably apply to most women. From those who doubt they are good enough mothers to their children to those who doubt they'd be good enough as mothers at all or simply just be themselves.

I hoped my story would also acknowledge and inspire those with eating disorders and other addictive behaviours.

There were so many reasons to publish the book and I wanted it finished. As far as I was concerned, I'd shared what I wanted to share. I had my potential 'happily ever after' relationship with a man and an intention to get Phil back into my life.

My intention was to create a wonderful, exciting story that left readers inspired and happy. I didn't want the story spoilt by what I feared would be coming my way. I was loath to share the pain of more disappointment. So I finished off a different version of this manuscript and sent it off to publishers thinking I'd done my share. The testimony was written.

I didn't write again for a year.

PART THREE –
RETURNING TO TRUTH

A rude awakening

It had been a month since my return from the States. Since dropping the investigation into the charity, I'd heard nothing from the lawyers with regard to Phil's social worker. There had to be some way to trace him. From what I had gathered, there was some sort of 'continuity plan' when a social worker resigned. A new social worker would be allocated all the cases, so it was likely Phil had a new social worker who had lost track of him somehow. Phil's identity number would be needed to trace this person, if he or she did indeed exist.

I called the charity. Moira answered the phone. I was sure she'd be accommodating, especially since she'd witnessed the favourable response from Nox. I was wrong.

"No, Ruby. Barbara's not in. And I will not give you any of Phil's details or ID number. I will do anything to protect him from you."

It was as if I'd been slapped. It was unbelievable. I tried again, "Moira, there must be a social worker. What was the name of the place of safety he was at previously?"

Again, she responded that she had absolutely no desire or wish to assist me in any way. It was most disappointing and annoying. Barbara had done a good job brainwashing Moira. From what I also could gather, they hadn't received the correspondence from my lawyers requesting access to Phil, either.

A few weeks later, the letter obviously did arrive, as Tracy was called by somebody at the charity and told that her cooking services on Wednesdays were no longer required, which was devastating as Phil would now truly have lost all contact with me.

That wasn't the only upsetting thing that had happened in my life lately.

Since arriving back from the States, I discovered many creditors were looking for me. If I didn't find employment, and submit a formal offer of employment, the Jeep was likely to be repossessed. Now that I had the Jeep back, I had to find gainful employment. I couldn't afford to move back into my apartment just yet, so I moved in with Tracy, who very kindly also offered the second guest room to Phil in the event I got access to him somehow.

I fought a rising panic, but calmed myself down and reminded myself of how I had survived up until then. My every need had been provided for, and was still being provided for.

When I hesitated at a pharmacy over a glass nail file I wanted to buy, rejecting it because the R30 was better spent on airtime or petrol to an interview, I had a wonderful experience that reinforced my faith. The following day at an interview I received a complimentary glass nail file, exactly like the one I had picked up the day before!

Alan had very little contact me throughout the week, but I appreciated he was busy and looked forward to weekends. I was certainly on my best behaviour and doing my best to make up for being away. He seemed much caught up in his own life, however. If I didn't make an effort to see him at Desiree's house, I wouldn't get to see him. He was very close to Desiree's father and seemed to prefer spending time at Desiree's house, with her family. Something didn't feel right.

In Knysna, he had spent the entire weekend playing golf with his friends. On the last day of our trip, when I'd asked if we could go to a spa or go on a picnic alone, he had said he felt he needed to get back to work. I couldn't understand, as I was now fully committed to the relationship.

I suspected he had lost some of his ardour when I had kept him waiting. Possibly he was one of those people who enjoyed the hunt, then lose interest when they get the prize. I was worried about having another bad experience, and eventually pressed Alan to talk to me on the phone about what was going on, and why he wasn't making time to see me.

"I really didn't have the easiest upbringing and I battle with the concept of love," he explained on the phone. He didn't say he was breaking up with me or that it was over, but I knew it was fizzling out. Somehow, I was all right with that, as the relationship had never really gotten off the ground. It would hurt for a day or two, but I'd be fine. I just wanted to pay him back for my ticket and get on with rebuilding my life. Sorting out Phil's situation once and for all was most important to me.

Ignoring the familiar little twinges of rejection in my heart, I got on with life. I also suspected that, in my absence, Alan had switched his affection to Desiree – which was not reciprocated by her, however. It didn't bother me in the slightest, and a part of me was relieved as I'd been unsure about committing to Alan from the very beginning. I had tried to force myself into something I wasn't ready for.

What did disturb me was my excitement at seeing Eugene, my actor friend, again. He had reconnected with me since my return. We had the strangest relationship. Without a doubt we had grown to love each, which surprised me. We were incredibly physically attracted to each other, although both of us acknowledged that a physical relationship was dangerous ground. It was difficult to keep the relationship platonic, which was sad in a way, as it meant we couldn't spend as much time together as we normally would have done.

I tried to not to put a name to what we had. However, once again when I'd been rejected, Eugene had been the one to help pick up the pieces. This time with no suave banter, but with a gentle touch and a kind word. He lifted my spirits up and kept encouraging me to continue the fight for Phil.

I realised that I had a developed a hopeless and ridiculous crush on him, which from what he said was unreciprocated. Looking back, it was a good thing. I had a huge task ahead of me, in finding work, sorting out Phil's situation and re-establishing myself. There was no time for the opposite sex. For a time, I desperately fought the crush and dated a few men too quickly to try to get over it. But I realised that was unfair, too. In fact, on reflection, I had been as guilty of using and abusing men as they were of doing the same to me!

After a time, I accepted my feelings and decided to honour them, until they eventually left, which I hoped would be soon. Unrequited love as exhausting as it can be, was a much better alternative for the time, than dealing with the teething problems of a new relationship. I remained faithful to my feelings, which ultimately proved to be a protection and allowed me to focus on more important issues, such as finding meaningful work and getting Phil back.

Finding a job and getting established again

Finding a job was daunting. I had no choice but to find work in the advertising industry again, which felt like an anti-climax. I hadn't completed my kinesiology studies and wasn't quite sure how I would make a living without being in the advertising industry.

If I were to adopt Phil, I had to prove that I was stable. However, one thing was clear to me: whatever medium I was to represent needed to mean something to me, or it would be impossible for me to sell it. I submitted my CV and went for numerous interviews, but couldn't find anything suitable.

Whilst searching for a job, I received an email back from David. He attached correspondence from the charity's lawyers. Apart from implying that I never had a regular arrangement with Phil, and that he was one of many children I took occasionally for weekends from time to time, the letter also stated that a Sotho-speaking family was in the process of fostering Phil. It was a shock to my system. As annoying as the other lies were, the fact remained that I had been too slow and another family was taking Phil into their lives.

I was devastated, but partially relieved. The lawyers had finally done their job and I had no choice but to let go. I had to move forward with my life. The battle was over, and Phil had finally gotten what he deserved. I hoped that once he was settled with his new family, I would get to see him from time to time. It was a selfish desire, but one that I would risk expressing, if and when I could get proper access to his new family and social worker. I finally let go, confused but accepting.

It had been three exceptionally lean months, during which I had even auditioned for a reality TV series. A friend of mine, Toncah, had called me to give her moral support while she auditioned. The reality TV show was set on an island, where people could either turn into savages or turn to God (I could see myself doing both, although not quite sure in which order!) with the winner becoming a millionaire.

It sounded like fun and I decided to give it at a go, too. There were literally thousands of people queuing outside at the audition venue – all hoping for a shot at fame, adventure or whatever it was they hoped to achieve.

After eight gruelling hours in the sweltering heat, it was my turn to be interviewed. When asked why I wanted to be on the show, I simply answered that I had a beautiful story to tell that would inspire others to reach out to children, and that I needed a platform to tell it. When questioned further about how I would cope in extreme conditions, I relayed my travel stories, which seemed to do the trick. I was through to the second round!

Walking back to my car, I was elated and shocked! I hadn't taken the whole experience seriously for a moment. Here, I'd literally gone and signed up for a situation where there would be no food or shelter and I'd have to expose my body and face to the world. My very pale white skin was likely to be burnt to a crisp! I shuddered.

If there was a message to get out there, God had to find another way without frying me!

Funnily enough, that was exactly what happened. I never did get through to the third round, but one of the finalists in the show turned out to be an adoptive mother. She was a well-known actress in a soap opera, and in the aftermath of the show was able to share her happy adoption story and what it felt like leaving her children behind for a month.

Overall, I found the results of that particular show to be immensely satisfying, spiritually. God certainly hadn't needed my 'lily whites' there on that island!

However, my sojourn into reality TV was far from over. I met up with Tessa, my old boss from the SABC, and she informed me of another opportunity to audition as a presenter on a magazine-type show, which featured beautiful houses and exotic destinations. That sounded like fun, too! While unemployed, I was game for anything, and by the looks of it I'd already lost Phil. I therefore had nothing to lose.

Again, there were thousands of people lined up for their shot at fame. On arrival at the venue, I felt nervous and reluctant. I really didn't need to be on television that badly – there had to be a better way to tell my story.

Tessa called me. "Florence, don't you dare go home! I've actually spoken to the producers and they are waiting for you."

Talk about pressure! I went into the audition room half-heartedly. I just couldn't get excited about houses and travel when I had so many more important things to say. Needless to say, I did badly in the audition.

Tessa called again, "What happened, Florence?" I responded "Tess, I can't do this. I have children I need to reach out to. I just don't know how I'm meant to do this. I have a book to complete, which I don't want to finish because it hurts too much, and I need to find real work. That's my truth."

She sighed on the other end of the phone. "Okay, love, we'll let it go this time." Five minutes later, she called me again. "Listen Florence, I've spoken to Patience the producer, about your real story. She wants to interview you on one of their shows when your book is ready."

I perked up a little. "All right, Tess, but that could take ages. Right now, I need to get on with my life, but I'll let you know the minute I'm ready and have something of real value to share."

And with that, I forgot about reality television, and continued applying for work. One day I received the most exciting phone call I'd had in years. I was sitting in Desiree's garden, praying for meaningful work in a notoriously superficial industry. It felt hopeless, and I was losing the battle to stay positive. To keep my faith, I turned my attention to the singing of the birds and the tranquillity of Desiree's garden.

My phone rang. It was the employment agency saying *O*, the Oprah magazine, was interested in my CV. It was perfect! Within five days of the call, I started my first day at the magazine. I resolved to put my heart and soul into the job, deeply grateful for the income and the wonderful opportunity.

Over the next few months I was extremely busy selling advertising space for the magazine. Now that I had to let go of Phil and the charity, I was trying to decide how best to contribute to society without getting hurt again. One day, one of the editors from *O* requested I attend a shoot. They had covered a story about a group of women called 'The Fairy Godmothers' who went into impoverished areas and threw parties. It was an intriguing concept, and one I was very glad to witness.

The Fairy Godmothers would cook up a feast, bring bubbles, tiaras and glitter and take the whole experience with them into what we would call squatter camps' or slums. The children would run out to take part in the festivities, and the Fairy

Godmothers would play with them and show them how to have a party.

This appealed to me enormously. This was exactly what I believed in. Not just sending money, but creating an opportunity to reach out and touch. There was, of course, the prospect of a child's 'coming down' from that exuberant high the next day when the party was over. But when I recalled what I was like as a child – I would have re-created the party as often as possible! This would likely have led to cakes made from mud, with flowers stuck on them, paper tiaras and flower petals as fairy dust. I believed it to be a wonderful opportunity, with the rest being left to the children's active imaginations.

I contemplated joining Fairy Godmothers when I felt strong enough and was back on my feet. That's what charity was all about. It was safe. I realised that Phil was not 'charity' – he never was. He was the child I'd fallen in love with. A completely different concept altogether.

Needing to see his glorious smile just once more, I downloaded the charity's homepage. I had no doubt that Barbara would upload photos of him in the arms of his new Sotho mother and I'd feel a pang of jealousy. I imagined a happy family surrounding him, standing outside his new place of residence. The page slowly opened. I wasn't far off the mark, but the reality of what I saw made my body go into high alert.

There was Phil, with 'Mama Moira' behind him! The caption on the photo referred to Phil becoming an extension of 'Mama Moira's' family. Moira was unofficially his new foster mother. It was astounding.

I quickly took the whole situation in. Clearly, Phil still didn't have a social worker, and nothing in his life would actually change, save for going with Moira to her grandmother for the occasional visit. He would remain exactly where he was. It appeared to be an informal arrangement, but nevertheless a red herring, thrown by Barbara to get rid of me.

I wondered if it was what Phil wanted. I vowed to do whatever it took to make sure he was given a fair opportunity to be heard. We needed a good lawyer and I would find the money to pay for it.

The night the police caught a fairy

I'd only been back for three months when I got into trouble one night. My behaviour had been exemplary – I had been leading the life of a monk living on rice, green tea and oats with no partying. An old friend of mine, Estie, invited me over to her home, which was a refurbished apartment in Johannesburg CBD. Developers had converted old office blocks into modern, fashionable apartments. Estie had assured me that it was safe at night, and I had nothing to fear.

I looked forward to dinner all day, and got through my work and appointments happily. At my last appointment, I had parked my car underneath a beautiful old oak tree. On arriving back at my car, I discovered an enormous branch had broken off and landed on the canvas roof of my Jeep. I picked up the branch, and looked to see if there was any damage.

Thankfully there was none. Picking up the branch, I decided to take it home with me. It would make lovely firewood, and in true tree-hugger style I thanked the old tree for giving me one of its precious branches. Oak trees have always represented wisdom and maturity to me. I hoped the tree had shared a little of both.

I arrived at Estie's apartment at 7pm. We tucked into dinner and a bottle of red wine. It was wonderful to see her after so many years and there was plenty to catch up on. She opened a second bottle of red wine, which we only drank half of, but I could feel that I was a little over the limit. There were definitely a good three glasses of wine in my system.

At 10pm it was time to leave. We said our goodbyes, and I made my way over the Nelson Mandela Bridge towards the lower end of Braamfontein, a rather more dangerous part of town. Suddenly, there were flashing lights ahead of me and I could see a roadblock. A female traffic officer stepped out and pulled me over. She approached the car, as I wound down my window.

"Good evening, ma'am. Have you been drinking?"

"No" I lied, hoping she'd let me go. It was dark and there seemed to be many unsavoury characters mulling around.

"Would you let me breathalise you?"

Oh dear – I was regretting my decision to lie.

"Okay," I answered meekly, getting out of the car. She looked me up and down in my little pink skirt, which seemed to be falling off me, due to the zip's being broken. I suddenly got nervous, looking at all the thugs that were being arrested and put in the police van. There were no women being arrested. In fact, there were no women at all, save for a few police officers.

The police woman walked beside me. I turned to her with a bit of anxiety. "I have had about three glasses of wine!"

She stopped and sighed. "Why did you lie? I thought you were okay. If you had have told me the truth, I would have let you go. This situation is not safe for a woman like you, and now my boss has seen you walking with me, and will see the result on the breathaliser."

Suddenly, a peace and calm came over me. I knew I could handle anything. I turned to her, "I have broken the law. I don't mind if you arrest me. Because even if I am to go to a cell there will be somebody there God wants me to talk to. There is probably somebody I have to help."

She looked at me strangely. "You're not scared?" she asked, now reaching out to hold up my skirt as I stood in the queue to blow on the breathaliser. "No, God will take care of me."

I blew on the breathaliser and it was established that I was over the limit. I expected to be cuffed and thrown into the police van with the thugs. But that didn't happen.

The police spoke amongst themselves in language that I wished I understood. The police lady came to me and explained that they would drive me in my car to the ATM to withdraw bail money. Then they would drive me to the Braamfontein police station where I'd be convicted and have to pay bail. I doubted I had even a third of what would be required for bail in my bank account. I explained this to the police officer, who didn't respond. She and two other officers all attempted to get in my car but of course, I had the big oak branch in the backseat.

"Please, I need to keep that branch. I want to burn it to give thanks to God," I said. I also had some pretty feathers I'd collected, as well as a few semi-precious stones on the dashboard.

The police lady looked around at all my bits and bobs. "You say you speak to God? Do you hear? Are you a sangoma (witchdoctor)?"

I thought about it, not quite sure how to answer. "I speak to God, and I hear His voice in my head. I've seen an *ingelozi* (angel) once," I answered slowly. All three police stopped. The police woman, who had taken to holding my skirt up full time, asked me sincerely, "Can you help me? What do you see?"

I looked at her carefully, and prayed deeply to God to find whatever it was I needed to tell her. There was a deep sadness in her eyes, a sadness I recognised, but hers was much worse.

"You've lost a child," I said with a lump in my throat, knowing that her loss was more permanent and terrifying than mine. "I'm so sorry," I said, throwing my arms around her.

We held each other, both weeping. Stepping back from her, I took both her hands in mine.

"God is with you. He sees your pain. He is healing your heart right now, and won't stop until it's well again."

She thanked me, while her two colleagues chatted excitedly amongst each other. Both wanted to know what I 'saw'. A few other officers made their way over, curious as to what all the commotion was. News quickly spread that I was a healer or prophet. And before I knew it, I was surrounded by people all wanting help. It was quite overwhelming, and I started hoping they'd rather arrest me than persuade me to try to solve their problems.

"I can't speak or hear God clearly because I'm drunk, remember?" I tried to reason my way out. But they were hearing none of it. I had to see ancestors, cheating partners, new jobs and who was going to win the lottery.

It was very taxing, and I couldn't answer all their questions, but I offered to pray with each one of them. I used a piece of the oak branch to sweep over their chakras, and cleared their energy fields as well. I don't believe God needs us to wave branches over others' heads in supplication to Him, but people are ritualistic creatures and we all appreciate some form of gesture or act to solidify our prayers.

Sometimes, I wonder if it's more of a placebo effect that we need to strengthen our own faith and conviction. If one believes healing is taking place, most likely it will become a reality.

After a few hours of listening and counselling the traffic department, I was sober and allowed to drive myself home. I was exhausted, but completely overwhelmed on the way home. "What the hell just happened there?" I asked aloud. God works in mysterious ways, but one thing's for sure; I'll never drink and drive again!

Little did I know how that incident would protect me, and how important it was. In months to come when applying for Phil's adoption I would need a police clearance certificate. Being arrested for drunken driving would have sealed mine and Phil's fate. I would never have made it through the first round of the adoption application. The commissioner would have thrown it out before it even got to the interim stage.

It was a very humbling experience indeed, and faith-strengthening all at once. I would never take the law, or the privilege of motherhood, for granted ever again. And I would forever feel the greatest compassion for the officers of the law, and the stresses they face on a daily basis.

The adoption process

Because my house was still rented out, I was living in Tracy's spare room, which became a sanctuary. I had made contact with an excellent children's lawyer. Her name was Leona. She was brisk and interested in the case, provided I was first prepared to go through an adoption screening process, regardless of whether Phil came to me full time or on weekends. We agreed on an affordable fee, and she set to work on developing a strategy.

She sent me to a social welfare organisation to start the screening process. This made sense, as when we got to court, I'd already be 'approved' as an adoptive parent and there would be no room or time for Barbara to discredit my character, which Leona believed she would do.

Coincidentally, Leona mentioned that she had also been approached by Barbara some time ago with a case relating to another child. Leona had refused to take the case. She didn't explain why.

The only problem was that, during this process, I was not to have any contact with Phil. The strategy was for me to go through the process and not let Barbara catch wind of it, in case she rustled up a real foster parent this time, to block my progress. Furthermore, Leona believed that I shouldn't get Phil's hopes up, either, in case I didn't qualify as an adoptive parent.

The adoption screening took an agonizing five months, which included psychological evaluation, chest X-rays, counselling, blood tests, a house visit and disclosure of my financial situation (which was under control thanks to our government's debt review programme).

Melissa Banks

During the five months I continued to work at *O* magazine, and fitted in the adoption screening process as best I could. My boss accommodated the time off I needed. While busy with the process I still managed to make my sales target, which was a huge relief.

After a year of being away from my apartment, I was finally able to move back in. I was able to afford new beds and basic furnishings, which satisfied the social worker when she visited to ensure I had adequate housing for Phil.

Keeping sane and away from Phil was exceptionally difficult. With Tracy no longer cooking on Wednesdays, all contact or links to Phil were lost for five months. I kept myself busy with work, while I prayed that Phil would stay strong and not lose heart. Each day, I had fed the birds in Tracy's garden, trying to focus on gratitude for the small things. I contemplated how the birds were always taken care of and took comfort that my son would be cared for by the same loving creator, the one who looked after his delicate skull every day.

Every now and then, I'd get a call from Leona, or Sally, the social worker who had been assigned to my case. The situation had become very complicated. Barbara was refusing to disclose Phil's ID number, and we needed his birth certificate. To force her to disclose the ID number in court was going to draw the process out further, and be an unnecessary expense.

I knew Barbara had to have his number as it would have been a prerequisite to obtaining a passport when he left the country to go to Germany for surgery. There was still no sign of any social worker, and the lead Leona eventually got from Barbara was most confusing. We received a copy of the 'body receipt' that had accompanied Phil on arrival at the charity. It was the most awful document I'd ever seen, without an ID number. It was literally a body certificate that would accompany an unknown corpse. It was sickening.

300

Furthermore, when tracing the name of the safe house he'd been at previously, according to Barbara's records it turned out that the institution hadn't existed when he was supposedly there. When trying to trace his case and social worker at the local magistrate's office of that jurisdiction, it turned out that at that time the children's court was being investigated and all files pertaining to that time had somehow vanished. Unfortunately this included Phil's file, if he was indeed ever there. Leona used the term 'bizarre' often when referring to the case.

I looked for signs from God, from the universe, from nature to keep my faith buoyed. But in doing so, I received confusing messages often. My brain and heart were filled to capacity with issues of faith. Doubt and faith fought a vicious tug of war within me. If Phil was truly meant to be with me, why had there been so many obstacles? People would ask me when last I'd seen him, and I'd feel a lump rising in my throat. A few even questioned whether what I was doing was right.

One person said, "So much time has passed. Maybe you ought to just let it go. When things are that difficult, perhaps it's not meant to be." Another commented, "Maybe he has karma with Barbara, and you're actually interfering and trying to play God."

I recalled what Ocean had said about Phil not coming to me. Even Sally, my social worker and now friend, gently suggested that there was a little burn survivor who had just come to their organisation who needed a home – perhaps I ought to consider her? But I couldn't. That was Phil's spot – nobody else could take it, and I wouldn't consider another child until I had some kind of resolution with Phil.

In spite of all the confusion, I had to get back to basics, and what I believed in. Whether I wanted to admit it or not, I trusted what I heard the preacher's wife say in church that

Mother's Day. I had gone to great lengths to figure out the secrets of the universe, and in the process thoroughly confused myself.

As much as I had my doubts about religion and investigated alternative philosophies, Christianity was ingrained in me, whether I liked it or not. It was obvious when I prayed to the God of the Bible I had more faith, and things happened. That was my truth – maybe not everybody else's but certainly what I had no choice but to accept. And there was one thing I was sure of. My love for Phil was of God and absolutely on purpose.

The psychological evaluation was wonderfully enlightening. This was a huge relief, as I finally understood that I was all right. My report stated that I would make a good, empathetic parent. That was the main objective. But the feedback was very interesting. I was viewed as highly self-assured, very creative but to mild psychosis, which would manifest in an inability to be grounded and fear of alienation. The psychosis wasn't in the clinical range, but it was there. The report stated that I was over-sensitive and deeply troubled by injustice. It also indicated that I would do well in artistic endeavours, and do not function well within an environment that is too highly structured.

It was a powerful experience. I realised what was 'wrong' with me and what my triggers for psychosis were. Injustice and an inability to express myself creatively. It was so simple!

The counsellor asked me if my sense of injustice was leading me towards psychotic behaviour as adopting a child with so many problems was quite an extreme thing to do. I smiled at her, "In that case, my psychosis is mine and Phil's best friend."

She smiled back at me. "I think you're going to make a wonderful mom," she said warmly.

Confidentially, the therapist told me that Barbara had been in a few months earlier for the same appraisal. "I don't know which child it was for, but I think it was for a girl."

I hoped it wasn't for Phil, but thanked her all the same, and wound my way home through the traffic. Adopting Phil was challenging indeed. And maybe I was a bit psychotic. But why on earth would God have sent a child such as Phil across the path of a creative, overly sensitive woman who had psychotic episodes sparked by injustice? It had to all mean something.

I smiled on the way home, thinking how creative God gets with me. He is the ultimate alchemist, turning every mistake or weakness into something beautiful and of value. My mistakes are always rather 'interesting', and I've learnt to count on God's response being at least three times more interesting!

Who would have thought He would have used my 'psychosis' for so much good. (As you can tell, I've started viewing my 'psychosis' as a gift, much to my therapist's dismay! As for our mistakes, all I can say is that Jonah's story only really interested me when he went off and did his own thing, and God got really creative in response!)

I realised all I had to do to stay 'sane' was keep being creative, even if my work environment didn't allow for too much of it. And I had to try and stay away from situations where there was injustice. That was easier said than done. Especially with Phil's plight constantly before me. But at least I knew what my triggers were and I could identify the feelings and moments that disturbed me. I was able to 'watch' myself and observe my behaviour. And it all started making sense.

But it took time to change age-old behaviour. And a serious car accident.

The accident

It was a clear, crisp winter's day. The grass was yellow on the pavements I drove past. Happily it was a Friday afternoon, after five o' clock, and I had scheduled an appointment at the beauty salon followed by a drink with Tracy in Melville.

I contemplated the busy week while driving and mentally doubled checked all the tasks I had accomplished, as well as what I would have to do in preparation for my manager Storm's visit. As her name suggested, she would literally arrive from Cape Town in a hurricane of activity.

At times we'd work till late in her hotel room, frantically churning out proposals and trying to get as much done as possible. Her visits were always exciting, but a part of me dreaded the accompanying frenzy and adrenalin that her presence produced. I had worked very hard on the magazine, as well as managing to successfully complete the adoption screening process. But I was no closer to getting Phil back.

I had used every last cent towards preparing Phil's room, and paying for all the processes, which were expensive. Of course, I also had to make provision for the lawyer's bills which would undoubtedly make their way to my mailbox soon.

Every month, I would buy Phil an item of clothing, just to help me feel closer to his return. In my efforts to provide for all of this financially, I didn't take out a medical insurance for myself, believing it was an unnecessary expense, and would use up my precious, limited financial resources that Phil so desperately needed.

Having finished off at the salon, I hopped into my car, in such a hurry I forgot to put on my seatbelt. My mind was full of work and Phil, and making it to Tracy on time.

Whilst navigating the traffic circle I texted Tracy. (Yes, I worked for *O* Magazine and broke the law of texting while driving!)

As I drove out of the traffic circle my concentration slipped for a minute and I went into the back of another car at quite a high speed as I had accelerated. I lost control of my Jeep as it spun, went up onto a pavement, blasted into a concrete wall and landed in a koi pond. My last thought, as my face hit my steering wheel was, "Ooh, that hurt! There goes my face!"

After some time, I came to. I had many people around me, asking me who to call. I don't recall much, except asking for Tracy, in a daze. I wanted to get out of my car and survey the damage, but somebody with some medical expertise was preventing me from doing so. It was frustrating, having all these people around me, when it would be so simple to quickly get out of my vehicle, assess the damage, which I couldn't believe would be all that bad, go home, and wait for my nose to heal. I had no doubt my nose was broken.

But hands and arms from nowhere restrained me. The man with the medical expertise looked me in the eyes and said "You're more injured than you think. Please just trust me and stay put until the ambulance gets here."

I can't recall his face, but his interference was inconceivable to me, which led to my having visions of huge ambulance fees, as well as other costs that were unnecessary. "Please, don't call an ambulance, I really don't have money for it. I don't have medical insurance, either. Please, please just let me go? You don't understand, I'm trying to adopt a little boy. I can't afford this," I started sobbing.

I don't remember much from then on, except Tracy arriving on the scene, as well as an ambulance. I tried to get Tracy to reason with everybody to please leave me alone, and just let me go home. She responded in a calm but stern manner, "Rubes, look at your hands. Look at your clothes, and tell me you're all fine."

Looking down slowly, I comprehended that my injuries were very serious. My hands were soaked in blood. My jumper and trousers, too, were drenched in the red liquid. It was completely shocking to behold. The paramedics carefully lifted me from my car.

"Ma'am, we have to handle you carefully in case you have a broken neck," a very gentle female paramedic assured me. She strapped me into their harnesses and stretchers and lifted me into the ambulance, soothing me all the while.

I relaxed as we drove to the Garden City Clinic – an institution I knew I wasn't going to be able to afford. Upon arrival at the trauma unit, my brother, Greg and his best friend Nuno were there. I had tried to calm down, but became increasingly anxious about the bills this incident would bring my way.

Softly, Greg said, "Shhh... Ruby, we'll manage this, somehow, just stop moving your head."

He handed me his phone. "Please tell mom you're all right. She needs to hear your voice."

I spoke to my mother, who sounded calm. I told her that everything was fine, and she had nothing to worry about. Greg took his phone back, "they're going to send you for X-rays now. Just be calm, I'm right here." And with that, I was wheeled off to the X-ray department.

I heard the doctor describing something I wasn't sure I wanted to hear. I was wheeled back into the trauma unit, where the doctor delivered the devastating news to us.

"Noooo!" I screamed, "My neck is not *fucking* broken! I can't! I can't! I'm adopting a child!"

Greg tried to calm my hysteria, but I wouldn't hear it. "I can feel my toes! I can move! You're wrong! You're fucking lying! You're fucking lying!" I sobbed hysterically.

Greg was pale. The nurse intervened, "Now miss, I know this is bad. But please don't use that language any more."

Sobbing, I apologised, reaching out my hand to Greg, who gripped it tightly, while Tracy held onto my other. The doctor mentioned CT scans and possible surgery. Greg and Tracy stood over me, and decided that there was no way we could afford the treatment at Garden City Clinic. I'd have to be sent by ambulance, again, to a public institution – a terrifying prospect. One hears so many horror stories of people left to die, not enough beds and so on.

"Please Greg, don't leave my side when we get to Helen Joseph. I don't know what's going to happen to me there," I implored my brother.

"I'll be there, Rube, I'm not going anywhere," he replied firmly.

Whilst waiting for the ambulance, I was still in denial. Eventually, Nuno took a photo of my face, so that I could see for myself. It was horrific.

"Do you want me to tag you on Facebook?" he asked morbidly.

"Sure why don't you just tag my toe, too, while you're at it ... I'm going to a morgue, anyway" I replied morosely.

Greg and Nuno were leaning over me on either side of the bed, and the look of absolute mischief that passed between them wasn't lost me. Before long, my toe was tagged, a blanket put over my head and I was ready for the morgue. Happily they clicked away with their cellphones, discussing which of the other patients in trauma needed 'tagging' too. It was too funny, and I couldn't stop laughing. Seeing their comic relief was working, they searched for bed-pans, which they decided to wear as hats. It was an incredibly entertaining show they put on. And judging by the looks on their faces, they were delighted to be entertaining the entire ward.

Before long, the ambulance arrived. Thankfully it was the same ambulance with the lovely paramedic that took me to what I thought would be a morgue! This time, I was strapped into a different harness, which was very painful. I cried all the way to the hospital in agony and absolute fear. We arrived, and again Greg was there. Tracy had left while we were waiting at the previous hospital. She had constantly been on the phone to Storm, giving blow-by-blow updates. She was exhausted, and Greg assured her I'd be fine, and that he was handling everything.

I was wheeled into the trauma unit, where there had been a stabbing. Three men had gotten into a fight, and from the glimpses I could catch it was serious. In spite of my discomfort, I was curious to see what was going on, as there was much shouting and activity.

Greg and Nuno weren't allowed in, and they spent the night outside the trauma unit. I was given a shot of something very heavenly, while a catheter was inserted, which was painful. The nurse was rough, and I bled into the little bag. Shortly, afterwards I was wheeled by a chatty, black, male nurse, for yet another set of X-rays, which confirmed exactly what the previous had.

A female, Eastern European-accented young doctor was attending to me. She was kind, and explained that we'd need a CT scan and possibly surgery would be required. It was very reassuring that I would have the required medical attention, and so far had been treated exceptionally professionally, except by the nurse with the catheter. The doctor assigned me to Ward 17, a ward designated for patients having surgery. My chatty friend returned to wheel me away. He was an angel, and I told him so.

We stopped to say goodbye to Greg and Nuno, who looked exhausted, and were going home to fetch my mother. The nurse high-fived them, and we were on our way.

"I don't know how long I'm going to be here, but if it's six weeks, like they say, please will you come visit me?"

He grinned in response, "Of course I'm going to be there! I like you!"

Once we got to the ward, I was lifted by two other nurses and my friend onto the hospital bed, my neck and body still in traction. Everything was clean, from what I could tell. Once again, I berated myself for my 'white' ignorance. The hospital was well equipped to deal with my situation. My CT scan was scheduled for 11am the following morning, and a drip had been inserted into my arm. Things were under control ... or, as Greg would say, "sorted".

Before long, my mother arrived. She had obviously been briefed about how bad I looked, although I could see from her expression that she was upset, but attempting to hide it.

My face had swelled up with purple discolouration and bruising. Although my face had been cleaned, my hands, fingernails and hair were caked with blood. I was in traction, too, for a broken neck. Not an easy sight for any mother.

"Oh Ruby baby, what did you do to yourself?" she asked, her green eyes full of concern. Looking at her beautiful face, her auburn hair glistening in the sunshine behind her, I smiled. "Oh mommy, I was silly, texting while driving. But I'm going to get better, you'll see, my neck isn't broken." Reassuringly, I squeezed her hand.

Tracy arrived, and hugs were exchanged all round. Greg and Nuno were there, too, this time *sans* bed-pan hats, thankfully.

"I've told the nurses to hide the bed-pans from you guys, and no toe tagging in this ward," I grinned at them. "Ah, spoilsport!" they joked.

Before we knew it, visiting hours were over and everyone left. They had brought me food and extra blankets, as that was all that was missing at the hospital. Other than that, the medical attention was more than adequate.

At about three o' clock the next day, I was ready for my CT scan. I prayed that everything would be fine. I could not and would not accept anything else. Confident that my future was in God's hands, I went through the intimidating machine, relaxed. The scans declaring my fate were put into a big brown manila envelope and inserted into my file. It wouldn't be too much longer, and I'd be free of these weights around my head, literally and figuratively.

Just before four o' clock, the lady doctor arrived. She opened the envelope and smiled. "Your neck is okay, from what I can tell. Those were lesions – the fractures didn't go all the way through the bone, so you won't need surgery. In fact, we can take you out of traction."

My spirit soared and it was all I could do not to start screaming and whooping with delight. The nurses had to stop me from ripping off the straps and weights, myself. My hands were everywhere, trying to reach for the straps, and oh, that catheter had to go! Laughingly, the nurses settled me down and removed my trappings in a dignified manner.

The family returned to find me sitting up, purple-faced, with bloodied hair, but with the biggest smile they'd ever seen. The elation in the ward at that moment was indescribable. There were tears of relief, but mainly laughter.

That night, I was once again given my heavenly injection and I slept soundly. The sun woke me up. Sitting upright , I joyfully absorbed the yellow walls, golden sunshine, and the movement on the streets, which I would be part of again soon.

Across the street, an old church dwarfed the houses surrounding it. And alongside the church, the sunlight danced across the Westdene Dam, which had a special significance to me. In 1985, a great tragedy had occurred there. A colourful double-decker bus, carrying primary school children, went out of control and drove off the bridge that ran alongside the dam. The bus landed at the bottom of the dam. Forty-four children under 14 years old lost their lives that terrible, tragic day. My throat still constricts at the thought of what happened.

There were many people who rushed to the children's rescue, including one nameless teenage boy. He dived in and brought one child to the surface, then another and another, until he didn't come up again. This incident affected me deeply, and still does. At that moment it was particularly poignant. Had I been doing the same thing and had I been given a message that it was all right to come up for air? That brave young hero died, because he didn't know when to stop. Maybe he couldn't live with their stricken little faces in his memory. If only he could rescue one more child....

It stories such as these that give me faith in mankind's inherent love. It's truly remarkable that human compassion overrode a child's survival instinct like that. I believe most folks have it in them, too, but are afraid to 'dive in' and start any form of rescue operation in case they see too many stricken faces that they can't help.

I understood all too well how that felt. Perhaps if I could save just one, it would make a difference. And hopefully our story would inspire others. But I had to come up for air from time to time. As much as I admired that beautiful heroic child, I didn't want to meet the same fate.

Tracy came to fetch me a little later in the day. It was liberating to be able to walk out of the hospital. Tracy almost literally 'broke me out'. Within minutes, I had my doctor's note and Tracy was hustling me along – she'd had enough of the hospital, and waiting in queues to visit. She had constantly argued with the nurses that I wasn't getting enough painkillers. We didn't stop to make an appointment for surgery to fix my nose – which I'd later come to regret, as I had two little bones sticking out my nose.

I walked out into the open air, inhaling deeply, full of gratitude. I was still in my gown, but barefoot without having had a bath or shower in days. Tracy glanced at me alongside her, wrinkling her nose. "We need to get you into a bath! You smell really bad!"

Laughingly, we made our way home in the traffic.

The recovery

Tracy decided to move me back in with her at least for a week so I could recover. My neck and body still ached, and I couldn't bear my reflection in the mirror. It was grotesque. Unfortunately, both my purse and mobile phone were stolen at the scene of the accident, so I had to go to the mall to get SIM cards and bank cards replaced.

My 'angel' and Hawaii photos were lost forever, as I hadn't bothered to download them on my computer. But that was all right, too. The memories were in my mind. To this day, I've always been doubtful about the 'angel' photo, and actually never placed too much value in it, being hopeful rather than sure. But the fact that it appeared over George, and I ended up going to George's home to experience healing and the beauty of his children, makes me think twice. I had never for a moment based my decision to go to George's home for the summer job on that photo – I'd actually forgotten about it when making my decision to make the great trek across the continent.

It's one of those delightful unexplained mysteries that I'm happy to live with.

Walking into the mall with a battered face was very intimidating, to say the least. For the first time, I truly had compassion for how Phil must have felt when walking through public places. It took a lot of courage. People could see something bad had happened, and that it was obviously painful. It made me feel incredibly vulnerable. Fortunately, another good friend of mine, Praksha, was with me. After a few minutes in the mall, seeing my tears welling up, she reached for my hand and held it tight while walking close to me. Her strength and love made it tolerable.

It was a wonderful gift to have time off work. But because I'd been in such a work frenzy for the past eight months, it was impossible for me to relax. At first, I felt guilty for being off and costing the company, even though I'd been assured of its support.

My first week was spent in bed, dosed with painkillers. By the second week, my face was well on its way to recovery (apart from the two bones jutting out of the side of my nose). Inspecting my face daily had become a blessing – I appreciated every little part of it.

As a child, and even as an adult to an extent, a girl never is sure if she's pretty enough. The fact that I'm artistic and am able to draw portraits of people had made my self-inspection even more critical when I was growing up. I couldn't help but look at people's faces, taking in the distances between their eyes, noses and lips. Each face, even with its irregularities, was precious and beautiful to me and I wanted to draw it. But for some reason I couldn't extend that love and tolerance to myself. It was time to take my inner little girl aside and have a chat with her.

In my mind, I went back to a time when my inner child had been very concerned about her prettiness. I was seven years old and we were at church. My mother had bought me the most beautiful floral gypsy skirt and pale pink cheesecloth blouse. I had matching slides in my hair, which my mother had curled, and pink canvas shoes, which had laces that criss-crossed up around my calves.

There was nothing we could have done or added that would have made my outfit any prettier. I walked into the church feeling confident, and then noticed other very pretty little girls with equally pretty, if not prettier, dresses on. Suddenly, I felt disappointed and insecure. My mother couldn't understand this – and neither could I. Why did I have to be the prettiest?

Wasn't it vanity, wanting to be first or best? Something Jesus frowned upon?

As I spoke to my inner child, I showed her photographs of myself through the years. I took her to a private bathroom for disabled people so that we wouldn't be interrupted or she wouldn't be embarrassed to talk about this very private matter, in front of the mirror, for all to see. The sermon had begun, and she looked gleefully at me, pleased to be escaping for a clandestine adventure. She was ecstatic to see how she would turn out as a grown-up. She looked through the photos, and didn't seem to mind the 'fat' ones, although she did comment on my sadness in them. I showed her photos of friends who had been pretty and had somehow let themselves go; also, I showed her photos of friends who had blossomed into greater beauties.

My inner child responded, "But you're kind and gentle. You're fun and you make me laugh." I don't want to be anybody else. Not even Olivia Newton-John or the Abba girl! I'm happy to be you."

And with that, she ran off, excited about what she was to become.

It was a powerful exercise, and well worth the effort as I felt something shift inside of me. I no longer felt the need to plaster my face with make-up or look at other women, feeling threatened that I wasn't good enough. I could now walk confidently into a room without its being an act, which is what used to happen in the past. I feel beautiful inside and special in my own right.

Re-parenting myself was fun, and apart from regular updates in my gratitude journal, I kept a list of really fun activities to do when I felt my sparkle was dying. The list read:

Feed the birds, then hide behind the window and watch them eat. Give each a name, and bless them.

Eat a Salticrax biscuit with as much Tabasco sauce as I can handle.

Have a lovely warm shower, then quickly turn off the hot tap and run around screaming in the shower, dodging the cold drops.

Sing in the shower.

Wear a tiara.

Write a fairy tale about a horrible witch who had captured goblins and was stealing their powers (wonder who that could be!).

If too lazy to make a real chocolate cake, make one from mud and decorate with flowers.

When feeling brave, start illustrating the fairytale.

I even went as far as retrieving my favourite childhood doll. I recalled my mother's gentle voice, "You're a good mommy," as I washed and dressed my doll. Now 30 years later, I clung to my doll and wept, "I'm a good mommy! I'm a good mommy," into her hair.

It was very therapeutic.

Still unable to drive, I walked to the shops daily, where my post-concussion bewildered me. I found myself holding items that I couldn't remember selecting or picking up. It was a time of slow navigation as I was constantly disorientated.

By the middle of the second week of recovery, I had started re-writing my book. This had been very off-putting for some time, as I didn't want to revisit most of the memories. It was noticeable that I had enjoyed writing the first part, but by the second part the pain had been all-consuming. My writing was incoherent. It was inconceivable that I'd almost submitted my manuscript as being complete in that state.

I could have sworn I'd read every word before liberally dishing it out to friends or anyone who would read it, thinking the journey was over. But for some reason, my eye had skimmed over those painful parts, not wanting to absorb the words as they were too raw and confusing.

Clearly, being so close to the situation and turmoil had made me unable to write about it logically or coherently. The words had tumbled out all over the place, the emotions were scattered and confused. That was where I had been mentally.

Slowly, I started writing, thankful for the time off. I sat and hammered away at my keyboard, feeling like a piano player. The tears flowed, at the times they needed to, and true restoration of body and spirit took place.

While on sick leave, I got a call from Toncah, a friend who was the entertainment manager of a well-established theme park.

"Just to let you know that we've got children's charity event coming up. We're launching a Winter Circus, and various celebrities have invited charities of their choice to attend. One of them has chosen Phil's School. So he'll be there, and you will be able to speak to him freely. Would you like to come?"

My heart leapt. This was exactly what we needed. So far, I'd been exceptionally well behaved, listening to my lawyer and refraining from contact. It would be an excellent opportunity to update him on what was happening. I couldn't tell him about the possible adoption, as I didn't want to raise his hopes or unsettle him where he was for now. But he needed to know I was still on the case!

Visualising how he would react to me, after not seeing me for 10 months, was nerve-wrecking. Would he be ecstatic to see me? Or would he be disillusioned and distant, angry with me for my abandonment?

Then I considered running into Barbara. It was doubtful she'd be there, but what if the volunteers tried to stop contact or made a scene? Maybe Phil could tell me if a social worker had been appointed? I hoped his reaction would tell me whether to proceed further or not. After all, it was about what he wanted and felt comfortable with.

Leona was nervous when I shared my plan with her. I assured her that I wouldn't get Phil's hopes up, I'd just let him know that he'd soon have an opportunity to be heard.

That Saturday morning, I covered my bruising heavily in make-up. I didn't want Phil to be alarmed when he saw me. Tracy agreed to come with me, and the two of us made our way to the theme park. I was excited and anxious at the same time. Walking towards the entrance of the building, we saw the children forming a queue. And there, some distance away, was the most beautiful child I'd ever seen. Thankfully Barbara wasn't around.

"Phil!" I called as loudly as I could. He didn't hear me. I called again, shouting till I was hoarse.

"Phil!" He turned around, and at that moment somebody stepped in front me, blocking me from his vision. But he saw Tracy.

"Tracy!" he yelled, and at that moment he saw me. "RUBY! RUBYYYY!" he screamed, breaking into a wild sprint towards me. I ran with my arms out, ready to pick him up. We reached each other, and I scooped him up, threw him into the air and pulled him close to my heart, which was ready to explode.

Tears poured down my cheeks. He wasn't angry with me. He had never stopped loving me in spite of everything. I didn't deserve his love or forgiveness.

"Where have you been?" he asked breathlessly.

"Phil, I've been to school just like Barbara said I should. I had to go for tests at doctors and even the police had to meet me to check that I was a good person for you to visit." He was nodding, listening intently. I continued, "Phil, have you got a social worker yet?"

He rolled his eyes and said something profound, "No – that's the whole problem." It was amazing that he understood, and I was relieved that Barbara had taken that route with him, rather than telling him I had abandoned him. It was much healthier blaming all his problems on the government!

I responded, "Well, we are getting you a social worker. It's going to happen soon. Then we will have to see a judge. The judge and the social worker will decide when you can come visit me again, and how often. But you must tell them what you want."

"When are the judge and social worker going to meet me?" he asked tiredly. "Soon, my boy. Let's not worry about that for now. Let's just have a wonderful time today."

"Have you still got the Jeep?" he asked. This time, I rolled my eyes and responded, "No, kiddo, I had an accident. And I'm not sure if the Jeep is being fixed or not." He didn't ask if I was hurt, but was more concerned about which car we were going to drive around in.

At that stage, the assessor had wanted to write off the Jeep, but I was fighting to have it repaired. A write-off would have meant that although the Jeep would be paid for I'd have to get another car. The problem was that I was under debt review so

I wouldn't qualify for finance. I decided not to think about it that day.

Phil ran off to call his friends. They were ecstatic to see Tracy and I. They abandoned the confused volunteer, but we assured him everything was fine and if he wanted to he could take the rest of the day off.

There was no interference, and the children were ours for the day! It was a freezing, but an otherwise glorious winter's day. I felt God's golden glow of love all around me. A choir of Aids orphans from Uganda was performing, and singing like angels. The lyrics of the hymn they sang rang in my ears, heart and soul: "Always remembered, never forsaken."

We all went our separate ways later. I promised Phil that he would get what he needed and that he'd be heard. We hugged and kissed goodbye. It was a poignant parting, but enough to give us both the little boost of faith we needed. Walking back to the car, we passed a camera crew from the television show that Patience, Tessa's contact, produced. I made a mental note to call her with an idea that had been forming in my head. I finally had something of value to share.

Africa's Angels

While at home in recovery, I had been working on a presentation for a concept for a television series I had envisioned – I called the project, "Africa's Angels". Clearly, there was some need to take mine and similar stories of the beauty of what we'd experienced and share it publically. I just didn't know how. But thinking back to the other adoptive families I'd met (all normal people like me), I believed the only way to encourage adoptions in South Africa was to show the truth of what it meant.

Rather than be prescriptive, we would show wonderful stories of children being rehabilitated after being institutionalised. I had been required to attend an adoption workshop, and there I met families who were adopting due to fertility challenges, as well as other families who weren't struggling with fertility, but had decided to have another child. One particular family had two children, and had decided to give the third 'spot' to a child in need.

It was amazing to witness. I believe it's something to be encouraged in this country, where adoptions are actually on the decline despite the fact that we have so many orphans. It was an ambitious dream – but one that I believed needed to happen. I emailed the presentation, "Africa's Angels" to my old boss, Tessa, hoping she would pass it on to Patience, which she did.

A few days later, I got a call from Patience.

"We're very interested in your adoption concept. We can't do a series, but we will create a feature on our morning show. But it needs sponsorship. Do you think you can organise that?" I assured her that I believed it was more than possible. And with that she hung up, telling me that her co-producer, Brad, would be contacting me.

Brad called me and he, too, believed it was an exciting concept. He said over the phone, "You know, I was just thinking about what Oprah did that made her show a success. And it was her compassion. And here you are working for *O* magazine. I think it all fits together somehow." I heartily agreed with him.

Brad arranged to meet me when he was next in Johannesburg.

It was so exciting I could hardly breathe. I had so much to do. I had to get back to work, finish my book and now produce a regular television feature. And then there was the most important –issue of all: Phil's adoption, which was becoming more complex by the day. I had to take each day at a time and trust that I would be guided to the right people at the right time.

Brad arrived in town a week later. We clicked instantly. He was a tall, attractive ginger-haired man. But he was involved with someone – so no going there!

Brad not only wanted me to produce my feature, but they also wanted me to handle their airtime sales in Johannesburg – which would mean leaving my beloved job at *O*. I didn't count on having to leave my job to fulfil my dream, and said as much.

Brad responded, "But will they let you have time off for shooting the feature? And what if you pick up some sales along the way for the show when you call on clients?"

I still wasn't sold, until he played his final card. "You know you'd work from home if you worked for us, as we're Cape Town-based."

Now he had my attention, as I was concerned that I'd get Phil for a month or two before starting school and have to take him with me to the office. Where I worked currently, working from home was not an option. At the time the company was adamant we were office-bound from 9am to 5pm, except when we were seeing clients. But even if we were seeing clients late afternoon, we were still expected back in the office.

Brad and I parted, each with a lot to think about. I needed him to commit to a high basic for a minimum of three months while I got sales going. I also needed his commitment that they would allow me to create and produce the feature with or without a sponsor. In return, even if the feature went unsponsored, I would bring in sales for the rest of the show.

I still wasn't ready to leave *O* magazine, even though I had the opportunity to do exactly what Oprah did. I had found a comfort zone, and was preparing to adopt a child. The last thing I felt like was more turmoil, especially after the company had been so good allowing me sick leave and sending me flowers.

I decided not to make any decisions until Brad reverted with a proposal and accepted my terms and conditions. Once that happened, I would make my final decision.

Back to work

After two weeks of bed rest, and one week working from home, I got back to work. My body was still tired and sore, but I had no choice but to continue as best I could. Barbara had finally produced Phil's ID number, which was a major breakthrough. But not without trying to sabotage our efforts.

Leona immediately traced the magistrate from the district Phil was from and discovered Barbara had been there a week earlier, trying to get Phil's birth certificate, which was lost.

A social worker had been traced, but she refused to meet me or have anything to do with our case. Barbara had got to her first, telling her that Moira was applying to foster Phil, and that I was not to interfere with the process.

The social worker told Leona that she intended placing Phil in foster care with Moira that following week. It wasn't surprising that she, like Barbara, also hoped I'd rather just go away quietly. But Phil needed to be heard, and by the sound of it, the social worker hadn't even met him yet.

Leona sent a firm letter to Barbara's lawyers, stating that we intended to pursue the adoption, which took precedence over fostering. She also mentioned that we had recently discovered that not only did the child now have a social worker, but was about to be placed in foster care, which should have been disclosed.

This was obviously quite embarrassing for Barbara. I was aware that she was preparing for her major court case, where she intended to sue the television channel for defaming her a few years earlier. I wondered if she was using those same lawyers, and if they would want to continue working with her, as she hadn't been honest with them at all.

A few weeks later, I visited the charity's website and, as I thought, the hearing had been put off for another year due to Barbara's lawyers being unable to represent her. It wasn't surprising in the least.

Still struggling with the offer from the television producers, I prayed for guidance. Within my first week back, I opened an email from an advertising agency I often dealt with. They had a request for exposure or free advertising space for their pro-bono client, Adoption Voice SA. Excitedly, I opened the email to see what it was about. It turned out that all the orphanages and institutions in South Africa had a single 'voice' for the first time. Until now, they had all been running their own campaigns, operating in isolation. I immediately made arrangements to meet with the woman who headed up the organisation. Her name was Annemie.

She was bubbly, blonde and about the same age as me. I explained what I intended to do on television, and she was as enthusiastic as I was. We ran through exactly what her expectations were, which dovetailed with what I was trying to accomplish with the feature. It was crazy! Excitedly, like two little girls playing, we started putting a synopsis together. She had access to all the organisations and their stories. She could provide me with the appropriate families, right government officials and social workers to interview. It was perfect.

There had been some progress on the Phil front. I had to lodge my application for adoption at the children's court in Johannesburg. It turned out that the court wouldn't accept an application without a birth certificate. Sally couldn't get his birth certificate, as she wasn't his social worker and she doubted they would give it to me either. I decided to take my chances at Home Affairs in Johannesburg.

Outside the office, I was told that not only couldn't I get his birth certificate, because I wasn't his mother or social worker, but I would also have to go to Pretoria to get it, where it could take six weeks minimum for them to send it back to me. It was devastating news. I stood in the parking lot outside Home Affairs and sobbed my heart out. I had come so far, and now I was encountering yet another obstacle.

I was crying with my head in my hands, making a mess of the roof of the old borrowed Mercedes Benz I was using, when a man approached me. He was one of those people who earn a living by queuing at Home Affairs for others, and doing their paper work for them.

"Why are you crying? I don't like to see a woman crying like this."

I brokenly explained the situation. "I can help you. I have a sister here. Do you have your adoption application with you?" I handed it to him, grateful for his kind assistance. "Follow me," he said, approaching the man with a copier machine under the tree in the parking lot. He spoke to his friend and before I knew it copies of all my documents were being produced. He turned to me.

"Okay, the copies are R35. The birth certificate will cost you R150, and it would be nice if you could give me something for Christmas," he said with a big, white smile. I handed over R300, wondering if he would be able to assist me or if I'd never see him again. He promised to be back in 10 minutes. In exactly 10 minutes, he returned complete with a printed, unabridged birth certificate, and a triumphant smile. I hugged him and made my way back to the office happily.

I called Sally who was amazed that I had a birth certificate. "Now you need to get to the court and submit your application, Ruby. Understand they might not be that helpful. Depending on the clerk's mood, your application may sit for days, so just relax and try and take it all in your stride." She knew that was useless advice when it came to me, though!

The following day, I arrived at the Johannesburg Children's court armed with old copies of *O Magazine*, and some ethnic hair-care samples. I didn't care if it was seen as bribery, social workers and clerks needed some love, too.

Of course, the Oprah magic worked like a charm, and before I knew it, every clerk and social worker in the building wanted to be my friend.

Salma, the clerk on duty, was exceptionally helpful, and insisted that I complete the official court document with me there and then. "I know that woman, Barbara, she came here recently wanting to adopt that girl, Daisy. I didn't like her. Something was wrong. She didn't want to disclose her financial statements, insisting that she doesn't earn any money. I asked her how she got here, and who bought her the car she travelled in."

Salma stood up to collect the document she'd just typed from the printer and returned. "I'm going to get this stamped and approved by the commissioner for you tomorrow, Ruby. If Phil wants to be with you, the court will give him to you. Don't worry!" she said, hugging me goodbye.

Sally chuckled over the phone when I told her about my meeting at the court. A day later, she called me to inform me that the commissioner had accepted my application, and in fact approved the enquiry. I didn't think much of it, but Sally assured me it was huge.

"The fact that she's approved this is massive, Ruby. Phil's social worker has until the 30th September to get a report submitted to me. And then I need to submit another report. This document demands it. But the commissioner has made notes on your application that she is concerned about your debt review, as well as your ability to provide for Phil's medical needs."

I quickly responded, "I've already been in touch with Operation Smile. They are prepared to help me with Phil's surgery, and I can get proof that since starting the debt review process my financial behaviour has been impeccable. How long do you think all this is going to take from here, Sally?"

Sally responded, "Once the court has had a hearing with Phil, and established that he is adoptable, we have to place an advertisement for his biological parents to come forward. And we have to give them a month to do that. But don't get disheartened, just carry on being patient. It's all good."

I put down the phone a little disappointed, but triumphant at the same time. I called Leona and updated her on the progress. She sounded happy in her crisp way.

"Don't worry about the debt review, Ruby, they would much rather have a child placed with a mother in a squatter camp than have a child institutionalised. If it's a problem, we will fight it. Just keep the faith. I'm very happy with the way things are going." I had to go back to the court the next day, as I'd left my passport behind. Salma was waiting for me with news. It was obviously confidential. "Listen, Ruby, I'm not supposed to tell you this. And it's up to you what you want to do with it. But I heard the charity and that woman, Barbara, are being investigated. These are the details of the officer investigating. He might need your emails as proof. But it's up to you."

She handed over the little blue piece of paper.

"Thank you so much, Salma. I'm not sure I should follow up. I just need Phil back. Maybe once I've got him back, I can make a decision."

She hugged me again. "Whatever you decide, God is with you."

I left uncertain as to what I was meant to do with the information. I certainly didn't want to see Barbara lynched. I wasn't sure if she truly was committing any crime other than not allowing a child to be heard.

I contemplated how she raised money overseas, which was deposited into a trust fund in Daisy's name. As the trust fund had been active for a number years, it was surprising that Barbara had only adopted Daisy recently. I found it quite ironic and hypocritical how she'd put so much pressure on me to adopt Phil, giving me ultimatums and 'punishing' me for not complying with her wishes earlier, when she herself had only applied to adopt Daisy after many years.

Unless of course she had never meant for me to adopt Phil at all, but had merely used this as a ploy to get money and whatever she could out of me.

Barbara also had plans to launch a specialised hospital in another African state. If she was hoarding money, she could easily prove it was for that, which I believed it most likely was. All this while, the children at the school lived in impoverished circumstances. As Salma said, something didn't feel right. A little voice inside me said, if it quacks like a duck and walks like a duck, chances are it *is* a duck.

I made a decision. I believed Barbara had received her come-uppance with her lawyers withdrawing from the law suit. I didn't think she deserved anything worse to happen to her. What she needed was to have the charity properly managed.

I recalled bumping into one of the 'trustees' of the charity who had been made a trustee after assisting with some electrical work. He had never been involved, or called into a meeting, either. He had literally interacted with Barbara once.

I suspected many of the trustees were actually trustees in name only, and neither the government nor the trustees were managing Barbara. As much as I believed she thought it suited her needs, it was actually destroying her, and turning her into an abusive person with too much responsibility to handle.

I decided not to disclose my evidence of her dealings with me, but rather to alert the investigating officer to keep an eye on her. The children deserved to be kept in a state of dignity and their needs met. They didn't need some white elephant institution to be built. Just recently it was discovered an extremely sophisticated hospital facility built for charity had become defunct due to lack of staff.

Although the way Barbara had handled Phil's case had been high-handed and cruel, I couldn't help but think that at the same time I hadn't been ready to assume full responsibility and in a strange way things were working out for the best.

Waiting in silence

The commissioner's request for the enquiry and subsequent reports had a six-week deadline. Those six weeks were incredibly long. I kept myself busy working, writing my book and selling advertising space for *O*. It didn't feel right to be so undecided about my career at the magazine, and I had started avoiding Storm, my boss, as I didn't want to resign just yet.

Storm knew me too well, though, and called me. In her typical no-nonsense way she asked straight out, "What's happening, Ruby? Have you been offered another job?"

I quickly told her all about the offer at the television production house. To my surprise she sounded delighted for me. "I'm going to respond to you as your friend Ruby, not as your boss. It's terrible for the magazine to lose you, but this is right. Don't be scared, and hide away here at the magazine. Don't get me wrong, we love you and don't want to lose you. But I can't see the company allowing you time off for shooting or working from home. It's just against policy at this stage."

"Okay, but can I please think about it some more?" I responded.

"Sure, but for everybody's sake try not to take too long," she advised. "We're hitting a busy time of the year and we'll have to make contingency plans." I respected that and promised to give her my answer as soon as possible.

I tried to put off my final decision, but felt a need to work on the adoption television project. It seemed like something constructive to do while I waited for Phil's situation to be resolved.

There was nothing I could do to speed up the adoption process, and I was instructed to stay away from Phil until the judge decided his fate. It would all come down to what Phil wanted, and it was important I wasn't seen as trying to influence him.

Phil's social worker was still refusing to see me, and had told my social worker Sally that she would submit her report directly to the commissioner, and not to Sally. But the good news was, she had finally met Phil. Sally reported that she had said at least five times, "This child knows what he wants."

She wouldn't disclose what he had said he wanted, which I found out soon enough.

I sent Kelvin a message, updating him. He sent a message back saying he'd forgotten to tell me but he had walked past the green fence and spoken to Phil. Apparently Phil had stated outright that he wanted to come and live with me. Kelvin had advised him to be strong and say that, if anyone ever asked him. Phil had promised that he'd do exactly that. It seemed my beautiful child had done precisely as he had promised.

"How did he sound, Kelvin?" I asked, worried. Kelvin sighed deeply on the other side of the phone. "Frustrated."

I prayed for Phil to continue being strong. It wouldn't be long now, but it was incredibly frustrating.

I didn't believe there was any reason for me not to have access to Phil in the meantime, or for us not to sit around a table with the charity and discuss his requirements like mature adults. I certainly needed access to him for him to be interviewed by the Hope School. Their intake for the new year was happening right then. Operation Smile had requested his medical files, so they could assess his injuries and give me an indication of their involvement.

I sent both Leona and Sally emails stating my frustrations and my requirements. They told me I had no choice but to be patient.

I was counting on the government to come through for Phil, and the other children for that matter. So far, government had protected my assets and cared for my physical body when injured. I love being South African. Fortunately, I have only pleasant experiences to relate. Although our country has a high crime rate, I've been lucky and have always felt safe. It may also be as a result of never expecting anything other than that. Sometimes ignoring the plight of somebody's suffering makes it easier for them to justify crime.

One can't always assist, but sometimes it's a matter of acknowledging the youth at the street corner, who is caught between begging and crime. I make a point of greeting every one of them, and telling them when I can't help, but that I see them and I see their suffering (even the angry-looking ones). They will often reply with a hopeful "tomorrow?" which you both know might never come.

I make a point of responding, "Yes, if I can". I hope that my loving intention and acknowledgement helps ease their hunger pains or their anger when the hunger becomes unbearable and I can't assist.

After two weeks of deliberation about my job at *O*, I decided to take the plunge and resign. It was a heart-sore moment for me. But I was obsessed with adoption, Phil, and a message I believed I had to work on. It wasn't right for me to stay with my heart in two places.

I submitted my resignation, and was asked to please give notice. At first, I was alarmed, as I felt it would be impossible for me to focus properly my job for another month. But I decided to do the best I could. The timing would be perfect, as I anticipated

Phil's coming home round about the time I started my new job working from home. It all seemed to fit together. But I was still sad.

The following weeks were a time of deep reflection. I felt I was being tested because I was on a mission of great significance. The greater the mission, the greater the tests! Some of the tests come as a result of fear-based beliefs – I like to call this 'the lie' because one ends up focusing more on the negative than the positive. The lie that often threatened my faith during this period included beliefs such as, "I can't afford to adopt Phil, I'm not worthy of his being his mother. I'm irresponsible because I was injured in an accident."

A part of the lie that saddened me was the fear that I'd never be loved by a man in the way I needed to be. In fact, the lie had showed me that I could expect to be lied to, cheated on and not taken out for dinners or spoilt. The lie told me I was worthless, and nobody would want me with another person's child, especially one so incredibly disadvantaged.

These beliefs were dangerous to my psyche. I chose to distance myself from situations or people that could possibly compound them. I became something of a hermit, working, writing, praying and hoping. I surrounded myself with affirmations, objects, memories of God's goodness and only very close friends and family. I meditated on how I had been delivered from my mistakes so very often, and how I would access exactly what I needed to proceed with Phil's adoption and the television feature on adoptions.

Every time I lost hope, there would be another breakthrough or some obstruction in the path would be removed.

The 'adoption' message grew louder by the day. Working with Adoption Voice SA, I grew to understand just how important it was. South Africa had been a magnificent example of reconciliation and forgiveness. Subsequent to the release of Nelson Mandela we had proved that to ourselves and each other that we were God's people, and that we could rise above hate, prejudice and discrimination. Now many years later, a generation of children had been born to parents dying of Aids. A generation without parental love and guidance threatened the very existence of our society.

What very few people knew was that the government was aware of this and had been working on an 'adoption' plan together with Adoption Voice SA, where the message was that you don't need anything but love to adopt a child in South Africa. A poor home, where there was love, was better than no home at all. Just as we as a nation had been 'adopted', delivered by grace and love, so we in turn could do the same.

With adoption being something of a Western concept, there was a great need to "Africanise" it. Adopting a child with uncommon ancestry was a concern in both black and white African communities. We had to de-mystify the process, and show the happy stories of children finding their way 'home.' There was no other way to do it than visually, I felt.

I did away with all my little prayer rituals. God knew I meant business – it was my lack of faith that had needed re-enforcement. I concentrated on what I believed was true, and the message I'd been given, which would assist many children. There was no space in my mind for any other philosophy other than what I felt deep inside of me.

Breakthrough

The end of September came and went with the social workers missing the deadline for the report. They explained that because it was a difficult case, and they hadn't met me, they couldn't complete the report. They suggested a round-table discussion, which is what had been proposed to them in the first place. The round-table discussion eventually happened in November.

Barbara and the charity were invited, but declined to attend. We met with a panel of three social workers and were astounded to hear that Phil had never been missing in the system. They had been his social workers all along, and had even given approval for his earlier trips overseas. Apparently they were as shocked as we were that Phil had even had such an arrangement with me in place for so long without their knowledge.

As they questioned me, one could see their shock and dismay at what had happened.

"Barbara had no right to make the decisions she did on his behalf!" one lady exclaimed furiously.

The emails from Barbara requesting me to adopt Phil and donate money, and those declaring me an unfit parent who could have no contact with Phil, caused gasps of astonishment all round. It was evident we'd all been had. Barbara had conveniently 'owned' my relationship with Phil, and milked it for what she thought it was worth.

Although the social workers confirmed that Phil had indeed told them he definitely wanted to live with me earlier in August, they were nervous to make the decision based on his injuries and Moira's application to foster him. They admitted that when they visited him the second time to confirm that he still felt the same way about living with me, that he seemed to have changed his mind and didn't want to admit to anything.

"That's because he wasn't heard the first time," I interjected bitterly.

"We don't want to make this decision. We've never had a situation where there are two applicants competing for the same child. And because of his injuries, we'd rather have the judge decide where he goes," the manager of the social workers explained.

"At least, let me have some access to him in the meantime over the December holidays," I pleaded. They shrugged in response and promised to revert to me. It was obvious from my correspondence, and the timing of it, that Moira's application had been rustled up by Barbara. However, in spite of this, it was still a legitimate application.

As I walked out, one of the social workers, a young black woman, pulled me aside. There was sincerity in her voice, "Ruby, there are things I want to say to you that I obviously am not allowed to officially. Phil loves you. Don't give up. God will take care of this."

Her words were soothing, and I took great comfort in them. In fact, they were a lifeline.

Another two weeks passed, and it seemed I wasn't going to get any access to Phil. I called Sally in dismay.

"Sally, if I don't get Phil, would it be possible to host another child over December?" I suggested, half-heartedly, loath to give Phil's spot to another child but unable to face the disappointment of a child's empty bedroom. The longing for Phil's laugh and the silence in my home would have been enough to drive me insane.

Melissa Banks

"We'll see," Sally responded, and we left it at that.

It was the first week in December when I got the news. Phil's social workers had agreed that, in fairness, I was to have the same access rights to Phil as Moira. Apparently Barbara was overseas, and the social workers decided to make a call in her absence. After reading the email twice to ensure I wasn't dreaming, the tears started flowing. There were no words. My gratitude and excitement knew no limits. I called everyone with the good news.

The social workers had arranged for me to visit Phil for three days on the charity's premises. Then, the following week, I would take him for three days off premises, returning him at 5pm. The final visit would consist of seven consecutive nights, where he'd be staying with me. It seemed too good to be true.

Sure enough, not long after that, Barbara must have discovered what was happening, and the volunteers started trying to persuade the social workers that it wasn't in Phil's best interests to visit. The social workers were admonishing in their response, indicating that obstruction would not be tolerated. I was relieved, but nervous to venture back to the property behind the green fence.

My first official visit back to the premises of the school would arrive soon enough. But in the meantime, there had been another development. Sally the social worker called.

"Ruby, I heard the good news about Phil. But does your offer to have another child still stand? You see, a children's home has just closed down and we've had to accommodate 25 small children. We're short of social workers because some of us are going on leave."

I hesitated, but knew in my heart that I couldn't say no when this was something I'd requested. "That's absolutely fine" I heard myself respond. "A little pre-school girl would be lovely if you could organise that."

"All right I'll call you back shortly," she promised.

A few hours passed, when the phone rang. "Hi Ruby, we don't have toddlers, only babies. We've got a four-month-old baby boy. Do you think you can handle that? We can help you with sponsored nappies and formula." Again, I heard myself respond with a yes. "That's great. We're actually quite desperate, so thank you," Sally finished off.

I put down the phone in shocked excitement. Could I really do this? Could I really handle both a baby and Phil? Clearly God thought I could, or I would never have been given the opportunity.

The following week was a frenzy of activity, preparing for both children and finishing off my work. Thankfully the television series closed over the festive season, so I would be able to give my full attention to two little busy bodies.

The day to see Phil arrived. I was shaking with excitement. I emailed the charity and told them I'd bring lunch for all the children, which would consist of wholewheat rolls and sausages. I couldn't really afford anything more elaborate. Nervously, I made my way to the school and pulled up in front of the green fence. Nobody was there. Five minutes later, a blue car arrived, full of children. Phil was the last one to get out. But this time, he didn't run towards me. He looked away.

My heart sank. It was too late. The damage was done.

I made my way into the kitchen. The rest of the children seemed very pleased to see me. However, Phil kept his distance. Eventually, after preparing lunch, I called him aside.

"Phil, you know I'm actually here to see you." He nodded silently and walked towards the outside bathroom, reaching for the mop. He started mopping, slopping water all over the floor, with his back to me. The despair inside me was all-consuming; I had to somehow reach him.

"Phil, you asked me to adopt you, remember? I promised you I'd come back for you and now I'm allowed to."

He turned to me, "Yes, you said you'd come back and you did," he acknowledged. Throwing the mop on the floor, he sat down and sighed, the deep sigh of an old person.

"You know my mom's coming to visit. And my sister phoned me." His pride in being able to tell me he had a family was evident. I understood that it gave him a sense of comfort, but the flip side was that, according to the social workers, he would never return to his family as his mother was unable to take care of herself. Her children were living in a shelter. It was unlikely she would ever come for him.

"That's wonderful news, Phil," I said gently, "but you can still visit me, you know. You can even live with me if you want to. I have some news for you. The social workers have promised that you can come visit me next week at my house."

He seemed surprised. Nobody had told him.

"So I'm going to fetch you next week. But I will first come back to visit next Sunday again. The social workers said I could."

He looked hard at me, distrust in his eyes, and exclaimed, "The social workers are stupid!"

He suddenly jumped up and ran off to play with his friends. My heart sank. There was nothing more to say. I would just have to continue to show up.

I had no doubt this was going to be a long process, and that there would be sabotage from Barbara's side. Little did I know just how much sabotage was coming our way.

Diapers and drama

The following day, it was time to fetch the baby. I kicked off my high heels, put on some flat shoes, and filed my nails down. I had borrowed a cot, baby car-seat and stroller from a friend. I was about as ready as one could be for a four-month-old baby.

His name was Thabang, which means 'happiness'. Sally handed him to me, and my heart skipped a beat. Lying in my arms was the most precious, chubby little angel. He was black, but with a very light complexion. He was solid, and looked like he could have been Mike Tyson's son.

Strapping Thabang into the baby car-seat, I smiled all the way home, constantly checking on him in the rear-view mirror. It was unbelievable that I actually had a baby in my car!

That night, I bathed Thabang and sang to him. I was in heaven. It felt natural and beautiful. He woke up three times throughout the night, but it didn't matter. I would hear him gurgle and I'd feed and change him. Then he'd go back to sleep almost immediately. In between feeds, I'd get heart-melting big grins with little gums showing. It would be so exciting to introduce Thabang to Phil.

My second meeting with Phil at the school went a little better than the first. Phil was genuinely excited to be coming to me. I had left Thabang with a friend, so I could break the news to Phil, that we had a little visitor.

"Phil, we have a baby coming to stay with us for three weeks." Phil was surprised. "Are we going to adopt him?" The "we" in that sentence excited me enormously. "No Phil, we're just helping out while the social workers are going on holiday. Besides, we've got to adopt you first."

He did a little dance of excitement. I jumped up and down with excitement with him. There could not have been two happier hearts on the planet at that moment. I left the school promising to fetch him the following week.

Throughout the week, I adapted to Thabang's routine and found myself in a very happy space, until Wednesday. There was a loud knock at my door. With Thabang in my arms, I opened the door.

It was the sheriff of the court. "Are you Ruby Florence?" he asked, holding a stamped document that looked like it weighed five kilograms.

"Yes," I responded, knowing in my heart that something drastic was about to happen. Below the big official purple stamp the document screamed in bold, black writing: "Urgent interdict, Barbara Johnson versus Ruby Florence and The Department of Social Development".

The sheriff looked apologetic. "I'm sorry, miss," he said flipping through the pages, "this seems like horrible news for Christmas. I'm only doing my job. I'm really sorry."

Shakily I took the document and closed the door. I gently put Thabang in his cot and sat at my kitchen counter, unable to pick up the document that lay there.

Eventually I plucked up the courage to read through it. It was a request for an urgent hearing in the High Court, preventing Phil from coming to my house over the festive season. The court date granted was the 23rd December, in two days' time. I was accused of drunken behaviour, promiscuity, neglect and many more crimes. The bile rose in my throat, and my legs were shaky. I wanted to hide. My phone rang. It was Leona. She had received the document via email.

"I cannot believe she is requesting an urgent high court hearing just before Christmas!" she screeched. "We're going to have to get an advocate and prepare an answering affidavit by Friday! This is going to be damn expensive! Phil's social workers are going to freak when they realise she's trying to overturn their decision."

"Phil is going to be devastated. But I'm not sure I can afford an advocate, is there anything else we can do?" I replied helplessly.

"The problem is she is requesting full parental rights with this application, Ruby. It's ominous. We don't actually have a choice. I know a good advocate and I'll negotiate with her for you. Don't you worry about my bill. I'm going to fight this, with costs for her account. Let's take her to the cleaners!" Leona declared passionately.

"Okay, I'll get on to responding to each allegation, and email you all Barbara's emails requesting money and so on," I replied. We said our goodbyes, and I started drafting a response. It was tedious and painful, and each accusation wounded me deeply. But for Phil's sake, I pressed on.

This was about my promise to him.

Friday arrived, and I left Thabang with my friend once again. Leona looked nervous. "I'm not usually nervous, but today I am. It's become personal for me, but the affidavits about Barbara that your friends sent through should make the difference," she said as we drove to the centre of Johannesburg to the High Court.

She was dressed in a smart blouse and denim skirt. The advocate, Alexis, greeted us. She was in a robe and white collar. Her long, curly dark hair was tied in a loose ponytail. We waited in the court room. The attorneys and advocates representing Barbara arrived. She was absent. I took my seat at the back of the courtroom. The clerk of the court announced the arrival of the judge.

An attractive middle-aged lady in a black robe walked out. We all bowed and were instructed to take our seats. The war began.

A young male advocate started explaining the need for an urgent high court application. The judge wasn't moved. "I don't believe this is urgent at all. It's the day before Christmas eve, please explain further – why the urgency?" she demanded of the advocate.

He spluttered his response. It was clear he hadn't been briefed about the case properly.

Alexis stood up, agreeing with the judge that due to there being a court hearing in the children's court early in the year, the motion was entirely unnecessary and certainly not urgent. She responded to all the allegations against and fought for me. With every word, she lifted the load off my shoulders, until I felt as light as a feather.

The judge swiftly declared she certainly didn't think it appropriate the hearing be brought to her court and, in light of this, she would not grant parental rights or guardianship to Barbara. My heart did a somersault of relief. The judge continued in a level voice, "The long overnight stay should be broken up, however. Please consult and establish a more suitable visitation schedule from now until the children's court hearing."

And with that she stood up, bowed and left the court for recess.

Alexis and Leona turned around to me gleefully. Alexis couldn't contain her excitement. I rushed over to my two angels and we hugged each other tightly.

We quickly worked out a visitation schedule, which gave me even more access to Phil. Alexis handed the paper over to Barbara's attorneys, who looked crestfallen. Leona offered me some jelly beans, which we were all chewing on excitedly as we watched Barbara's attorneys walk out of the courtroom, phones in hand. I almost felt sorry for them.

They returned, reporting that Barbara was devastated and had only agreed to half the visitation schedule. The judge returned. Alexis explained that we were unable to agree on a visitation schedule. Both advocates submitted their schedules. The judge put her spectacles on and came to a decision. Holding up Alexis's piece of paper, she declared that she would grant me my request. Alexis walked back to her seat, winking at me.

The battle was almost won. We had one final hurdle – costs. The judge read her verdict, announcing the first applicant (Barbara) had abused the high court system with her urgent request and the first respondent (which was me) had won the case. My costs would have to be paid by Barbara in her personal capacity! I couldn't believe it!

The judge left the courtroom. I dashed over to Leona and Alexis and once again we hugged, thrilled with our victory. Now nobody could stop me from spending time with Phil. The High Court had ruled in my favour and I had proper access to Phil until the children's court hearing. All that I had to do was collect him, and give him the proper medical care for his left eye, which was apparently blind. In the hearing the lawyers had made him sound completely blind.

As per the ruling, I arrived to collect Phil on the Tuesday. He was ready for me in a lime-green shirt, and turquoise shorts.

He had a little cooler bag with him. Barbara's biological son came out with a list of instructions for his care.

The list was tedious, starting with how to wash one's hands properly. It instructed me that Phil wasn't allowed to swim in chlorinated swimming pools due to his eye problem (suddenly his eye problem was worse than ever) and he was not allowed to be given sweets or fatty carbohydrates. He was to eat dinner at 6pm every night and be in bed by 8pm. I was to purchase eye ointment, eye patches and medicated cream for his scalp, which proved to be very expensive. However, I was so thrilled to have him that I didn't care what it cost me.

Phil had been given a cellphone to call, as the list stated, his 'family', being Moira as well as her aunts and uncles. Phil was thrilled with his new toy. When I looked at the numbers saved on his phone, my jaw dropped. There were a few numbers for Barbara and Moira. The rest were for child line, my local police station, the charity's local police station and a number saved under 'help' for the social worker.

What was interesting is that Barbara hadn't saved Moira's number under 'mama', but rather her own. Clearly, there was no intention of Moira ever being Phil's mother.

Phil played around with his phone, and I was terrified he'd dial all the incriminating numbers and it would be used against me. So I purchased him a cheap little phone to play with and told him to keep Barbara's phone for emergencies. Within the first 24 hours of Phil being in my care, he received many phone calls. And when we were busy or out, and he didn't answer his phone, there would be text messages asking him where he was. It was as bad as having a tracking device.

Sensing the threat, I called Leona who immediately contacted Barbara's lawyers to state that we were not going to be on call, and that they could call Phil at 8pm. The phone calls slowed down, but the texts didn't stop. I didn't read them, but Phil told me that it was Barbara and Moira constantly telling him they loved him. I didn't doubt that.

Keeping Phil busy and looking after Thabang at the same time proved quite challenging. At night, I'd be exhausted, contented and nervous all at the same time, aware that I was being 'watched' through that phone, but happy to have two beautiful little souls in my care. It was quite nerve-wrecking, but somehow I managed to get through it with a babysitter for Thabang now and then, so I could take Phil to movies or for lunch.

Phil loved his new room, and was thrilled to ride his bicycle again, and watch all the old movies he had enjoyed two years before. The only strict rule I personally put in place for Phil (amongst all the others from Barbara) was that he wasn't to play with my BlackBerry.

On discussing his adoption, he asked "Can't I have all my surgery first, then you adopt me?" I smiled, "I'm sure we can make a plan. But don't worry. I have other people who can help us with surgery too if you need it." He didn't look convinced.

In between all of this, Phil asked me to help him with Barbara's phone to text Thabo. He handed me the phone and a text from Barbara was still open. It read "I love you as much as all the grass in the world. There will not be privacy while she is there. She will read your messages. So delete what you need to."

I wasn't surprised, but smiled to myself that they were communicating in text when she had insisted in his care instructions that I was to supply him with a braille-writer. He had suddenly started braille lessons in the last week of the school term, clearly another ploy to keep him at the school and in her care. His reading was as good as ever.

It was confusing, as there were so many messages of love on his phone. I started feeling like I was intruding on his life, with my application to adopt him. Phil was getting increasingly nervous of what to say to Barbara regarding my care of him, and what to say to me. It was heart-breaking to see him so torn.

What made matters even worse was at night Barbara would sometimes call at 8pm and tell him none of the children were there, as they were out for pizza. And here I'd fed him grilled chicken and rice at 6pm and had him in bed by 8pm as per the list of instructions, which I was terrified to slip up on.

I could see more and more disappointment register in his eyes, as I obeyed the prohibitive list and he heard all the exciting things his friends were doing at the school. It was also challenging to entertain him all the time, with a four-month-old baby. It was an impossible situation. I looked forward to Phil's social workers being back in January and ridding myself and Phil of this horrible vampire ruling our lives and sucking the fun out of them!

The last day of Phil's five-day visit arrived. He was looking forward to seeing his friends. I could see he was weary of being in my home and having to watch what he said to Barbara. That morning, he put on his Spongebob T-shirt and red shorts I'd bought him. He walked purposefully out of the front door with his little cooler bag.

"Where are you going, Phil?" I asked, stopping him. "Barbara wants to speak to me privately," he replied somewhat sheepishly. "Well, you can go upstairs to the top balcony and make your call, Phil. I'm not having you standing speaking to her in the parking lot. It's dangerous."

I went into my bedroom, closing the door to give him as much privacy as he needed.

A few minutes later, he came down the stairs with his phone, asking, "What's your address here?"

"Why? Who do you want to give it to?" I responded a little testily.

"Jonathan, the volunteer who cooks for us on Friday night," he said innocently.

"Does he want to visit?" I asked.

"He said he might be able to," was the response. I gave him the address which he punched into his phone, sending off the message.

Half an hour later, he came to me again, "Can I please go and visit the security guards?" he asked. He had visited them every day at the entrance to my complex, so I agreed, thinking nothing of it.

"Just don't be too long, I'm making mashed potatoes for you, like you asked," I responded, peeling the potatoes. Thabang was asleep.

After 20 minutes, I ran outside to see if I could catch sight of Phil. Running to the security guards would mean I'd have to leave Thabang unattended for a few minutes. Something didn't feel right, so I took my chances. I ran as fast as I could to the security guard's kiosk. Phil wasn't there.

"Have you seen Phil?" I asked breathlessly. "He was here for a while. We don't know where he is. We'll go and look at the main swimming pool," the kind security guard said, walking towards the pool area. "Thank you, Sizwe, I will run and look at the other pool," I said dialling his number for Barbara's phone. The phone rang, unanswered. My heart was pounding.

My phone rang. It was Sizwe. I hoped it was good news. "We have him on camera, he sneaked past the gate out the boom. He left the premises."

The last sentence hit me in my stomach. Where could he have gone? Racing back, I woke Thabang, practically threw him into the baby seat and drove out the complex like I had the devil on my heels. Sizwe rang again, "Ruby, he was seen by the other security guards at the complex around the corner running up Hornbill Street." I wanted to scream. It was New Year 's Day and Phil had run away.

Racing towards where he was last sighted, I called Leona who didn't answer her phone. I called the social workers who didn't answer their phones. The last person I wanted to call was Barbara. Phil was nowhere in sight. It was as if he had vanished into thin air.

My phone rang. It was Leona. I tearfully broke the news to her.

"You're going to have to call the police, Ruby. I've no doubt this was orchestrated by Barbara and it's in contempt of court. Call their police station and see if he's back there."

Turning the car around, I made my way home. Thabang was awake but silent. I climbed the three flights of stairs, put him on my bed and reached for the telephone directory. I called the Brixton Police and was put through to the captain. I explained the whole story, and he remarked, "Oh, we know that woman who runs the charity. We'll go and check it out and see if he's back there." His tone of voice suggested annoyance. I was relieved that he knew exactly what he was dealing with.

The next half an hour passed in a state of disbelief, fear, confusion, and a deep sorrow that I kept swallowing back. Numbly, I changed Thabang's diaper and fed him. The mash

351

potatoes were cold in a pot on the stove. My phone rang again. It was the captain and he confirmed what I knew to be true in my heart – that Phil was safely back at Barbara's house and had run away from me, with only two hours to go before I was meant to return him anyway

I spent the next few days in utter disbelief and disappointment. I poured all the love I had to give into my care of Thabang. I fought the tears I needed to cry, whilst Thabang was with me. I was fearful that once I started crying I'd never stop.

Six days later, Thabang's social worker returned, with an adoption application for him from some other people. I handed him over tearfully. He had been a precious gift to me in my darkest hour.

Driving home from the orphanage, I finally allowed myself to cry properly. I wept for everything. For Thabang and Phil both being abandoned; for Phil, who had endured so much pain and further abandonment, when I wasn't allowed back two years ago; and for the relationship that had existed, which had possibly been completely ruined. I cried over the injustice of it all. And finally, I wept for myself, and the disappointment and love that had come all rolled into one.

A new chapter

A lawyer's letter arrived a few days later accompanied by a psychologist's report on Phil. It stated that he never wanted to come to my home ever again. The reasons given were that he was bored, and that I had shouted at him for playing with my BlackBerry.

I had no doubt there was more to it, but didn't believe it fair on either of us to push any harder, or probe any deeper. There was no doubt in my mind that when the adoption hearing came around he would choose to stay where he was.

He had never liked change at the best of times, and having two mud-slinging adults quarrelling over him when all he wanted to do was get on with life was proving just too much for him to handle. I sincerely doubted Barbara would ever change her antagonistic stance, and Phil would always feel compromised if he allowed himself to love me or enjoy his life with me too much.

For now, Phil has a home, and good care. He has friends and people who love him. It does worry me that he won't be given an opportunity to integrate properly with other children, but his peace of mind right now is more important than that.

Hopefully, my returning to him and delivering on my promises will assist him in trusting the outside world one day. If I hadn't come back, he may have become even more damaged and mistrusting of people. I believe our encounter was meant to open both our hearts to the world.

Phil knows I love him. His situation is complicated, but it doesn't change the truth of what was shown to him. No matter how others try and twist and darken the truth, love prevails.

Phil knows my heart and home will be forever open to him. He doesn't need to choose it, but it's there for him.

Fighting Barbara is not what I want to do for the rest of my life. But at the time, fighting was something I had to do for Phil's sake. For now, for Phil's sake, and mine, I have to stop the fight.

From here on, all I can do is give the choice to Phil, and trust that the Children's Court will make the right choice for him.

My life has changed for ever. I have conquered an eating disorder, started a new career in television production, been successfully screened as a parent, fostered a four-month-old baby, written a book and gotten involved with many children and charities through Africa's Angels. I haven't solved the riddles of creation or seen God, but I've seen proof of His existence in the love and everyday small miracles in my life.

My dreams haven't all come true in the way I thought they would. We don't always get what we want, but we always get what we need. And sometimes, it's getting what we need first that prepares us for living out our dreams, which I believe eventually come true.

I will consider adoption again, when I'm ready, and of course Phil may always be just a moment away. But right now, I'm enjoying the new chapter in my life, which I am free to embrace in any way I wish.

And that excites me no end.

Epilogue

January 2017

Five years had passed. I looked at my husband playing with our daughter, and couldn't quite believe how fortunate I was to have such a blessed life. It was still inconceivable that I hadn't recognized my soul mate when we first met eight years earlier. His behaviour had certainly improved since that fateful night I had drugged him, with Desiree, before leaving for Hawaii! He had resurfaced in my life, a changed man. Then again, I certainly was a changed woman.

There was a loud knock at the door. "I'll get it," I shouted to father and daughter, walking towards the entrance of the house. I opened the door, and there standing before me was a young man with the most beautiful smile. His face was slightly disfigured from old scarred tissue. He had a beautiful nose and unmistakeable eyes.

"Hello Rubes!" he chimed brightly.

"Oh my darling boy!" I grabbed him, hugging him tight. He was much taller than me. I stepped back to look at him again. "Wow! Barbara did a magnificent job! She certainly got the best surgeons out! And you've outgrown a lot of the old scarred tissue" I exclaimed holding his face, examining him from all directions. He seemed proud.

"Phil! You came!" screamed our daughter running towards him, immediately knowing exactly who he was. He picked her up and planted a kiss on her cheek. Still holding my daughter, he continued in his now deep voice, "Rubes I need to talk to you." "Absolutely," I ushered him inside.

Melissa Banks

He sat down, and I waited anxiously for him to start.

"I need you to help me. Teach me all you know about film and television production, please?" he implored. "Of course! I've got a few colleges and courses in mind. What would you like to produce?"

With a big grin, he responded, "I want to make a movie about a boy who walked through fire and the many mothers who loved him."

"Sure, but under one condition." He rolled his eyes, while I continued, "show me that you can still skip." He let out a whoop of delight, and went skipping off. It was just his way.

Acknowledgements

So many people have made this journey possible. I could not have done it without the love of family and friends. My first thanks must go to Aleksandra, who read and edited my first draft of the book. My family, Mommy, Greg, Claire and Troy – you are my light and my inspiration.Carol, Chris, Cilma, Desiree, Elandre, Hykie, Jackie, Liesel, Michele, Patience, Peter, Precious, Reena, Storm, Tessa, Toni, Toncah, Zenette – my deepest thanks to you for your support. Sincerest apologies to anybody I may have left out.

To my partner and soulmate, Robbie, thank you for believing in me, and getting me through the most difficult part of this project.

Finally, thanks and glory to my Heavenly Father. Thank you for delighting me with life and the beauty of it.

And a word for "Chocolate" the beautiful large Rhodesian Ridgeback who sadly passed away. She will always be remembered.